JANE AUSTEN'S
LOST LETTERS

ALSO BY JANE K. CLELAND

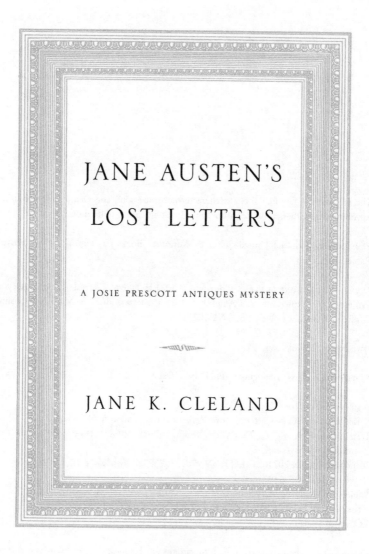

JANE AUSTEN'S
LOST LETTERS

A JOSIE PRESCOTT ANTIQUES MYSTERY

JANE K. CLELAND

MINOTAUR
BOOKS
NEW YORK

First published in the United States by Minotaur Books, an imprint of St. Martin's Publishing Group

JANE AUSTEN'S LOST LETTERS. Copyright © 2021 by Jane K. Cleland. All rights reserved. Printed in the United States of America. For information, address St. Martin's Publishing Group, 120 Broadway, New York, NY 10271.

www.minotaurbooks.com

Library of Congress Cataloging-in-Publication Data

Names: Cleland, Jane K., author.
Title: Jane Austen's lost letters : a Josie Prescott antiques mystery / Jane K. Cleland.
Description: First edition. | New York : Minotaur Books, 2021. | Series: Josie Prescott antiques mysteries ; 14
Identifiers: LCCN 2021027413 | ISBN 9781250779380 (hardcover) | ISBN 9781250779397 (ebook)
Subjects: GSAFD: Mystery fiction.
Classification: LCC PS3603.L4555 J36 2021 | DDC 813/.6—dc23
LC record available at https://lccn.loc.gov/2021027413

Our books may be purchased in bulk for promotional, educational, or business use. Please contact your local bookseller or the Macmillan Corporate and Premium Sales Department at 1-800-221-7945, extension 5442, or by email at MacmillanSpecialMarkets@macmillan.com.

First Edition: 2021

10 9 8 7 6 5 4 3 2 1

For Jane Murphy, who planted the seed,

and Sarah Melnyk, who encouraged me to write the book.

And of course, for Joe.

Greely Woods

Pastor Ted's
Garden

Reynold's Woods

Mimi's Copse

Rocky Point
Congregational
Church

Ocean

Vaughn's Weald

AUTHOR'S NOTE

This is a work of fiction. While there is a Seacoast Region in New Hampshire, there is no town called Rocky Point, and many other geographic liberties have been taken.

JANE AUSTEN'S
LOST LETTERS

CHAPTER ONE

The operator assigned to camera one rolled the dolly toward me, framing the shot. I smiled at the lens as if it were a friend, the way Timothy, my TV show's producer and director, taught me.

"Welcome to *Josie's Antiques*!" I said.

Timothy had assured me that on camera I didn't sound all gooey and mawkish, as I'd feared. My cheeks had reddened with embarrassment when he'd raved that the camera loved me.

"In this segment," I continued, "we're going to appraise what might just be a first edition of one of the best-loved children's books ever published, Beatrix Potter's *The Tale of Peter Rabbit*. I'm thrilled that two world-renowned document appraisers are here in our beautiful New Hampshire studio for a battle of the experts."

I took five steps to the right, stopped on the small masking tape X on the floor, my mark, and turned slowly to face camera four. I now stood in front of a room-size, tempered glass arched window that provided an unobstructed view of Greely Woods, the ancient hardwood forest that separated Prescott's Antiques and Auctions headquarters from Highbridge, a newish residential development a quarter mile away to the north. The window offered us the opportunity to show off New Hampshire's spectacular scenery—the pristine snow in winter, the redbuds in spring, the verdant growth in summer, and the gaudy leaves in fall. Right now, we were at the peak of the autumn foliage season, early October, and the forest was ablaze with the colors of fire.

"I'll introduce you to both experts," I continued, "then we'll discuss their appraisals, with an eye to identifying and sorting through any differences."

I leaned in toward the camera and lowered my voice, delivering my last line as a gossipy aside. "Doesn't that sound fun?"

I turned toward Oliver Crenshaw, one of the experts, who was sitting in an old-style red leather wing chair, one of three arranged to form a cozy conversational grouping. The middle one, facing the window, was mine. I walked to join him, the camera following me.

Oliver, who was in his midthirties, looked like a tweedy professor with his head in the clouds, but was actually the third-generation owner of Portsmouth-based Crenshaw's Rare Books, Prints and Autographs. After his dad died and he took over the business, he got himself certified as a forensic document examiner and approved by half a dozen courts as an expert witness, with an emphasis on materials published or produced from the late eighteenth through the early twentieth centuries, an impressive accomplishment at a relatively young age.

Oliver was also a buddy, an industry pro I'd known for as long as I'd been in New Hampshire, from when he'd manned the cash register for his dad during college. He was popular with the ladies, too. I ran into him at half a dozen benefit galas a year, and he always brought a date, never the same woman twice. He was tall and fit, with short brown hair and regular features. He wore a brick-red collared shirt and Dockers.

Because the TV studio was small, each expert was allowed only one guest. Oliver had brought his mom, Rory, which charmed me no end. Rory was around fifty-five, maybe a little older, tall, and sinewy, like an athlete. She wore a tan-and-navy CRENSHAW'S RARE BOOKS, PRINTS AND AUTOGRAPHS baseball cap.

About a year earlier, I had taken a flyer and asked Timothy whether we could do more filming at my company's headquarters in Rocky Point, New Hampshire. We'd always shot a fair number of segments in my company's massive warehouse using our fully equipped workstations, but I figured that if Timothy was okay with the idea, I'd build a mini-studio where we could film entire episodes on site, sparing me weeks away from home. Timothy thought it was a great idea, and sold the concept to the network—not such an easy task since they'd have to cover the crew's travel expenses.

Timothy, who knew the ins and outs of TV production, oversaw the entire process. Construction began within a month, and we were up and running six months later. The studio was housed in an addition that abutted the auction gallery, the luxury venue where we held our monthly antiques auctions. The wall separating the two spaces folded like an accordion allowing us to livestream our auctions. The studio contained a state-of-the-art soundstage; storage rooms and cabinets galore; a crew wing, complete with a small gym; a guest area, including dressing rooms with full bathrooms and a green room; an office suite for Timothy; and a dressing room suite for me. We'd also had brackets installed on the outside wall, so we could attach a big tent for team meetings and meals. The tent was fancy, with clear plastic windows that could be rolled up to allow summer breezes to waft through. When it was cold, we brought in freestanding heaters.

"I hadn't expected it to be so posh," I'd whispered to Timothy during our initial tour. "You worked wonders with the budget."

"Don't tell the network . . . I might have given them the impression we were roughing it up here in the boonies."

With the cameras rolling, I took my seat next to Oliver. "Hello, Oliver! I'm delighted you could join us for today's battle of the experts. Tell me about the appraisal process you used."

The team would insert a photo of the book cover to run alongside our conversation in a split-screen view. They'd already taken what Timothy called the "beauty shots," a series of photos designed to showcase an antique's attributes, from sheen to shine and from scratches to scruff marks.

Oliver, a polished performer, kept smiling, which isn't as easy as you might think, especially if you're expected to talk at the same time. "Thanks, Josie. It's a pleasure to be here. Time is more valuable to me than money, so many years ago I developed a four-step procedure for appraising antiques, including rare books, prints, and documents. I first consider known anomalies, such as typos or copyright peccadillos. Second, I look at the tangible elements, the paper and ink, for example. Third, I assess the content itself to determine if it's complete, correct, and appropriate. Finally, I trace provenance."

"Thank you, Oliver." During my conversations with people, I didn't need to think about camera placement. Camera three was aimed at my face all the time, so I simply had to look up to be on camera, and the only time I did so was if I wanted to make a specific point to the viewers. I did so now. "Provenance refers to clear title—tracing ownership from creation, production, or manufacture to the current day. Now let's meet our second expert, Dr. Gloria Moreau."

Gloria Moreau, a former supermodel, was a tenured professor of archival studies at Hitchens University in nearby Durham. Gloria had quit modeling when she was thirty, and now, fifteen years later, she was still drop-dead gorgeous, but I had the sense that she couldn't care less about her appearance. Her ash-blond hair was streaked with gray and cut in a short wash-and-wear bob. She wore black slacks, a sky-blue tunic, and a blue-and-ivory silk scarf—professional garb, but not stylish. She allowed the hair and makeup team to do their thing, but barely glanced in the mirror as they worked.

Gloria was one of the world's leading experts on signature authentication, having made her mark while still in grad school by validating a previously unknown letter from Thomas Jefferson to French geologist and explorer, Barthélemy Faujas de Saint-Fond, in which the president shared an update on the Lewis and Clark expedition, and proving another was a fake. Gloria had found the letters misfiled in a university library while working on her dissertation. Using her findings as exemplars, she'd developed a unique method of verification related to pressure points—a reliable way to identify not only the forgery, but the forger, something I hoped to learn more about during my interview. While the Jefferson letter forger was never publicly identified because of some kind of plea agreement, Gloria's protocol became the gold standard in signature authentication. Overnight, she became a cause célèbre in the rarefied antiques world.

Gloria's guest was Ivan Filbert, her graduate assistant. Ivan was about Oliver's age, midthirties, and thin, with brown hair swept back and long sideburns. He was curiously quiet, which was hard to interpret. Possibly, he was simply reserved and self-contained; or perhaps he was bashful, even timorous; or maybe he was just taking it all in.

I returned to the window where Gloria was waiting, standing on her mark.

Oddly, since she was based less than half an hour away and we both worked with rare objects, this was the first time we'd met, and I was, to my dismay, intimidated. She wasn't merely beautiful—she was breathtaking. Also, she towered over me. I didn't feel petite; I felt small, diminished, insignificant, the way I had in middle school when some of the taller girls had picked on me.

Determined to suppress the flare-up of my childhood insecurities, I drew in a deep breath. My dad always told me to fake it till you make it, words that had helped me survive more than one emotional gully.

Before I could speak to Gloria, Timothy cut in, "Makeup! Take a look at Josie."

Marie, my regular makeup gal, appeared in front of me, wielding a fluffy brush and a tub of translucent powder. Timothy couldn't bear a shiny nose. Marie had a white stripe running through her waist-long coal-black hair and three gold studs running up her right ear. I often wondered if the stripe was natural or dyed, but I'd never asked. She flicked the brush over my face, narrowed her eyes to seek out sheen, then zipped back to the makeup area.

"Starr!" Timothy shouted, calling to his pink-haired assistant director.

She rushed to join him, and he lowered his voice, pointing to his clipboard. I knew from experience this was a minor glitch. He wanted a new shooting sequence or a reshoot or a substitution or something that would delay us, but only for a few minutes. When the delay was longer, he was more upset.

Starr nodded, then called, "Five minutes, everyone!"

"I bet this brings you back to your days of modeling," I remarked to Gloria.

"God, no! In those days, I had to sit for hours and hours getting primped. Boring to the tenth degree." She raised her arm, gesturing toward the set. "There's nothing boring about this."

"Not even all the waiting around?"

"Not to me. Here, the hair and makeup stations are out in the open, and the staff adapts to you. If I want to stand for a few seconds, they step aside and wait. Back then, I was wedged into a small room and told not to move. It felt like jail." She smiled, and I thought of Helen of Troy, whose face had launched a thousand ships. Helen had nothing on Gloria. "Also, I'm a people-watcher. So long as I can observe people, I'm never bored."

"To you, a deserted beach is a nightmare."

She laughed. "Totally."

"Yet you live in New Hampshire, not known for its crowds."

"You go where the jobs are. Tenure track professorships in archival studies aren't so easy to find."

"I never considered that. You've been here for what . . . ten years?"

"Eight. I got tenure last year."

"Congratulations!"

"Thanks. It's the single hardest, most stressful thing I've ever done, and my proudest accomplishment."

"I can imagine . . . or maybe I can't."

"And please . . . don't get me wrong . . ." She turned to face the window wall and raised a hand, a silent toast to the scenery. "This place is spectacular."

"True, but when I first moved here, I struggled to make friends. I bet you did, too."

"Yes, that's an issue. I don't blame New Hampshire, though. Moving any-where as an adult is hard. Most people have long established relationships that date back to childhood. They're not in the market for new friends." She grinned. "It's not an issue, though. When I'm not people-watching, I'm a real homebody."

"Me, too."

"You? I never would have guessed."

"Shh! Don't tell anyone."

"I somehow got the impression you have a million friends."

"Not a million, or anything close. Part of it is business, of course. As soon as I started my company, I joined a lot of business groups to get the word out, and I still attend a bunch of those meetings and events. I'm friendly with a lot of the people I've met that way. 'Friendly with' is different than 'friends with,' if you know what I mean."

"I know exactly. Do you have any real friends?"

"A few. Lucky me."

"Was it just luck?"

"Not only luck . . . I suppose it's a combination of luck, timing, and be-ing open to the prospect. I rented a small house for a long time and became really close to the landlady. Also, I began volunteering for New Hampshire Children First! It's a wonderful organization. I help them with fundraising." I thought about Mo, who died too young, Mona, who ran the therapeutic horse riding program, and Helene, the director, one of the finest women I knew. "Connecting with them is one of the best decisions I've ever made."

"I wish—"

I'd have to wait to hear what Gloria wished because Starr shouted, "Josie! Urgent message for you."

I excused myself to Gloria and hurried toward Starr. No one had ever interrupted our filming before. Not once. Good news could wait, so this had to be bad news. The only question was how bad.

Starr pointed toward Cara, Prescott's grandmotherly office manager, standing near the corridor that connected the studio with the warehouse.

"What's wrong?" I whispered when I reached Cara.

"Nothing. Maybe nothing. There's a woman to see you. She said . . . well, I had her repeat it because I could hardly believe my ears . . . oh, Josie . . . she said she has to talk to you about your father."

I stared at Cara, confused. I assumed I'd misheard. "My father?"

"I know," Cara said, reaching out a hand to touch my arm, then pulling back. "I told her you were busy, but she insisted. She said it was urgent, and that it would only take a minute."

"Who is she?"

"Veronica Sutton. She's waiting for you outside, on the bench."

It had to be a joke, but that someone would joke about my dad, who'd been dead for twenty years, was silly. Then what was it? A hoax? A con?

Time, I knew, was money. Timothy's five-minute delay was bad enough. For me to further impede production as if I were a prima donna was an appalling thought, but I had no choice. I thanked Cara, apologized to Timothy, promising to make it quick, and dashed outside, exiting through the tent.

As I sprinted across the parking lot, one of my dad's favorite sayings came to mind—expect the best, but prepare for the worst. I wondered which side of that equation this woman represented.

CHAPTER TWO

The woman sitting on the wooden bench near the willow tree looked to be about seventy. She stood as I approached. She was elegantly dressed, but pale. She wore a honey-colored Burberry trench coat over a black blouse. Her auburn hair hung to her shoulders in soft waves.

"Hello," I said, a little breathless, smiling. I introduced myself, and she did the same. "Cara said you wanted to talk to me about my dad."

"Yes. I was a good friend of your father's."

Something was out of whack. She couldn't have been a good friend of my father, since I'd known all his friends.

I took a few seconds to gather my thoughts, then sank onto the bench. "Forgive my surprise . . . I don't recall him mentioning you."

"It was a long time ago." She fingered her pearl necklace, as if she were nervous. "I came to give you this." She extracted a brown paper–wrapped package about the size of a large shoebox from an oversize tote bag resting on the bench and handed it to me. "I'm very glad to meet you, but I have to go."

Without another word, she took the bag and walked away, disappearing behind a U-Haul truck the New York City–based crew had driven up for the shoot.

I leapt up. "Wait!" By the time I circled the truck, she was already at her car, a black Mercedes. She slid behind the wheel and fired the engine. I ran toward her, clutching the package under my arm like a football. "Wait! Please!"

She drove to the exit. I stopped and concentrated on reading her license plate, but it was so streaked with mud, I couldn't even identify the state that had issued it.

She turned right, east toward Rocky Point Congregational Church, toward the ocean. I dashed into the street and watched her car until a curve in the road blocked my view. Dazed, I walked slowly back to the bench and sat. *I was a good friend of your father's*, that's what she'd said.

My property was surrounded by woods, and staring into them helped me think. In back of me, to the west, the woods were called Carter's Forest. To my right, at the rear of my building, was Greely Woods. To my left, across Trevor Street, the woods were known as Vaughn's Weald. In front of me, Mimi's Copse connected my property to the Congregational church's parking lot a quarter mile to the east. The copse had been deeded to the church a century earlier by a congregant named Mimi Jones to provide the congregation with a place for reflection, and that's what I needed now. I focused on the boscage, my brain trying to process what had just happened, but I couldn't. My mind kept replaying that one line, over and over again, like a needle stuck on an old vinyl record: *I was a good friend of your father's. I was a good friend of your father's. I was a good friend of your father's.* After a few minutes, I gave up and went into the office, entering through the front door.

Cara was at her desk. She waited for me to speak.

"Did Veronica Sutton give you her contact information?"

"No. I'm sorry."

I dredged up every ounce of professionalism I could muster and smiled. "Thanks." I reached for the heavy door that led to the warehouse. "If anyone needs me, I'll be upstairs."

I crossed the warehouse to the spiral staircase that led to my private office on the mezzanine level. If I continued straight, I'd reach the corridor that led to the TV studio. Hank, one of Prescott's cats, frisked alongside, then bolted up the steps ahead of me. Hank was a platinum Maine Coon, handsome and sweet. By the time I reached my office, he'd settled onto the yellow brocade love seat.

"Sorry, Hank. I'm going to sit at my desk."

He meowed, voicing his disappointment.

I texted Timothy an apology for further delay, explaining that I needed ten minutes or so. I turned to the package.

It took a fair measure of self-control to stop myself from ripping off the paper. I am naturally impatient, but I'm also a realist, and I knew that proceeding cautiously now might pay off later. I snapped on a pair of plastic gloves from the supply I kept in a desk drawer. The oils on human skin are murder on antiques.

Timothy texted back that I should take as long as I needed.

I examined all sides of the box. The brown paper was neatly folded and sealed with ordinary cellophane tape. There was a small, hard lump on the top, but no markings of any kind on the paper. I used my phone to take still shots and a brief video, partially out of habit—at Prescott's we record every object we appraise—and partially out of devotion. If my father was somehow involved with whatever was inside, I wanted to memorialize every bit of it.

I used the point of a sterling silver letter opener to pierce the tape holding down one corner, then eased the blade under the flap. I moved slowly, methodically, slitting the tape on all sides, examining the paper's underside to confirm there were no writing or marks. I moved the paper aside carefully, wanting to preserve it for further study, if and when appropriate, and leaned back in my chair. Removing the paper revealed an olive-green leather box with an ornate brass escutcheon. This particular shade of green had been my father's favorite color.

Oh, Dad. He'd been dead for decades, yet often my grief felt as fresh, as raw as if he'd died yesterday. Sometimes, like today, my heartache was stirred by a specific memory, leading to a yearning for his strength, his smarts, his sensibility, followed by a sorrow as bitter as day-old coffee. Other times, it manifested itself as more of a generalized longing. I sat up straight, willing the melancholy to subside, and it did.

A clear plastic bag containing a shiny brass decorative key lay on top, the lump I'd felt through the brown paper. I unlatched the small metal tape measure clipped to my belt, and wrote the box measurements on a scratch pad: 14" by 10" by 8".

I dropped the key into the palm of my hand, turning it over, looking for a stamp or etched mark of some kind, but it was blank. From its pristine condition, I conjectured it was either new or recently buffed and polished.

I couldn't imagine what was inside the box. My dad had been an amateur photographer, a world traveler, and an inveterate correspondent, and he'd saved scores of favorite photos, souvenirs, and letters, but the plastic tubs where he'd kept his treasures were safely stored among other memorabilia.

After a minute, I realized that I hadn't moved, that I was in some kind of stupor, no longer thinking about his possessions, not thinking at all. I felt fuddled, as if I'd been jerked out of a deep sleep. I was a key turn away from learning something about my father, but I was torn, as hesitant as I was curious. I wanted to know, of course I did, but I was also scared to my kneecaps that whatever I'd find would disrupt my memories. Veronica Sutton had already thrown me for a loop. What if I was about to open a Pandora's box?

I slid the key into the lock.

It turned smoothly, culminating in a satisfying click.

I lifted the lid and stared—too stunned to move. I blinked. It couldn't be, but there it was.

On top of a padded envelope was a notecard-size white envelope, unstamped, that had been addressed to me at my old New York City address.

I recognized my father's graceful script, his handwriting as familiar as my own.

My heart pounded against my ribs, yet my body felt sluggish, as if I were slogging through knee-deep mud. I slowly drifted into autopilot, ready to cope, as I always did. In some remote corner of my mind, I knew I'd fall apart after the crisis passed, my modus operandi.

With trembling hands, I turned the envelope over. My father had handled this paper. Wild ideas of steaming open the flap so I could preserve his DNA to keep the last little bits of him close flicked through my brain.

I slit it open and eased the notecard out. The handwritten message read: *Hey, Josie! You're not going to believe what I found! I was poking around a shop in Portsmouth, and ended up buying a portfolio of sketches—it wasn't until I got back to my hotel room that I saw two letters in the mix. Trust me . . . you're going to be happy! I'll get them into archival sleeves and give them to you when we have dinner on Tuesday. Can't wait to see you!*

I clutched the note to my chest, gold and silver flecks dancing before my eyes like slow-moving confetti. My dad was referring to a dinner we'd never eaten, the dinner scheduled for September 11, 2001.

His note ended: *Love you, Dad,* followed by a P.S.: *I can't find a stamp. Never mind. I'll hand this to you in person next week.*

I set it aside, breathless, weak.

Suddenly parched, I drank some water, then sat quietly for a few seconds. When I felt more poised, I removed the padded envelope. Below it were two transparent plastic sleeves, each protecting a letter written on personal-size stationery. I picked them up, tilting them toward my desk lamp. The ink was brown, the paper yellowed. One letter was dated 1811, the other 1814. The first bore the salutation, "My dear Cassandra," the second, "Dearest Fanny." I squinted to read the signatures, and when the name came into focus, I gasped. *Jane Austen*. I dropped the plastic sleeves as if they were on fire, then stared at the name. Could my father really have found two previously unknown letters written by one of the world's most beloved authors? No way. Absurd.

I reached to pick one up, saw I was trembling, and grasped the edge of the desk to steady myself. A minute later, a bit calmer, I eased the plastic-encased letters toward me and studied the handwriting. The script was elegant, the letters well-formed with period-appropriate clarity. When a lowercase *d* ended a word, long left-leaning swashes embellished the ascender. In Cassandra's letter, the words "lend" and "changed" included the swash. In Fanny's, the swash adorned "need" and "bind."

I read the 1811 letter.

The tone was chatty and witty, filled with amusing descriptions of the minutia of home life, written while Cassandra, Jane Austen's sister, was off visiting relatives. Jane spoke of her success at bilbo catcher. I'd had a similar toy when I was a kid. I still owned it, and I played it occasionally. The modern American version was called cup-and-ball. A wooden cup sat atop a wooden spindle. A wooden ball sized to fit snugly inside the cup was attached to the spindle by a string. The idea was to let the ball dangle, then swing it up into the cup, landing it cleanly in one motion. Jane boasted that she made the shot ninety-eight times in a row. My record, which I'd thought was decent, was nine. Jane also discussed playing spillikins, what we call pick-up sticks, and putting up blackberry jam. She mentioned gussying up a hat and the cabbage pudding and vegetable pie she'd eaten for lunch. She also included a scathing review of Rachel Hunter's novel, *Lady Maclairn, the Victim of Villany*. In the review, Jane referenced the book she'd written in 1791, "The History of England from the reign of Henry the 4th to the death of Charles the 1st, By a partial, prejudiced, & ignorant Historian." She joked that she was less ignorant now, but just as prejudiced. According to Jane, *Lady Maclairn, the Victim of Villany* was verbose and overly melodramatic, yet, she confessed, she'd enjoyed it hugely.

I laughed. Apparently Jane Austen had enjoyed trashy novels, just like the rest of us.

She ended with, "Yours very affectionately."

The tone in the 1814 letter was quite different—less frivolous, more serious. Fanny, Jane's niece, who would have been twenty-one at the time, was considering marrying a man she didn't love. Jane started by summarizing Fanny's description of "Mr. S," stating that she couldn't believe Fanny would consider marrying a man where the best she could say of him was that he was the eldest son of a good family, that there was nothing repulsive about him, and that she was certain he would be a kind husband, neither tyrannical nor oafish. Jane wrote:

Anything is better than marrying where there is no attraction. You don't need to despise the man you marry to become an object of pity. Mild affection will take the trick. Better to live in poverty or endure the contempt of your friends and wrath of your family than bind yourself to a man you cannot admire. Know that I do not speak without experience.

The letter ended "Yours affectionately."

I couldn't believe what I was seeing. The ramifications were simultaneously humbling and overwhelming. Under normal circumstances, I'd dash downstairs and run through the warehouse to the front office, where I'd screech and shout and do my happy dance, the one I performed when I was euphoric, too jubilant for words. But this circumstance, where the letters had been delivered with a message from the grave, my father's grave, was far from normal.

I touched the plastic-sheathed letters, awestruck, dumbfounded. As the magnitude of this offering sank in—this package had really, truly come from my father—the maelstrom of emotions left me reeling, grappling for safe harbor as if I were on a dinghy in rough waters.

I placed the letters on my desk and turned to the padded envelope. Inside was a black-metal framed photograph of myself, taken during my junior year at college. I remembered the day Dad snapped it. He'd come to campus to take me to lunch. I'd been squinting into the sun, excited to see him, proud of the A I'd earned in statistics. No one but my father had that photo, and he never traveled without it.

I glanced at my computer monitor. It was almost eleven thirty. I'd already been absent forty-five minutes. I had to get back to the studio. I took photos of every object and recorded another short video, annotating it by describing what I'd discovered in the box, then replaced all the items inside the box and wrapped the paper loosely around it. I returned the key to its plastic baggie, slipped it in a zippered compartment of my tote bag, and stood, so unsteady on my feet I tipped back into my chair.

"Whoa," I said aloud. "Get it together, Josie."

Hank sauntered over and jumped into my lap, his purring machine rocketing on to high. I petted his back, using gentle, sweeping strokes, and I felt the topsy-turvy world begin to right itself. I needed to find a way to compartmentalize this situation, so I could continue recording the show. I had to. I kissed Hank's furry little head and told him he was a good boy, then lowered him to the ground. He walked back to the love seat and curled up again. Life was tough for Prescott's cats.

I stood again, and this time, I was able to walk without stumbling. There is no more effective tension reliever than petting a cat.

Downstairs, I left the package in my company's walk-in safe and returned to the front office. I told Cara I was going back to work, and left, glad for the two minutes of fresh air my walk to the studio would afford me.

Just after I rounded the corner of the building, a good-looking blond man in his forties stepped out from behind a car, his eyes fixed on the tent. He saw me and stopped short.

"Sorry," I said. "I didn't mean to startle you."

"It's okay . . . maybe you can tell me . . ." He paused to shift his gaze to mine, his intensity unnerving. "Is this where they film the TV show?"

"Yes. It's a closed set, though."

"Do you know when they'll be done?"

"No, sorry." I nodded and continued on, unsettled.

I greeted Lenny, the ever-present TV-network-provided security guard hovering just inside the tent's entry door.

Before I stepped into the studio, I glanced back, peering at an angle through one of the plastic windows in time to see the blond man disappear behind the U-Haul truck, then poke his head back out, his eyes riveted on the tent entrance.

He looked more California surfer dude than New Hampshire outdoorsman. His hair wasn't merely blond; it was streaked with lemony highlights, as if he'd spent a lot of time in the scorching sun. He wore a heather-blue long-sleeved collared T-shirt, untucked, and jeans. A few seconds later, he realized I was watching him, as if he could feel my eyes on his face. Before I could react, he tore across the parking lot, zigzagging as if he were under fire in a war zone.

I pushed past Lenny, shouting, "Follow me!"

I charged past the truck, but by the time I reached the open lot, he was gone. For the second time in a matter of hours, I ran onto Trevor Street and looked both ways. At least with Veronica Sutton, I saw a car. The blond man had simply vanished. I peered into Vaughn's Weald, the forest across the street, listening hard, but didn't hear anything more than an occasional chirping of a bird. Trevor wasn't a bus route, so the man must have parked somewhere out of sight. I couldn't imagine why. I supposed it was possible someone had dropped him off, but again, I couldn't see why.

"What can I do?" Lenny asked when he caught up to me.

"Did you see him?"

"Some guy running, blond, tall, normal weight, that's all."

"Have you ever seen him before?"

"No. What did he do?"

"He tried to hide behind the U-Haul, and when he saw I'd spotted him, he took off." I scanned the parking lot. "It's strange . . . if he didn't drive in . . . how did he get here?"

"Good question."

"Just keep an eye out, okay? Let me know if he shows up again."

Lenny said he would, scanned the surroundings with professional acuity, then jogged back to the tent.

I followed more slowly, trying to rationalize what this man could possibly be up to. One thing I knew for sure was that I didn't like the idea of a stranger prowling around my property, asking about the TV studio and our shooting schedule. I didn't like it one bit.

CHAPTER THREE

I entered the TV studio. People were scattered about, sitting or standing, looking at their devices or chatting in hushed tones. Timothy was sitting in his director's chair, reading from his phone. He was tall and lithe, with angular features. I'd never seen him wear anything other than black, and today was no exception. I crossed the room to join him, and hoisted myself up into my chair, a match to his.

"Sorry about that," I said.

He looked up. "Hey, cutie! How goes it?"

"I'm good. Ready to go."

He scanned my face, taking his time. "Something is wrong."

"No, really. Nothing."

"Well, then, something isn't right."

I touched his arm. "I got a little bit of a shock, that's all. No bad news, I promise."

"You're sure?"

"Yeah."

"Okay, then!" He gave my hand a quick pat. "Let's do it to it."

He dashed away, and I could feel the shift in energy as everyone geared up. His first stop was Starr.

A moment later, Starr called, "Ten minutes, everyone! Hair and makeup touch-ups now."

Starr's ten-minute call stretched into twenty, but I was used to waiting on set. Inside the studio, I lost all sense of time.

Marie finished her touch-ups, and I walked to where Gloria leaned against the wall near the arched window, watching the crew prepare.

"Hey," I said.

"Hey."

"Were there this many delays on photo shoots?"

"At least . . . maybe more. I learned to be productive, to work in ten-minute increments. Just now, I did some research on New Hampshire Children First! You aren't just a volunteer—you're on the board. And you were named fundraiser of the year the very first year you volunteered."

"I worked with great people, incredibly supportive."

She smiled radiantly. "Have you ever noticed how many successful people give others the credit for their own work well done? And take responsibility for screwups?"

"Thanks, but I'm not being falsely modest. They truly are a great group."

"I can tell. Giving a newbie an important award makes a dramatic statement—they're open to newcomers and new ways of thinking. I'd love to learn more about the organization."

"Wonderful! The development staff organizes a luncheon for all the volunteers every quarter. We hear reports on what's up, what's planned, what they need, that sort of thing. The fourth quarter luncheon is scheduled for next Wednesday—a week from tomorrow. Noon to two. I'd love to bring you as my guest. I can introduce you around, show you the facilities."

"Wednesday works." She tapped into her phone. "Done! It's on my schedule."

"Perfect!" I said, hoping this small first step might lead to friendship. "I'll email you the particulars."

Starr shouted, "Quiet on the set!"

"Here we go!" I said to Gloria in a near whisper. "Are you ready?"

"Always."

I envied her sangfroid.

Gloria assumed a model's position, back straight, shoulders down, three-quarter's profile, chin slightly raised, a Mona Lisa smile. I glanced at the ground to confirm I was on my mark, then beamed at camera three.

Starr counted backward from ten, and when she hit "one," Timothy called "Action!"

I counted to three, as Timothy had taught me, then turned to face Gloria. "It's great to meet you, Gloria. Thanks for coming in."

"My pleasure."

"You have a Ph.D. in archival studies," I said. "How does your academic orientation affect your work as an appraiser?"

"I start with history. I want to know why this particular object was created at that particular time by this particular person. Once I have context, I can move on to more concrete factors, such as condition, rarity, and so on."

"What's the most important factor?"

"Authenticity. Until and unless you confirm that an object is genuine, you can't determine its value."

"One of your specializations is signature verification. Tell us how that process works."

"Again, I start with history. Was this person known to sign this kind of document or object? What types of pens and ink did they typically use? From there I move into more technical issues, using a proprietary process I developed that assesses pressure point patterns."

"Thanks so much, Gloria." I took three steps away from her, moving toward the red leather chairs. I smiled at camera one, letting my enthusiasm show. "Now let's hear what the experts have to say about Beatrix Potter's *The Tale of Peter Rabbit*."

"Cut!" Timothy walked toward me, both hands extended. "You just keep getting better and better!"

I laughed, simultaneously thrilled and embarrassed at his praise. I'd never admit it because it sounded so lame, but even in my sixth season, I was still a little amazed that I actually had my own TV show.

He gave my hands a little squeeze, then turned to Starr. "Check the shadows, will you? Let's soften it up some." Starr replied that she was on it.

Timothy called, "Okay, everybody, listen up. I want to start filming scene eight at two sharp, so grips and hands, let's get the set change going."

Starr hollered, "Be back on set at one forty-five."

"You were great!" I told Gloria. "Concise and clear, a host's dream." She thanked me, and I added, "I think I'll go for a short walk, just to stretch my legs a bit, then grab something to eat. Want to come?"

"Rain check, please. I need to go over my notes with Ivan. I planned on doing it during breakfast, but stupid me, I brought the wrong ones, so I had to send him dashing to my office this morning to fetch them." She smiled at Ivan. "Thank you again." Spots of red blossomed on his cheeks. She lowered her voice one notch, implying she was sharing a confidence, but it was mostly for show since neither Ivan nor I had to struggle to hear her. "I know enough about Oliver to get all my ducks in a row before we get on camera live." She leaned in closer. "We've clashed a couple of times before—once in a courtroom. We were opposing experts on a fraud case about a year ago."

"Oh, my," I said. "I had no idea."

She smiled like an angel, her innocent look belied by her twinkling eyes. "It's okay—my side won."

I laughed.

"What's the joke?" Rory asked as she and Oliver walked up.

"A silly one that actually isn't the least bit funny . . . but I'm in a silly mood, and Josie indulged me."

"Now you have to tell us," Rory said. "I love silly."

"What goes clump, clump, clump, squish?" Gloria asked.

Rory and Oliver exchanged looks. I glanced at Gloria. Talk about quick on your feet.

"I give up," Rory said.

"An elephant with one wet sneaker."

Everyone laughed, including Ivan, which pleased me. I hadn't heard him speak more than half a dozen words all morning, and I'd never seen him smile. I also admired his ability to roll with Gloria's little white lie as smoothly as she delivered it.

"I love your shop, Oliver," Gloria said. To me, she added, "I went in there last week for the first time."

"The first time?" Rory demanded. "How long have you lived here?"

"Long enough so there's no excuse."

"My problem," I said, "is that Oliver's research is so thorough, and his prices so on-point for full retail, I can never find a bargain."

"Coming from you," Oliver said, "that's high praise."

Buying high-end antiques for resale is much harder than selling them. Typically, more than half of a dealer's quality inventory sells to another dealer, sometimes because you have a specific collector in mind, usually because you have to maintain a steady influx of prime stock, or top collectors stop coming by.

"Have you noticed a decline in in-person sales?" I asked, always eager to talk shop.

Oliver snorted. "A plummet is more like it. Everything is online now. I freely admit I was late to that party."

"Maybe you're ahead of the curve, not behind it. Online is more common at our auctions, but in-person traffic is up at the tag sale."

"That's interesting," Oliver said. "How do you account for it?"

"We think the trend has to do with the role of kismet. Everything we sell at auction is warranted. Everything we sell at the tag sale is sold strictly 'as is.' Buyers of high-end items typically attend the auction to buy a specific object or lot. Tag sale customers are a whole different breed. They rely on serendipity, not planning—they see something that intrigues them or fits with their collection. For them, an open shop is key."

Oliver laughed. "No wonder I'm on the edge of oblivion—I'm doing the exact opposite of what you just said. I don't sell low-end objects *and* I have an open shop."

I scrunched up my features. "Ouch."

"Time to rethink that puppy."

"Not necessarily," Gloria said. "I came in to say hello, and look what happened . . . I bought a President Garfield autograph for top dollar." She held up a hand. "I'm not complaining. The letter was signed while he was in office. You know how rare those are."

"Our second shortest serving president," Rory said. "Four months before he was shot. So he didn't have time to sign a lot of things while in office."

"Do you collect presidential memorabilia?" I asked Gloria.

"No, my interest was—and is—professional. I appraised President Garfield's signature on a letter from when he was in the military, and he wrote with distinct and unusual pressure points, a very different style than what I identified in the Thomas Jefferson letters lo those many years ago." She smiled at Oliver. "Looking at this Garfield letter through a loupe in your shop . . .

well, let's just say that I can't wait to get it under a microscope!" She glanced at her watch. "And now, if you'll excuse me, it's time to review my notes." She turned toward Ivan. "All set?"

Ivan said he was, and Gloria led the way to the tent.

Rory faced the set. "It gives me quite a feel to be here." Her gaze took in the cameras, the overhead lights hanging from black piping, the cables and cords snaking around the floor. "Never in a million years would I have thought I'd be inside a TV studio."

"Me, either," I said.

"What? You're the star!"

"Completely unexpected, I assure you." I issued the same invitation to go for a walk to Rory, and got turned down again.

"I can't walk worth a darn." Rory gently tapped her left knee. "I took a nasty tumble last week on my dirt bike."

"You rode a dirt bike?"

"I don't like your choice of tense or your tone of voice, young lady," she said sternly. "I *ride* dirt bikes. I'm on a brief hiatus while my knee heals."

I laughed. "My apologies." I turned to Oliver. "What a mom."

"Best ever." He kissed the top of her head.

"*He's* the best ever. Best son a mother ever had. His only flaw is that he doesn't ride dirt bikes." She patted Oliver's cheek. "Go with Josie. You don't need to babysit me. It would do you good to get some fresh air."

Oliver laughed. "She's been telling me that since I was four."

"You always had your nose in a book, starting when you were old enough to pick one up. You've stayed with it, I'll give you that."

"I was a prodigy," Oliver said. "If you doubt it, just ask my mom."

"Well, you were. That's enough of memory lane. I'm going to head out to the tent and sit this creaky old knee of mine down. Byzie!" She limped toward the exit.

Oliver and I followed. He paused by the lunch buffet, which had been set up on the long side of the tent. Round tables—some designed to seat eight or ten, most smaller—filled the space.

"I'll have to pass on the walk, too," he said, his eyes resting on Gloria and

Ivan, who were sitting with their heads together at a small table in the corner farthest from the studio entrance. Gloria was reading from a brown leather portfolio and nodding at something Ivan was saying. "I want to make nice to Gloria, to let her know I have no hard feelings—the last time we met she cleaned my clock."

"I'm sorry to hear that."

He waved his loss aside. "I had the bum side of a lawsuit, defending a so-called expert's authentication of a George Washington letter." He lowered his voice. "Since I couldn't endorse the authentication without perjuring myself, I had to rely on a lofty discussion of process—my job came down to helping the jury understand the complexity of verifying the signature. The truth is all I had was sizzle—Gloria got the steak." He held up a hand. "She won fair and square, but I sure didn't like having my lunch handed to me in public, so maybe I said some things I shouldn't have." He grinned. "You've never seen that side of me."

"The competitive side? Never! Would you like some pumpkins?"

He gave a shout of laughter. "Talk about a non sequitur!"

"My walk takes me to the Congregational church next door. Pastor Ted grows pumpkins this time of year, available for the taking. Want me to collect a few for your shop?"

"A nice thought, but too late. Mom has already decorated the shop to within an inch of its life. Halloween is her favorite holiday. Mine, too, now that I think of it. I'm going as Andy Warhol this year. My date is going as Edie Sedgwick. Very avant-garde." His gaze shifted to Gloria. "How did you happen to invite Gloria anyway?"

"She's the best. Just like you."

"Thanks. I hope she remembers her audience. Sometimes she's too pedantic for nonacademic settings."

I had no way of gauging whether Oliver's comment sprang from professional jealousy, sour grapes, or whether he was genuinely concerned for the quality of my show.

"I'm not worried," I said. "The bits we taped yesterday and her comments just now were fine. Besides, the crew can always edit out jargon or whatever."

"What did she say yesterday, anyway?"

I laughed at his not-so-subtle attempt to get me to share the skinny with him in advance of their on-air "battle." "Wouldn't you like to know."

"Hey, no harm in trying." One corner of Oliver's mouth shot up and he faux shot me with his index finger, then wove his way through the tables toward Gloria and Ivan.

CHAPTER FOUR

I was a walker. I liked bicycling, too, taking the back roads, watching the world go by, but walking was my favorite way to see the world close up. I liked the slower pace. I trekked along the beach most mornings, a new habit since my husband, Ty, and I moved to the shore. This morning we'd walked to Maine, a private joke, since our house was at the north end of Rocky Point Beach, only about a half mile from the state line, marked by a long jetty.

Now, I entered Mimi's Copse. The air was cool and dry, a perfect autumn day. The birch and poplar leaves glowed like spun gold. A month earlier, the packed dirt path had been obscured by soft pine needles, and I'd swished as I'd walked. Today, the needles were covered with crackly fallen leaves, and I crunched my way along.

I was glad for the quiet time to think about the next segment, the actual battle between the experts, invariably the toughest to manage. The primary difficulty in facilitating a three-person discussion was keeping a bunch of different-size wheels spinning simultaneously. I needed to allow both experts adequate time to talk, without either one dominating the debate; ask questions designed to foster lively interactions, while maintaining civility; and delve into the nitty-gritty, without boring viewers. The responsibility was, to say the least, nerve-racking. Timothy never shut me down. He wanted me to get people talking and keep them talking. If our conversation lasted an hour for a six-minute segment, so be it. During the post-production stage, it was his job to work with the editors to make the segment fit within the time allocation, whatever it was, and they were masters at the task.

I was also glad to have some time to think about Veronica Sutton, this stranger who appeared out of nowhere and disappeared without an explanation, with barely a goodbye. There was so much I wanted to know. The genesis of her relationship with my dad, its nature and duration. What she knew about the Jane Austen letters. How she came into possession of the box and objects, and why she'd delivered them today. Everything.

I stepped out from under the leafy canopy into the sunlight. No one was around. At the back of the lot, Pastor Ted's community garden was packed with fall produce. The tangled vines enveloped plump pumpkins and long zucchini, aromatic chives, thyme, and mint, and a few late-growing tomatoes. The garden was raised, fenced, and covered to keep critters out. A hand-painted sign on the gate invited folks to take whatever they could use.

I pulled my phone from my back pocket and called Ty. He was in charge of regional training for Homeland Security and today he was running a workshop in Manchester, New Hampshire's largest city, so I wasn't surprised to get his voicemail. I left a message saying I was calling to say hello, that all was well, and that I loved him.

I exited the church grounds onto Trevor Street, walking farther east for about ten minutes, then headed back, retracing my steps across the church parking lot and through Mimi's Copse. When I reached my property, I glanced at my phone. It was a little after one—enough time to grab something to eat, check in with my staff, and be ready for the one forty-five call. With maybe a few minutes to try to locate Veronica Sutton.

I chose a small chicken Caesar salad and an iced tea from the buffet in the tent, then stopped in the front office. Cara told me that nothing required my attention. Upstairs in my private office, I slipped in my fancy new earbuds, the ones with noise cancellation capability that delivered on the promised immersive musical experience. I was in a jazz mood, and decided on Dave Brubeck's "Take Five."

Googling "Veronica Sutton" turned up nearly thirty-eight million hits. I added "New Hampshire" to the search parameter, and still got more than nine hundred thousand. When I added "age seventy," I was back over a million. Hopeless. I searched all the social media platforms I could think of, and tried to sort through the plethora of Veronica Suttons, but didn't make any headway.

I brought up the security camera footage from the units mounted high on the light poles that ringed the property, selecting images as I ate. Decent quality color photos were snapped every three seconds. I started at ten thirty, my guess as to when Veronica had arrived.

According to the time stamp on the security footage, she drove in at ten thirty-four, parked, and entered the front office. Six minutes later, she settled herself under the willow tree. After reviewing all the footage, I choose three images: one full length, one full face, and one a profile, taken when she reached into her tote bag for the brown paper–wrapped box. I also captured an image of her vehicle's mud-streaked license plate. Even enlarging it, I couldn't distinguish any numbers or letters. We'd had a fair amount of rain earlier in the week, but I didn't for a minute believe the license plate had gotten muddied because she drove through a puddle. The rest of the car was pristine, which meant she'd smeared mud over the tag on purpose.

I continued my review, looking for the blond man. I fast-forwarded until I saw him walking along Trevor, coming from the west, where the interstate intersected Trevor a mile away. That was at eleven twenty-one. At eleven twenty-eight, he stepped onto my grounds near the tag sale venue entrance, having hiked through Carter's Forest, the woods that bordered my property to the west. My brow creased with puzzlement. We only ran tag sales on Saturdays, so there was no reason for him to be there. There was no reason for him to be in Carter's Forest, period, or on my grounds. I'd felt uncomfortable observing his odd behavior in person, and I felt more than uncomfortable now.

He edged his way toward the six-foot-six high fieldstone wall that hid an assortment of mechanics from public view. Why would he care where we housed our air-conditioning condenser and backup generators? He glanced over his shoulder as if he wanted to be certain no one could see him, then walked furtively around the wall toward the back. At eleven thirty-seven, with his creeping around apparently finished, he reappeared and walked across the parking lot. That's when he spoke to me. Five minutes later I had him on camera sprinting into Carter's Forest, and passing out of my camera's range.

I captured an image showing him full face, and saved that photo to the cloud, along with the three I'd selected of Veronica and the one of her car, then downloaded them onto my phone.

I ran through the rest of the images, hoping I wouldn't see anything else disturbing, and I didn't. I saw myself exit the tent en route to my walk. Five minutes later, Starr came out for a smoke. After crushing her butt under the heel of her boot, she picked it up with a tissue. One of the cameramen came out, too, a minute later, also to smoke. He left his butt on the asphalt.

I felt weirdly voyeuristic.

I enlarged the full-length photo of Veronica, and leaned back in my chair to study it. Elegant was a fitting description, with her manicured nails, her makeup tastefully applied, her hair coiffed. She was an attractive woman by any measure, but she must have been a stunner when she was younger. I examined every inch of visible skin—her face, neck, hands, and legs, even the few inches above her wrists where her coat sleeve ended, hoping to spot a birthmark, a tattoo, anything that would help me locate her. Nothing. Her skin was the color of milk, as if she hadn't been in the sun in years, with no marks, not even a few freckles or a tiny blemish. She wore diamond earrings, studs. They were large, but not ostentatious, maybe a karat each. Her necklace was lovely, but not distinctive, a diamond eternity circle pendant. She wore no rings.

"Why don't you want to talk to me?" I asked the photo.

I glanced at the corner of my monitor. It read one forty. I had to go.

"I'm going to find you," I told her.

I walked through the warehouse, passing rows of shelves stocked with collectibles and antiques, inventory for the tag sale and a series of worktables. The kitty domain came next, with its plush rug, cushy kitty beds, food and water stations, and a litter box hidden behind a privacy screen. Cordoned-off areas, devoted to purchased or consigned lots ready for appraisal, took up most of the rest of the space. I reached the door that led to the corridor that connected the warehouse to the TV studio. I tapped in the security code, and stepped inside. The door closed behind me with a soft whish. The hermetically sealed space was dimly lit and eerily silent. When I reached the studio entrance, I pasted a smile on my face, and opened the door.

Timothy stood behind the bank of cameras talking to one of the operators. I waved as I joined Marie at her station. Oliver was already getting primped, and I greeted him as I hopped into my chair. Marie inspected my face, then settled in to work. Normally, I loved her constant flow of comfortable chitchat, but today I only listened with half an ear, and I didn't listen at all once Gloria stomped in and took her place next to me.

"What's wrong?" I asked.

"Do you remember the fable about the farmer and the viper? The farmer took pity on the half-frozen creature and tucked him into his coat to warm him up."

"And then the viper bit him."

"Killing him."

"Who's the viper?" I asked.

"Sorry . . . I'm in a mood, that's all. It'll pass." She shut her eyes and crossed her arms across her chest.

I refocused on Marie, but not for long. While she whisked a powder puff over my cheeks, happily babbling about her plans to go to the Diamond Cowboy later with some of the crew for wings, brews, and line dancing, I watched a little drama playing out in the shadows.

Ivan, Gloria's grad assistant, stood near a small utility table, staring at the floor, nibbling his lip. Rory stood next to him. She tapped him on the upper arm and when he looked up, she said something. He shook his head, his forehead wrinkling, evidently distressed.

Marie used her pinky to blend the foundation at my hairline. "Look down."

I looked down.

"Look up."

I looked up.

"Look at me."

I looked at her.

"You're gorgeous!" she said. "My work here is done!" She bent at the waist, arms out, hands fluttering, a ballerina's bow.

I laughed and thanked her.

Ivan said, "No!" loud enough so Marie turned to see what was going on. He traversed the studio, disappearing into the tent.

Rory's shoulders shot up, then sank, and she flipped her palms in an "Oh, well" gesture, but from her icy expression, I doubted it was a shrug of frustration, disappointment, or indifference—she was mad.

I considered whether I, as the host, should do something about any of the ill will swirling about, and decided no. Everyone involved was an adult, and I didn't have the mental energy to deal with other people's problems, not today. The questions that burned inside me, that caused my heart to hammer against my ribs until I felt sick, weren't related to Gloria, Rory, or Ivan—they were centered on Veronica Sutton, my dad, and the Jane Austen letters.

I decided to follow Gloria's lead. I shut my eyes and tuned out the world.

Twenty years of not knowing that my dad had been thinking of me in the days before he died. Twenty years of wondering what happened to the photograph I knew he'd carried in his briefcase, placing it on hotel bedside tables around the world, a routine as familiar to him as brushing his teeth. It seemed needlessly cruel to have kept it from me for so long, but Veronica hadn't struck me as spiteful or vindictive.

But that was all on an intellectual level.

Emotionally, I was a wreck. Did Veronica have something against me? If she'd been a good friend of my dad's, why wouldn't she talk to me? It felt as if she were punishing me. I knew I was overstating it, that I was immersed in the agitation of the moment, with inchoate thoughts coursing through my mind like a lit fuse. Once I'd gotten over the initial shock, I was certain I'd be better able to assess the situation objectively, but at this point, I couldn't. I told myself to focus on the positive. I had these objects now. I could hold the notecard my dad had touched, and feel his caring. I could place the photo on my desk, and remember how much we'd loved each other. I swept aside a tear, as such noble thoughts dissipated like early morning fog, replaced by pricks of anger. From the day my mother had died a horrific cancer death when I was thirteen, my dad had been my rock, guiding me through the eddies of a complicated and unpredictable world. Yet now it seemed I'd hardly known him. If Veronica had been nothing more than a random acquaintance, a business colleague or a friend of a friend, why had she held on to the box for twenty years before giving it to me?

I swiveled to face the window and watched the sun dapple the maple's gold and russet leaves.

I supposed it was possible that Veronica hadn't withheld the box from me on purpose. Maybe she'd forgotten all about it until she happened upon it again, when she'd moved or cleared out a storage facility. Perhaps she just came into possession of it, say, through an inheritance. Possibly, she'd been in a coma all these years. Or had suffered from amnesia. I shook my head at the futility of my guessing game.

Whatever circumstances had driven her to deliver the box today, if she and my father had actually been good friends, then I had to face the fact that I'd been wrong in thinking I knew all his friends. And if I was wrong about that—what other secrets had he kept from me? It was as if the world I'd experienced as colorful had dulled to black-and-white, the vivid videos of my life transmuted into a series of chiaroscuro still shots. I felt unmoored, adrift in a sea of uncertainty.

"Josie?"

I heard my name, but it didn't fully register.

"Josie?"

The voice was familiar, but intrusive, an irritant, like a mosquito buzzing nearby.

"Josie?"

The mosquito hovered closer, its drone louder. My temper flared, and I was tempted to swat it away. I was typically a model of grace under pressure, but not today. Today, I was a model of jagged nerve endings and bristly irritation.

"Josie?"

I opened my eyes.

Greg, one of the audio guys, stood in front of me with a lavalier mic. Greg was short and wiry, with a mustache that drooped over the corners of his mouth.

"Sorry," I said, slipping into my professional persona. I was good at it, even though I didn't feel very professional. "I was zoned out."

"No worries."

I stood so he could clip the mic to my lapel and the transmitter to the back waistband of my slacks.

"Give us a test talk, please," Greg said.

I spoke in my normal tone. "Testing one two three. Testing one two three."

Greg waited for a thumbs-up from the guys at the sound board, and when he got it, he told me I was good to go.

"Everybody!" Starr called. "It's show time!"

I stepped over and around the thick cables to another masking tape X on the floor, this one facing camera four. Oliver and Gloria followed Starr's instructions and stood at either end of the butcher block worktable to my right, facing camera two.

Timothy reviewed the scene, taking his time, as thorough and diligent as always.

I wondered how Veronica had met my father and what their relationship had entailed. Over the years, Dad had told me hundreds of stories about his colleagues, who was an ally and who was a pain in the neck, who was an up-and-comer and who was on a downhill slide. He talked about their personal lives, too, sharing who got married and who got divorced, whose child got into college and whose was arrested. Never once had he mentioned Veronica's name. My dad had traveled all the time for work and for pleasure, consulting with clients, attending conferences, haunting museums and art galleries, and hiking through city parks and along mountain trails. He could have met her anywhere, but his not mentioning her could only mean one thing: Veronica had been his girlfriend, his lover, not merely a work associate or friend.

"Quiet on the set," Timothy boomed. Silence descended like a shroud.

Why hadn't my father told me? Had he worried that I'd be jealous or upset, that I'd see it as a betrayal of my mother? Surely he'd known me better than that.

Starr gave the countdown, then Timothy called, "Action!"

My father and I had supported each other consistently and unconditionally, or so I'd thought. I would have been thrilled for him.

"Josie?"

That my father had, apparently, kept such an important part of his life secret, that he hadn't trusted me to be happy for him, crushed me.

Timothy stepped into my line of vision. "Josie? Are you all right?"

Everyone was looking at me, some eyes curious, others confused or worried.

I met Timothy's empathetic gaze. "Sorry," I whispered.

"No prob!" He turned toward camera four. "Cut!" The red light went dark. "Kill Josie's mic."

"Done!" someone called a moment later.

Timothy came on set and spoke to me, his tone soft and compassionate. "What's going on?"

"I got some news," I whispered, "not bad, just startling. I guess I'm having more trouble than I expected concentrating on anything else. I'm sorry."

"What do you think . . . can you do this?"

I had to tell Timothy the truth. This was not a fake-it-till-you-make-it moment. The camera outed phonies faster than a lie detector. "I don't know."

"What can I do to help?"

I glanced around. So many people depended on me. "Nothing."

He clasped my hand. "Seriously . . . let me help."

I laid my hand on top of his, and looked him straight in the eye. "There's nothing you can do, Timothy, but thank you." Unexpected tears filled my eyes. "I'm sorry to be mysterious, but now's not the time for me to share what's going on. When I can, I will." I forced a smile. "I really am okay. Everything really is okay. I promise. I'm just a little rattled."

"Okay then, here's what we're going to do. I'm beat. We did a marathon day yesterday and were up with the roosters today. I'm calling a time-out. You take the rest of the day. We'll reconvene in the morning."

"We started at eight, which proves you know nothing about roosters. Thank you, Timothy, but I don't need that long. An hour, maybe."

"An hour's fine. And if you need longer, you'll take longer. My priority is you." Timothy lowered his voice to a whisper. "Don't worry about the guests . . . their honorariums cover the entire day."

"I'm sorry to be such a problem child."

"You're perfect." He gave me a little hug. "It's okay to need time to process whatever is going on." He lowered his voice to a conspiratorial whisper. "I won't tell a soul that you're human. It'll be our secret."

I laughed and went up on tiptoe to kiss his cheek.

He walked to center stage and spoke to the room. "We're on a short break, everyone. Be in your places at three thirty."

"Touch-ups at three fifteen," Starr called.

Greg ran up to remove my mic.

I blew Timothy a kiss and left through the inside corridor.

I work best with structure. I don't do well with ambiguity. I flounder when I don't know what to do. I needed to locate Veronica Sutton.

"Hi, Veronica," I said in a friendly tone, trying it on for size. *No way.* She wasn't a friend, and I knew in my bones that she never would be. That said, once I talked to her, once I heard her story, whatever it was, I suspected that everything else would fall into place.

CHAPTER FIVE

Back upstairs, I brought up the photos I'd selected earlier, including the one of Veronica's vehicle. Comparing the photo of her car to online examples, I determined she'd been driving a 2016 Mercedes C 300. It didn't matter—New Hampshire's motor vehicle registration database didn't allow for a search by vehicle type. Neither did Vermont's, Massachusetts', or Maine's.

I considered whether my security company could help. I called Russ, the account manager Sterling Security had assigned to my company. While I waited for Russ to pick up, I stared at Veronica's full-length photo on my monitor. After Russ and I exchanged greetings, I asked if he could use facial recognition software to identify a woman I needed to locate.

"Sorry, Josie. That's not a service we offer."

"Oh, wow! Really? Can you refer me to someone who does?"

"I'm afraid not. We're actually in the middle of an internal review on the topic. There are a bunch of legal and ethical issues associated with using biometric data."

I'd think about ethics later. Right now, I needed to find the woman who said she'd been a good friend of my dad's. I thanked Russ and called Ty.

Before Ty took the job with Homeland Security, he'd been Rocky Point's police chief. Between the two positions, he'd banked unparalleled knowledge of law enforcement tools and capabilities, and I knew that if he could help me, he would.

"No, of course not," he said, when I explained what I needed.

"I don't think you understand, Ty. Veronica Sutton told me she'd been friends with my dad. I have to find her."

"First, accessing the databases used by facial recognition software programs is regulated, and you're not on the list. Second, no crime was committed that might justify an exception. Third, private companies and individuals using the software face all sorts of thorny issues. There are ethical concerns relating to privacy and liability questions related to accuracy, which, taken together, lead to legal exposure on multiple fronts, and I really don't think you want to wade into that quagmire."

"I'll consider your objections. My question is who to call."

He chuckled. "I love you, Josie."

"You're not going to help me."

"Help you how? Break the law? Risk falling off an ethical precipice? Set yourself up for a lawsuit? No. Of course I'm not going to help you. And don't even think of accessing it yourself on the dark web. That would open you up to every con and scam known to man."

"I'm frustrated."

"That I understand. What did you think of Veronica Sutton?"

"I don't know. Nothing. I only spoke to her for a minute, not more. I'm mad at her. She acted like she didn't want to talk to me, but that doesn't make any sense. She could have shipped the box. She hand-delivered it for a reason. Either she chickened out or something spooked her."

"What?"

"I don't know."

"Maybe she just wanted to meet you," Ty said. "You know, to look you in the eye."

My father always said to look a person in the eye, that eyes truly were the windows to the soul. Maybe he'd said the same thing to Veronica and that was why she'd wanted to meet me.

"You're saying I didn't pass muster, and that's why she bolted?" I asked.

"Not at all. She might have intended to hand you the box and skedaddle all along."

"That isn't logical," I said, irritated.

"Just because you don't know her motive, doesn't mean she doesn't have one, you know that."

Years earlier, I'd asked Ty how the police could possibly hope to catch a random serial killer when there was no motive. His answer had chilled me then, and it chilled me now as I thought of it. He said there was always a motive. You may not know it or understand it. It may not seem logical, or rational, or even lucid—but there's always a motive.

He was saying that the same truism applied here, but I couldn't see it. "Give me a scenario where handing me the box and running away is logical."

"When you find her, you can ask her."

I exhaled, my frustration growing. "How can I find her?"

"You tell me."

I turned to face my window. White fluffy clouds floated across the cerulean sky. "I don't know."

"You'll figure it out." I heard muffled voices in the background. "I have to get back to the workshop. Are you okay?"

"No."

"But you're coping."

"That's what I do."

"You know I adore you, Josie."

"I adore you, too, Ty. Even if you won't help me."

He chuckled again, adding to my annoyance. "See you soon."

The rage that had blazed inside me just minutes earlier dwindled to a slow, steady simmer. I tried hard never to judge people, certainly not without understanding their perspectives. I could easily lather myself into a frenzy fueled by white-hot fury at the mere thought that Veronica had withheld my father's memorabilia for two decades, but until I knew why, I needed to call on my objective, analytical self, and temper my emotional, impulsive self. It didn't work. As my anger toward Veronica Sutton diminished, my resentment toward my father increased. If I was right that their relationship had been romantic, then the two of them had conspired to keep me out of the loop. Which meant he'd either suggested the idea or endorsed it. Unshed tears burned my eyes. I was so hurt, I felt like flinging myself to the ground, thumping my heels, and screaming *How could you have done this to me?* I leaned back in my leather chair and closed my eyes, willing my normal calmness to return and, after a minute, the rancor that threatened my equanimity loosened its grip.

I ran through Ty's arguments. I got it. I could see every one of his points, and I could even agree that, theoretically, he was right. But that didn't get me any closer to finding Veronica Sutton. I knew there were companies that would provide information on people for a fee—often an astonishing amount of information, sometimes a horrifying amount. A momentary twinge of revulsion stopped me. I was a privacy fiend, so the magnitude of what I was considering wasn't lost on me, but I had no choice, not really. I *had* to locate her.

I vetted alternatives by checking well-respected review sites and the Better Business Bureau, and selected the provider that seemed the most aboveboard, yet effective. I filled out the form, or tried to. I had hardly any information about Veronica Sutton. As I skipped box after box, not knowing her address, phone number, date of birth, car registration number, or anything else, I realized how unlikely it was I'd get the info I sought. My finger hovered over the keyboard for a few seconds, while I suppressed another flare-up of the ethical conundrum I was trying to ignore, telling myself that this occasion was the exception that proved the rule, that my desire to find her went beyond the personal, that I had to learn what she knew about the Jane Austen letters. As soon as the flare-up quieted, I authorized the charge on my credit card and sat back to wait.

It didn't take long. They were unable to provide even the most rudimentary information. It was what they called a failed search. They automatically refunded half the fee, as per their agreement, and that was that. I slapped my desk. I was irrationally enraged, and I worked to tamp it down, drawing in slow, deep breaths, repeating the silent promise that I'd find her, over and over again, like a mantra. I kept at it until my self-control returned, at least enough of it to proceed for the moment.

I had one last hope—I could ask Wes Smith for help. Wes was a reporter for the local paper, *Seacoast Star*. He was a sometimes ally and a frequent thorn in my side. Wes was connected to a web of sources that defied description. He was able and resourceful, with the journalistic habits of a terrier, adept at discovery and pursuit.

"Whatcha got?" Wes asked, skipping hello like always.

"I need a favor. Your paper uses facial recognition software, right?"

"We use a variety of investigative tools," he said, sounding snooty.

"I need to reach a woman about an appraisal. I have her photo, the name she gave me, and the make of car she was driving, and nothing else."

"Why didn't she give you her contact info?"

"I don't think she expected me to need to talk to her again," I said, shading the truth.

"What's in it for me?"

"The antique involved is huge. It will position your paper as an international player."

"What is it?"

"I can't tell you now."

"Josie!"

"I'll owe you, Wes. You know I always pay up."

Our quid pro quo relationship was informal, but carried the weight of our word, a commitment neither of us took lightly.

"You'd better. Email me the photos and whatever else you've got and I'll see what I can find."

And that, I told myself, *is how you do that.*

I walked to the front office a new woman, reinvigorated, charged with hope. I'd seized the moment. Picasso said that the foundation of all success was action. I'd learned over the years that doing something, even if it didn't lead to the outcome I'd hoped, was better than diddling around waiting for inspiration.

I still had thirty minutes before I needed to report to Marie for my retouch. I sat at the guest table in the front office, gratified to see my staff engaged in normal activities, a comforting counterpoint to my internal turmoil.

Cara was on the phone giving someone directions to Saturday's tag sale. She waved as I got settled.

Sasha, Prescott's chief antiques appraiser, shook her head dismissively at her computer monitor.

"Is everything okay?" I asked her.

"Yes. I was just reading a catalogue note for some outdoor statuary. It's fair to say that their research isn't up to our standards."

Fred, Prescott's other antiques appraiser, turned a page of a competitor's auction catalogue, and his nose wrinkled. Fred was an antiques snob, so I conjectured that he considered one or more of the objects unworthy. The cover showed an Audubon bird print. I couldn't read the title, a no-no. You want prospective buyers to understand an auction's theme from one glance across the room or as they're surfing around your website. We spent hours nailing down every one of our auction titles and cover designs.

"Is the auction's theme related to Audubon's *Birds of America*?" I asked.

"No." Fred pushed up his black square-framed glasses. "Guess again."

"Nineteenth-century art prints?"

"Nope."

"I give up."

"Birds."

"Birds?" I repeated. "I suppose you could infer that theme from the cover art."

"Maybe, but since this is the only Audubon print in the auction, it feels more like a bait and switch to me. There are bird chandeliers, bird-handled flatware, and lots of nothing-special bird miscellany. It's a mess."

"Are you reviewing it because you think we should run a bird-themed auction?"

"No, but Sasha does. She asked me to look at it."

"Birds?" I asked Sasha.

She pushed her lank brown hair behind her ears. "Fred is exaggerating for effect."

"I'm here," he said. "I can hear you."

"What I *said* was that a forest creature theme might be interesting. We have that serving tray with olive wood inlaid birds and a few Victorian bird Christmas ornaments. Owls continue to be popular, and we have some nice outdoor statuary we could include, including a rabbit family and a deer. And unlike this other gallery, *we'd* research everything properly."

"You can't have my acorn thimble case," Fred said, continuing to flip pages in the catalogue.

"It might make sense to include it."

I turned to Fred. "What acorn thimble case?"

"Sally Cruz has an eighteen-karat gold thimble case designed to look like an acorn," Fred said, referring to a client. "A squirrel charm is perched on top."

Over a span of thirty years, Sally Cruz had amassed a world-class collection of thimbles. She was planning to retire, and hoped to earn enough from the sale of her collection to fund a bungalow on a Bahamian beach.

"I just know Sasha's going to call dibs, claiming my acorn case fits her woodland critter theme better than my thimble theme."

"Which auction will garner the higher price for the client?" I asked.

"The thimble sale," Fred said. "Offer quality objects to specialized collectors and they'll beat a path to your door. It's a no-brainer."

"What do you think, Sasha?"

"The acorn case would make a charming addition to the auction I have in mind, but . . ." She flipped a palm. ". . . I agree with Fred."

"Me, too. A unanimous vote."

He grinned, gave me a thumbs-up, and swung back to his monitor.

I leaned back, more relaxed than I'd felt since Veronica Sutton had driven into my life. I was about to walk to the studio when Starr texted. Timothy had taken a quick look through the last segment, and he wanted to "pink it up," so the crew was switching out the gels. They needed an extra half hour. I returned to my private office.

I assumed it was too soon to have heard from Wes, but I was wrong. He'd already sent an email. The woman in the photograph was indeed named Veronica Sutton. She had a Sarasota, Florida, address. A black Mercedes was registered to her at that location. Her phone number started with a 941 area code—Sarasota.

I stared at my monitor, my mouth ash dry.

I'd found her.

CHAPTER SIX

I'd located Veronica Sutton, but I didn't feel relieved or excited. I felt guilty. The ethical dilemma I'd managed to brush aside came rushing back. I was breathing too fast, and I couldn't stop.

What have I done?

I'd breached the privacy wall Veronica Sutton had built.

When it came to morality, I tended to see issues as black or white, rarely perceiving even the slightest hint of gray, all while knowing that other people might view the same situations through a more flexible lens. I never judged. I wasn't arrogant. I didn't believe I was the global arbiter of what was best or appropriate for other people, only myself. As such, I had to face the fact that I had contravened my own standards.

I'd done the wrong thing, but I couldn't put the genie back in the bottle, so I had a decision to make as to whether I should proceed or retreat, except it wasn't really a decision at all. The idea that I would give up searching for the truth about my father was ludicrous.

I copied Veronica Sutton's number onto a pad of notepaper. I reached for my phone, then paused mid-motion. Impetuousness was my enemy. I needed a plan, and I didn't have one.

I had no idea how to get Veronica Sutton to change her mind about talking to me. Simply calling her out of the blue was a fool's errand. What could I say? *Hi, we met earlier today. I have a few questions.* She'd hang up on me. I needed to frame my call in such a way that she'd *want* to talk to me. This moment felt like one of the few instances in life when I had to get it right the first time.

I ran my finger over the notepaper where I'd written her phone number.

I could ask, demand, or beg.

Asking was neutral, and made it easy for her to refuse to talk to me.

Demanding was aggressive, and would put her on the defensive and make her even more determined to avoid me.

Begging weakened me, but might work, except I didn't know her capacity for compassion, for empathy.

Hank interrupted my musings. He sauntered into my office followed by Angela, the newest feline addition to the Prescott's family. Angela was black with a small white triangle under her chin. I'd named her Angela because angels wear white. Hank leapt onto the love seat, walked in a circle, then stretched out, covering his eyes with his right front paw. Angela leaped into my lap and mewed, asking for a cuddle.

"Good girl," I said, stroking her. "How's my sweet angel?"

She settled against my chest, purring.

Ask, demand, beg.

Ask, demand, beg.

I needed to know more about Veronica Sutton's disposition and personality before determining a strategy. I tried Googling her again, adding her Florida address, and hit the mother lode.

The first result led to a Sarasota, Florida, chamber of commerce newsletter from eight years ago. The president of the chamber had interviewed Veronica Sutton on the occasion of her retirement from the children's clothing line she'd founded twelve years earlier. Her company, called Together by Ryan B, was based in Sarasota.

My mouth opened, then closed. I stared at the monitor, transfixed. "Ryan B." That's what it said. *Ryan B.* The letters blurred, then danced. I gripped the chair arms amid a cacophony of silent screams pinging through my brain with the clarity and terror of bullets hitting metal.

My father's name had been Ryan Benjamin Prescott.

Ryan B. Veronica had named her company for my dad.

I closed my eyes to stop the world from spinning. The shrieks in my head quieted, then stopped, and I opened my eyes. I'd read it right. *Ryan B.*

"Look at that, Angela," I whispered.

The accompanying photograph showed a younger version of the same woman I'd talked to this morning, confirming that this Veronica Sutton was the one I'd been looking for. Her hair fell in soft waves to her shoulders and was closer to a chestnut brown than today's auburn. In the photo, she had a good tan, passé now, and even then, which said something about her, though I wasn't sure what. That she was vain, perhaps, or shallow, or maybe anti-science, disdaining sunblock, dismissing the danger of overexposure to the sun. None of which could possibly apply to a woman who'd been a good friend of my father's.

I read on.

Veronica had been a partner in a New York City–based private equity firm that specialized in the fashion industry. Her firm had been located in the World Trade Center. The chamber president asked if she'd been nearby during the 9/11 attack. "No," she was quoted as saying, "I had an appointment with a lingerie designer in Midtown, so I wasn't there. I lost dear friends that day."

The interviewer asked if that's why she moved to Florida, and she said no, explaining that was why she moved out of New York City, but not why she moved to Florida. She chose Florida because it offered her business an educated work force, reliable infrastructure, and convenient access to suppliers. She moved to Sarasota in mid-October 2001, only weeks after the towers fell, after my dad's death.

I still couldn't locate a social media presence for her, other than a basic LinkedIn profile. The company, Together by Ryan B, had more than 380,000 followers on its Instagram account and nearly a quarter of a million likes on Facebook. The clothes displayed on the company's website featured colorful prints and exquisite tailoring—and expensive price tags. Positioned just below the company name, a tagline read, "Trendsetting fashion for trendsetting kids." The "About Us" page explained that Veronica Sutton had founded the company to celebrate children's individuality as an antidote to bullying, and I found myself warming to her.

Angela vaulted to the ground.

I brought up Veronica's full-face photo. She appeared to be affable, but looks can be deceiving. Shakespeare knew: *Look like the innocent flower, but be the serpent under 't*. I chastised myself for my unwarranted cynicism. Here I was again, disparaging her, after I'd just a minute earlier praised her. I didn't like that I was seesawing from one emotion to another, especially since my conclusions were based on mere speculation. I needed more information.

I minimized the photo and turned back to the window. The church steeple rose above the trees. Maybe learning more about her wasn't hopeless after all. If she'd been a good friend of my father's, I knew several things about her, conclusions I could trust. I knew she was kind and considerate. My dad wouldn't be friends with a woman who wasn't. She was also smart and articulate, qualities he relished in his friends. She'd be adventurous, too, not so much in a zipline sort of way, but in a sure-let's-try-that-new-restaurant sort of way. She'd be a straight shooter, too, giving her opinion directly when asked.

I dialed her number, crossing my fingers for luck that she would answer, and that she would talk to me, and waited for the ring.

It never came.

Instead, I listened to a stock message informing me that the number I had dialed had been disconnected and that no additional information was available.

I felt deflated.

I'd been so sure of myself, so confident. I tried the number again, in case I'd misdialed. I hadn't.

A few hours ago, Veronica was in New Hampshire, not Florida. Maybe she'd driven up to admire the foliage, but it was also possible that she'd moved north. Perhaps she got a local phone number and hadn't yet had a chance to register her car. A good idea, but another bust. My search didn't turn up a landline phone number for her in New Hampshire, or any nearby state, and I had no way of finding a cell phone number.

I had another idea—if I could discover when Veronica had left Florida, maybe I could follow her trail.

I checked with an online real estate site for information about Veronica Sutton's Florida home. It had sold two months earlier. The county records confirmed it, and provided the names of the new owners, Hilda and John Potts. They had a listed phone number.

An older woman answered with a cheery "Hello!"

"Hi. My name is Josie Prescott. I'm an antiques appraiser from New Hampshire. In connection with an appraisal, I need to reach the former owner of your house, Veronica Sutton. I was hoping you might have contact information for her."

"Oh, my, how interesting! What's the antique?"

"I'm sorry, but I'm not at liberty to say. Are you Mrs. Potts?"

"Yes, that's right . . . call me Hilda."

"Do you have a phone number for Ms. Sutton, Hilda?"

"I'm afraid not. We never met. The closing was conducted by mail, well, email and wire transfer, but they call it mail. Our lawyer mentioned she moved north. Johnny and I laughed about it, saying we should have just exchanged houses. We moved here from Ohio. Too cold!"

"Would you mind telling me your lawyer's name?"

"George O'Neill. Do you know him? He's such a nice young man."

In response to my request, Hilda gave me Mr. O'Neill's phone number.

"By any chance is Ms. Sutton's lawyer listed on the closing documents?" I asked.

"I don't remember. Hold on. I have to go into the other room."

Three minutes later, Hilda read off the name: Yvonne Philbin.

I thanked her. "You've been very helpful," I said.

"Good luck!"

I suspected there was zero chance that either lawyer would give me Veronica's phone number or email address, but maybe I could convince one of them to pass along a request that she contact me.

I was right—and wrong. I received two point-blank refusals to discuss any client or contract in any way. Mr. O'Neill seemed affronted that I might think otherwise. Ms. Philbin was amused. Neither would acknowledge knowing anyone named Veronica Sutton, so of course neither one would agree to pass along my message, although I suppose it was possible one of them would do so on the QT.

As an antiques appraiser, I knew all about false leads and wrong turns, but that didn't lessen my disappointment.

I scanned through the photos I'd taken of my father's green box and its contents, stopping at the Jane Austen letters. Tracing provenance was going to be hard. While all her letters had been written in England, several had found their way to the United States. My dad had said he found these letters in Portsmouth. How had two Jane Austen letters crossed the ocean and ended up in a small New Hampshire city?

The first photo of the letter to Cassandra showed pages one and four. Pages two and three were on the reverse. The left side, page four, included the conclusion of the letter and the address panel. The right side, page one, included only text. The address panel took up most of the center of page four, with text to the left and right of the panel, and below it. The letter would have been folded so that only the addressee showed, and the corresponding creases were visible. The letter to Fanny followed the same format, but seemed a bit more tattered. I spotted a small tear in the center crease, but since it didn't reduce legibility, nor was the damage beyond reasonable wear and tear, it wouldn't diminish fans' appreciation of the artifact or reduce its value. My pulse quickened. I couldn't believe what I was looking at. I just couldn't! Two Jane Austen letters!

I glanced at the clock on my computer monitor. There were no more leads to follow, but that didn't mean my hunt was over. My strategy was when in doubt, poke around and see what flies out. I hoped a closer examination of the contents of the green leather box might provide a hint. I had to go back to the TV studio, but at least I knew my next steps, and with a plan in hand, I felt more composed.

As soon as I stepped outside, I heard a familiar voice call my name.

Eric, Prescott's facilities manager, stood twenty feet away. His eyes radiated worry, but that was par for Eric's course. He was watching me like a puppy that wasn't sure whether he'd get a kick or a pat. I walked to join him.

Eric had been one of my first hires, starting as a part-timer while still in high school, going full time as soon as he graduated. He took his job like everything else, super-seriously. He'd worked his way up steadily, which pleased us both, but the responsibility weighed on him.

"There was a man," he said when I reached him. "About fifteen minutes ago. I was on the loading dock platform and I caught him hiding in the bushes in Greely Woods taking photos of the arched window. As soon as he saw me looking at him, he took off into the woods. I couldn't go after him because the loading dock door was up. By the time I got it lowered, he was out of sight. I didn't know what to do, so I locked up, and came to find you."

"You did the exact right thing, Eric. Never chase an intruder—period. It's far too dangerous." He nodded, hangdog style. "Locking up the loading dock—perfect. And remember, you're authorized to call our security company or the police any time you think it's appropriate."

I tapped my phone to reach the photos I'd downloaded earlier, scrolled through until I came to the blond man and showed the image to Eric.

He nodded. "That's him."

I thanked Eric again, told him I'd take it from here, and he marched off toward the front door, relieved.

CHAPTER SEVEN

Lenny, the security guard, said he didn't recognize the blond man in the photo. I thanked him, and walked into the studio.

Starr was chatting with Greg, the audio guy.

"I'm late," I said to Starr. "I'm really sorry."

"You're fine. Timothy is on the phone with the network. He wants to buy extra lighting gear." Her expression remained neutral, but her tone communicated an eye roll and a wink. "That's never a one-minute call."

"I feel his pain." I held up my phone. "Do you recognize this man? Have you ever seen him?"

Both gave the photo a good look.

"I saw him outside earlier," Starr said.

"What was he doing?"

"I don't know. Nothing. Just standing around. I had the idea he was waiting for someone, because why else would he be hanging around, you know?"

"How about you?" I asked Greg.

"Don't know him."

"Have you ever seen him?"

Greg glanced at the image again. "No."

Marie tapped me on the shoulder. "Time to touch up, gorgeous!"

I held up my phone and asked her the same questions.

She touched my device with two fingers, angling it under the light. "No, I've never seen him, but I'd like to. He's cute!"

"Proceed with caution," I warned her, laughing a little. "I don't know anything about him. I just need to finish up here . . . I'll be with you in a minute."

"Sure!" she said, and walked back to her station.

I emailed the photo to Starr. "Show it around to the crew, okay?"

She said she would and I hurried to where Marie was waiting.

Marie was as chatty as ever, but again I struggled to pay attention. A stranger brazenly parading around and near my property, hiding in a thicket, taking photos of a window . . . was he checking out access points? If he was planning a break-in, he was doing a bad job of secretly casing the joint. His behavior seemed bizarre, aberrant.

Marie tickled my neck with her big puffy brush, and I giggled.

"I love to hear you giggle!"

Marie was always so congenial. Today, her chitchat was more than pleasant—it soothed me like a steaming hot cup of tea.

Marie finished, and I thanked her.

The set was quiet. A few members of the crew were sitting behind cameras kibitzing or reading. Starr was talking softly on her phone, gazing out the window, her back to me. Neither Gloria nor Oliver was in sight. Timothy was talking to one of the lighting guys. Rory sat on a low chair, rubbing her knee. Ivan sat a few feet away on one of the high director's chairs reading something from a slim book.

"Sorry to interrupt," I said, walking to join him.

Ivan slid his finger into the book to hold his place. The book was bound in red leather with gilt tooling on the spine and cover.

"The binding is beautiful."

"Thanks. It's an early edition of Byron's poem, 'Don Juan.' It deserves a beautiful binding."

"You're a Regency man."

"For context, sure. Mostly, I'm a Lord Byron man."

"What's your dissertation topic?"

"How Byron's relationship with Contessa Guiccioli informed 'Don Juan.'"

"I'm not familiar with her."

"She was one of Byron's most important muses. They had a passionate love affair starting just after he moved to Italy, and within days of her marriage."

"Either they had some chemistry," I said, "or hers was a marriage of convenience."

"Both, I think. Marriages of convenience were the norm among certain social strata during that era. Love was irrelevant. Marriage was a way of consolidating power and building wealth."

Ivan reminded me of Sasha. She was painfully shy and totally tongue-tied, unless she was talking about antiques. Then she was transformed, confident and articulate, and sometimes, ferocious.

"I bet there was an age disparity between the count and countess," I said. "That was common then, too."

"She was eighteen, maybe nineteen, when she married," Ivan said, "and her husband was sixty-eight, roughly fifty years her senior."

"That's disgusting, actually. The poor creature."

"I don't know . . . no one forced her up the aisle. I suspect she'd never been in love before meeting Lord Byron, so she probably thought she was getting a good deal by marrying Count Guiccioli—the title of contessa, an important place in society, and plenty of money. That all changed, once Byron entered the picture. They experienced a magnetic connection the first moment they met. Their romance was fraught with danger, though, since Count Guiccioli was ruthless. That's the aspect I'm studying—how the danger inherent in this passionate, long-lasting, secret affair informed Byron's poetry. I'm researching a series of fifteen letters Byron wrote to his friend, Alexander Scott, in which he describes how loving Contessa Guiccioli freed him to write in ways he never knew he could. There's the dichotomy—what had to be secret turned out to be liberating."

"I'm not sure I know what to think of that. On the one hand, it's a beautiful story, touching. Who wouldn't want to be a great writer's muse? On the other hand, it's so self-centered! What about the contessa? Did Byron inspire her, too? Or was her role simply to serve him?"

"Yes, that's part of the complexity I'm wrestling with," Ivan said. "Since these letters were written by Byron, they offer only one point of view—his."

"But they're authentic?"

"Unquestionably."

"So you work with documents from that period, the early eighteen hundreds?" I asked.

"Sure. All the time."

"If you wanted to authenticate a letter written in 1811 by a literary luminary, what would you do?"

"Ask Gloria."

I laughed. "Come on, now. That's no answer . . . not from a man who authenticates letters written by Lord Byron."

He shot a nervous glance at the outside door. "Gloria is the expert. I'm only an extra set of hands."

I smiled. "I'm just asking a hypothetical question."

He smiled back. "Hypothetically. Okay. Please repeat the question."

"If you wanted to authenticate a letter written in 1811 by a literary luminary, what would you do?"

"Who's the literary luminary?"

"Indulge me by leaving that question for later."

His attention fully caught, he closed the book and stepped down from the chair. "Is this person known as a letter writer?"

"Yes. All the author's letters are catalogued, so if this is a new one, and it's genuine, it would be huge—financially, culturally, and academically."

"Individual letters written by Lord Byron have sold for upwards of a quarter of a million dollars."

"Then you can imagine the reaction of fans and scholars."

He grinned. "We'd go nuts."

"So? What would you do after confirming the author was known to write letters?"

"I'd analyze the content to confirm it's the kind of thing this person would write at that point in their life and stage of their career. At the same time, I'd consider whether the specific cultural references and word choices are known to have been used by that writer."

"There are artificial intelligence programs that do those sorts of analyses, aren't there?"

"Yes. They're good at it, too. They've outed more than one author who published as 'Anonymous.' The programs also check for plagiarism."

"Let's assume the content is apt and familiar, and not plagiarized. They could still be the work of a savvy forger. I need hard evidence of authenticity. What's next?"

"I'd investigate the paper. That's a quick and easy way to identify fakes."

"And if the paper proves to be period appropriate?"

"I'd do a chemical analysis of the ink."

"And if the ink is right?"

"There are two options at this point—confirm provenance or continue with the physical examination." He stroked his chin for a few seconds. "I'd probably opt for provenance because it's important both to confirming authenticity and maximizing value. If we hit a brick wall, we may decide further physical examination is too expensive since without clear provenance we can't expect to recoup the expenditure at sale."

"You're both a scholar and a pragmatist. Stick with the physical examination for a minute. What's next?"

"I'd compare the handwriting with known examples. At this point, I'd also try to determine if the signature is genuine. That's part of the handwriting analysis, but a separate step. I'd look for pressure point differentials the way Gloria documented in her analysis of the Thomas Jefferson letters, and what I call writing hesitations, a subtle indicator of individuality. It's another reliable way to identify a forger." He pulled his shoulders back and raised his chin, a warrior ready for battle. "I'm working on standardizing the technique now."

"Congratulations."

"Thanks. With any luck, my analysis of writing hesitations will get my name out there the way pressure points did for Gloria."

"What does she say about it?"

"She thinks I need more examples before claiming it's a pattern." His shoulders shot up a half-inch, then lowered. "She's probably right. Anyway, depending on the analysis of the signature, I might jump back into provenance— sometimes walls can be taken apart, one brick at a time."

"Provenance of what?" Gloria asked, holding a cup of coffee.

I hadn't heard her walk up, but I was glad to include her in the conversation. "We're talking shop—theoretical shop. I asked Ivan about appraising an early-nineteenth-century letter written by a literary giant."

Timothy walked up. "Sorry for the delay . . . we'll be ready to get going in just a few minutes." He nudged my shoulder with his own. "When next we meet, we'll have better lighting." He glanced around the group. "Carry on! Don't mind me! Pretend I'm just the proverbial fly on the wall!"

"You're always welcome," I told him, touching his upper arm. "We're talking ways and means for appraising a letter from a famous author."

"Am I going to love it?" he asked, his eyes lighting up.

"Yes."

"Were you talking to Ivan because the letter is from Lord Byron?" Gloria asked.

"No, I was talking to him because he's knowledgeable about that era." I turned back to Ivan. "Let's back up to provenance. What's your first step?"

"Gloria?" he said, bobbing from one foot to another.

She flipped a palm in a "be my guest" motion, but when she spoke, there was an edge to her voice. "She asked you."

"I'd interview the current owner," Ivan said. "We need to know how the letter came into that person's possession."

"What are we appraising?" Oliver asked, as he walked toward us. Rory limped along beside him.

I decided to tell them. I had no reason not to. I silently repeated her name: *Jane Austen*. The mere thought that these letters might be authentic made me woozy. I fought an urge to whisper, as if I were in church. I wasn't used to feeling this way and I paused for a few seconds to give the reverence time to settle.

"I have two letters—" I broke off, my solemnity growing. Everyone waited, picking up on my mood. "There's a chance they were written by Jane Austen."

Ivan gawked.

Oliver lowered his chin and tilted his head, a sure sign he planned on playing his cards close to his vest.

"I love Jane Austen," Rory said. "*Pride and Prejudice*! Colin Firth, that's what I call eye candy."

I laughed, and glanced at her, trying to decide if she was joking.

"Well, well," Gloria said, a glint in her eye, cutting right to the chase. "You're saying you have two previously undocumented Jane Austen letters?"

"It's possible." To help them assess the challenge of appraising the letters, I was going to have to reveal my personal connection to 9/11. I dreaded the prospect. No one knew how to react; how could they? Horrors like the one I experienced that day are unfathomable, and the people who survive them are inconsolable. It had been twenty years, but my wounds still weren't fully healed, and maybe they never would be. "Let me tell you how they came into my possession."

I explained that a woman had stopped by without an appointment and handed me a gorgeous leather box containing, among other things, those two letters. I took in a deep breath and braced myself for their shock and condolences. I shared the contents of my dad's note.

In the days following the 9/11 attack, everyone was so traumatized, it was as if we were wraiths plodding through a miasma, which, it turned out, we were, both literally and figuratively. Back then, I'd lived three miles from the World Trade Center as the crow flies. The ash and grit were omnipresent, suffocating. The stench lasted a week. On hearing that my dad had been at a client meeting on the seventy-first floor of the South Tower, everyone I knew offered support and condolences. I'd stared at them, watching their mouths move, not hearing a word.

I held up a hand. "I know. It's horrendous." I smiled as best I could. "I can see the concern and sympathy in your faces, and I appreciate it more than I can say. I only mention my connection to nine-eleven because it's relevant to the appraisal we're discussing . . . but, really, I don't like to talk about it, so I appreciate your understanding if I shy away from the subject." I paused for another second to let my revelation sink in. "Back to my dad's note. He didn't name the shop where he bought the portfolio, and the portfolio itself wasn't in the leather box. I cleaned out his hotel room about a week after he died, and it wasn't there, either. What this means is that I have no information about the store he referenced in his note, the portfolio, or how the letters ended up amid a collection of miscellaneous sketches. I've already tried to locate the woman who dropped the box off—so far, without luck. Our next step is to track down owners of shops from that era that might have sold a portfolio of sketches, even though that seems unlikely to bear fruit. Another avenue I'll pursue simultaneously is authenticating the letters themselves."

"I'd love to take it on," Oliver said.

Gloria smiled like a supermodel. "Me, too."

Ivan, standing a step in back of her, his eyes round with wonder, licked his lips. "Maybe I could help . . . I have period-specific knowledge."

Oliver laughed, but it sounded more scornful than amused. He spoke to Gloria. "Trolling for business doesn't become you." He turned to Ivan. "Everyone knows you do most of Gloria's work, so don't worry . . . if she lands the gig, you'll get the grunt work." He laughed again. "None of the glory, of course . . . she'll keep all of that." To me, he added, "I'm not trolling. I'd love to partner with you, my friend."

His emphasis on partnering and his referring to me as his friend were nice touches, I thought. Ivan's chin jutted and his shoulders hunched, a pugilistic stance, as if he'd love to respond to Oliver's taunting with his fists. Gloria seemed equally enraged, but from her crooked smile, I inferred she planned a subtler approach. Rory looked excited—apparently she liked a good fight. I found their blatant ambition unseemly. Business was business, but the underside of fervor is frenzy, and frenzy has no place in the analytical, methodical process of appraising antiques.

"Thank you," I said. "As you might expect, I'm not making any decisions yet."

"Whenever you're ready," Oliver said.

"Ditto," Gloria said, her eyes aglow. "And of course, needless to say, Ivan doesn't do most of my work, and I don't troll."

"Why don't you do the appraisal on your show live?" Rory piped up. "Have Oliver discuss it with you, one-on-one, maybe throw in a psychic or two. You could get the psychics to help you trace provenance, ask them about past owners, that sort of thing. Wouldn't that be a hoot and a half?"

Timothy made a noise, a kind of gurgle, which he quickly shuttered. I met his eyes, then looked aside, fighting an urge to burst out laughing. Oliver chuckled. Gloria's lip curled contemptuously. Ivan kept his eyes on Oliver's face, maybe deciding where to land the first punch.

Rory laughed. "Lighten up, guys. Have a little fun!"

Gloria smiled politely, then turned to face Ivan. "Did you mention comparing Josie's letters to known examples?"

"Not in detail."

"As you know, that's an important step," she said to me. "Once we review the letter, we'll create a list of comparable exemplars."

"Did you smell them?" Rory asked.

We all looked at her.

"The letters . . . give them a whiff." She surveyed our faces. "If they're that old, I bet they smell musty. Unless someone sprayed them with Febreze."

For a moment, no one reacted in any way.

"We don't use air fresheners on antiques, Mom," Oliver said.

Rory winked at me. "Don't mind Oliver. He's always been a bit of an old fogey."

"Five minutes!" Starr called from across the set.

"Thanks, everyone," I said. "I appreciate all your support."

Timothy walked me onto the set, keeping his voice low. "I love her!"

"Me, too. She rides dirt bikes."

"Of course she does."

I laughed, and it felt good, normal, and I was relieved to have something feel normal.

CHAPTER EIGHT

The lighting designer used seashell-pink gels to diffuse the overhead lights' harsh glare, and everything was washed in a pale rosy hue. From past experience, I knew that to the viewer, the gels added a mood, not a color. When discussing one of Picasso's many drawings showing a mournful mother and child bathed in a blue-green wash, this one from 1902, I was suffused in soft turquoise light, as if I were underwater, a visual metaphor for the artist's worsening depression during that period of his life. During an appraisal of a wheat motif caneware butter dish, the designer chose a pale yellow wash.

I stood next to the arched window with Gloria. Starr gave me a prompt to bring me back to where we'd stopped earlier. I waited for Timothy to call "Action," then said, "How about you, Gloria? Do you use a structured appraisal process, too?"

"Not a rigid one, like Oliver," she said.

Out of the corner of my eye, I saw Rory fold her lips and cross her arms across her chest.

Gloria continued: "I customize every appraisal depending on the object, the history, and so on. I like to start with context, what is known and what we can infer about the writer's communication habits. That generally helps with provenance, too. Then I examine the handwriting, especially the signature. Finally, I look at the technical issues, paper, ink, and the like."

I thanked her, and smiled until I heard "Cut." We took our positions behind the worktable. Oliver stood to my right, Gloria to my left. We were ready to record their opinions of each other's work. This exchange comprised the true battle portion of the "Battle of the Experts." Afterward, I'd get the last word—a quick thank-you, and a longer summary and reflection. We'd film most of my solitary work and some of my segues tomorrow, once Timothy and the editing team had reviewed the rough cuts overnight.

I raised my eyes to camera three and waited for Timothy's signal that we were ready to start. "The question before us is whether this book is from the first printing of the first edition, what's known as a first first, or whether it's from the second printing of that first edition. Let's see what rare book and document experts, Oliver Crenshaw and Gloria Moreau, have to say." I turned to face Oliver. "Let me start with you, Oliver. What did you discover?"

"At first glance, both printings of the privately published edition seem identical. They both feature gray covers, and they both include forty-one black-and-white pen ink illustrations, with a frontispiece, a color illustration opposite the title page."

I looked up at camera three. "The illustration shows Peter's mother serving him tea in bed." That image would appear on screen in the final cut.

"The second printing includes three easy-to-spot differences," Gloria interjected.

"Yes," Oliver said, adding a little ice to his voice. "In the second printing, the gray is a bit greener in tone, the spine is rounded, not flat, and the date 'February 1902' appears on the title page. In this copy, the gray is purer in hue, the spine is flat, and there is no date. This is a first first."

"That sounds definitive," I said.

"Only if it's not a replica," Gloria remarked.

"Is there any evidence, Gloria, that it's *not* a fake?"

"Yes, actually." She smiled, adding a luminescent glow to the room. "Many of the pages are foxed."

I spoke to the camera again. "The term 'foxing' refers to brownish spots or streaks that appear on paper and indicate oxidation, part of the natural aging process." To Gloria, I said, "Implying the book is authentic."

"Exactly."

"Unless the foxing has been faked," Oliver said. "All it takes is the judicious use of an iron."

"Or a smoker," Gloria said. "But fakers tend to over-age. It's pretty obvious. What's more of a tell is *no* foxing."

60

"Oliver, what conclusions would you reach if there's *no* foxing in a book from that era?" I asked.

"Either it's been stored perfectly, or it's a forgery."

I turned to camera three. "Which means you can't judge a book's authenticity by its appearance alone. You need to assess all the factors that come into play." I thanked Oliver, then turned toward Gloria. "So, Gloria, how can you be certain this *isn't* a replica?"

"On page fifty-one, we find that Peter 'cried big tears.' For the first trade edition, Beatrix Potter changed it to 'wept big tears,' and in later editions, 'shed big tears.' This book uses 'cried.'"

"Which doesn't prove anything," Oliver said, his tone sharp. "That same word, 'cried,' appears in the second printing of the first edition. All it suggests is that if this book is a fabrication, the forger copied either the first or second printing of the first edition."

"That might be true, if that one word was all we had to go on. It isn't. It seems that Oliver didn't examine the signature and handwritten note thoroughly enough, or he didn't fully consider the implications. Those two elements alone prove the book is a first first. Certain pressure points make the signature verification indisputable, specifically the crossbar on the lowercase *t* and the dot over the letter *i*. The note asking someone to buy the book to help the charity makes the authentication indisputable, too."

I spoke to camera three. "Ms. Potter donated the book to help a hospital raise money."

"If I may make one additional point," Gloria said, smiling like an angel. "As an added bonus, I learned that Beatrix Potter didn't often write in books, thus, the rarity of the note adds to the value. As to the possibility of it being a replica . . . it strains credibility to think that someone would have bothered to create a forgery within weeks of the first publication of a children's book by a previously unknown author, or that Ms. Potter would have autographed and annotated a fraudulent copy of her own work."

"Thank you, Gloria. Oliver, what's your conclusion?" I paused to add a little drama. "Is this copy authentic?"

"Yes! And because these books were read and reread, it's rare to find one in such good condition. This is a very special find."

"This book," Gloria said, leaning forward, resting her elbow on the table and her chin on her fingers, eying the camera lens like a lover, creating an intimate connection with the audience, "is a treasure!"

I took a step toward camera three. "This copy of Beatrix Potter's *The Tale of Peter Rabbit*, is an authentic first first, one of two hundred and fifty copies printed. It's in wonderful condition and it comes with a charming story." I smiled more broadly, including the viewers in a moment of appraisal joy. "We also have solid proof of provenance. This copy is owned by a direct descendant of the person who bought it at that charity fund-raiser." The camera rolled in for a close-up. "These two renowned experts, Oliver Crenshaw and Gloria Moreau, and my staff here at Prescott's, have all validated the book, the inscription, and the provenance, a triad of perfect. I asked Oliver and Gloria for their auction estimates—if the book was sold at auction today, how much would it likely fetch. Let's take a peek!" An animated graphic of an envelope would appear below each of the experts' photographs. Oliver's card would pop out first, showing his estimate of $47,000. Gloria's envelope would open next, reading $50,000. Prescott's envelope—appearing below a photo of me standing in front of my company's headquarters, would be opened last. Our estimate was $51,000. "As you can see, we're all within a few thousand dollars of one another." The graphic would slip away and we'd be back to live action. "Needless to say, the owner is thrilled!" I kept smiling and didn't move until Timothy gave the word.

"Cut!" Timothy called. "I love you! I love you all." He stepped on set and spoke to Oliver and Gloria. "Both of you are fantastic! Thank you. You're wrapped for today—I think we have everything we need, but we'll review the takes overnight and confirm that in the morning. Starr will text you by six one way or another. Josie, your call is for nine fifteen." He waved goodbye, jogged to the center of the stage, and raised his voice. "Grips, hands, break it down! Wardrobe! Strip 'em down! Editing, see me now."

Within seconds, organized chaos erupted. Editors and assistants huddled around Timothy as workers disassembled the set, moving cameras off to a corner, coiling cables and cords, replacing stage lighting with work lights, with an additional half a dozen people scurrying around doing I don't know what.

Timothy's directive to "strip 'em down" was literal. As soon as he gave the instruction, Jackie, a middle-aged woman of comfortable proportions, with short curly brown hair and rosy cheeks, appeared out of nowhere to pack up our outfits for overnight cleaning. Jackie was in charge of wardrobe, which, since most of us wore our own clothes, mostly meant continuity. If Timothy wanted to reshoot any of our lines in the morning, it was her job to ensure we looked the same as we had the day before. Her eagle eyes were legendary. I'd seen her catch a hanging thread and a change in nail polish from fifty feet away.

I told Oliver and Gloria I'd meet them in the green room in a few minutes—they'd brought changes of clothing, too—and went into my private dressing room. I hung up my outfit on one of the gold satin-padded hangers Jackie provided and changed into my everyday work uniform, khakis and a maroon collared T-shirt with "Prescott's" embroidered above the pocket. Guests who hadn't brought a change of clothes could wear the "Josie's Antiques" branded running outfits included in the swag bags we gave all guests. I blushed every time I saw the lightweight cloth totes with *Josie's Antiques* silkscreened on the sides or any of the promotional items the team chose. It seemed so pretentious, but anytime I ventured to suggest that we should skip it, Timothy shushed me.

As I exited my dressing room, I saw Rory and Ivan standing behind the bank of cameras.

"It's just like Oliver said," Rory whispered. "You do all the work, and she takes all the credit."

"No, no, not at all," he said.

"I overheard you talking to Josie about making your bones with writing hesitations. You validated the Beatrix Potter's inscription using that technique, didn't you?"

"Well, sure."

"See, that's what I mean. Gloria didn't mention it on air. She didn't mention you at all. She's a charlatan."

"I don't know why you think that. It's not true."

"She regurgitates other people's work. What are you afraid of? That she'll flunk you? Man up and stand your ground."

"I have to go."

Ivan walked toward the tent with more speed than decorum. I had no idea why Rory thought Ivan was a lackey, or why she felt comfortable saying it, but it was clear to me that she was some piece of work.

She noticed me, and limped my way. "I hate men who dodge tough questions, don't you?"

"That's one of those questions, Rory, that is impossible to answer. If I say yes, I'm tacitly agreeing with you that Ivan is in that category. If I say no, I'm implying that I have no problem when men dodge tough questions, which isn't true, and again tacitly including Ivan as an example. So, you'll have to excuse me from answering. Instead, tell me why you're so angry."

Her lips pressed together. "I don't like liars."

"Is that directed at me?"

"Should it be?"

"No."

She looked me square in the eye, her wrath fading. "Sorry. I get riled up and I say whatever comes into my head. It's a bad habit."

"Who's lying?"

"Gloria. Oliver tells me that Ivan does most of her heavy lifting. You just heard him admit it."

"I heard him say he studied the Beatrix Potter note for writing hesitations. That's not doing Gloria's heavy lifting."

"Why didn't she mention it?"

"Why do you care?"

"Gloria makes Oliver look bad, and it just burns my britches every time I think about it. She's a real slick talker, I'll give her that, but that's all I'll give her."

"I thought Oliver did a terrific job."

"I'm not stupid. Or better put, he did a terrific job at the role you assigned him—patsy." She punched the air again, this time aiming at me. "You'll get good ratings, which I'm sure is all you care about. Good for you. Not good for Oliver. You should have slapped that Gloria person down for making Oliver look bad. She did the deed, but it's your fault for letting her do it. You hung Oliver out to dry."

"I don't see that at all."

"Then you weren't looking."

"I'm sorry you feel that way, Rory. I think they both nailed it—two top professionals going back and forth."

"I saw a lot more back than forth."

"I think you're biased."

Rory gave a crack of laughter. "You got that right, at least." She took a step toward the tent, then looked back at me. "Don't worry. I won't start a brawl. Oliver wouldn't like it."

I laughed. "Implying you would?"

"Implying I wouldn't mind."

"You're wrong on all counts, by the way," I said, smiling. "I care about way more than good ratings, I didn't assign Oliver a role as a patsy or anything else, and I genuinely think he did a terrific job."

"I'll tell you what . . . you're a good girl." She tapped her forehead with her index finger. "I know these things."

I laughed, inordinately pleased at her tribute. "It was a pleasure meeting you, Rory," I said.

"Ha!" She cackled as she limped off. "Tell Oliver I'll meet him in the tent." She raised her arm over her head and waved. "Ciao!"

Rory might not be everyone's cup of Earl Grey, but I thought she was rather wonderful, although I didn't know what to make of her rant. From what I could tell, her antipathy toward Gloria derived solely from hearsay— from Oliver's accusations. Oliver's conviction that Ivan was nothing more than a hapless fool didn't make it true. To be fair, it didn't make it false, either.

Starr came up to me carrying the swag bags.

"I showed the photo of that blond man around," she whispered. "No one recognized him. No one even remembered seeing him."

"Thanks for trying."

We walked into the green room together.

The green room was actually green, a soft sage. The furniture had been selected for casual relaxation. There were comfortable chairs scattered here and there, all covered in a coordinating green-and-navy-plaid twill. The lighting was diffused. There was a large round oak table with six Parsons chairs suitable for shared meals, work, or playing cards during long delays. A tiny kitchenette took up part of one wall.

Oliver entered from the men's dressing room wearing jeans and a black crewneck sweater, very sharp. Gloria stepped out from the women's dressing room a moment later, wearing brown slacks and another tunic with coordinating scarf, this one mint green, as professional and unstylish as before. She started to twist the scarf around her neck, but it slipped and fell to the ground. She, Oliver, and I all reached for it. Oliver got there first and handed it back.

Gloria accepted the scarf with a quick thank-you.

"From the *Josie's Antiques* family," Starr said, passing the bags to Gloria, then Oliver. "With thanks for doing such a great job."

"How nice," Gloria said. "Thank you."

"I need to apologize," Oliver told me, after thanking Starr. "I heard snippets of my mother's tirade. Sorry about that. She lacks a filter."

"Don't apologize!" I said. "I want to clone her. I love that she says what she thinks. You always know where you stand with her."

"And how, and then some," Oliver said, "They say weirdness skips a generation. Makes me scared for my children, if I ever have any."

Gloria laughed. "I can only imagine what it would be like growing up with a mother like that—perpetual laughter, a wonderful thing."

I didn't think it would be wonderful to have a mother known for her mercurial temperament and acid tongue. It was one thing to enjoy her rapier wit as a disinterested adult. It would be another thing altogether to have her as a mom. You'd spend your childhood apologizing and embarrassed. My dad had been the exact opposite, stable and gracious, which is what made Veronica's revelation so astonishing, and why I found myself bewildered and anxious. As I started to edge my way toward the door, I had another thought—I wondered if what Oliver described as "weirdness" was actually "dangerous if crossed."

CHAPTER NINE

Gloria and Ivan left the green room first, followed by Oliver. I brought up the rear. Halfway down the hall, Oliver placed his hand on my arm to stop me. I turned toward him and he looked into my eyes, his gaze penetrating, as if he were trying to see inside me. He smiled, not his usual friendly smile. This one was man to woman, rippling with fire. I was amused. Apparently, Oliver could turn on the heat at will.

"Any chance I can get a look at those Jane Austen letters?" he asked.

I laughed. "Sorry."

"Just a peek?"

"Soon."

"The curiosity is killing me."

"It'll pass." I continued down the hall and caught up with Gloria, Ivan, and Rory in the tent.

Rory spotted Oliver's goodie bag, and asked, "What's that?"

"A thank-you from the team," I said.

Oliver handed the tote bag to his mom, and she began pawing through it.

To Gloria and Oliver, I said, "Thanks again." I nodded at Ivan, and at Rory, although with her preoccupation on the bag's contents, she didn't notice.

"Say it again, Sam," Rory said. When she registered our confusion, she added, "Joke. Get it? From *Casablanca*. 'Play it again, Sam,' which isn't actually the line, by the way, but that's a separate conversation. Would you say whatever you just said again, Josie? I didn't hear you, and don't tell me I'm deaf. I'm not . . . you're a quiet talker."

"Sure." I repeated my "thank you" comment.

"Okeydokey!" She stood and handed the bag back to Oliver. "I've got to get to my physical therapy appointment." She patted his shoulder and kissed his cheek. "Ta-ta!" She left.

Lenny held open the door, and the four of us trooped outside together. When we reached the parking lot, Oliver and I pulled a little ahead. Ivan and Gloria slowed their pace and were talking.

"I enjoyed our conversation," I told Oliver as we walked. "You're very comfortable on camera."

"Thanks," he said, stopping near his cargo van.

I told Oliver goodbye and continued on toward the front. I waved to Ivan and Gloria, but they weren't paying any attention to me. They were still walking at a snail's pace, and whatever Gloria was saying seemed intense. Ivan shook his head, no, no, no.

Timothy caught up with me just before I reached the office door.

"I know today wasn't easy for you," Timothy said, "and I wanted to tell you that you're such a complete joy to work with."

"What a nice thing to say. You are, too. How did Gloria and Oliver do, for real?"

"Medium. Simmering isn't as interesting to watch as boiling, and they left out the funny. The only sweetness came from you. No blaze, no humor, no charm . . . overall, it was a little flat."

"What could I have done to make it better?"

"Let that firecracker Rory fill in for Oliver."

I laughed.

"When have you ever heard me refer to someone as a firecracker?" Timothy asked.

"Never."

"She's a pistol."

"I've never heard you call someone a pistol, either."

"I love her."

"Maybe we should go ahead and invite a psychic," I said.

"Maybe you should smell old books on camera."

"And then spray them with Febreze."

"It's a thought." Timothy lowered his voice. "Are you okay, or do you just have your professional face on?"

Timothy was an ally, a trusted confidant, so I could let down the façade. "Between you and me and the gatepost, I could use a long soak in my hot tub, a big hug, and a martini, not necessarily in that order."

"I'm in. When do we start?"

"In about an hour, as soon as I can get myself home. Want to come for dinner?"

"What will I miss?"

"Nothing if you come."

"Tease me."

"Steak. I'll stop at the butcher."

"You're killing me. With sautéed mushrooms?"

"Of course. Also, double-baked potatoes and a big salad."

"Oh, God. What kind of martinis?" he asked.

"What's your favorite?"

"The Third Degree. Gin. Vermouth. And with a few dashes of orange bitters instead of absinthe."

"I have gin and vermouth at home. I'll pick up orange bitters en route. I'll make a pitcher."

"I wish. Ah, the glamour of television. I get to eat pizza, drink water, and watch the rough cuts."

"I'm sorry."

"Don't be. I'm going for broke—I'm ordering pepperoni."

I laughed.

Gloria and Ivan walked to the middle of the parking lot, and stopped. After a few seconds, they walked a few more steps, and paused again. Gloria said one last thing, then walked to her car, a silver Honda. Ivan, still biting his lip, watched her drive away. She turned right, toward the ocean. Ivan trudged to his old gray Toyota, then drove out of the lot, turning left, toward the interstate.

"The situation with your dad," Timothy said, "you must be all atwitter."

"All atwitter, and then some." I brought my gaze to his face. "Why would this woman have withheld his note all these years? Why give it to me now?"

"On the face of it, it's a terrible thing, isn't it? But it might turn into a beautiful thing."

"You're as much of an optimist as I am."

"Shh! Don't tell a soul. What about those letters? Are they as good as they sound? You know me . . . if an antique doesn't set my hair on fire, I'm yawning."

"Consider yourself scorched."

He kissed my cheek, told me to call if I needed anything, and sped away, back to the tent.

Shortly after Ty and I married, we bought a sprawling Victorian house on the beach, known throughout Rocky Point as the Gingerbread House. We spent close to a year renovating it, keeping as many of its original decorative details as possible, while upgrading the infrastructure to handle modern technology and the layout to suit our style. One of my favorite changes was to the second-floor porch, which overlooked the ocean. We converted it into an all-weather room by installing floor-to-ceiling windows with removable glass panels, and that's where I found Ty. He was sitting on an Adirondack rocker, with his legs stretched out, reading something on his tablet. He'd opened the window in the corner, and as soon as I mounted the steps, I could hear the rhythmic lapping of the tide.

I checked my phone. It was five thirty. "You're home early," I said.

He lowered his tablet. "You, too, given that it's a filming day. The shoot must have gone well."

"I guess." I sank onto the chair next to him, and exhaled slowly. "I'm exhausted."

"Physically or emotionally?"

"Emotionally. I'm still off-kilter about my dad. And those letters."

"Anyone would be. What can I get you?"

"Timothy's favorite martini, called the Third Degree. Gin. Vermouth. A few dashes of orange bitters. I left the bitters on the kitchen counter."

Ty laughed. "There's a story here . . . I can smell it."

"That's because you're smarter than everyone. Timothy can't come to dinner, so I'm drinking it in his honor."

"You're thoughtful and sentimental." He leaned in for a kiss. I shut my eyes and lost myself in the moment, luxuriating in his tender touch. He straightened up. "I'm on the case."

After he left I walked to the open window, zipping up my sweater. A steady breeze was blowing in from the east, sending sun-touched sparks dancing across the ocean surface. The sun was low on the horizon, clouds stippling the sky with streaks of orange and red. *Red sky at night, sailor's delight. Red sky in morning, sailors take warning.* Tomorrow would be another beautiful day.

By the time Ty got back, I was ensconced in my chair, a match to his, covered by a double-wide, cream-colored afghan crocheted by Mona, my friend from New Hampshire Children First! I'd won it at a silent auction I'd helped organize.

Ty slid a tray on the small table between our chairs.

"I love this afghan," I said.

"It's a beauty."

"We need a love seat so we can sit together and cuddle."

"Okay. Let's get one this weekend. We can go after Bristol's."

Bristol's Rifle and Pistol Club housed the finest shooting range in the region, and Ty and I went most weekends. My favorite part was the old-fashioned gallery with moving targets, just like they'd used at the club where my dad taught me to shoot. *Oh, Dad!*

I touched Ty's cheek. "Have I told you lately how great you are?"

Ty poured a martini into a chilled glass and handed it to me. "Because I like the idea of cuddling with my sweetie?"

I sipped. "And because you make a mean Third Degree."

He poured his own drink, then took my hand. We sat there, lulled by the water's ebb and flow. After a while, I told him about my day and my fears and anxieties, skipping most facts, focusing on my feelings.

"How did you locate Veronica Sutton?" he asked when I was done.

"What makes you think I did?"

"I know you. I can tell by the gleam in your eye and what you didn't tell me."

I laughed. "I didn't do anything wrong. I asked Wes for a favor. It took him about a minute and a half." I brought up the image of Veronica Sutton on my phone and handed it over.

Ty tilted the phone to catch the light from the orange lanterns we'd strung around the porch, just below the ceiling. "She looks like someone we'd know and like."

"I agree. She doesn't look mean or conniving." I took the phone back and assessed the photo again. "Except . . . I know this is an off-the-wall question, but do you think she looks a little too perfect?"

"What do you mean?"

"I don't know exactly." I stared at the screen. "Something about her appearance and demeanor, her posture, her perfectly belted Burberry trench coat . . . everything came together a little too well."

"Like she's an actress dressed for the part?"

"Exactly. There's no way to tell, of course, and it doesn't matter, since whether she's playing a role or not, she has information I want. Information I *need*." I finished my drink and placed the glass on the tray. "There's more." I told Ty about the blond man who'd roamed around my parking lot and grounds, showing him his photograph.

He enlarged the photo. "This I don't like."

"Me, either. Do you think I should get my security company to send a team to patrol the grounds tonight? We have security cameras, but . . . I don't know . . ."

"Why not? Better safe than sorry."

I made the call, and Russ assured me there'd be a Sterling Security team in position by seven. Teams of two would continue the patrol until the network's security detail took over. I told him there was no "detail," there was only one man, Lenny. I emailed Russ the photo of the blond man, and asked to be notified immediately if anyone saw him. We agreed to meet at my company in the morning at eight thirty, and I would decide at that time whether to keep the patrols going. I texted Timothy and Starr to let them know about the additional security, and asked them to alert Lenny, so he wouldn't wonder what was up when he found a pair of guards patrolling the grounds in the morning.

As soon as I was done, Ty said, "I have news, too."

"Good news, I hope."

"Complicated news."

My heart beat an extra thump. Complicated news didn't sound like good news. I skewed around in my chair to face him, and waited for him to speak.

"I've been offered a promotion."

"That's great! Congratulations! That's not complicated."

"It's the job that's complicated. Head of training."

"You're already the head of training."

"I'm head of training for the tristate region. I've been offered head of training for all of Homeland Security. It's a four-step bump in title and pay."

I understood why he thought the news was complicated—any promotion or new job Ty might accept at Homeland Security or FEMA would require his relocating to Washington, DC. My stomach clenched. I loved our house. I loved New Hampshire. But I loved Ty more, and I was as committed to his success as to my own. If I had to move, I would, and I'd be fine—and so would Prescott's. As the face of Prescott's, I was already less responsible for day-to-day management than I had been when I first started the company. My team was strong, and I was confident that Gretchen, Prescott's general manager, could handle it. That said, there was another potential fly in the ointment.

"What's the travel expectation of the job?" I asked.

"Seventy-five percent."

"I'd be in a new city, and you'd never be home."

"More and more training is moving to web-based platforms, so the seventy-five percent may drop some. Or not."

"Do you want the job?"

"No, but I want a promotion, or new responsibilities, or something. This opportunity has obvious advantages, but there are a lot of cons, too. Too much travel. Having to leave New Hampshire. Changing our life from one we love to something else, which is to say, the unknown. Dealing with more meetings, more paperwork, more bureaucracy."

"The last cons would come with any promotion."

"But if I could stay in New Hampshire and not travel all the time, they wouldn't feel like such big cons."

"Don't undervalue the pros: more money, more prestige, more power, more ability to do good works. The pros win."

"Are you trying to get rid of me?"

"Of course not. I'm trying to empower you to do what you want."

"You're a woman in a million."

"Ten million."

"A hundred million." He exhaled loudly. "Do you hate the idea of moving as much as I do?"

"Honestly? Yes. Maybe more. But I'd hate it more if we stayed and you ended up depressed or resentful because you didn't take a promotion you'd earned."

"Which means we're caught between a rock and a hard place."

"We'll wiggle our way clear." I smiled and poured an inch of martini in my glass. "When do you have to let them know?"

"A week. They know the intricacy of our situation. I'm going down tomorrow to discuss it further."

"Aren't there any companies in New Hampshire that need you?"

"No."

"Start a security training company."

"I don't want to start a company. I'm not an entrepreneur like you."

"If you could have any job in the world you wanted, what would it be?"

"Some big-cheese position with FEMA. My heart has always been with emergency management."

"Why don't you talk to the FEMA people while you're in DC?"

"To what end?"

"To check out options. If you meet with someone at your level or higher, like Sheila, you can ask about future initiatives and gauge whether there might be an appropriate opportunity." I'd met Sheila Zerof and her husband, Mitch Porter, a couple of times. She was FEMA's deputy associate administrator for Response and Recovery, number two in the division. She and Ty had worked together for almost a decade, ending up on the same cross-agency task forces three times over the years. Ty thought she was brilliant. "Based on any scuttlebutt she passes your way, you can assess which division or department might be hiring, and when. Knowledge is power. Don't make a decision in a vacuum."

"That is one fine, fine idea. I'll do it. In fact, I'll text her right now." He touched the rim of his glass to mine, offering a silent toast. "Just so you know . . . I'm the luckiest man on earth."

"I'm the luckiest woman."

Later that night, I fell asleep to the whisper of the ocean, and to my amazement, I didn't dream of my father, or rare letters, or Jane Austen, or Ty's potential job change. I slept solidly and awoke refreshed, ready to face the day, maybe because I hadn't heard a peep from the security team. When it came to guards patrolling my property, no news was definitely good news.

CHAPTER TEN

B y the time I stumbled into the kitchen at six, Ty had left for Boston's Logan Airport. He'd made a pot of coffee and left a note: *Sheila and I are on for lunch at one. You're the best! XXOO*

"Fingers crossed," I said aloud, although I didn't know what I was hoping for.

I pulled on a heavy Irish fisherman's knit sweater, and allowed my thoughts to drift from my father to my need to find Veronica Sutton. I was having trouble reconciling my relationship with my dad, which had always been grounded in truth and openness, with his relationship with Veronica, which had been, evidently, a closely held secret. The disconnect was jarring, like stepping from solid ground into an ankle-deep puddle without warning.

I slipped my keys and phone into my back pockets, and walked outside. The sun was just rising, stripes of gold and amber marking the horizon. Dewdrops dotted the flagstone path that led to the beach. It was cool, in the fifties, at a guess, a clear, windless beauty of a day. I picked my way through tall beach grass to reach the sand.

I turned left, toward Maine. I loved walking along the craggy shoreline, stepping over and around the slick twisted ribbons of seaweed and selecting silvery gray curls of driftwood for holiday decorations. I loved watching the waves batter the jetty, too, sending sprays of water shooting into the air.

Before I'd walked ten feet, Starr texted to thank me for the heads-up about the security patrols, that she'd passed the info along to Lenny, and that my nine fifteen call was unchanged. I replied that I'd be there.

The water was near black. Soon, when the sun was high enough to set diamonds tripping along the surface, the water would appear bluer—still dark, but not the color of night. The tide was high.

I knew when Veronica moved to Florida, and why; that she'd started a business and run it for years; that she'd recently sold a house in Sarasota, and was in New Hampshire yesterday, but had no domicile I could find; that she'd wanted to hand deliver the green leather box, but hadn't wanted to explain anything to me; and that she'd been a good friend of my father's—or said she had. From her photos I could tell she was well-dressed and well-groomed. That was a lot of information to have collected in less than a day, but none of it got me closer to finding her.

Because of the curve of the shoreline, I heard the water smacking the jetty before I saw it, a stentorian slap, followed by a thunderous whoosh as frothy spray exploded toward the heavens.

Witnessing Ivan, Oliver, and Gloria's fervor about the Jane Austen letters comforted me. I thought about my father's long-held belief that you need to look a person in the eye to gauge their candor. I wasn't so sure he was right. Windows can be screened, tinted, or blocked. Still, the expressions on their faces were heartening.

While I'd talked about the letters, Oliver kept his eyes on mine with fever-ish intensity, like a seagull that espies a fish. Gloria's reaction was more nu-anced, less overtly savage, a cat preening itself, pretending it wasn't the least bit interested in that cute little mouse creeping along the baseboard. Ivan looked guarded, but game, like a schoolboy so keen to play hockey with the big boys, he was willing to swallow his fear of skating on thin ice. Rory, too, was a player here. She had a blast, as amused at watching the oh-so-serious adults spar as she was by her own jokes.

The jetty came into view, a gazillion man-size granite boulders jumbled together in a ragged line stretching from the beach out into the ocean for a hundred yards. I stood on a dune near the street, safe from the spray. I stayed a while, until I was half hypnotized by the rhythmic crashing and retreat of the water, then turned back toward home.

A glint of light caught my eye, and I picked up a piece of pale blue sand-glass, the shard's edges softened and smoothed by years of exposure to gritty sand and salty water. The glass was translucent, and backlit by the rising sun.

It became, effectively, a mirror. I stared at my image, but saw Veronica. Someone knew where she was, but they had no way of knowing I was looking for her. I could fix that. I watched my eyes sparkle. Ty said I'd figure out how to find her, and he was right.

I pocketed the sandglass and called Wes. He agreed to meet at eight.

Ocean Avenue ran the length of New Hampshire's coast, all eighteen miles. The dune where Wes and I usually met was located at about the halfway point, a little closer to Maine than Massachusetts. I parked on the sandy shoulder, pushed through rambling rosebushes and scrubby grass, and half-walked, half-crawled up the shifting sand. From the top I could see a quarter mile in either direction, not that there was much to see, which was the point of meeting here—we could have an uninterrupted, private conversation. I got there first, just before eight. Wes screeched to a stop a minute later.

"Whatcha got?" he asked as he scrambled up.

Wes was tall, and he'd slimmed down some in the years since he'd gotten married. He'd cleaned up his act, too, wearing chinos and button-down shirts instead of ratty jeans and old T-shirts, carrying a real notebook instead of scraps of dirty paper, and driving a newish sedan instead of an ancient rattletrap. He hadn't lost a bit of his rough-and-tumble style, though, or his tenaciousness.

"I need help finding Veronica Sutton."

"Old news. I already located her for you."

"No. You located where she came from, not where she is now."

He cocked his head. "This must be some antique if you're this hot on finding her."

"That's one way of putting it."

"Talk to me."

"If and when, Wes. If and when."

He shook his head sadly. "You're all take and no give, Joz. Not good."

"Sometimes I owe you, Wes, and sometimes you owe me. We have a working partnership. Don't get snippy."

Wes sighed. Over the years, I'd become fluent in translating Wes's sighs. The deeper the sigh, the more profound his disappointment. This one came in at about medium.

"I can't promise something open-ended like that in a vacuum," he said. "What's the antique?"

"It's big. What you would call an info-bomb."

An infallible rule when marketing antiques was that the more you build anticipation, the more collectors you'd draw to your auction, the more bidders you attract, the higher the price you'd realize. Typically, I waited until I was further along with an appraisal before I began publicizing the object, so I could tease potential bidders' interest with facts, but the more I thought of it, the better I liked the idea of capitalizing on the suspense factor. Jane Austen's name would garner interest, no matter what.

"Josie?" If Wes had been standing on solid ground, I would have heard his foot tapping impatiently. "What gives?"

"Sorry." I smiled. "You want a scoop? I'll give you a beaut."

He waggled his fingers. "I don't need the hype. Just give me the facts. Whatcha got, and what do I have to do to get it?"

"Nothing onerous. Interview me about the complexity of documenting provenance. Let me announce a reward for information that will lead me to the woman named Veronica Sutton who has knowledge about letters purported to have been written by Jane Austen."

"Jane Austen?" He stared at me for several seconds. "No wonder you've been so cagey."

"I haven't been cagey. I've been circumspect. Ms. Sutton dropped them off yesterday, then disappeared."

"Why?"

"I look forward to asking her that very question as soon as I locate her."

"What's your offer?"

"Five hundred dollars for the first verified sighting I receive."

"I don't know, Joz. Publishing her name sounds a little dicey to me."

"Why? We're not publishing any personal information. I'll be the only one who'll know how to contact her. I don't think it's dicey at all."

"How will you decide who's first?"

"By the time stamp on the email or phone log. I doubt I'll get all that many."

Wes's chest puffed out and his chin lifted, the picture of pride. "The *Seacoast Star* has more than twenty-three thousand subscribers, and my blog is the most popular feature. More than sports. More than food. People want hard news. And don't forget I do news spots on Hitchens's classical music radio station, too. Which means thousands of people are going to descend on you. Tens of thousands. Word will spread. Hundreds of thousands."

I laughed. "When it comes time to sell the letters, I hope you're right. It won't happen now."

"Even if it's only a couple of hundred, you'll end up with people who feel stiffed—certain they were first."

"I think you're overstating the response, but if it becomes an issue, I'll go public with the info. You can publish a list of responders—not their names, their initials—and the time we received their tips. That should reassure people that everything is on the up-and-up."

Wes tapped his notebook against his thigh. "With the Jane Austen connection, I think my boss will go for it . . . when will I get the info?"

"Today. Soon."

"How will you vet the responders?"

"I thought I'd put together a photo array and get people to ID her."

"That's good, but it means I can't publish her photo."

"True, but you can use a photo of the two letters. You can position the story as a two-hundred-year-old mystery your readers have the opportunity to help solve."

His eyes lit up, and as his gaze shifted to the ocean I could almost see the wheels turning.

I followed suit and watched a tanker steaming north. The sun was bright, but the ocean was growing restless, whitecaps dotting the water far out to sea.

I hoped Veronica would understand why I felt I had to go to such lengths to find her that, while I needed information about the letters, I *craved* information about my father. I was also aware that the public nature of this call for sightings might spook her into fleeing and burrowing deeper somewhere far, far away, where I might never find her. I had no reason to think she would disappear again, but she might. Yet it seemed to me that I had no choice. Doing nothing got me nowhere, and this was my only idea. Sometimes you have no choice but to cast a wide net and hope for the best.

"Why would this Veronica Sutton person just hand over the letters?" he said, turning back to face me. "Something's not adding up."

"I agree. She told me they were mine, and I need more information about that, too."

"If I do this, I get an exclusive on the provenance once you know it."

Wes and I both knew there was zero chance he would turn down the opportunity to break the news, but I played along.

"Yes, and I'll cite your article in our marketing materials: Small-town support leads to big-time success."

His brow cleared. "You're the bomb, Joz!"

I touched his arm. "We're a good team."

"Don't get all mushy on me."

"Me?" I asked in mock horror. "Never."

Wes shook his index finger at me as he started down the dune, a tough guy making his point. "See you don't." He paused halfway down, his expression back to kid brother. "Thanks."

Wes was, by any objective standard, cute as a bug.

When I reached my company, just before eight thirty, breakfast was still being served in the tent, but most of the crew were already at work in the studio. Ripples of laughter wafted into the parking lot. Before I joined the team, though, I met with Russ, our Sterling Security rep, and Mel Gold, the shift lead. Russ and Mel both wore Sterling Security–branded windbreakers and navy blue slacks.

"We had two shifts of two men each on duty all night," Russ said. "One team worked from seven to two. The other started at two and is scheduled to finish at nine. I asked Mel to join me for the debriefing in case you had any questions."

"Thank you both." I turned to Mel, whose perfect posture and silvery crew cut suggested he'd spent a long time in the military. "Is there anything I should know?"

"We maintained an open presence, which is to say we kept the overhead lights on all night, patrolled with flashlights on, didn't worry about making noise, and so on. There were no infringements or attempted infringements reported by the first shift team. Same with us. All was quiet."

"That's a huge relief. I think that's—" I interrupted myself, turning as a car pulled into the lot. Ivan waved and I waved back. "Thanks, Mel. Russ, I'd like the patrols to continue. Lenny sticks close to the tent, to cover the entrance to the studio, and I'd be more comfortable if I knew professional eyes were looking in other places, too."

"Done," Russ said. "Any idea how long?"

"No. Let's take it day by day—and night by night."

"You got it. I'll let Lenny know."

I was glad Prescott's was having such a banner year—the extra expense wouldn't pinch.

I thanked them again, then walked to where Ivan had parked, not far from the front door. He was reaching for something on the passenger seat.

"Ivan!" I called.

He straightened up, his phone in hand. "Hi."

"Good to see you again. If you're here, that means Gloria must be up for some retakes. Was there a glitch in the filming?"

"I guess Gloria's audio got wonky. Oliver's, too."

"Annoying, but not surprising. This kind of snafu happens all the time."

He glanced around. "I don't see Gloria's car." He tapped his phone. "It's almost quarter of nine. She said she and Oliver had eight fifteen calls for a nine o'clock start. She's usually very prompt."

"Maybe her car died and she took a cab."

"No way. She would have called me for a ride."

"We'll know soon enough. Do you feel like breakfast? They're still serving."

He said he was always ready for coffee, but didn't move. "Can I ask you something?"

"Of course."

"Two things, actually. Will you be soliciting proposals for the Jane Austen letters appraisal?"

It wasn't hard to imagine Gloria's reaction to Ivan's ambition. He didn't come off like a snake, but maybe he was the viper Gloria had referred to. It's often the quiet ones who cause the most trouble. I felt an imbroglio in the making, and if I wasn't careful, I'd end up in the middle.

"I'm sure we'll discuss the project with a few experts," I said.

"I'd like to throw my hat in the ring," he said, his eyes reflecting unexpected determination with perhaps a hint of nervousness, not a surprise given the situation. "As you know, I specialize in Regency-period document authentications."

"Duly noted. What's your second question?"

"Do you ever bring in interns?" he asked.

"Yes . . . what's your interest?"

"Gaining experience in all facets of the profession," he said, a good answer to a tough question. "Could I apply? I'm a hard worker and reliable."

I didn't know whether we needed any interns now, nor if Ivan's skill set and interests would be a match. Sometimes an internship satisfied an academic requirement for a specific course or degree. Other times people applied because of a personal interest or career aspiration, or as with Ivan, to learn the business.

"I don't do the hiring myself," I said, "but I'll put you in touch with the people who do."

"Thanks," he said like he meant it, and set off toward the tent.

I checked my phone as I walked to the front office. I hadn't heard from Gloria, either.

Cara stood by the coffee machine, watching the pot fill. "Good morning," she said cheerfully. "The coffee should be ready in a minute."

"Thanks, but I'm all set. You haven't heard from Gloria, by any chance, have you? She's running late."

"No. Oliver was here, but he dashed out—he forgot his notes."

"I can see the schedule getting pushed further and further back in front of my eyes."

"He said he'd be back in a few minutes."

"Famous last words," I said, but as soon as the words were out of my mouth, a car drove into the lot. I opened the front door in time to see Oliver hop out of his car.

"You made it!" I said.

"My notes! I'd forget my head if it wasn't attached!"

"You probably won't need them."

He lifted a manila envelope shoulder high. "This guarantees it. If I didn't have them, I'd need them."

"So true!" I waved. "See you in the studio."

He ran for the tent.

Cara poured herself a cup of coffee. While she got herself situated at her desk, I sat at the guest table to email Sasha and Fred, cc'ing Gretchen about Ivan's interest in interning.

Sasha emailed back saying she'd reach out to him. I replied: *Good.* After a moment, recalling how Ivan asked to be considered for the Jane Austen letters appraisal assignment when Gloria wasn't around, I added: *Check references carefully, from Gloria especially.*

Just as I was leaving, Hank and Angela sauntered up to say hello. "I'm sorry, babies," I whispered, giving them each a little pat. "I promise you'll both get proper petties later."

Unconcerned, Angela started batting a red felt mouse, her current favorite. Hank stared at me in patent disbelief that I could think anything took precedence over his unspoken demand for an immediate cuddle.

I told Cara I'd see her later and left, trying not to take Hank's chagrin personally.

CHAPTER ELEVEN

I van sat alone in the tent, eating an English muffin, reading from his phone. Inside the studio, Oliver stood by the makeup table, his eyes closed, while one of the hair and makeup crew fluffed a brush over his cheeks. He was in the same outfit he'd worn yesterday, go Jackie! She had my outfit ready, and I changed in a flash. Back in the hair and makeup section, I lifted myself into my chair, ready for Marie to do her thing.

While Marie worked, she chatted about her kid brother who was calling her every other minute for help in high school biology, a favorite subject of hers from way back when, and a dating show she'd watched last night at the hotel, saying she was thinking of applying, why not? I shut my eyes, listened with one ear, and let the rest of my mind drift into planning my submission to Wes.

As soon as Timothy finished the morning's shoot, I'd select photos of the letters and draft something for Wes to publish, a Q and A, perhaps.

Wes was right about one thing—the minute the word was out about a never-before-seen pair of letters alleged to have been written by Jane Austen, I'd be inundated with requests for interviews, offers to help with the appraisal, and pleas to submit preemptory bids. This was all good news, but managing the onslaught required forethought. I needed to provide word-for-word instructions so my staff knew how to respond to each request, offer, or plea. They already knew never to talk to reporters, and this certainly wasn't our first high-profile antique, but the possible connection to Jane Austen had the potential to catapult us to a new level—or, if I mishandled any facet of the situation, to make us a laughingstock. I was confident, but I knew enough about Murphy's Law and human nature to know I'd better prepare carefully.

At nine forty-five, Marie said, "You're gorgeous!"

Starr came over and leaned in close to my ear. "Have you seen Gloria? She's up next."

"No," I whispered back. "Have you heard from her?"

"Just a text acknowledging my crack-of-dawn message, saying she'd be here between eight and eight fifteen."

I checked my phone again. Nothing. "Let me talk to Ivan."

Ivan was still in the tent, but he'd moved to a table by a window, and was staring into Greely Woods.

"You look deep in thought," I said.

He spun toward my voice, drawing his legs in, preparing to rise.

"Don't get up," I said, holding up a hand to stop him.

He settled back. "Sorry . . . I was four thousand miles and two hundred years away."

"You were spending time with Lord Byron in Rome."

He leaned back. "Busted."

"I admire your enthusiasm." I lowered my voice. "Have you heard from Gloria? It appears she's gone AWOL."

He tapped his phone. "No." He raised his eyes to meet mine. "It's odd . . . totally unlike her."

"Do you have another way to reach her?"

"I texted her and left a voicemail message."

"Did you have any contact with her this morning?"

"Yes. I texted her just after six, to see if she'd heard from Starr. She texted back that she had, but that I didn't need to come in." He licked his lips. "I just thought . . . moral support or if she picked up the wrong notes again . . . you know, anything I could do."

"That's very thoughtful of you."

He looked down, and I empathized. I get embarrassed when I'm praised, too.

"How about a second phone?" I asked. "Does she have one?"

"Not that I know of."

"Could she have fallen back asleep?"

"I don't see how. She keeps her phone on her bedside table for note taking. She told me that she sometimes gets ideas in the middle of the night and doesn't want to risk forgetting them, so she dictates into her phone then and there."

"Maybe the ringer's off."

"It's possible. When I've been with her in meetings and she gets a call, her phone vibrates."

"How about a boyfriend? Could she be at someone else's home with her phone in her purse?"

"I don't think so. She had a rough breakup a few weeks back."

"I'm sure there's a reasonable explanation—a minor fender bender, something like that. I don't mean to make a mountain out of a molehill."

Ivan's brows drew together. "She would have called or texted."

"I know." I met Ivan's eyes. "Between you and me, I'm a little worried. If you hear from her, let me know right away, okay?"

He said he would, and I returned to the studio. Oliver was just wrapping up, shaking hands with Starr. He walked toward me with a jaunty gait and a big grin.

"Josie!" he said. "What a great setup you have here. Thanks again for including me."

"My pleasure." I took in the room. "Where's your mom?"

"Swimming. She was bummed to miss it, but getting back on her bike is her number one priority."

"That's hysterical."

"Which part? That she's bummed? Or that dirt bike riding is more important to her than watching her son on camera?"

I laughed. "Honestly, that she's your mom. You're so different from her."

"I know. Always have been, too. I was born studious and rather formal. She's . . . well . . . neither. I suppose I could be a changeling."

"It's wonderful to see how much she adores you, changeling or not." I looked around again. "You haven't seen Gloria, have you?"

"Today? No. I know she expected to be here. We texted this morning, comparing notes, and spoke on the phone for a minute."

"Really? When?"

"Around seven." He extracted his phone from an inner pocket of his jacket and tapped a few times. "Seven-oh-four, to be exact." He grinned again. "I can tell from the look on your face that you're wondering why I contacted her. I was worried I'd screwed up big-time, and if so, I was hoping that she had, too. Misery loves company, and all that. Starr's text made it clear that it was the audio that was the problem, not me, but by seven, self-doubt was gnawing at me." He gave a self-deprecating laugh. "Being an insecure malcontent, I had about convinced myself that Starr was being diplomatic, that I'd totally mucked up the works. Luckily, before I had worked myself into enough of a dither to throw my sorry self into the Piscataqua, I got Gloria's side of the story. Starr told her the same thing—it was the recording that was at fault, not us. Crisis averted."

"You're funny."

"The laughter that hides the pain."

He raised a fist for a friendly bump, waved around the room, and left.

"I'm disappointed Rory wasn't with him," Timothy said.

"I said the same thing."

"I want to wait a little longer for Gloria. If we can't reshoot her lines, we'll either edit around the issue or have you slip the missing info in your monologue or one of the segues. Which is to say that I want to hold off until we know one way or the other about Gloria. I've already talked to Fred. We're going to do the thimble beauty shots while we wait." He patted my shoulder. "Stop fretting. We're not losing time. Everything is under control."

"Thank you for reassuring me. I'll tell Ivan."

I checked my phone again, then sat at Ivan's table, and repeated what Timothy told me.

"I don't know what to do," he said.

"I don't think there's anything we can do. Is she scheduled to teach today?"

"No . . . not until tomorrow at noon. But she's usually on campus all day on Wednesdays working on her research or writing."

"How about calling over to the department and asking someone to knock on her door? Maybe she's deep in research and lost track of the time."

"I don't know. Gloria's really private. She wouldn't like me making waves."

For a trusted graduate assistant, Ivan seemed oddly reluctant to get involved.

"I'll take care of it," I said. "If I haven't heard from her by noon, I'll stop by the college and talk to someone in the office. That way, if she's fine and resents the intrusion, she'll blame me, not you."

"You must think I'm scared of my own shadow. It's not that . . . it's just . . . well . . . it's that I know her. She hates a fuss. But there's no reason for me to stay here. I'll head over to campus. I can knock on her door and see if she's there. If she is, I'll text you."

I thanked him, and walked to the exit.

I decided to loop around my building to see if I could identify what yesterday's interloper might have been after.

"Everything copacetic?" I asked Lenny as I passed by.

"Seems so."

Outside, I took a careful look around. A Sterling Security guard stood by the entrance to the parking lot, facing out, studying Vaughn's Weald. The other guard wasn't visible.

As I walked, I repeated Timothy's words: *Everything is under control.* It showed how little he knew. Between Veronica's shocking revelation about my father, the Jane Austen letters, and a stranger on the prowl, I didn't feel that everything was under control, not by a long shot.

I stayed in the middle of the wide driveway, with the back of the building on my right and Greely Woods on my left. I passed the window to Timothy's private suite, which was always shrouded with blackout curtains because, he said, seeing things like trees and bushes made him nervous, a New Yorker's view of the world. The window in the TV studio was uncovered. Under the dim inside lighting, all I saw were shadows and silhouettes of cameras, chairs, and people. When the work lights were on, you could see inside as clear as day. I continued the circuit, passing the windowless auction venue, the loading dock—big enough for trucks to back into—and the warehouse. Six security cameras were mounted high overhead. Red dots assured me that they were operational.

At the end, I turned right onto the flagstone pathway that led along the west side of the building past the tag sale venue entrance, ending at the parking lot. The fieldstone wall that hid the unsightly equipment was to my right. Carter's Forest loomed large to my left. I lightly dragged my fingers along the cool, coarse stone as I walked by. Two steps farther along, and I'd reached the section of wall where I'd seen the blond man. I stopped to investigate. The wall was intact. Everything seemed normal—the security cameras, the overhead lights, the building. When I reached the end of the wall, I saw the other Sterling Security guard, a woman. She aimed a flashlight held high above her head at a window beside the tag sale venue entrance, and peered inside.

I called hello and she turned. I introduced myself, and she told me everything seemed fine.

I thanked her and walked on. The bench by the willow tree where I'd met Veronica came into sight a hundred feet ahead. When I reached the place where the blond man had dashed into the woods, I paused to face Carter's Forest. I stepped closer to the trees, examining the ground, but amid the reticulation of low growth, latticed vines, thick bushes, and feathery ferns, I couldn't see any trace of his flight, not one single trampled bush or stomped vine.

Something caught my eye. Fifty feet from where I stood, a stripe of mint green lay on the ground, partially hidden by the welter of low growth. Nothing mint green grew or lived in the forest.

I felt suddenly breathless, unable to draw in enough air.

I spun back toward the tag sale venue entrance, but the guard had moved on, continuing her patrol. I stepped into the woods, pushing through a bramble bush and ducking beneath low-hanging branches. I tripped on a bulging root and nearly went down, making enough noise to scare the birds into silence.

A body came into view.

It was Gloria, except it wasn't. Her eyes were open, fixed on the sky. Her mouth was frozen in a silent scream. Her skin was blotched with dark purple bruises.

I looked away, and swallowed hard. I was afraid I might get sick.

There was no question she was dead, strangled. Her scarf, the green one she'd worn yesterday, was wrapped around her neck so tightly, it disappeared into folds of skin, the ends snaking alongside her torso.

I kept my eyes on the mint green scarf and dialed 9–1–1.

CHAPTER TWELVE

G riff, the Rocky Point police officer first on the scene, was as brusque as ever. I'd known him for years, ever since I'd first moved to New Hampshire. He herded the TV crew, Timothy and me included, into the tent for the initial round of questioning. Prescott's staff was holed up in the front room with a young officer named Darryl. Griff stood by the door scowling at us until two additional police officers arrived, both women—a tall ice blonde named F. Meade and a short, chunky brunette I didn't recognize.

Griff told us to listen up. When he had our attention, he instructed us to answer police questions directly and honestly, and to stay put. No one made a peep.

Officer Meade and the other woman started on opposite ends of the tent and moved from table to table, entering everyone's name and contact information into some program on their tablets. They asked each of us what we knew about Gloria or the situation. No one within my hearing had met Gloria before we began filming, and none of us knew anything about how she'd died—rather, none of us admitted knowing anything.

As soon as the responding officers were finished with me, I walked to a corner and turned my back to the room to call Ty. I got his voicemail and left a long message, filling him in, then called Gretchen and reached her at our other location, Prescott's Antiques Barn. She was empathetic and upset, wanting to know if I was all right. Once I assured her that I was fine, or as fine as I could be under the circumstances, she steadied herself, and calmly took charge, reassuring me that she'd communicate with the staff in both locations about what was happening. She'd also remind them of Prescott's policy regarding talking to the press—don't. They were to refer all requests for comments to me. For the umpteenth time, I patted myself on the back for hiring Gretchen the first day I started my business, and for promoting her ever since. Life would be far harder without her even-keeled competence.

I returned to my seat next to Timothy. He was reading something on his phone. Starr was texting. Other people clustered in small groups, whispering. I tried to read the spate of emails that had arrived in my in-box, including one from Wes wanting info about Gloria's death, but I couldn't concentrate. I'd experienced so many shocks during the last twenty-four hours that I felt numb, yet I couldn't stop thinking, conjecturing, speculating. Facts spun through my brain like bingo balls in a cage, never releasing, leading nowhere. It was exhausting. Every once in a while, Timothy patted my hand.

Police Chief Ellis Hunter entered the tent around eleven fifteen. Ellis was tall, broad, and nice-looking, with brown hair cut short and a jagged red scar near his right eyebrow. I'd never asked him how he got it, but suspected it was an on-the-job injury from his days as a New York City homicide detective. He wore a beige sports coat, dark brown slacks, an off-white shirt, and a gold tie. We'd been friendly for more than a decade, and were closer now that he and Zoë, my best friend, were married. He met my eyes for a moment and nodded, acknowledging me. He spoke to Griff, then walked to the middle and asked for our attention.

"I understand from the officers that you've answered our preliminary questions. Thank you for your cooperation. For now, you can all get back to work. We'll be in touch as needed. Please don't leave Rocky Point just yet."

Timothy stood and introduced himself. "How long do you need us to stay? We planned to leave for the city—New York—tomorrow."

"Understood. Let's you and me stay in touch about schedules." Ellis was a master at saying things that sounded good, but actually promised nothing and revealed even less. He turned to face me. "Josie . . . can I see you?"

"Sure." I followed Ellis outside.

"Josie!" Wes yelled as he tore across the parking lot toward me.

"Not now, Wes." I didn't listen to his protests. Instead, I wagged a finger at one of the security guards. When the guard reached me, I said, "This is Wes Smith, a reporter. Escort him out. Keep all reporters out."

"Let's go," the guard said, gripping Wes's elbow.

Wes sputtered angrily as the guard steered him to his car and hovered over him until he drove out of the lot. Ellis, a disinterested spectator, didn't comment. Once Wes left the lot, Ellis and I walked to the front office.

Ellis sat on the yellow brocade love seat upstairs in my private office. I took the wing chair facing him.

"You look a little worse for wear," he said.

"I've had a lot of surprises drop in my lap over the last twenty-four hours, and now this." I closed my eyes for a moment. "I can't believe I said that. Gloria's death is appalling, and finding the killer is all that matters. I didn't mean to sound callous. It's just that—how can this possibly have happened within sight of my property while guards were on patrol?"

"Speaking of which . . . why did you call in the cavalry?"

"Stuff that happened yesterday spooked me a little. Have you talked to the guards?"

"Claire did. Detective Brownley. They say they didn't hear or see anything."

"Was Gloria killed in the woods or was she brought there after the fact?"

"Unclear. We need to wait for the ME's report."

"People walking through a thicket wouldn't make any more noise than a deer moving through the brush. Ditto someone towing or carrying Gloria's body."

"In any event, it's moot, because no one heard anything."

"If someone dragged her, there'd be signs of the disruption."

"True, and if that's what happened, we'll find it. What spooked you yesterday?"

"You don't want to hear my problems in the middle of a murder investigation. It's probably nothing, just me overreacting."

"Is there some reason you don't want to tell me?"

I examined the rug, getting my thoughts in order. "It's not that." I raised my eyes. "It's emotionally taxing and totally unrelated to Gloria. Poor Gloria." I shook my head. "I can't believe she's dead—murdered."

"Tell me anyway. Sometimes things connect in ways you don't expect and can't see until after the fact."

I couldn't think of how to explain, of where to start. It felt as if my brain were wrapped in gossamer fuzz. I took a few seconds to recalibrate. "A woman named Veronica Sutton appeared out of nowhere to tell me she'd known my father and deliver a package, a beautiful leather box filled with things she must have known I'd cherish. She said, and I quote, 'I was a good friend of your father's.' Can you imagine? She shows up without notice and dashes away before I can ask her anything. Who does something like that? It's sadistic." I tried for a smile, but it came out closer to a grimace. "In case you can't tell, I'm upset and hurt and hopping mad. How dare she tease me like that?" I described the contents of the green leather box. "I've confirmed her name and that she used to live in Florida. I'm determined to find her—not only because I want to know more about her relationship with my father, but also because she probably knows something about the Jane Austen letters, something that will help me trace provenance." I raised a hand, then let it drop. "Forget it. While very important to me, all of this is insignificant in the face of Gloria's murder."

Ellis rubbed his nose, a sure sign he was thinking hard, his brain firing on all cylinders. "You didn't hire security guards because of Veronica Sutton."

"What are you? A cop or something?"

He smiled. "Or something."

I told him about the blond man who'd been skulking around, adding that I'd asked Starr to show his photo around, but that no one had recognized him, and that I'd distributed the photo to the guards, but the man hadn't been seen again. I brought up the images of him and Veronica Sutton on my phone, and handed it over.

He scrolled through the photos, taking his time, then enlarged one shot and studied it for several seconds. "May I email these to Detective Brownley?"

"Why?"

"Two unusual events occurring the day before a murder. It's worth seeing if there's a connection."

"Will you tell me what you learn?" I asked.

"If I can."

"That's not good enough."

"I will keep you apprised to the full extent possible."

I held out my arm, palm up. "Give me my phone."

"Don't make me sorry I told you I wanted to check them out," he said.

"Don't make me sorry I showed you the photos."

Ellis cocked his head, looking at me through narrowed eyes. "You have an answer for everything."

I glared at him, annoyed.

"May I send the photos?" he asked again.

I leaned back in the chair, resting my head on the wing. Getting angry at Ellis was counterproductive. He had information I wanted, or he might. Certainly, going forward he would. "The man, okay. Veronica Sutton, no."

"Why hold her back?"

"Wes is going to publish an interview in which I'll request help in locating her. The idea is that Prescott's needs to find her in connection with an antiques appraisal. I'll announce a five-hundred-dollar reward for the first verified sighting. Wes will print photos of the Jane Austen letters to whet the world's appetite and convince people it's a genuine offer. I need her photo to separate the wheat from the chaff. I don't want to take any chance of it getting out."

"Thanks for the vote of confidence."

"I'm not worried about you. I just know that the only safe secret is the one you never share."

"What makes you think Wes will help you? He seemed fairly agitated just now."

I waved Wes's attitude aside. "Wes always plays offense. No way will he pass on an opportunity to be the first out of the gate with a story of international significance."

"You're on target there, but you can't just snap up people's photos from the internet. There are privacy issues."

"We subscribe to a propriety website for just this reason—we pay them for the rights to their photos."

Ellis examined Veronica Sutton's photo for a few seconds. "Okay . . . you've convinced me. I'll email the photo of the man, not her."

He sent the photo, then returned my phone. "What if you can't locate her?"

"I can. I will. I have to."

"Did you talk about this yesterday on set?"

"Some, yes. I told Gloria, Oliver, Ivan, and Oliver's mom, Rory, about the letters. Timothy was there, too." I anticipated his next question by adding, "I know you're going to ask if anyone reacted oddly. Not that I noticed. Only the usual skirmishes between competitors."

"Skirmishes?"

"Gloria and Oliver pitched themselves within seconds of hearing about the letters, then swatted one another down. It didn't strike me as anything surprising or especially vicious. It was simply a real-world battle between experts vying for important work. A little aggressive maybe, but the stakes are big. They were on me like cats on cream, but to each other they were more like two dogs competing for one bone."

"What can you tell me about Ivan Filbert?"

"Not much. He seems serious about his work—ambitious, quiet."

"I can tell by the look on your face that you're holding back."

"You know how much I hate gossip." I raised a hand. "And I know you're going to tell me that sharing facts in a murder investigation isn't gossip. So okay, I'll tell you what I know, which isn't much. Except for Oliver, I met them all for the first time yesterday. Ivan seems determined to make his mark, but not ruthless or anything. He's developing a new technique for document authentication, something to do with writing hesitations. He told me he wanted to submit a proposal to appraise the Jane Austen letters, which, while not unethical, might well have alienated Gloria."

Ellis made a note. "And Rory Crenshaw?"

"She's what could politely be called a handful. She got into it with Ivan, telling him to man up, that since he was the brains of the operation, he was a fool to let Gloria take all the credit. He looked mortified and scurried away as fast as he could."

"Did he say anything?"

"Just that it wasn't true. He was . . . discreet."

"What was he being discreet about?"

"Talking out of school about his boss, I assume. Rory comes on strong, yet Ivan didn't waver."

"I can tell there's more. What *didn't* he talk about?"

"This morning, I was a bit surprised that he resisted checking on Gloria. He explained that she'd set clear boundaries, and he respected them. I suppose you can't argue with that, except that when someone's well-being is involved, it's time to bend some rules."

"If they just met, how could Rory know he was the brains of the operation?"

"I have no reason to think Ivan was the brains or that Rory thought he was. She said Oliver told her so, which makes sense since he said the same thing himself, and he did it in a kind of snide way. At the time I assumed Rory and Oliver were simply stirring the pot, trying to get a rise out of Ivan, to mess with his relationship with Gloria. Whether he complained to her, or apologized, or assured her that he'd done nothing to deserve their accusations, Gloria might get riled up, which, in turn, might throw her off her game."

"How Machiavellian."

"That's Rory. She didn't limit her ire to Ivan. She was peeved with me, too."

"Peeved?"

"Annoyed. Irritated."

"I know what 'peeved' means," he said. "It's just not a word you hear every day. What was she peeved about?"

"She thought I manipulated the situation so Gloria would look better on camera than her son."

"Were you peeved back?"

"No. A, she was wrong, and B, I thought her protectiveness toward Oliver was kind of sweet. She isn't sweet, but her motivation was."

"What do you know about her?"

"Rory? She's one of a kind, but once I got over the shock of her personality, I found her hilarious. Rory thought the episode was terrible, that if I couldn't see it, I wasn't looking. That's how she talks."

"Was she right?" Ellis asked.

"Not about me. I try to make both guests look good. If it didn't work out that way, that's the way the cookie crumbles. As to Gloria, I guess you could say there was a little one-upmanship with Oliver. Gloria got a couple of sharp digs in. Oliver handled them well, I thought, smoothly, which made them seem less pointed. Timothy said the episode was medium, code for better than some, not as good as most."

"Was Gloria spoiling for a fight?"

"That's an interesting question. I don't know. She got some digs in when we were off camera, too. Gloria goaded Oliver openly, bragging that she'd beat him at a recent trial—they were expert witnesses on opposite sides of a case. To be fair, he told me about himself. He was charming, actually . . . self-deprecating, you know? At the time, I just thought they were jostling for position."

Ellis crossed his legs, resting his right calf on his left knee. "How did Ivan get along with Oliver?"

"I doubt they exchanged more than a dozen words."

"How about with Gloria?"

"Ivan? I'm not sure. He acted wary and a bit intimidated, but his reaction didn't strike me as over the top. Gloria was a bigwig in his field, a big fish in a pond where he's a minnow. Actually, he was fairly assertive when you consider the power she wielded over his career. Without her stamp of approval, he wouldn't get his Ph.D."

"What'll happen to him now?"

"He'll get another advisor. It's hard to switch horses halfway down the track, but it happens. He'll be fine."

"Any hint that she wasn't going to give him that stamp of approval?"

"I don't know. Maybe." I repeated Gloria's comments about the viper. "Betrayal is a strong word." My shoulders lifted a half-inch, then sank. "He's going to apply for an internship here."

"Really? Doesn't that represent a conflict of interest?"

"No, it's common practice. To reach expert status, you need the widest possible range of experience."

"Do you like him?"

"I guess I liked him all right," I said. "But you know me . . . I like most people when I first meet them."

"And it's downhill from there."

"Ha ha."

Ellis shifted position. "Speculate for a minute on what the blond man wanted."

"I have no idea. That's why I walked the perimeter, looking for signs of an attempted break-in . . . sabotage . . . anything that was off." I paused for a moment. "Who owns Carter's Forest, where Gloria's body was found?"

"Why?"

"Maybe the murder was intended as a message to the owner. Do you want me to check the county records?"

"I'll do it." He typed into his phone for a minute, then said, "Carter's Forest is owned by the city." He tapped and scrolled for a while. "They bought it, and Greely Woods, the land in back of you, more than fifty years ago. The historic statement says they wanted to prevent overdevelopment."

"Good for them. Good for us all." As I spoke, my phone vibrated. Wes had left a voicemail reminding me in a cold and clipped tone that he had deadlines, and if I wanted my story in the next edition, I had to get him the material right away.

"Wes is chastising me for not having sent him my story."

"Go ahead. I have nearly a hundred texts and emails to read."

I relocated to my desk and drafted a Q and A. Wes would change the wording to get the copy into his voice, and he might rearrange the order of the questions. So long as the key points were included, that was all fine with me. I pasted the text into an email, attached still shots of the letters, and sent it off with a message apologizing for the delay and thanking him for his help. If I knew Wes, and I did, he'd be clamoring for payback within the hour.

I rejoined Ellis in the seating area. He held up a finger, signaling he'd be a minute. He read a long message, then said, "Nothing popped on the blond man."

"Frustrating."

"Give it time," Ellis said. "Patience is a virtue."

"So the old saying goes. From your scattershot questions, I infer you don't have a motive for Gloria's murder."

"Do you have any ideas beyond what we talked about?"

"No, but I have a question. Is her car parked on Trevor?"

"We haven't located her vehicle. Did you see it? A silver Accord? I'd like to confirm that's what she was driving."

"That's what she drove yesterday."

"It's not on Trevor, at her apartment, or in her college lot. It's possible she spent the night with a friend, and once we identify that person, we'll find the car."

"So how did she get here?"

"Good question." He stood. "I need to check in with Detective Brownley."

"Give her my regards."

He said he would. I walked him downstairs. He greeted my staff and asked if anyone had remembered anything that might help with the investigation. No one spoke up. I stood by the open front door as he strode across the parking lot to his SUV. Detective Brownley leaned against the hood, watching the techs working in the woods, her ink-black hair swaying as she dipped her head to gain a better view.

Ellis said patience was a virtue, but I wasn't convinced. In fact, I thought patience was often overrated. Persistence and perseverance when working toward a specific goal, sure. Telling someone to be patient, though, was all too often simply a ploy to keep them out of your hair. The worst was when people dressed it up as righteousness.

I had no idea how I'd identify the blond man, but I knew that if Ellis didn't, I would.

CHAPTER THIRTEEN

I shut the door. My staff was looking at me expectantly. After so many years working with them, I could read their moods from their body language. Right now, anxiety was writ large on every face. They needed to know the ship was secure and steady despite rough seas.

I turned to Gretchen, standing by the warehouse door, and asked, "Have the police finished talking to everyone?"

"Yes. Officer Darryl Rilnick asked us each a few questions and that was it. No private interviews. It all seemed pro forma."

I nodded, then met each person's gaze, taking my time. "Gloria's death is heartbreaking. Later, once we know more about the circumstances, we'll work out some way to honor her memory, a donation, something. Now, though, let's just take care of each other. If you need some time away from the office to process what's happened, that's fine. Otherwise, carry on as best you can. Don't be shy about asking for help." I touched my chest, my heart. "I can't tell you how fortunate I feel to have you all on my team. Each and every one of you. Thank you." I faced Gretchen. "Is there anything I need to know or do?"

"No."

"Walk outside with me, okay?"

"Sure." She shrugged into a black sweater coat.

The police were everywhere, but no one stopped us from crossing the lot to the bench.

"I'm really upset about Gloria," I said as we walked. "I thought I'd found a new friend."

"It's just so horrible."

"I feel terrible discussing business in light of Gloria's murder." We sat on the bench. "The thing is, some wheels were put in motion, and that motion is going to continue." I filled her in about Veronica Sutton and the Jane Austen letters.

"Oh, Josie!" she exclaimed, her eyes growing moist when I spoke about my father.

I touched her arm, the nubby wool from her sweater coat rough against my skin. "The bottom line is that I need you to do something for me."

"Of course. Anything."

I described my arrangement with Wes and the photo array I wanted to show people who responded to my request for sightings. I emailed Veronica's photo to her, and asked her to prepare three copies of the array, one for me, one for her, and a spare, just in case.

She told me she'd take care of it right away.

I thanked her, and after a quick hug, she left.

I sat for another few minutes, trying to quiet my mind. I thought about Gloria—a magnificent woman at the height of her intellectual prowess. I wanted to think about her, to allow myself to mourn a friend that might have been. That wasn't the only sonorous voice plaguing me. I also needed to slow the rush of seemingly unrelated facts rocketing through my brain. I needed tranquility, but that wasn't in the cards, not now, not here.

From the murmurs and crunching emanating from Carter's Forest in back of me, I could tell that the technicians were still at work. I could hear other sounds, too, distant gulls, an occasional car, footsteps. I stood and surveyed the scene. Two men wearing Rocky Point CSI–branded jackets squatted near where Gloria's corpse had lain, examining something I couldn't see. Uniformed police officers were conducting a grid search in the woods twenty feet farther west from the CSI techs, moving slowly toward the interstate. Turning toward my building, toward Mimi's Copse, I saw Ellis standing near the tent, talking on his phone. I couldn't hear anyone or anything distinctly, but I felt a sense of generalized urgency, and that added to the pandemonium inside my head.

Back in the office, I asked Sasha and Fred to meet me upstairs in ten minutes. En route, I retrieved the green leather box from the safe. At my desk, I extracted the two plastic-sheathed letters.

I wasn't an expert on Jane Austen, but I was a fan, and as part of my job, I maintained a casual interest in the value of ephemera related to all literary giants. I was aware, for example, that no one knew how many letters Jane Austen had written. I did a quick online search. Experts thought there might have been as many as three thousand letters. Of those, only a hundred and sixty-one were known to exist, the rest presumably having been destroyed. Evidently, members of Jane Austen's family had discarded or burned many of them shortly after her death in 1817. Jane's sister, Cassandra, had burned an additional trove in the 1840s. Most of the remaining letters recounted the mundane incidents of her daily life.

While I waited for Sasha and Fred, I continued reading. Interestingly, a six-line chunk of one of her letters had been mysteriously cut out. The missing section had resurfaced a few years ago, found in a collector's scrapbook, creating quite a flurry of excitement. Experts and devotees alike had hoped to discover some titillating secret, an illicit love affair, perhaps. Instead, the clipped lines were about counting linen, begging the question of why that snippet would have been cut out in the first place. Fans and scholars might have been disappointed, but I was thrilled: If six lines could reappear two hundred years after disappearing, so too could two letters—with one of them offering a nugget fully as tantalizing as any fan could ask for: Jane offering her niece Fanny advice about a romance.

I sent the article links to Sasha and Fred.

Gloria had mentioned studying exemplars, an important step in the appraisal process. Since every extant letter had been documented and analyzed multiple times by top scholars, we could study a variety of examples matching the time frame and subject matter of my letters. If we could get a handle on provenance, we might even be able to trace them, too, an awe-inspiring prospect.

Sasha and Fred climbed the spiral stairs and sat on guest chairs, across from me. Sasha looked worried. Fred looked curious.

"I only have a few minutes," I said, "but I wanted to share a remarkable occurrence and ask you to get started in developing a recommendation as to how we should proceed. I know it's hard to pay attention to business when we're in the middle of such a horrific event as Gloria's death, so if you need a time-out, all you have to do is ask. For me, work is an antidote to trouble, but I know many people take a different view. Tell me honestly . . . are you okay to work?"

"Yes," Sasha said, twirling a strand of hair.

"Always," Fred said, pushing up his glasses.

I slid the letters toward them. Fred's eyes went straight to the signature of the one in front of him. He grinned and reached for it. Sasha's eyes rounded as she lifted the other one. They read them silently, then exchanged letters.

"Yowza," Fred said.

"I can't believe it," Sasha whispered.

I gave them a two-minute explanation of how the letters had come into my possession and detailed my arrangement with Wes, then said, "We should expect a flood of inquiries about the letters. Sasha, I want you to take the lead here, but Fred, you'll be immersed in this project, too. You can tell anyone who asks that we have these letters, adding that we're not yet ready to announce any details yet. Get their contact information so we can create a database of interested parties for our marketing push."

"I'll tell Cara and Gretchen," Sasha said, "so everyone knows to direct all inquiries to Fred or me."

"Thank you. My dad wrote that he'd purchased the portfolio at a shop in Portsmouth. That was a regular stop on his travel schedule, but he might not have been speaking literally. His client was in Portsmouth but it's possible he found the shop somewhere off the beaten path. If we're going to build a list of likely places, it should be as inclusive as possible. How far from Portsmouth would a busy management consultant venture? Ten miles? Twenty?"

Sasha nodded. "All we'll need is a phone book of the Seacoast Region from that year. We'll look up anything that your dad might have called a shop: art galleries, bookstores, thrift shops, antiques stores, flea markets."

Fred agreed, adding, "We should include southern Maine, too."

"Once we have the list, we can call any that are still in business."

"Right," Fred said, "and we can try to track down the owners of any place that has closed."

"I know it's unlikely that any shop would have records about the twenty-year-old sale of a run-of-the-mill portfolio containing no-name sketches, but maybe it's not as far-fetched as it sounds. My dad was an art collector, so it's completely possible to think that he stopped in at certain shops and galleries every time he was in town. The owner might have known him by name. Perhaps Veronica Sutton kept him company on his art search crawls. Perhaps she'd been friends with the owners, and still was." I raised a hand. "I understand that the odds of finding anyone who remembers the sale are somewhere between slim and negligible, but they aren't zero. Do you agree?"

"Yes," Fred said.

"Absolutely," Sasha concurred. "How about if I ask Cara to build the list of shop owner possibilities?"

"Good. Also, put a list together for me of experts who could handle the overall authentication process. The three of us will work on the appraisal in-house, but I want a top expert overseeing the project, someone with gravitas."

"Should we put Oliver on the list?" Fred asked.

"If you think he belongs there, sure."

Sasha asked, "Should we consider Jane Austen experts from out of the country, or only US-based?"

"That's a good question. Include everyone you think should be included. Annotate the list with your opinions. This is a once-in-a-lifetime opportunity. We want to be both prudent and bold, which I know is an oxymoron, but there you go. It would be interesting to know what was going on in Jane Austen's life when she wrote these letters."

As we walked back to the front office, Sasha mentioned that Ivan had already submitted his internship application, which she took to be an encouraging sign.

Downstairs, I told Cara that I'd be back in a while.

"Would you like a cup of tea before you go?" she asked. "I didn't have a chance to tell you before, but I brought in gingersnaps."

No one, having tasted Cara's gingersnaps, could doubt their curative value, and I had enough experience with her nurturing nature to know that allowing her to fuss over me would serve as balm to her own upset, but I needed to be alone.

"Thanks," I said. "Maybe later."

Outside again, I leaned against my car. Before I could go for a walk and try to shake out the mental kinks, I needed to talk to Timothy about how we should proceed. I texted him, asking if he had a minute to talk. He replied that he'd be right out.

When Timothy joined me at my car, he asked, "How are you holding up?"

"About as you'd expect. You?"

"Same."

"I was wondering . . . after what happened, should we use the footage of Gloria?"

"I had the same thought," he said, his expression grave. "I don't know. I could argue either side. Are we capitalizing on a tragedy or eulogizing a colleague? It may be moot—I'm reviewing the bumpy audio to see if editing is even possible. It's one thing to splice in a rerecording and a whole other thing to salvage an existing one."

"Let's table the decision until you know for sure." I stood up. "Do you need me for anything?"

"No, not now. Everyone's pretty shaken up, but the consensus is we should power through in an effort to keep depression at bay. We're working on the thimble beauty shots."

I thanked him and we agreed to touch base in an hour or so.

We walked to the tent together. He continued into the studio. I snagged a slice of meatball pizza from the buffet, and left. I crossed the parking lot to Mimi's Copse, and started down the packed dirt path that led to the church, nibbling as I walked.

Five paces in, the human babblings receded as the forest sounds grew louder and more distinct, the chirpings of small birds and the rustlings of a rabbit bounding through the brush. Together, they soothed me like a lullaby. I scuffed along, sending fallen leaves flying. A gust of wind ruffled my hair, and I looked up, turning my head this way and that until I found an opening in the lattice of crimson and gamboge leaves. The clouds had thickened since my walk on the beach. Two minutes later, I reached the church parking lot. Three cars were in slots near the service entrance. Pastor Ted was on his knees in the community garden, weeding.

"Hey, Ted," I called.

He looked over his shoulder. "Hello, my friend." He leaned back on his haunches. "Want a pumpkin?"

"I already helped myself to several. Thank you."

He stood and brushed the dirt from his knee pads, then scanned my face. "You look like you could use a cup of coffee and a friendly chat."

"Thanks, Ted. I'm all right, all things considered. Did you hear what happened?"

"Yes, so sad. Are you sure you don't want to talk a little?"

"Another time. I need to clear my head, and you know my motto: When in doubt, go for a walk."

"That's a good motto. If I can help, just let me know."

I told him I would, and continued on. I glanced back as I rounded the corner of the church, heading for Trevor Street. Ted was already back on his knees pulling weeds.

I stopped short. There was only one car parked in the side lot—a silver Honda, an Accord, the same kind of car Gloria drove.

I examined the car on all sides from three feet away, then inched my way closer until I was about a foot from the vehicle. A Hitchens University parking sticker was affixed to the front windshield, in the center, just below an E-ZPass transponder. Looking through the windows, I could see that there was nothing on the dashboard, the center console, the seats, or the floor.

I texted Ellis.

CHAPTER FOURTEEN

I sidestepped to the back of the church, keeping the car in sight. Ted was still in the garden.

I shouted his name, and when he looked up, I asked if he would join me for a sec. Something in my tone, or maybe in my expression, must have communicated urgency because he jogged toward me, stripping off his gardening gloves as he ran.

"What's wrong?" he asked.

"How long has this car been here?"

He looked at the vehicle. "I don't know. I don't recall seeing it, but I don't come around this side all that often."

"Could it have been here since this morning? Or overnight?"

"Maybe. We can ask Winnie Thornton. You remember Winnie—she helped you organize those wonderful window screens you donated last year. She still works here part time, and she still notices everything. She's inside now. Why?"

"I think this car . . . I think it belongs to the woman who was murdered, Gloria Moreau."

"Oh, how awful! The poor soul."

I scanned the roofline. "I don't see any security cameras."

"No. We never felt the need."

"Would you ask Winnie about the car? I've already contacted the police. I'll wait for them here."

"Of course," he said and sped toward the rear entrance.

Gloria could have stopped by the church on her way home last night or early this morning to take some produce from Ted's community garden. Maybe Gloria had already known about his "help yourself" policy, or maybe someone had overheard me asking Oliver if I could bring him some pumpkins and mentioned it in her hearing. Then what happened? She decided to leave her car at the church and . . . and what? No ideas came to me.

Perhaps Gloria met someone here and she was murdered then and there. But after killing her, why go through all the hoopla of getting the corpse into a car, driving it a mile or so down the road, and towing her body a hundred yards through thick undergrowth?

I turned my back to the Honda.

The church, like my property, was surrounded by acres of forest, this section known as Reynold's Woods. If the killer wanted to delay the discovery of her body, he could have left her there.

So she probably wasn't killed here.

The only other alternative I could think of was that Gloria had been strangled in Carter's Forest, near where her body was discovered, and the murderer drove her car to the church to help delay finding the corpse. If we'd discovered her empty vehicle on the street or in my parking lot, we would have been far more worried than when we thought she was simply late.

My phone vibrated.

It was Timothy, asking if I had a minute to brainstorm.

"A minute, yes, but not much longer. I found what I think is Gloria's car, and I'm expecting the police to show up any minute."

"Oh, boy. No prob. We can talk later."

"No, no. Now is good—it's just that I may just have to get off the phone quickly."

"Are you safe?"

"Yes. I'm fine." Sunlight filtered through the clouds, adding a weak yellow sheen to the silver car. "No one is here. There are no obvious signs of violence. How about you? Any luck with the audio?"

"Not a bit. We couldn't recover enough to make a difference, which is something Greg and I will be talking about back in the city. Right now, the place where Gloria explained her views of how the Beatrix Potter inscription impacted the overall value of the book needs to be revamped. I was thinking that if you're all right with using the footage, we could have you draft an approximation of what she said and read it—pulling a few heartstrings along the way, which sounds crass, but isn't—she was a pleasure to have on set, and I'd love to pay tribute in this way. What do you think?"

"I think it's a great idea. I want people to see her final performance. Maybe we can add . . . hold on . . ."

Ted was walking toward me.

"Anything?" I asked him.

"Winnie saw the car when she got here this morning around nine thirty. She didn't think anything of it, assuming it was someone here for the garden."

"Thank you for checking. I'll be off the phone in a minute."

"Don't rush on my behalf." Ted walked several paces away.

I returned to the call. "Sorry about that, Timothy. I was saying maybe we can add a short interview with Ivan about her research process, not just the facts, but her thought process, too. Our viewers might like a bit of a deep dive into the how and why, not simply the what."

"I love that idea."

"Great! I'll need her notes, though. I don't want to put words in Gloria's mouth, as it were. Plus, if I'm going to interview Ivan about her work, consulting her notes is the only way we can verify that what he says is true."

"Aren't we cynical."

"Cautious, not cynical."

"Don't tell anyone, but me, too. Belts and suspenders, it's the only way to be sure your pants stay up. Do you want to contact Ivan about getting a look-see at Gloria's notes and appearing on camera, or should I?"

"Let me. As soon as I'm done here, I'll track him down." Ellis's SUV swung into the lot. "I need to go."

"Keep me posted. Love ya, sweetie."

Ellis rolled to a stop on Trevor, far from Gloria's vehicle.

"Ted," Ellis said as he walked toward us. Ted returned the greeting, calling him "Chief," then Ellis turned to me. "Tell me you haven't touched the vehicle."

"I haven't touched the vehicle. Is it Gloria's?"

He read the license plate, then the vehicle ID tag on the driver's side inner dash. "Yes." He examined the ground, slowly, carefully, crouching to study something by the trunk. When he stood, he asked, "How close did you get?"

"About a foot."

Ellis extracted a pair of plastic gloves from his pocket and put them on. He tried the trunk, then all four doors. Everything was locked. He cupped his eyes and leaned in until he was an inch from the glass.

He stepped back and glanced at his watch. "The tech guys should be here any minute."

While we waited, Ellis asked me how I happened to be on site, and after I explained, he asked Ted what he knew about the car. Ted repeated what he'd learned from Winnie.

"Has the ME determined the time of death yet?" I asked.

"Why?"

"I was thinking . . . Gloria was wearing the same clothes this morning as she was when she left the studio yesterday. I wonder if she was killed last night. No, wait, that's not right . . . Oliver spoke to her and Starr and Ivan got texts from her this morning."

"Can you account for her wearing the same outfit?"

"For multiday shootings, we keep the clothes people wear on camera on site for continuity purposes, so we ask guests to bring a spare outfit to go home in. Maybe Gloria only wore those clothes long enough to change into sweats or pj's, so this morning she just threw them on. No muss, no fuss."

Ellis jotted a note.

Ted asked if it was all right if he went back to puttering around the garden, and Ellis said that was fine, that he'd find him there if he needed him.

Ted took my hand for a moment. "I'm available to talk anytime, Josie."

"Thank you, Ted."

He left, drawing on his gloves as he walked back to the garden.

A minute later, a technician arrived. According to the lanyard dangling from his neck, his name was Phil. He told Ellis the CSI team would be there shortly. He'd brought some kind of master key and had the car opened within seconds.

Ellis shone a flashlight under the seats and into the door storage pockets, lifted the floor mats, and pulled down the visors, but he didn't find anything, not even the car keys. He opened the glove box, revealing its meager contents, a small stack of fast-food napkins and an old Avis-branded map of New Hampshire, an anachronism in our device-driven world.

"You can tell a lot about a person by what's in their glove compartment," I said.

He glanced over his shoulder. "What do you conclude about Gloria?"

"That she was frugal and nostalgic. I bet the map was from her very first time in New Hampshire, for her on-campus interview."

"Maybe she wasn't a neat eater and didn't trust technology."

"Good point."

Ellis walked toward the back of the car. "Josie, I'm going to ask you to stand beside my SUV. Phil, if you'd pop the trunk."

Ellis obviously feared something—or someone—dangerous was in the trunk. I coughed, my mouth as dry as sand. He glanced at Ted, apparently deciding he was a safe distance away. I walked to Trevor Street, as instructed, then turned to face Gloria's car. My hands were damp, and I wiped them on my slacks.

Ellis stood off to the side, drew his gun, and aimed it at the trunk. Phil used the inside lever to open it. The lid rose smoothly, silently. I went up on tiptoe to try to see inside, but I was too far away.

Ellis holstered his weapon, and I ran to the car.

Inside were a large clear plastic bin with a latching cover, a spare tire and jack, and a blue-and-white-floral-patterned cotton blanket, probably for picnics on the beach or evenings listening to music on the village green. Ellis unlatched the bin cover and set it aside. Neatly arranged inside were a bag of clay kitty litter—useful to gain traction on ice—emergency flares, a thermal blanket, and an ice scraper with a brush attachment, standard fare for a prudent New Hampshire driver. Ellis gently lifted out the blanket, and hidden in a fold was Gloria's purse, a Michael Kors mini-tote. Hidden in another fold was a brown leather portfolio.

"Spread a tarp on my hood, will you, Phil?"

As soon as Phil had ripped open the packaging and laid out the tarp, Ellis lowered the two items to the center of the hood. We stood on the shoulder as Ellis went through them.

Ellis opened the portfolio first. A few of Gloria's university business cards were tucked into a small pocket on the left-side flap. There was a pad of lined paper on the right. Ellis peeked under the inside flaps, a perfect spot for secret notes, but both sides were empty. He slid the portfolio into a clear plastic evidence bag that Phil held at the ready. Ellis opened the mini-tote next. After he examined each object, he placed it in its own evidence bag. Gloria's iPhone was protected by a black leather case. She'd hidden a hundred dollar bill under the flap. She carried a full-size brown leather wallet. Ellis opened it, revealing two credit cards, a debit card, a driver's license, and a Hitchens University faculty ID card, each in its own slot. Ellis eased cash from the dollar bill section and fanned the bills out. I counted forty-two dollars. Next out of the bag were a key fob and a comb in a blue plastic sleeve. He pressed the UNLOCK button on the fob and the Honda's car lights flashed. Gloria carried a fortune-cookie-shaped, red plastic coin purse. He pushed it open and spilled out the change, eighty-seven cents. He tossed the coins back in before dropping the purse into its evidence bag. Ellis unzipped a pocket, peeked in, and whistled softly. He extracted a small black handgun.

"Holy moly," I said.

"Did you know she carried a weapon?"

"No. That's tiny."

"That's part of its allure. It's a Springfield nine millimeter subcompact, about six inches long. A favorite with women for the ergonomics and power. It has a reputation for shooting true despite its small size." He examined the chamber, and checked the magazine. "Fully loaded. No sign of any recent shooting."

"I wouldn't have pegged Gloria as a gun gal."

"Why not?"

"She was so cerebral."

"So are you, and you like to shoot."

I pictured the Browning 9mm I kept in my bedside table. My dad bought it for me for my twenty-first birthday, and it was still my favorite weapon for target shooting. "True, but that's not a hobbyist's gun or a hunter's weapon. That's the kind of gun you carry for personal protection." I paused for a moment, thinking. "Does she have an order of protection against anyone?"

"No. No arrests, warrants, or court filings of any kind. Not even a speeding ticket."

Ellis dropped the magazine and chambered bullet into their own evidence bags and eased the gun into another, then gave the mini-tote a final look and pat down. "That's it."

"No makeup, not even a lip gloss. That really makes a statement—when Gloria left modeling, she completely jettisoned the trappings."

Phil gathered all the bags together, dropped them into one large evidence bag, sealed it, and handed it back to Ellis. He signed it and returned it to Phil.

Phil said he'd arrange for the Honda to be brought into the police garage on a flatbed once CSI was done with their part of the investigation. Ellis thanked him and me, then led me a few steps away.

"I didn't want you to think I'd forgotten the blond man. Our investigation is underway."

"Anything so far?"

"I don't deal in 'so far' assessments. Today's update is tomorrow's mistake."

"Understood."

I turned toward Ted. He was still on his knees, weeding, his back to us. "Did Gloria have a license to carry a concealed weapon?"

"No, but none is needed in New Hampshire, you know that. If I recall right, you don't have one for your weapon."

"I do now, at Ty's suggestion. It makes carrying it out of state easier, and we're talking about going target shooting in Maine. If Gloria doesn't have a license, she must not have planned to leave New Hampshire. Which means the danger she perceived was here, with her."

"We don't know enough to conclude that. Maybe she was paranoid or obsessed with someone. She also could be a rule-bender. Maybe she planned to carry it into another state, licensed or not."

"If so, I didn't get a hint of any of that."

"You didn't get a hint that she was scared enough to carry a handgun, either."

"True. I wonder if the reason she wanted it came up in conversation with the seller."

"When we trace the sale, we'll ask."

My phone vibrated. I glanced at the screen. "It's Timothy. I should take this."

"And I should leave."

We said our goodbyes, and I took the call.

"Did you reach Ivan?" Timothy asked.

"I haven't tried yet. I've been with the police. I'll call him now."

"Not a prob. We'll work on the thimble beauty shots."

I promised to keep him posted and texted Cara for Ivan's number and email address.

CHAPTER FIFTEEN

I caught Ted's eye for a goodbye wave, and headed back to my company. A few paces down the path, my phone vibrated. Cara got Ivan's phone number and email address from the liability release he'd signed in order to enter the TV studio. I called, but the phone just rang and rang until an automated voice stated the phone number and invited me to leave a message, which I did, requesting an urgent call back. It seemed sufficiently odd that he wouldn't have set up a personal voicemail message that I called Cara to check the number again. It was correct. It was, of course, possible that he had transposed digits himself when he'd filled out the form, but that and a dime didn't get me any closer to reaching him. I emailed him with the same message, writing "Urgent" in the subject line. I continued my walk, then, annoyed at the delay, called Cara back. Ivan hadn't listed a work phone number on the form, but Gloria had. I thanked her and called Gloria's work number, hoping whoever picked up would be able to help.

Gloria's line was answered by a pleasant-sounding woman with a faint British accent. "Archival studies. Arlene Stevens speaking. How may I help you?"

I introduced myself, then said, "As you may know, I've been working with Dr. Moreau. She taped a segment for my TV show, *Josie's Antiques*."

"Oh, yes. We were all so excited—and now this. We were shattered to hear of her death, totally shattered. Do you have any news?"

"No. I wish I did."

"It's hardly the time to mention that I'm a huge fan of your show, but it's true. My sister and I have a standing date to watch it together."

"You're very kind. I know what you mean, though. It's hard to think of a TV show at a time like this." I paused. "I hate to intrude with a business issue, but I have a rather urgent question about her research into the Beatrix Potter book she discussed during the taping. I'm hoping you can help me get a look at her notes. They're probably in her office."

"Oh, heavens, no, I couldn't possibly."

"Hmm," I murmured, hoping to change the conversation from her flat no to a discussion of how. "Maybe you could help me think this through. Did Dr. Moreau have a private office on campus?"

"Certainly. All professors do."

"How about her graduate assistant, Ivan Filbert? Is he allowed to go into her office?"

"Ivan doesn't have a key . . . I know because I let him in earlier today—Dr. Shield, the chair of the department, said it was all right. Ivan needed to get in right away so he could locate her lecture notes for the classes he's taking over. Gloria kept them all in three-ring binders, one per class."

"She taught on a Tuesday-Thursday schedule, isn't that right?"

"Yes. I looked up both their schedules for Dr. Shield. Ivan teaches an evening class on Wednesdays. Gloria teaches two classes during the day on Tuesdays and Thursdays. That is, she *taught* on Tuesdays and Thursdays."

"I know. I made the same mistake."

"It's dreadful." She cleared her throat. "Well, then . . . her next class isn't until tomorrow at noon." Her voice lowered. "Dr. Shield is in Davenport, Iowa, for a conference. He was quite upset."

It was hard to hear her while tromping on fallen leaves, so I stopped moving.

"Of course," I said.

"Yes. Quite upset." She resumed her normal speaking voice, and I walked on. "Which is perfectly understandable, of course. We're all upset."

I didn't want to prod, but if she wanted to talk, I was glad to listen. "Besides the obvious—Gloria's death—why was he upset?"

"The police." Her voice dipped even further, to a whisper this time, and again I stopped. "He was appalled that the police wanted to go into Gloria's office. He flatly refused, then left it to me to tell them."

"That doesn't seem fair. He's the boss."

"Exactly! Finally the director of public safety arrived—that's our on-campus police department—so I didn't have to argue with them any longer. The director also refused to authorize entry without a warrant, but he allowed the police to seal her office. The police were cross that Ivan took Gloria's binders from the office after her death and with me for letting him in and returning the binders after I made copies."

"That's so unfair!"

"That's what I told them. I did as I was instructed, yet everyone is annoyed with me."

"I'm sorry you're having to deal with this . . . how is Ivan handling things?"

"As best as might be expected, I suppose. He told me he felt fortunate because Dr. Moreau had prepared for her classes so thoroughly." She lowered her voice again as a rabbit scampered by and leapfrogged over a thorny bush. "Louise—that's Professor Louise Lee—she lives in the same apartment complex as Dr. Moreau. She called a few minutes ago to tell me that the police have sealed Gloria's apartment, too."

"I think that's routine in a case like this. Do you happen to know if Ivan is still on campus?"

"I don't know . . . I don't think so. He called me a few minutes ago to check on an a/v order, and said he'd follow up with media services in the morning. He wants to show slides in tomorrow's class. He's rather nervous."

"That's natural, but Ivan seemed very knowledgeable to me. I suspect he'll do just fine."

"That's what I told him . . . he's ready and I'm confident he'll rise to the occasion."

"That was kind of you. Do you have any idea about how I might be able to reach him?"

"He was on his cell phone."

"I tried calling him earlier . . . I wonder if I have the right number." I stepped onto my parking lot. Nothing seemed to have changed—in Carter's Forest, the technicians worked the crime scene and uniformed police officers searched the ground, their eyes sweeping back and forth. In the parking lot, Ellis and Detective Brownley had their heads together, talking, standing next to his SUV. One of my private security guards was moving out of sight around the tent. I refocused on Arlene Stevens. "What number do you have for Ivan?"

"I'm sorry. I'm not allowed to give out any personal information. I'd be glad to call him to deliver a message, if that would help."

"Thank you. If you'd let him know I need to reach him urgently, that would be great."

"I'll pass it along."

"I appreciate it. If I tell you the number I have for him, could you confirm whether it's the same one you have?"

She thought about it for a few seconds. "I can't see any harm in that."

I called out the number.

"No, that's not it."

"Could it be a transposition error?"

"No. It's not even close."

"Interesting." I didn't bother asking for his home address. "You've been very helpful, Ms. Stevens. One last question . . . where is Ivan's office located? That's public information, isn't it?"

"Certainly. He's in Johnson three-four-one. Johnson is the name of our building. We're located at the east end of the campus. The department is on the third floor. He shares it with Jonathan Duggal, another graduate assistant."

I thanked her again, and said goodbye, ending the call.

I walked into the front office.

"Gretchen left this for you," Cara said, and handed over a nine-by-twelve envelope. I eased the contents out, a sheet of stiff cardstock covered with a protective flap, about the size of a hardback book.

I lifted the paper and viewed six headshots of women around Veronica's age, each equally pleasant-looking. Veronica's photo was in position number four.

I raised my eyes to Cara's face and held up the booklet. "Did you see this? It's awesome! How did Gretchen do it so quickly?"

"She's so ingenious! She looked through the copyright-free photos, but didn't think they were right for this purpose." She laughed. "Her grandmother just went to her high school's fiftieth reunion, and Gretchen thought the photos on Facebook were perfect, so she asked her grandmother to line up volunteers." She laughed harder. "Her grandmother's classmates loved the idea of being in a photo lineup! Everyone she asked signed the waiver. Gretchen didn't think there was any chance anyone around here would recognize the other women because her grandmother went to high school in Topeka, Kansas."

"Brilliant!" I eased the array into the envelope and slid it into my tote bag. "I need Ivan's home address, if you would be so kind, and I think I'll take one of those gingersnaps you offered earlier."

"Take two," Fred said. "She's outdone herself with this batch."

"Twist my arm right off," I said, carrying the tin to the guest table. I bit into the sweet crispy-soft cookie, and murmured yum. "Oh, wow. You are so right, Fred."

"Stop!" Cara protested. "You're making me blush!"

"It's your own fault for being the best baker in Rocky Point." I turned toward Fred. "Where are you with the thimbles?"

"Timothy is taking the beauty shots. That's all I know."

I nodded my thanks, and texted Timothy that I hadn't reached Ivan yet, but was hot on the trail.

Timothy texted back a thank-you for the update. Cara read off Ivan's address from the form. He lived on Islington, no doubt in one of the scores of two- and three-family wooden row houses crammed together just outside of Rocky Point's central business district.

"I'm taking a gingersnap for the road—and you can't stop me!" I said, closing the tin.

Cara laughed, her cheeks rosy with pleasure.

Before I drove to Ivan's house, I took another look at the photo array, homing in on Veronica's image. "Is there something about my dad or the Jane Austen letters you don't want me to know?" I asked aloud. "Is that why you won't talk to me?" Her eyes were expressive, and in the photo she appeared concerned— not panicked, just uneasy. I slid the array back into my tote bag and headed off to Ivan's house.

During the ten-minute drive, I listened to Hitchens University's classical music radio station. Wes was discussing the Gloria Moreau murder investigation with the station's news anchor. Wes didn't offer any new information, but he did mention my call for sightings, implying that the appraisal I was working on was somehow connected to Gloria's murder. I hoped his innuendo would generate some word-of-mouth sharing of the request. The more leads, the better chance I'd find Veronica Sutton.

Ivan's duplex looked well cared for. It had been painted gray with white trim within the last couple of years. Gold and maroon chrysanthemums lined the walkway, the hedge was neatly trimmed, the leaves recently raked. Before getting out of my car, I texted Wes: *Thanks for the on air mention. I have some info for you. Let's meet.*

His reply came as I climbed the steps to the porch. *When?* I answered, *30 min. Our dune*, and tossed my phone back in my bag.

Two separately numbered doors opened onto a shared front porch. Ivan's unit was on the right. I pushed the doorbell next to the frame and a tinny chime sounded. A few seconds later, the door was opened by a tall, slender woman. She was around thirty-five and pretty, with alabaster skin, short, dark brown hair, big brown eyes, and a wide smile. She wore a long-sleeved white T-shirt and low-rise jeans. Her feet were bare.

"Hi," I said, matching her welcoming smile. "Is Ivan home?"

Her smile receded, replaced by suspicion, her fount of goodwill turned off like a faucet.

"Who's asking?"

"I'm Josie Prescott, an antiques appraiser here in Rocky Point. I need to talk to him about Gloria Moreau's presentation on my TV show, *Josie's Antiques*." I paused, uncertain how to ask if she'd heard about Gloria's murder. "I don't know if you've been keeping up with any news today."

"No. I've been working. Why?"

"Then I'm afraid I'm the bearer of bad news. It's about Gloria."

"What about her? What's going on?"

"I'm sorry. Gloria is dead."

"What?" She gawked, then fell against the door jamb.

"I know. I can't imagine what you're thinking."

"Is Ivan okay?" she asked, sounding years younger.

"As far as I know, he's fine."

A girl of about six or seven and a woman old enough to be her great-grandmother came onto the porch of the house next door, chatting and laughing as they shook out plastic Halloween decorations, a skeleton, a witch, a ghost. The older women raised the witch to the soffit and asked the girl how it looked.

"May I come in?" I asked softly.

The young woman hesitated for a moment, then backed up a few steps. "I guess."

I followed her inside. We stood in a square entryway. The walls were covered with masks, puppets, and wigs, artfully displayed. I recognized a white and red kabuki mask; a pair of shadow puppets; a mischievous jester Mardi Gras mask; wigs evoking Elvira, Mistress of the Dark, Marilyn Monroe, and Katy Perry's long blue do; and other items: a lute, a series of Polaroids of sunsets, and an elaborate lace doily.

"Souvenirs from your travels?" I asked.

"I wish. Sadly, the farthest I've ever traveled is Boston, shame on me. I buy them at local flea markets and garage sales." She scanned the walls. "I like artifacts that reveal a culture's values, like these shadow puppets. In Indonesia, they're used to tell stories about good versus evil."

"They're superb," I said.

"Thanks." She walked down the corridor. "Come this way."

I recognized the linear layout of the apartment. I'd bought antiques and collectibles from dozens of people who'd lived in units like these. The apartments ran from front to back with the bedrooms and bathroom opening off a hall that ran half the length of the unit, T-boning into a sitting room, which itself led to the kitchen. I could see the dinette table and back windows from where I stood.

"What did you say your name was again?"

"Josie Prescott. And you are . . . ?"

"Of course. The TV show. Ivan told me. I'm Heather Adler, Ivan's ex."

"Oh, golly. I'm so sorry."

"Don't be." She waved it aside. "What happened to Gloria?"

"She was murdered, strangled, sometime overnight or this morning. Her body was found in some woods off the interstate, Carter's Forest."

Heather stared at me, wide-eyed. "Who . . . who did it?"

"I don't know. The police just started their investigation."

"Come on in." She continued down the long hall. "Ivan mentioned he hoped to work with your company on an appraisal. The Jane Austen letters."

She didn't stop until we reached the sitting room. Modern black steel bookcases lined one wall. An off-white twill couch sat in the middle of the room facing a fifty-five-inch flat-screen TV mounted above a black wood media center. Windows on the third wall overlooked the house next door, which couldn't have been more than a dozen feet away. An arched doorway in the fourth wall led to the kitchen. The only color came from the red throw pillows on the couch.

"He seems well-qualified," I said. "He was fortunate to train under Gloria. She was a leader in the field, a true visionary."

"Ivan admired Gloria a lot," Heather said, but her tone belied her words.

"It sounds like you didn't."

"I didn't get a vote. Ivan was grateful for the opportunity to work with her, so I should be grateful, too." An impish grin transformed her face. "I hate the word 'should,' don't you?"

"Yes." I laughed. "As soon as you hear it, you know you're not going to like whatever follows."

"Exactly. Ivan is going to be listed as an author on two upcoming articles already accepted for publication. I don't know anything about archival studies, but it seems to me there's something off when one person writes the drafts of articles for another person's review, she makes minor changes, then attaches her name as lead author. At some point you've got to stand up for yourself."

"What a miserable position to be in."

"You're only in a bad position if you think you're trapped. I told Ivan that. You're not a tree, that's what I said. If you're not happy—move. He didn't want to hear it. He said those publications would help him land a tenure-track position. Maybe he's right. I don't know. What I do know is that exploitation goes by various names, including co-author. Ivan said I was just looking for trouble, that this was the way the game was played. I told him that disrupting a norm is always scary and often necessary. I thought I had him convinced, but I was wrong. Trying to fire him up wasn't just idle chatter on my part, either—I apply the same principles to myself."

She shoved up her left sleeve to show me a hard-to-spot tattoo. I leaned in to read the white lettering. "Be bold" was written in an elegant script, the kind used for wedding invitations. The tattoo ran vertically on the underside of her arm, ending two inches above her wrist.

"I've never seen a white tattoo before."

"I picked white ink so it wouldn't stand out. It's not a conversation piece. It's a reminder to myself. I got it when I was in my early twenties and flipping burgers. It's disastrously easy to just go along. I need to constantly remind myself that fortune favors the bold." She folded her lips together, stopping herself from expressing her next thought, then glanced again at her tattoo before pulling down her sleeve. "Never speak ill of the dead, but Gloria held some kind of Svengali-like power over Ivan. He and I had one last blowout about her this morning, then we broke up. After eight years—*finito*. So if I sound all bitter, sorry."

"You just broke up today! I had no idea. I'm so sorry."

"Don't be. It's for the best. I'm just still a little raw."

"Oh, gosh . . . I hate to ask questions now, but . . ."

"I'm okay," she said. "What do you need?"

"There's some urgency or I never would interfere like this." I paused for a moment. "I need to speak to him about yesterday's TV episode . . . do you know where he is?"

"Try his car."

My stunned expression didn't faze her.

"Didn't you ever hear that old joke? What do you call an archivist without a girlfriend?" She waited a few seconds before delivering the punchline. "Homeless." She lifted her hand. "I know . . . not even mildly amusing. Tasteless, too."

I didn't know how to respond, so I walked over to the bookcase. The shelves were packed, mostly hardbacks wedged together vertically, but there were several horizontal stacks positioned here and there, and a few paperbacks tossed into the mix.

"Someone likes books."

"Ivan."

I scanned the titles. Most of them were related to document authentication, conservation, and book production. There was plenty of general history, as well, spanning the millennia from ancient Egypt to the twentieth century. A small collection of leather-bound books sat in the center of the top shelf, mostly tan leather with gold tooling on the spines, but one was a folio volume, larger than the rest, bound in dark red with gilt embellishments. They were all nineteenth-century classics. It was a library appropriate for an archivist.

I turned to face her. "I'm sorry about your breakup."

"Thanks."

"Do you still work in the restaurant business?"

"No. I got bold, just like I said. I'm a self-taught graphic designer. I specialize in rock band branding from logos to websites to corollary materials, but I'm trying to expand into more mainstream clients, hospitals, government agencies, and so on."

"Diversification is key."

"Except established organizations only want to hire people who already have experience. How are you supposed to get experience if no one will hire you? It's such a crock. And a racket, too. I've supported myself for fifteen years with only a high school diploma and grit, but you can't even submit a proposal for some of these projects unless you have a B.A. So I go back to school to take courses I could have taught, and what do I get for my trouble? A useless piece of paper and forty-four thousand dollars in debt. Sorry to rant, but it just burns me up, just completely burns me up." She lifted a hand and let it drop. "Ivan's in worse shape—he's got more than sixty thousand dollars in student loan debt. And he's only halfway through the program! What a rip-off! And for what? A job he'll never get."

"Why do you say that?"

"Because he has a personality like a fish." She laughed. "He comes across like a profound thinker. Another crock. He's just inarticulate and weak. I thought we were in sync, but I was wrong." She laughed again, but not like she thought something was funny. "You know what they say . . . losers try, winners do. I tried to make a winner out of him, but he just didn't have it in him."

"I'm sorry," I repeated, not knowing what else to say.

"Don't be. It's for the best. No blood was drawn. No one has bruises. I kissed him goodbye as he walked out the door. It could have been worse."

"So the breakup was amicable."

Her nose scrunched as if she'd smelled rotting garbage. "Is any breakup amicable? I've had lots of girlfriends go through lots of breakups, and I've had my share myself. None of them was good. This one was more civilized than some, that's all."

"Even when the breakup is your idea, it's still a loss."

She snorted, a quasi-laugh. "You're delicate with your words. Loss sounds flat, like you've misplaced your keys. Ending a relationship is giving up on a dream."

"You're right. A hundred percent."

"But then it passes. It always passes." She lifted a hand again. "It's all good. So you want to know where Ivan is. I haven't got a clue."

"Does he have any friends he might be staying with?"

"As far as I know, he has no friends. I'm not exaggerating. All he does is work."

"Got it. I appreciate your talking to me." I started back down the hall, with Heather trailing along. I paused midway. "One question before I leave . . . could you give me Ivan's phone number?" She rattled it off. "That's the same one I have, and it just goes to one of those robotic voices saying you've reached this phone number. I left a message, but so far, he hasn't called back."

"When I gave him the boot," she said, "I gave his phone the boot, too. He'd been on my family plan. I assumed he'd keep the number, at least for a day or two, but apparently I assumed wrong. The company gives you a month's grace period before they shut the number down for good, so I guess Ivan's phone will ring for thirty more days, then sayonara, baby." She opened the door. "If you find him, do me a favor, will you? Tell him to come get his stupid books."

CHAPTER SIXTEEN

Ty called as I was latching my seat belt. He was going to stay in DC overnight because Sheila Zerof, his pal at FEMA, had to cancel lunch—he was meeting her at ten in the morning.

"Are you excited?" I asked.

"That's too strong a word. Gratified is better, I think. I'm pleased Sheila agreed to meet me."

"Did you bring a change of clothing?"

"Of course."

"Once a Boy Scout, always a Boy Scout. I bet you were a gorgeous Boy Scout."

"I have photos that prove otherwise. I was gangly."

"Maybe, but still cute."

"I'll be home tomorrow in time to grill chicken for dinner."

"I'll buy the fixin's."

"Good. I was sorry to hear about Gloria," Ty said. "Any news?"

"No. It's just so horrible—such a loss."

"You liked her."

"A lot."

"How about Veronica Sutton?"

"No news there, either, although Wes mentioned my search on the radio, so I'm hopeful." I filled him in, explaining that I was on my way to meet Wes now. "Then I'll go to Hitchens to see if I can find Ivan. Timothy is champing at the bit. I assume Ivan isn't checking his old phone, so he wouldn't get my voicemail message or text, but I don't understand why he won't respond to my email. Probably he's immersed in prepping for the classes he's taking over tomorrow."

We chatted for another minute, then I drove to the beach. I thought about Gloria and her murder the whole way, and arrived at the dune unsettled and sad.

Wes was already standing on the dune, and I trekked up to join him.

"Whatcha got?" he asked.

I didn't answer right away. Instead, I turned toward the ocean. The water was choppy, churning, like my mind.

"Gloria's scarf," I said, my eyes on the whitecaps. "It was wrapped tightly around her neck, but the ends stretched down her sides."

"Good, good," he said, scribbling in his notebook. "Love the image. What else?"

I asked to meet Wes not to share information, but to gain information, and now was my opportunity. "What about her ex-boyfriend?"

"Neighbors say they fought a lot—not physically, as far anyone knows, but lots of shouting."

"What about?"

"No one heard words, or at least no one admits they heard words. You know how it goes . . . you're curious as all get-out, so you listen, but you don't want to admit you eavesdropped or get involved, so you say you didn't hear anything."

"Surely, someone would come forward. She's been murdered!"

Wes shook his head. "You're so naïve."

"Are you saying it's naïve to be ethical?"

"That's a question to ponder over a drink."

I laughed. "I look forward to it. What about Gloria's finances?"

"She withdrew eight thousand dollars cash each month on the first," he said, proving yet again that he had contacts everywhere.

"That's a lot of money!"

"Tell me about it. No one I've talked to knows where it went."

"Gambling?" I mused. "Drugs? No way!"

"She's not wiring it to a distant relative, at least not through any local provider. What else could it be for?"

"A secret lover. Maybe he's married and the money covers their love nest."

"And she's footing the bill? Come on!"

"It happens."

Wes grinned. "And you know this how?"

"Funny man! I read a lot. How about blackmail?"

"Over what?"

"I don't know."

"Nor anyone else. From all reports, Gloria's a straight arrow, squeaky clean."

"She must have made a fortune when she was modeling. Who inherits?"

Wes flipped back to an earlier page in his notebook. "She has a hefty amount in a brokerage account, which lists her mother as her beneficiary. The thing is that she gave her mother's address as her own, and the neighbors I spoke to say she's never had anyone living there, certainly not her mother."

"Maybe Mom died and she didn't change her beneficiary."

"No death certificate that I can find. And the cops haven't found a will, but it's only been a few hours. If she had one, they'll find it."

"Look at all you've learned in those same few hours. What do you think happened?"

"I think squeaky clean can be a good cover story," Wes said. "There's a lot about her we don't know."

"We could say that about everyone. We only know what people show us."

"And what we can ferret out. Anything else for me?"

"No."

His voice took on a stern tone. "Anything you learn, *anything*—I'm your first call."

I laughed and he slid-walked down the dune. I followed. By the time I reached the street, he was revving up his engine.

I reached Ivan's office at three o'clock, but there was no answer to my knock. I turned my back to the wooden door, trying to decide what to do next. The utilitarian corridor walls were painted pale blue. The linoleum floor was speckled cream. The lighting was fluorescent and harsh. Every office door was closed, and they were all covered with taped-on flyers, announcements, cartoons, and other ephemera. Professors came and went. Students stopped at professors' doors to knock, most gaining entry. Several clusters of students chatted as they cruised by. I turned back to Ivan's door and knocked again. No answer. I'd need a good story to convince Arlene Stevens to let me into his office, and I didn't have one.

A young man with short, curly red hair walked up. "Did you knock?"

"Yeah . . . no answer." I introduced myself, explaining that Ivan had been on set during yesterday's filming.

"I'm his office mate, Jonathan Duggal. He told me he was fascinated at the process and structure of the filming. He also said he'd applied for an internship at your company. Do you have room for one more?"

I took a business card from the sterling silver card case Ty had given me for my birthday a few years back, flattered at the implication that interning at Prescott's was a plum assignment. I told him that I didn't know our current needs, but that he was welcome to get in touch with me, that I'd pass his name along to the right person.

He accepted the card. "Thanks. This is great." He slipped the card into his shirt pocket. "Ivan's probably got his headphones on. He listens to opera when he works. He says it helps him concentrate."

"Can you check if he's in there?"

"Sure. He should be back from Pease by now, though."

"What's Pease?"

"The gym building . . . indoor track, all the equipment money can buy, that sort of thing."

I smiled. "Somehow Ivan doesn't strike me as a gym sort of guy."

"You never can tell. He just signed up, said he needed an outlet now that he and Heather split up." He dug out a key from his pants pocket. "I have to pick up a folder for my class." He unlocked the door, and pushed it open.

Ivan looked up, saw me, and lurched up as he whipped off his headphones.

"As expected," Jonathan said, grinning.

I thanked him.

"No prob," he said. He took a manila folder from a desk near the windows, smiled as he passed me on his way out, and left.

"Sorry to interrupt," I said, taking in Ivan's messy desk.

"No, no—did you knock? I'm sorry I didn't hear it. Come on in."

I released the door and it swung closed on a hydraulic arm, but didn't latch. The office was cluttered. Jonathan's desk sat perpendicular to the left wall, facing the window. His back would be to the door. Ivan's desk extended into the room, the left side of the desk touching the wall to the right of the door. A bank of tall, tan, metal four-drawer file cabinets, two facing Ivan, two facing Jonathan, ran from the right wall to about four feet beyond Ivan's desk, and served as a room divider. The remaining space was plenty wide enough to allow access to Jonathan's section of the room. It was a clever layout, I thought, providing decent privacy and a fair division of the space.

Ivan moved a pile of books and papers from a guest chair near the file cabinets onto an unwieldy stack on his desk. An old-fashioned brass banker's lamp, the kind with an elongated green glass shade, sat next to his laptop.

He brushed off the chair seat. "Sorry . . . everything's a mess."

"You look busy."

"Too busy."

I sat down and smiled. "You're a hard man to find."

He looked startled and a little concerned. "I've been on campus all day."

"I've called, texted, and emailed. Ms. Stevens said she'd leave you a message, too."

"Sorry. I'm not as good at checking messages as I should be."

"I have an old phone number for you, anyway. May I have your new one?"

"Sure. Sorry. I just got the new number."

He called out the number. I tapped it in and sent a text.

After a few seconds with him simply watching me, I said, "How about checking to see if it arrived?"

"Oh, sorry." He reached into a leather satchel that took up a chunk of his desk and rooted around for a while, finally coming out with his phone. "Yup, I got it. I see the one from Arlene, too." He dropped the device into his bag. "I rarely get any messages, let alone urgent ones, so I'm not in the habit of checking. How did you know I have a new number?"

"I spoke to Ms. Stevens. She wouldn't give it to me, but she confirmed it was different from the one I had. Heather told me about canceling the family plan."

Ivan leaned back, his concern deepening. "You spoke to Heather?"

"Yes. I didn't mean to intrude, but with what happened to Gloria, well, the problem with the audio isn't fixable, so Timothy and I were thinking I could interview you to fill in the missing bits. We could add a little about Gloria's process."

His eyes radiated panic. "Me? On camera?"

"Yes. You're certainly knowledgeable enough."

"I don't think I can. I'm not really a good talker."

"You did fine when we discussed Byron."

His eyes brightened. "That was Byron."

"You did fine when talking about your approach to authenticating rare documents."

"That's rare documents."

"And, of course, you'll receive an honorarium. Everyone on the show does."

"Well then," he said, smiling a little. "Do you really think I can do it?"

"Yes."

He smiled again. "Thanks. Okay. I'm in."

"Excellent! Now to the particulars: Do you have Gloria's notes?"

"Me? No . . . I mean, why? I can talk about the subject without her notes."

"I understand, but since the audio is all mucked up, we need to pinpoint exactly which talking points need to be replicated."

"I don't know . . . I'm not sure if I'm allowed to show you her script."

"Script?"

"Sorry," Ivan said, flustered. "I shouldn't have said that. She hated it when I called it a script, even though it was. When she told you we were going over her notes, what she meant was she wanted me to follow the text as she rehearsed. She liked to deliver her part word for word. She didn't want to sound scripted, but she wanted to be certain to include everything and express it in just the right way."

"No wonder she was so good on camera. She was prepared."

"That's exactly how she put it. She wanted to sound natural, but prepared. It was an important lesson for me, especially since I'm such an awkward talker."

"I don't think you're awkward. I suspect the only thing you lack is confidence."

"Thanks," he said, looking down.

"If you were cuing her using those notes, you must have them."

"Yeah, I do. She emailed them to me so I could print them out."

"I promise I won't use any of her work outside of this limited application. I respect both copyright and intellectual property rights."

"I guess that's fair." Ivan turned to his laptop, tapped for a few seconds, then swung back to face me. "I just emailed it. Do you want me to print it, too?"

"That would be great. Thank you. I'll work with Timothy to determine what parts of Gloria's presentation need to be rerecorded, and how you and I can cover the material. We'll probably include Oliver, too, to let him share in the mini-eulogy." The printer whirred to life. "You mentioned that Gloria had a bad breakup a few weeks ago."

"Guess it's something in the air. Heather must have smelled it, too."

"I'm sorry . . . are you saying Gloria broke it off with her boyfriend?"

"So she said."

"How come?"

"I'm not really comfortable . . . I shouldn't talk about her personal affairs."

"I understand, and I agree. I hate gossip, too. I know what the police would say, though . . . this isn't gossip. This is information that might be relevant to a murder investigation. She didn't confide in you, did she?"

"Gloria? No way. I didn't even know she was dating someone until I heard him shouting on the phone. We were in her office, meeting about something, I don't remember what, when she answered her phone. She didn't screen the call. She just picked it up, you know how when you're in the middle of something where you're concentrating, you just react, you don't think. As soon as she realized who had called I could see she was kicking herself for answering. She shut her eyes and kind of winced. She listened for a while, a minute, maybe, then said she'd have to call him later. That's when he went ballistic. He was yelling so loudly, she moved the phone away from her ear. He was haranguing her about how she owed it to him to let him explain. I started to leave, but she patted the air, telling me to sit back down, so I did. It was embarrassing to the max. I picked up a book and tried to read. A minute later she told him she was going to hang up, and she did. The phone rang again almost immediately, then another two or three times before it was over. She shook her head a little and said, 'Sorry for the interruption. Where were we?' And that was that."

"What's his name?"

"I don't remember, maybe Fitch or Butch or something like that."

"Thank you," I said, as I digested Ivan's revelations. I extracted my phone again and brought up the photo of the blond man. "I know you said you'd never met him, but maybe you saw him hanging around." I held up the phone.

Ivan took his time, then said, "Sorry."

I returned the phone to my tote.

He handed me the printout, and I slid the pages into my bag. I pushed back my chair, preparing to stand. Two large suitcases were wedged under his desk. I pretended not to notice.

I stood. "I know Timothy was thinking he wanted to finish tomorrow, but between writing the new material and your teaching schedule tomorrow, I don't think that's realistic. How's Friday? Ten o'clock at my company?"

He stood, too. "That'll work. Thanks."

I walked to the door. "It just occurred to me . . . how about coming to the front office at nine, so we can get you set up as a consultant."

"Nine it is."

I swung open the door, stepped out into the corridor, and turned right, toward the staircase. I heard the click as the door latched completely shut. Ivan must have pushed it closed. A sign indicated I was heading the right way to reach the archival studies department office. I passed the administrative offices for psychology, sociology, and philosophy, before reaching archival studies.

A woman with short brown hair and a pug nose sat behind a desk. Stacks of three-ring binders covered half the available space. A computer and printer took up most of the rest. As she typed, her eyes darted back and forth between a legal pad and her monitor. A brass name placard read ARLENE STEVENS.

I said, "Hi! I'm sorry to interrupt you. We spoke earlier. I'm Josie Prescott."

She shot up, smiling, and extended her hand for a shake. "Don't apologize. I'm tickled pink to meet you in person!" Her smile faded. "Despite everything."

I paused, acknowledging the somber moment, then said, "I won't keep you long." I brought up the photo of the blond man on my phone, then handed it over. "Can you put a name to the face?"

She looked at the image for less than a second before handing it back.

"That's Dutch Larkin, Gloria's friend. Where did you get his photo?"

"Dutch Larkin!" I exclaimed, ignoring her question. "Do you know how I can reach him?"

"He owns Rocky Point Quarry, on Baylor Street. I know because Sue, my sister, is getting ready to renovate her kitchen, so we went to look at granite options for the counters."

"Was he nice?"

"Yes, and professional. He assigned us to a designer who was very helpful."

"Thank you. Another question—how did Gloria seem lately? In the days before she died?"

Arlene sat back down. "She seemed fine until yesterday. She called around one, I think it was, really upset." She lowered her voice. "She wanted to meet with Dr. Shield, the chair of the department, right away, but of course, she couldn't, since he's at a conference in Iowa. She made an appointment for his first day back, next Monday."

"What was she upset about?"

"I don't know."

My phone vibrated. It was Cara. "I have to take this. Thanks again."

I stepped into the hall, out of earshot, and answered the call.

"I'm sorry to bother you, but I thought you'd want to know. We've received a response to your call for sightings about Veronica Sutton, and just now . . . well, Ms. Sutton called herself and asked me to deliver a message."

"From your tone, I infer I'm not going to like the message."

"She was quite firm." Cara cleared her throat. "She said it didn't matter if you found her or not because she had nothing to say to you. She asked you to please leave her alone, to just let her be. I'm sorry, Josie."

"Oh my." I closed my eyes for a moment. "I certainly didn't intend to upset her."

"Of course not."

"Thank you, Cara. I'll think about what to do next. Email me the information from the person who replied, all right?"

I walked slowly to my car, fighting tears. I'd learned early on that all rejection hurts, and that the memories of rejection long outlast the incident. Veronica Sutton's wanton denunciation would, I knew, leave indelible scars. Her rebuke felt more than merely personal; it felt mean, as much a dismissal of my father's significance to her as an affront to me.

By the time I reached my car, I'd calmed down enough to consider whether her right to privacy transcended my right to know about my father. That calculation came out a tie. What tipped it over the edge in favor of continuing my search was my need to discover what she knew about the Jane Austen letters.

I would meet with this first responder, and with any luck, I would discover Veronica Sutton's location. I didn't know how or when I'd unearth the key to unlocking her tongue, but I knew I would. Failure was not in my lexicon.

CHAPTER SEVENTEEN

I leaned against my car, waiting to regain my composure. The sky, which had been sunny earlier in the day was now leaden, the moisture in the air leaving a film of dampness on my skin.

I wasn't good at giving up. It wasn't that I was stubborn per se. That was the wrong word. I thought of myself as tenacious, and I frequently had to remind myself that when you swim upstream, you're lucky if all you get is exhausted. If you're not careful, you may well find yourself dragged under or swept away.

After a few more minutes standing in the chilly air, breathing deeply, I was able to consider what to do next. I got behind the wheel, and texted Ellis about Dutch Larkin, summarizing what Ivan and Arlene had told me, then extracted the papers Ivan had turned over to me from my tote bag and flipped through them. Gloria hadn't merely prepared a word-for-word presentation; she'd also written an extended Q and A—if I asked question x, she was prepared with answer y. No wonder Ivan called it a script. This level of preparation is how professionals make things look easy. I forwarded Ivan's email to Timothy so he could find the specific sections we needed to reproduce, then called him.

"Bless you," he said, after he scanned the document. "I was feeling a little bit like I was back in junior high school, wondering how on earth you could possibly look up a word in the dictionary when you didn't know how to spell it. How could I determine what was missing when it was, you know, missing?"

"I had the same thought, but we don't have that worry now. Gloria was a real pro. If you can tell me what we need to cover, I'll write up a draft of how we can address it. What do you think of asking Oliver to join us?"

"Sure! The more the merrier!"

"I booked Ivan for Friday. I know you wanted to leave tomorrow, so I'm sorry."

"That was always an aspirational deadline. We're all fine staying an extra day. Tomorrow we can work on the thimbles. Fred tells me he's ready with everything except the final estimates. We'll segue you in later, and add an interview with him after the auction."

"Sounds good," I said, relieved that I didn't have to get up to speed on the collection overnight.

The first responder to my call for sightings of Veronica Sutton was Vincent Dillard, who worked for Supa-Kleen, a cleaning service headquartered in a strip mall not far from Hitchens. Before heading out, I texted Gretchen to stand by to verify Veronica Sutton's location if Mr. Dillard had the goods.

I stopped at my bank en route, withdrew five hundred dollars in hundreds and placed the bills in a money envelope.

A young man in his twenties, tall and dark, stood as I entered Supa-Kleen. He was alone in the office, but there were three desks, all facing the entry door. The walls were bare except for a series of sheets torn from an old-style desk calendar tacked to the wall on the left. A litter of brightly colored Post-it Note flags filled most of the day-to-day space. The notes each bore a name: Kazinski, Carson, Fields, Stern. When the man spoke, I took a step toward him.

"You like my calendar? That's Supa-Kleen—organized up the kazoo, all for you. Each girl has her own color, so she can see at a glance which clients are on her schedule on any given day. I don't mind telling you, I invented the system—my dad, he started the company thirty years ago, he did it on the computer—but my girls, they don't know from computers."

I wondered how his employees liked being called "my girls." I also wondered how many of them were more computer literate than he was. I wished I could run away, but you can't pick your sources, and if he had information about Veronica Sutton, I wanted it.

"So welcome to Supa-Kleen . . . whatever you got dirty, we get clean." He smiled like a snake oil salesman from days of yore. "How can I help?"

As soon as I explained who I was and why I was there, his eyes lit up. He dragged up a guest chair. With its wooden arms and worn turquoise plastic cushions, I conjectured it had been in use for a couple of generations.

He patted the top rail. "Take a load off." He sat behind his desk, and smiled again, although this time it was more a baring of teeth than an actual grin. "Call me Vinnie. Nice to meet you, Joz."

Only a few people called me "Joz," and Vinnie wasn't one of them.

"Do you know Veronica Sutton?"

"Sure. I signed her up for biweekly cleanings. As soon as I heard about that reward, I thought, 'Call. Call now.' And I did. And here you are." He rubbed his hands together in anticipation of receiving the reward. "Yippee-ki-yay!"

I eased the photo array out of the envelope and laid it on the table. "Do you see her here?"

He rapped on photo number four with his knuckle. "That's her. Good looking cookin' for an old broad. Why'd you want her?"

"Where can I find her?"

"I think that radio guy mentioned a reward. Not for nothing, but five hundred smackers represents a lot of pie to this guy."

I forced the corners of my mouth up to keep myself from groaning, and tried to stop myself from judging. Everyone has his own style, and just because I didn't warm to him, didn't mean other people wouldn't.

"Of course." I opened the envelope and showed him the money.

"See the yellow flag?" he asked, pointing to his wall-mounted calendar. "That's Tina's color. Tina's been cleaning Veronica's house for almost two months now."

The timing was right. Veronica Sutton sold her Florida house about two months ago.

I struggled to make out the handwriting. "That says 'Carson,' not 'Sutton.'"

"Ginny Carson. She owns the property. This Veronica gal lives in the guest-house. Ginny arranged the cleaning and pays the bills."

"Oh, I see. Veronica Sutton is renting the guesthouse."

"Not my table, signor," Vinnie said, in a mocking faux Italian accent. "The check clears, the house gets cleaned, that's what my dad always said. Cash, check, debit, app, we got it all."

"What's the address?"

He called it out and tapped his forehead. "Like a steel trap."

Rusted in the open position, I thought.

"I'll just need to verify the information."

"You doubting my steel trap?"

"Not at all. It shouldn't take long." As I walked to the window and turned my back to him, I felt a twinge of guilt again. Veronica Sutton had made her wishes clear, but my hackles were up. Simply ringing a doorbell wasn't a crime, nor was it an intrusion. I texted the address to Gretchen, adding: *Find the guesthouse. Knock on the door. Ask for someone—make up a name. Verify ID from photo.* She texted back *10 min.* I crossed my fingers that Veronica Sutton was home.

I turned back to face Vinnie, watching me, his distrust apparent. I was tempted to step outside, but I suspected Vinnie would give me attitude, so I skipped it. I turned back to the window.

Eight minutes later, Gretchen texted: *It's her. Sitting on lawn chair, reading. I didn't need to approach her.* I replied: *Thx.*

"All set," I told Vinnie, handing him the envelope. He licked his lips as he opened it.

I was eager to get away. I managed a quick thank-you, then left.

Veronica Sutton lived near Rocky Point's central business district. I knew the area, which was mostly comprised of beautifully renovated colonial-era mansions. I suspected the guesthouse was magnificent as well, and having a good idea of Veronica Sutton's style, well-appointed. I had to restrain myself from driving there now. *I could simply drive by*, I argued to myself, *to see the lay of the land.*

I texted Cara to inform anyone else who responded to our call for sightings that the reward had been given out, and was ready to head home when a lengthy email from Timothy arrived. He gave me the specific line in Gloria's presentation where her voice got squirrely, asking for my help in finding it because he couldn't locate that line in the document I'd sent him. "The second printing includes three easy-to-spot differences," Gloria had said, and, Timothy explained, the next eighty-five seconds of audio was unintelligible. Timothy speculated that Ivan had given me an early draft. I called Ivan on his new number, and left a message simply asking for a callback. I followed up with a text.

I drove to Ellie's Crêpes, one of my favorite restaurants. I sat by the window, and ordered a coffee and an appetizer-size chicken asparagus crêpe with Mornay sauce, a perfect late-afternoon snack. I leaned back, glad to be quiet, to have a moment to consider how Cara was doing building the list of galleries; what I needed to do to make the reshoot of Gloria's meticulous efforts work, to honor her memory; and what I'd learned from Vinnie.

Many old New England properties included secondary residences. Until Ty and I got married and moved into the Gingerbread House, I'd rented a former dower house separated by a driveway from my best friend Zoë's more regal home. Apparently Veronica Sutton had moved into a guesthouse owned by someone named Ginny Carson, who must be a friend or relative, if Ms. Carson was paying for a cleaning service.

My phone vibrated. It was Ivan, and I hurried outside to take the call so I wouldn't disturb the other diners, signaling the waitress that I'd be back in a minute. It was cold and dank, the clouds thick and tumid.

"Sorry about that," Ivan said after I repeated Timothy's conjecture. "You're exactly right. The version Gloria emailed me was her original, but we did a run-through and she made lots of changes. She didn't email me the final draft, so all I have is the printout. I just found it in the mess of stuff on my desk."

"That's great—a huge relief, actually. Can you scan it in?"

"Umm . . . I don't have a scanner . . . and since it's not official college work, the office won't let me use theirs . . . I'm sorry. I know you need it right away. I can make a copy and drive it to you at home or wherever as soon as my class is done."

"When does your class start?"

"At six. Six to eight forty."

I glanced at my watch. It was five ten. "How about if I stop by and pick it up? I can be there around quarter of."

"That would be great, but I hate to inconvenience you like this."

I laughed a little. "Oh, Ivan. We all make mistakes . . . may this be the worst thing that happens to either of us all day."

He thanked me again.

I finished my coffee, paid the check, and left.

Ivan's office door was latched, not locked, but there was no answer to my knock. It was twenty to six. I scanned the hallway, thinking maybe he'd stepped out for a minute to use the photocopier or grab a coffee before class. The corridor was packed with students making their way to their classrooms, most downtrodden, bearing the look of too much responsibility and too little sleep, the lot of most night students. I knocked again, waited a few seconds longer, then pushed open the door an inch.

"Ivan?" I called. "Jonathan?"

I opened the door wider and stepped inside. I stopped, waiting for my eyes to adjust to the dimness. The overhead fixtures were off. One stark circle of bright white light fell on Ivan's desk from the banker's lamp and a few streaks of garish fluorescence flickered in from the corridor behind me. I saw myself reflected in the window glass, the image distorted by the diffused glow of distant streetlamps.

Ivan's desk was as messy as before, with teetering stacks of papers, books, folders, and journals covering most of the space. An envelope with my name on it rested on his closed laptop.

"Thank you, Ivan!" I said aloud, and stepped inside to retrieve it.

The door hissed shut as I walked the four paces to reach the envelope. I slid it into my tote bag, and was turning to leave when I saw a boot on the floor at the end of Ivan's desk, toes down and angled sideways. Confused, I leaned over to gain a better view. If Ivan had changed into shoes for his class and simply left the boots where he'd tossed them, they'd be on their sides or standing up. That a boot landed upside down and angled sideways, and remained in that position, defied the laws of physics.

I inched forward, transfixed, then stopped mid-step, gasping.

Ivan was lying on his stomach, his head turned toward me. His face was bulbous, splotched with red and purple. His eyes bulged. His fingers were stiff and curled, as if he'd been trying to claw his way free from the rope that circled his neck when he died.

I staggered backward and tried to yell for help, but I only squeaked. I spun around and ran for the door when something struck me in the lower back, hurtling me into the wall. I crumpled and rolled over, hoping to shield my head.

The door wrenched open, then slammed shut, and I was alone.

CHAPTER EIGHTEEN

I took stock. My back was throbbing and the top of my head was tender to the touch, but everything moved as it was supposed to. Nothing was broken. I hadn't lost consciousness.

I sat up, then scrabbled up the wall to get myself to a standing position. Even in my panicky eagerness to get away, I knew not to touch the doorknob with my bare hands. I wiggled a tissue loose from the pack in my tote bag and gingerly turned the knob.

I stepped into the hall, and closed the door behind me, but left it unlatched. It felt surreal to step from dim gruesomeness to bright normalcy. The corridor was marginally less crowded than before, and much less sedate. My watch told me it was five minutes to six. People looked just as weary, but now they were in a hurry. Class was starting in five minutes.

I found my phone, and called Ellis's cell. I told him what happened, and that I would stay put to ensure no one entered Ivan's office. He said he'd be there in ten minutes.

As soon as I saw Ellis swing around the corner, followed by Detective Brownley, Griff, and a guard wearing a Hitchens University Public Safety uniform, my knees buckled and I pressed my hands against the wall to steady myself. Now that help was here, I no longer had to cope.

Ellis said something to Griff and Griff turned back the way they'd come, while Ellis walked toward me.

"How are you feeling?" he asked.

"Like somebody shoved me across the room."

"We'll get you to the hospital pronto."

"There's no need. I'm fine. I just wish I'd seen my attacker."

"Tell me more specifically what happened."

I recounted my experience, picking up the envelope, seeing Ivan's boot, then discovering his body, followed by the fierce attack.

"When the killer heard me enter and call Ivan's name, he must have stepped behind the file cabinets. Maybe he could peek between the units. If not, he heard me stagger toward the door. He had to get away, so he rammed into me. It worked."

Griff came up with a chair. He left again, this time with the Hitchens's guard.

Ellis moved the chair closer to the wall. "You look like sitting down might be a good idea," he said with a hint of a smile.

"Thanks." I sat. "When the killer fled, there were dozens of students around. Someone might have noticed him running out of the office, but maybe not. People were rushing to get to class on time."

"Do you have any reason to think the killer was a man?"

I raised my eyes to his face. "You mean why am I using a male pronoun?"

"Yes."

"No reason. Habit. Assumption. Except, maybe I have a reason after all. The murderer had to be someone big and strong, most likely a man."

"Why?"

"Do you think I'm wrong?"

"No. I just want to hear your reasoning."

"From what I know, the killings required physical strength. Wresting Gloria's scarf away from her, getting it around her neck, and pulling it tight enough to kill her, while she was fighting for her life. Lugging her body into the woods, if she was murdered elsewhere. Gloria was tall and fit. Ditto, getting a rope around Ivan's neck and strangling him. He was no featherweight."

Ellis thanked me and said, "I'm going to look at what we have here, then I'll talk to you some more. Are you sure you don't need medical attention?"

"Positive."

"Are you okay to wait around for a little while?"

"Sure," I said. I felt shaky more than battered. I was glad to sit quietly, to reflect.

Ellis and Detective Brownley put on plastic gloves and entered Ivan's office. Ellis kicked the attached doorstop down, leaving the door wide open. Griff and the guard reappeared, each carrying four folded blue plastic crowd-control barriers. Griff asked if I was okay to move, and I assured him I was. I swallowed a groan as I stood, my back reminding me that I'd been hit. I slid the chair to the other side of the corridor and eased myself back down. The two men set up the barriers, creating a crime scene zone. Griff wrapped yellow police tape around each one.

From where I sat, I had a direct view into Ivan's office. The overhead lights flashed on, showing Ellis crouched near Ivan's body. When Ellis stood, Detective Brownley took a dozen photos with her phone. Five minutes later, the medical examiner arrived. George Beaufort, called Beau, was young, new to the department. I'd never met him, but I'd heard he had a flair for gallows humor. Ten minutes after that, Ivan's office was crawling with experts and the hall was packed with civilians gawking.

My phone vibrated nonstop. Wes had picked up the story from his police scanner, with my name given as the person who called it in, adding that I'd been attacked, and had a head injury. Wes didn't merely have all-star sources, he obviously had them on speed dial. He had it on air as "breaking news" within minutes. Since then, he'd called, texted, and emailed impassioned pleas for information and photos. Gretchen and Cara called, wanting to know was I all right. Zoë called asking where I was so she could come and be with me. Timothy called, upset that I might be hurt. Other members of my staff, friends, and customers followed suit. It was gratifying, but I didn't want to talk to anyone. I didn't feel capable of dealing with multiple, repetitive conversations. I wanted to curl up in a ball and whine that they were to leave me alone, all of them.

After a minute or so, maturity kicked in and I texted Gretchen, letting her know I was okay, and asking her to spread the word, starting with Timothy, and to tell him that I'd call or email later, depending on how the time went. I texted Ty, too, keeping my message simple, saying only that I'd discovered Ivan's body, that I was fine, and that I'd call him later. Then I texted Zoë, thanking her and explaining that I was waiting to give a statement to Ellis, and would be in touch.

I dropped the phone into my bag, leaned back, and closed my eyes, willing the aches and throbs to subside, letting images and memories drift into my consciousness. Using only what I knew or could infer about motive, means, and opportunity, I tried to distill disparate facts and perceptions into logical conclusions, or at least, into the beginning of a logical conclusion.

I didn't know if the police had any official suspects in Gloria's death, but the mere fact that Ivan had been killed in a similar manner and within hours suggested a connection. That was a question for Wes, and I decided to ask it then and there, grunting a little as I retrieved my phone. I selected Wes's most recent demand for information, and replied: *Details later. Re: Gloria's murder—suspects?* I could picture Wes's teeth-grinding frustration, but I was confident he'd come through with an answer. If he didn't, our quid pro quo would be out of quid, and he'd worry that I'd close up shop as one of his most reliable sources.

In terms of motive, I suspected Gloria was a rich woman. During her modeling days, she'd had a bunch of multiyear multimillion-dollar contracts as the face of various brands. Her heirs, whoever they were, would be prime suspects, of course, but that didn't account for Ivan's death, and I was proceeding on the assumption that the two murders were connected. Ivan had debt, not assets.

I supposed that Dutch Larkin, Gloria's ex, might be the killer. Maybe he was insanely jealous and suspected Gloria and Ivan were having an affair. His unexplained presence at my company, his clandestine sneaking around, his frantic flight, and the story Ivan recounted about his explosive interaction with Gloria on the phone suggested that he might be one of those people for whom jealousy knows no bounds. It seemed far-fetched, though, that he would be jealous of Ivan. There was a difference between jealousy and paranoia. But then again, maybe Dutch was paranoid.

The person who'd killed Gloria was calm and methodical. Recalling the careful, meticulous manner in which her corpse had been laid out . . . that wasn't the hallmark of a crime of passion. Even if Dutch had strangled Gloria while in the throes of jealous rage, then lovingly tidied the scene out of some kind of twisted wish to show respect for the woman he'd loved, why on earth would he murder Ivan?

Beau, the medical examiner, came out swinging his black medical case.

Griff moved one of the barriers aside so he could leave. Beau winked at Griff and said, "It's official. He's dead."

Dark humor, indeed.

By process of elimination, if Gloria's and Ivan's deaths weren't coincidental, and Dutch Larkin wasn't the killer, the motive had to derive from some aspect of their professional interactions. Which left me with nothing other than the question: What about their professional interactions could have led to murder? Gloria had been upset enough about something to tell me she'd been betrayed and to schedule a meeting with the chair of her department. Gloria and Ivan had had some kind of intense conversation as they left the studio yesterday. Those three facts might be related to their deaths, or not.

Identifying the means seemed even less likely to bear fruit. Ivan had been strangled with what had appeared to be a length of thin, braided rope or cord. In the quick look I got, I hadn't noticed even a hint of plastic sheen, and I thought I would have noticed a gleam had it been there, so it was probably made of sisal or cotton or some other natural fiber. Thin cotton rope was ubiquitous along the coast, used by boaters, hikers, DIYers, and folks who liked to hang their laundry out in the sun to dry. It was found in everyone's basement or garage, and sold in every outdoor goods supplier, small hardware shop, grocery store, and big-box store in the state, in all states, in every country in the world. Maybe the police could trace the rope using forensics, but I doubted it. Everyone knew about fingerprints, and if I wanted to use an old skein of rope I kept in the basement, all I had to do was let it sit in bleach for a while, then toss it into the dryer while wearing gloves. Maybe I'd rinse it first, or not.

As for opportunity—forget that, too. Anyone could have knocked on Ivan's door and been admitted. If he hadn't closed the door all the way, the killer might not have even needed to knock. There were no security cameras that I had seen anywhere in the building or the parking lot. The halls were crowded with students, most bleary-eyed from having worked all day, unlikely to notice someone knocking on an office door or leaving quickly, just before class.

With no known motive, untraceable means, and ample opportunity, it looked as if the police had their work cut out for them.

Thinking about motives to kill made me think about other motives, too.

What was Veronica's motive for keeping me in the dark? I was as mystified by her actions now as I was the day I met her.

I shut my eyes for a moment, willing the blues away. What was Jane Austen's motive in writing her sister on that day in 1811 and her niece in 1814?

I opened my eyes, glad to turn my attention to work, to distract myself from the angst that threatened my equanimity anytime I thought about Veronica.

What had been going on in Jane's life at that time? *Sense and Sensibility* was published in 1811. She would have been working on final revisions and copyediting. Why hadn't she mentioned this momentous event in her letter to Cassandra? The same question applied to Jane's letter to Fanny. If I remembered right, Jane's brother, Henry, had helped her copyedit *Mansfield Park* in March 1814, before its July publication. Why hadn't she mentioned that in the letter?

I opened my eyes and emailed Sasha and Fred, asking what they thought of writing catalogue copy that addressed these questions.

Ellis appeared beside me. "How are you feeling?"

"Good," I said. "Two ibuprofen and I'll be as good as new."

"I need to ask you some questions. How about if I take you home and interview you there?"

"You don't need to take me. I can drive myself." I half smiled. "Maybe you can conduct the interview with me in the hot tub."

"That can be arranged. Are you sure you're all right to drive?"

"Yes." I stood, and when my muscles protested, I pawed the wall. "Ouch." I smiled again, as best I could manage. "I have leftover spaghetti and meatballs if you want."

"You don't need to be tough all the time, Josie."

"Sure I do."

"You really don't. Not with me."

"Thank you, but it doesn't matter who you are. It matters who I am."

"I give up," Ellis said. "How about if I meet you at your place in an hour?"

I told him that was perfect and wobbled out, still shaky, but resolute. The last thing I saw as I passed by the open door was Ivan's boot.

CHAPTER NINETEEN

Now that I was alone, I could let go of my crisis-competence, and allow the shock and trepidation I'd held at bay to bubble to the surface. I sat in my car and tried to quell my rising panic.

Ty had left a voicemail saying he'd read Wes's breaking news report, and to call him when I could, no hurry. I appreciated his patience. I wanted to talk to him, to hear his voice, but I could barely manage coherent sentences, so I held off.

I didn't want to risk driving, either, until I felt more in control. I leaned back against the headrest and closed my eyes. My bruising was physical, but I felt emotionally drained, too, as if I'd gotten out of bed too soon after the flu.

Wes had replied to my earlier inquiry: *Suspects = nada. CALL ME. NOW.* I sent a message to keep him at bay: *I'm bruised, but okay. Ivan was strangled with thin cotton or cotton-like rope. Horrible. What about Dutch Larkin?*

I texted Zoë to ask her to come over, to keep me company for the evening.

I texted Russ, too, to arrange patrols at the house overnight, as well as at Prescott's. I had no reason to think I was involved in whatever was going on, but my dad always told me to watch my back. Better to have guards on duty than rely solely on an alarm system someone might disable. Russ replied within a minute that he'd take care of it immediately.

As I started the engine, my phone vibrated—it was Zoë texting that she was on her way.

I parked in my usual spot on Ocean Avenue, near the walkway that led to our front door. I watched for traffic, then opened my car door. My back seized up as I swung my legs to the ground, and I moaned. I waited a few seconds for the spasm to subside, then locked the car and started the painful trip to the porch. Zoë was leaning against a porch column watching me walk with conscious care. She wore a cherry red long-sleeved scoop-neck sheath, black tights, and black knee-high leather boots, the red perfect with her olive complexion and short black hair, the shape flattering to her willowy frame.

"Don't look at me," I said. "I'm a mess."

"Amazingly, you look fine. Ellis told me you were flung across the room."

"'Flung.' I'm going to have to remember that word." As I passed her en route to the front door, I added, "The truth is I'm really, truly a mess. Thanks for coming on zero notice."

"Anytime."

I unlocked the door, punched the disable code into the alarm keypad, threw the deadbolt after she was in, and reset the alarm, leaving the back door unarmed so we could get to the hot tub. I pointed to her oversize canvas tote bag. "Swimsuit for the hot tub?"

"And a nightie, in case I decide to sleep over. And soup. Minestrone. Last of the tomatoes and basil."

I called her the "soup queen" for a reason. "Thank you."

She smiled. "I'll get it simmering."

I started for the stairs. "Fire up the hot tub, too, will you? I'll meet you there in a few minutes."

Upstairs, I took painkillers and assessed the damage. My scalp was tender from where I'd crashed into the wall, but there was neither bleeding nor a lump. Good news. I used a handheld mirror to examine my back. The bruising appeared minor. I used one finger to touch my skin, testing sensitivity and scope, and discovered more good news. Nothing really hurt, meaning I'd suffered no severe injury. My spasms and stiffness were, no doubt, the result of my tensing up during the attack, and would subside within a day or two.

I carefully stepped into my bathing suit, taking my time, wanting to avoid another cramp. Wrapped in my favorite pale blue chenille bathrobe and flip-flops, I walked out onto the second-floor porch to call Ty.

It was mizzling, my mother's word for misty drizzle. I switched on the soft orange mini-lantern lights. The ocean was churning, the waves thunderous as they thrashed the shore. My conversation with Ty was quick, just long enough for me to hear his strong voice and for him to know I really was fine. By the time I switched off the lights, the mizzle had morphed into rain.

Wes had replied to my text: *No news re: Dutch. Call me. NOW.* I'd call him tomorrow, maybe.

When I got downstairs, Zoë, gorgeous in a Japanese kimono robe, sat on the wide porch ledge chatting with Russ. Ellis stood nearby, listening in. Russ told me the guards had been deployed, a team of two, with others at the ready to provide continuous coverage, as needed. I thanked him for his quick work and asked him to let the security guards know that I would be in the hot tub for a while, and to simply ignore me. He said he would, and left.

Ellis followed us into the kitchen, where Zoë put plastic bowls of soup, spoons, plastic glasses, and the pitcher of Third Degree martinis I'd left in the fridge, on a tray.

We grabbed towels and walked quickly through the light rain to the hot tub.

Ty and I had built a heavy canvas pitched roof over the spa and surrounding pavers to protect us from the sun and rain, and to ensure that falling leaves tumbled to the ground, not into the hot tub. We'd also fabricated small side tables that attached to the spa shell with C-clamps, and Zoë set one up for me so I'd have easy access to my soup and drink. I dropped my bathrobe, kicked off my sandals, and tucked my phone between folds of my towel to safeguard it from errant splashes and wind-driven rain. I lowered myself into the steamy hot water.

Ellis sat on a lawn chair under the canvas roof. "You're feeling better."

"Being home helps. So does having Zoë here, and Russ on the case, to say nothing of the unbelievable aroma from this soup. How could I not feel better?"

Zoë set up her own side table and eased into the hot tub, sitting across from me.

"I know you're here on business," I said to Ellis, "and I appreciate your letting me give an official statement in such an unconventional location."

"I assume you're okay with Zoë being here."

"Yes."

"And with being video-recorded?"

"It's totally weird, but yes to that, too."

He turned on his tablet's video function and leaned it against a towel, aimed at my face.

He stated the date, time, and location, then asked me to tell him how I happened to be at Ivan's office and to explain again what I'd seen and heard from the moment I opened Ivan's office door until I'd called 9–1–1.

I answered his questions between sips of soup, sticking to the facts. The soup was thick and hearty, the tomato flavor rich and full-bodied, the basil piquant.

Footsteps echoed from the flagstone path on the north side of the house, and a moment later, a guard trooped by. He acknowledged us with a nod, then glanced around and continued his patrol. I was glad to see him.

I finished my explanation, and Ellis asked, "Where are Gloria's notes, the ones you picked up from Ivan's desk?"

"Oh, golly! I completely forgot. They're in my tote bag, in the kitchen. I'll get them." I placed my soup bowl on the table and steadied myself, preparing to rise, but he held up a hand to stop me.

"I'll collect them on my way out," he said.

"Timothy and I really need them to complete the segment."

"Sorry."

"Can I take photos?"

"Let me make sure the notes are what they're supposed to be, then okay."

Zoë stood and said, "I'll go." She slipped on her robe and sandals. A minute later, Zoë was back with my bag.

Ellis extracted the notes. He scanned every page, front and back, then settled in to read through the document.

I leaned back and closed my eyes, sinking lower into the hot bubbly water.

A few minutes later, Ellis said, "You can take the photos."

I opened my eyes. "Great." I reached for the safety handle, preparing to hoist myself up.

"You stay here," Zoë told me. She retrieved my phone from the towel. "I'll take the photos in the kitchen—the light's better."

"Thanks. When you're done, upload the photos to the cloud and email Cara, asking her to create one document and send it to me and Timothy. Apologize for the late-night request. Tell her it's urgent."

"Got it."

Zoë padded back to the kitchen, and I retrieved my bowl.

"Okay, then," Ellis said. "We've covered the facts. Now tell me what you think." One side of his mouth ticked up. "No gossip, just your expert opinion based on facts."

"Did you talk to Dutch Larkin?" I asked, jockeying for precedence. As soon as I was done with my statement, Ellis would leave. My best chance to garner new information was now.

"Gloria's ex," Ellis said. "Why do you ask?"

"Isn't he a suspect?"

"Should he be?"

"Sure."

Ellis's gaze intensified. "Larkin is cooperating fully. I tell you this so you won't tell someone—oh, I don't know, say, Wes Smith—something that turns out to be untrue or a false lead."

"I don't know why you assume I pass things along to Wes."

He tried and failed to swallow a laugh.

"You're snickering."

He laughed without trying to hide it. "I'd call it a derisive chortle, myself, not a snicker."

"Why are you chortling derisively?"

"You've told me yourself that you work with him. Don't be coy."

"I don't know why you're dismissing Larkin as a suspect. His behavior at my place was what I can only call peculiar. As for his motive . . . you don't seem to be taking his apparent jealousy seriously. Jealousy is a curse—it grows exponentially and destroys everything it touches, like cancer. What if Larkin thought Gloria was romantically involved with Ivan?"

"I'm not dismissing anything or anyone. All leads are taken seriously. What else do you wonder about?"

"Gloria's professional interactions. Ditto Ivan."

"Can you give me an example?" he asked. "What kind of professional interactions?"

"At a guess? Document authentications. When you're at the top of the pyramid, some people like to see you topple off."

"And Gloria was at the top of the pyramid?"

"Yes."

"Who was Gloria consulting for?" he asked.

"I have no idea, and no way of knowing."

"How can I find out?"

I paused for a few seconds, considering his question. "You could send an alert to all the major antiques auction houses and rare book and document sellers, I suppose, because those are the only corporate players that could afford her. You'd need to check museums and libraries, too. Not all of them . . . just the ones with relevant collections. You might need to look at private collectors, too."

"That sounds like a massive undertaking. Any ideas to get the information quicker?"

"She'd have emails with the client."

"None. The only emails about consulting work refer to your TV show. No texts or saved phone messages, either."

"A deposit in her bank account? She'd want some earnest money and maybe an advance against expenses."

"None."

I slid the now-empty soup bowl onto the tray. "Really?"

"Yup. What's my next move?"

"Check her files. Did she have a home office?"

"Just a desk with a few bills awaiting payment, all current. It looks like she kept all her work-related materials at Hitchens, and as crammed as those file cabinets are, I estimate we might find something useful in a year or two."

"How about letting me take a look?"

Ellis rubbed his nose. "With a police officer observing and a video camera rolling. Not that I don't trust you . . . it's a chain-of-evidence thing."

"Of course. Do you want me to do it now?"

"Tomorrow morning is fine—but only if you're up to it. We have the office sealed."

Zoë rejoined us. "All set." She handed Ellis the folder, then stepped back into the hot tub.

"Great. I'm really relieved." To Ellis, I said, "Tomorrow is fine. I'm sure I'll be in good shape. Zoë's soup cures all ills."

Ellis looked at her, and his features softened and his smile deepened, the face of love. "Not just her soup."

"You guys," Zoë said.

Ellis turned back to me. "What can you tell me about Ivan?"

"Almost nothing. He used to live with a woman named Heather Adler." I described my visit to her apartment and our conversation. "Heather is not a happy camper."

"Because of Ivan?"

"Because of shattered dreams. She thought Gloria treated Ivan like an indentured servant. She blamed him for not standing up to Gloria. Heather was resentful, but the breakup is fresh. It just happened today." I shook my head. "She still loves him—loved him. His death will hit her hard."

Ellis had me repeat her name and state her address for the camera, then asked, "How else can I find out about him?"

"Ivan would have had to list three references on his internship application. I can get you those names."

"Thank you. There is a text I wanted to ask you about. Gloria sent it to Ivan yesterday afternoon, about five thirty. It shows as read, but not responded to." Ellis tapped his phone, then read aloud. "'As to the other issue, I'll discuss it with Dr. S as soon as he gets back.' What was she was referring to?"

"I don't know, but Gloria made an appointment to see the department chair, Dr. Shield, for as soon as he returned to campus. Arlene Stevens, the department admin, told me that Gloria was upset."

"Did she say why?"

"She said she didn't know."

Ellis paused for a few seconds, then asked, "Do you have any other information that might be relevant?"

"No."

"How did Gloria act on set?"

"She was upset about the betrayal issue, as I told you. Other than that one comment, though, she acted in a completely professional manner. Maybe you can get some ideas by looking at Ivan's phone and computer and so on."

"Thank you," Ellis said. "You've been very helpful. This is enough for now." He turned off the video.

"I'll walk you out."

I started up, but crumpled when my muscles protested my sudden move. Zoë lunged across the hot tub to break my fall. I grabbed the rim, steadying myself.

"I'm okay," I managed. "Mental note to self: move slower." I read the concern on their faces. "I'm fine. Really. It's just my muscles' way of telling me they want to stay in the hot tub, that's all." I slid down onto the seat, the hot water lapping my neck, the whirlpool jets shooting pulsating water at my back. "It's amazing how when I'm not moving and letting the jets do their thing, I feel absolutely no pain."

Zoë asked if I was sure I was okay, and when I assured her I was, she said she'd walk Ellis out.

"When you go off duty, Ellis, come back. The beer is cold. The soup is hot, and I have plenty of other stuff to eat, too, not just leftover Italian."

He thanked me, but said he'd have to play it by ear. They walked together into the house, leaving me alone in the hot tub. I was glad Russ's security guards were on patrol, just as I was glad I kept my Browning 9mm in my bedside table. I leaned back and closed my eyes, lulled by the steady patter of the rain on the canvas roof.

Two people dead. Easy-to-access means. Ample opportunity. No apparent motive, except for Gloria's wealth and the one I floated for Dutch Larkin that Ellis seemed to dismiss out of hand. With any luck, I'd find evidence in Gloria's files that she was working on a controversial or fishy project, something that would explain the inexplicable.

CHAPTER TWENTY

I awakened to pelting rain just after eight, late for me. I rolled out of bed, girded for pain, and was relieved to discover that I wasn't nearly as stiff as I'd expected. I opened the drapes and looked out through thick fog to the Atlantic. I hoped Ty would be able to get home. The ocean was near-black and riotous, topped with blustery white froth. I dressed quickly and walked downstairs.

Before I even set the coffee brewing, I called Russ and told him I thought I'd like to continue the patrols, that I was in a better-safe-than-sorry kind of mood.

I sat at the kitchen table, watching the rain, checking messages, and eating a banana.

Ty had texted at seven, en route to a breakfast meeting with his boss. He planned to ask if he could accept the promotion, but be based in New Hampshire. He explained that he wasn't nervous—that the buzzards nose-diving around his stomach had to be from something he ate, that surely his boss wouldn't can him simply for floating the idea. He asked me to text him as soon as I woke up to let him know I was okay, which I did. I added that I understood buzzards' nefarious flights stopped in the face of courage, so given his bravery in asking his boss to accommodate him, I was confident they were already long gone.

Wes was as persistent as a yellow jacket, demanding the inside scoop. Other reporters wanted my comments on the murders, too. Another set had discovered the Jane Austen story and wanted to know what was what. I forwarded their contact information to Cara for the news release.

Timothy had emailed at midnight saying the notes Cara had sent earlier in the evening were perfect, that he now knew exactly what content was missing, and that he'd touch base in the morning. He added that the thimble beauty shots had gone well, and Fred's descriptions, while competent and delivered with panache, were about as exciting as watching an oak grow. "Give me something, Josie. Something intriguing. We need to sex it up a bit." I laughed. Timothy wanted me to "sex up" thimbles. I emailed back that I'd talk to Fred, that we would come up with something.

I'd finished scrambled eggs and a second cup of coffee when Ellis called and asked if I felt up to meeting him at Gloria's office. I assured him I did.

I smoothed the duvet over the bed and fluffed the pillows, my version of making the bed, and opened my bedside table. My Browning 9mm was nestled beside my latest book, Rex Stout's *Three Witnesses*. I confirmed the gun was cocked and locked, fully loaded with the hammer cocked, one bullet in the chamber, and the safety catch on, and secreted it in one of my tote bag's cavernous pockets. Nothing in particular was worrying me, but as I'd told Russ, I was in a better-safe-than-sorry frame of mind.

Gloria's office was roughly double the size of the one Ivan had shared with Jonathan. The desk was clear except for a desktop computer, a multi-line phone, and a framed cover of the August 1997 issue of *Ambience* magazine, known for memorializing the lifestyles of the mega-rich.

The cover showed Gloria on a chaise lounge under a latticed portico dripping with wisteria. She wore a strapless gold lamé cocktail dress. A wood and fieldstone mansion was behind her. She was gazing out over the ocean, the water deep blue and dotted with sequins. Everything about the scene was movie-set perfect, from the meticulously groomed lawn to the fit and tanned woman. The pewter frame was engraved: *Forget Past Mistakes*.

The desk faced two windows overlooking the quad. They were covered by sheer ivory curtains. Wooden bookcases lined one wall. Three old-fashioned wooden file cabinets stood against another. A worktable with a work light attached was in a corner. A box of plastic gloves sat alongside a microscope.

I turned to Ellis. "You said you went through her emails and texts . . . no intellectual or other kinds of squabbles?"

"Like what?"

"Another professor accusing her of plagiarism. A student who didn't like her grade threatening to challenge Gloria's findings about some document in a letter to a professional journal. A colleague who was so jealous of Gloria's accomplishments, he filed a bogus complaint to HR. Et cetera."

"No, nothing like that," Ellis said. "That's why you're here." He opened a palm to the filing cabinets. "For all I know, there might be evidence in there related to one of those intellectual squabbles. I'm not sure any of us would recognize it."

"So my job is to go through her files and see if I can find anything that seems like it might provide a motive?"

"Yes, but more broadly, to call our attention to anything that seems off in any way. For instance, some folders are full of documents. Others have only one or two sheets of paper in them. I have no way of knowing if anything is missing, but I'm hoping you'll be able to tell."

"I'll do my best." I pointed at the desk. "Do I check there, too?"

"You can, but we've already gone through it. There aren't any papers there, just supplies and some personal things—a tube of dry skin cream, an emery board, that sort of thing." He turned to Officer Meade, standing by a window. "The officer will stay as an observer. She'll give you plastic gloves. I want to introduce you on video, then I'll leave. Before we get started . . . how are you?"

"Rarin' to go."

He shot me a "who are you kidding?" look, but didn't comment.

Officer Meade handed me the gloves, and I wiggled my hands into them.

Ellis latched the video recorder into its tripod cradle and aimed it at the file cabinets. He positioned Officer Meade in front of the cabinet on the left and me in front of the one on the right. When he was satisfied we'd be visible on screen, he stood between us and used a remote to start recording. He introduced himself and us, stated the date and time, explained why I was there, and said that the police officer would be observing in person. He thanked me on camera, then left.

Having gone through every folder in Gloria's file cabinets, I could attest that she was as thorough, organized, and well-prepared as Ivan had said she was.

One entire cabinet was devoted to her doctoral work. In a folder labeled

JEFFERSON, THOMAS, I found the issue of *Antiques Insights* magazine containing the article that had shot her to fame, but no notes. I conjectured that once an article got published, she tossed her notes.

Another cabinet documented her consulting work and scholarly interests. I found a printout of her notes about *Peter Rabbit*, which, from the page count, appeared identical to the final version Ivan had copied for me. Her works-cited listing included twenty-seven sources. Another folder contained her appraisal and notes regarding the President Garfield letter from when he'd been in the military. I counted two appraisals of documents signed by President Washington, one from Zachary Taylor, and three from President Lincoln. No wonder she was considered a presidential signature expert. Other folders included her original handwritten notes, listing her source material and citations, along with copies of published articles and essays from years past.

The last cabinet was dedicated to her teaching. Binders of lecture notes were organized by class, one for each course she'd ever taught. There was nothing misfiled, that I could see.

Just before eleven, I turned to Officer Meade and said, "I'm done. There's nothing here that stands out to me."

Officer Meade clicked the camera's OFF button. "I'll text Chief Hunter."

"I have a question for him . . . has anyone gone through Ivan's files? He and Gloria worked closely together. Maybe there's something there that would raise a red flag."

"I'll ask." She sent the text.

I shrugged into my leather jacket and slung my tote bag over my shoulder.

Officer Meade's eyes stayed on her phone. "He says the crime scene team is still working in Ivan's office and the tech team hasn't finished analyzing his emails and so on." She raised her eyes to mine. "The chief will be in touch."

I thanked her and left, glad I'd worn my waterproof boots and carried a big umbrella. The rain was drenching.

I couldn't stop thinking about Dutch Larkin. I didn't know exactly what I wanted to ask him or say to him, and I had no illusions that he would reveal anything useful about why he'd crept around my property, but I needed to see him. I drove to Rocky Point Quarry on Baylor Street. If nothing else, I could offer my sincere condolences for his loss. I didn't think it was risky—I wasn't looking to meet him alone in a dark alley. I was going to a place of business.

I parked in his company's side lot, in sight of a football field–size yard filled with blocks and chunks of stone. Wide aisles allowed slab transport carts easy access. The showroom was housed in a huge, one-story free-standing building. I decided I would only go inside if there were other people around—I was curious to meet Dutch, and committed to learning why he'd been sneaking around my place, but I wasn't foolhardy.

I splashed my way across the parking lot to the showroom. Window displays exhibited before and after samples, raw and finished slabs of granite, marble, and quartz. Peering through the rain-streaked glass, I was reassured to see half a dozen customers scattered about, alone or in pairs, and four staffed desks. Dutch stood with his back to me in a model kitchen on the right.

Stepping inside, I lowered my umbrella into one of the plastic sleeves the showroom supplied, and pretended to look around, starting on the left.

A young woman approached me and asked if she could help. I said no, that I was just browsing, and she handed me her business card, saying that if I had any questions, I should feel free to ask. Evidently, Dutch Larkin cared about customer service and knew how to train his staff.

I surreptitiously watched Larkin as I wandered through the sample rooms and stone displays. Dark smudges under his eyes told me he hadn't slept much last night. Periodically, he massaged the left side of his neck. I recognized the motion and knew what it meant—his muscles were tight. After a few minutes, he left that model kitchen and walked into another one, squatting to examine the counter, maybe checking the seams or the overall fit. He's methodical, I thought, and conscientious.

When he stood, I walked over, and said, "Hi. I'm Josie Prescott. We met the other day . . . well, we sort of met. You were asking about where we film my TV show."

Recognition dawned on him. "Oh, yeah, sure." He extended a hand for a shake. "Dutch Larkin. Nice to meet you."

"You, too." I opened my arms and looked around. "This is quite an operation. I'm impressed."

"Thanks. Are you in the market for some stone?"

"Actually, no. I wanted to talk to you about Gloria Moreau."

He flinched as if I'd slapped him. "You know that she's . . . that she passed away."

"Yes . . . and one reason I'm here is to tell you how sorry I am for your loss."

"Thank you, but I don't see . . ." He paused and glanced around, then brought his eyes back to my face. "I'm sorry, but . . . you said that was one reason you're here . . . why else?"

"I'm just so horrified and confused. Gloria was a new friend. We really hit it off. I wanted to connect with someone else who cared about her."

"You came to the right place."

"Tell me about her."

"Gloria? She was a wonderful woman. A remarkable woman."

"In what way?" I read the doubt on his face. "That's a serious question . . . I only got to know her briefly . . . I'd love to hear more about her."

His expression shifted from inured to reflective when he realized that I wasn't looking for routine platitudes. He gazed out the window toward the quarry. "She was smarter than me, but she never acted like it. She liked that I work outdoors, that I work with my hands. We talked about everything. We exchanged questions of the week. It was her idea, a way to get to know one another, and then, after we'd fallen in love, a way to become even more connected. Her first question to me was, 'What's the best decision you ever made?' Mine to her was, 'Who was the best boss you ever had?' We emailed them to one another on Monday morning, took the whole week to think about it, and talked about it over the weekend."

"I love that idea. Thank you for telling me about it. Obviously, you were close."

"I adored her."

"I don't know how to ask this, and I certainly don't mean to add to your pain, but, well . . . I'll just say it . . . I'd heard you'd broken up."

He snapped his eyes back to my face. "That's a lie! Who said that?"

"Ivan Filbert, her grad assistant."

He snorted contemptuously. "That little twit wouldn't know a breakup from a take a break."

"I guess you haven't heard . . . Ivan's dead."

Dutch ran his fingers through his hair. "Yeah, I heard."

"Did you know him?"

"Only through what Gloria said about him. I never met him." He shook his head as if he were trying to shake a fly loose. "I can't believe she's gone."

"Me, either."

He ruffled his hair again, and looked around the showroom. "I planned on staying home to grieve, but I only lasted about five minutes."

"I'm the same way. Sitting around feeling sorry for yourself doesn't help anyone, but you're in too much pain to do anything productive, so you just sit like a lump. Finally, I do the only thing that seems to make me feel human—I work." I paused for a few seconds. When he didn't comment, I added, "It must be extra hard to know that some people thought your relationship was over."

"Not so much hard as infuriating. It wasn't over, and suggesting it . . . well, it's lucky for Ivan that he never said it to my face."

"Why did he think the relationship was over?"

"I haven't got a clue, but I'll tell you what I told the cops. Okay, so Gloria and I were having a little glitch in our relationship . . . it happens. Maybe she called it a breakup once or twice. I called it a pause." He raised his chin and stiffened his spine. "We were going to get back together." Giving voice to his conviction transformed him like an elixir. He was done with wallowing. "Right now, I've got to get back to work."

"Before I go . . . would you tell me why you were at my company the other day?"

"Yeah, I know. Not my finest hour."

"You were hoping to see Gloria."

"I just had to see her."

"Why take photos of the window?"

"She was inside . . . I saw her."

There was something ineffably sad about a man so desperate to see a woman, he was reduced to hiding in the woods so he could snap a photo of her through a window.

"You had to make certain she didn't see you. That's why you didn't park in the lot." He didn't say anything, so I changed the subject. "Just one more question . . . do you know anything about Gloria's will?"

"No. Do you?"

"No. How about her finances?"

Dutch tilted his head, assessing my intentions. "Are you a reporter?"

"No! I'm just who I said I am."

"Listen, I'm having a hard enough time keeping it together without you asking questions that are none of your business. You'd better go."

"I'm sorry. I really am. Please accept my condolences."

He nodded, then pulled back his shoulders, and marched across the room.

Arlene Stevens, the admin at Hitchens, said Dutch Larkin was Gloria's friend. Ivan referred to him as her ex. Dutch himself said they were in a "pause." No one can ever know what's in anyone else's heart or mind—or relationship.

His pain was evident, but that didn't prove anything. Lots of killers feel regret.

CHAPTER TWENTY-ONE

I decided to indulge myself. Veronica Sutton had refused to talk to me, but there was no reason I couldn't see where she lived. I didn't want her to worry that I was stalking her, but between the steady rain and thickening fog, I was certain she wouldn't be able to identify a driver in a moving vehicle.

Ginny Carson's house was, as expected, an eighteenth-century center entrance colonial, with a third-floor widow's walk and two side porches—one screened, the other long since converted to a sunroom. The house was painted pale lavender with butter-yellow trim. I couldn't see a guesthouse. I circled the block, then switched on my flashers and slowed to a crawl. Peering over an expansive lawn, I glimpsed the guesthouse at the rear of the property, behind a stand of evergreens, and recognized the design as an old carriage house, with stables on the ground floor and living quarters for the grooms on the second level. I circled the block again and rolled to a stop at the entry to a narrow street I'd never noticed before. It looked more like an alley than an actual road, one of many in this part of Rocky Point that had originally been designed so horse-drawn carriages could reach the stable yard without disturbing the residents of the main house. I squinched my eyes, trying to locate the street sign, but I couldn't. I turned in and inched my way along until I spotted it. The sign was nearly obscured by a fifteen-foot-tall fir tree. Veronica Sutton lived on Parker Mews.

I backed out and drove to the grocery store.

I bought chicken for dinner and a take-out roast beef sandwich for now. At home, I got the chicken marinating in my mother's special mixture, olive oil, lemon juice, pepper, and dried basil, put on my Irish knit sweater, and took my sandwich outside to the covered patio. The rain had slowed, but the sky remained dark, the ocean tumultuous.

I hoped Ty's meeting had gone well, however he defined that term. I called and got his voicemail. I told him I was thinking of him, and that the chicken was ready to go.

I'd delayed thinking about how to get Veronica Sutton to confide in me, or at the least, how to get her to answer some basic questions about the provenance of the Jane Austen letters. She'd made her position clear—she didn't want anything to do with me—but that position was unacceptable to me. I needed to change her mind, if not about helping me, then about helping with the appraisal. At the bare minimum, I needed her to tell me how she came in possession of the letters. Saying they were from my father wasn't sufficient. If she didn't want to talk to me about my dad, so be it. I would contact her with a professional request for information about provenance nonetheless.

I weighed whether she might be more forthcoming if I had one of my staff make the initial contact to ask about the letters. By separating the two issues—learning about the provenance of the letters versus learning about her relationship with my dad—I might have a better chance of achieving both goals. Once the technical side of the appraisal was finished, or at least well underway, I could renew my efforts to persuade her to talk to me about my father. For now, I needed to give her a little space. There was no immediate urgency, though. I could proceed on other fronts and decide who should reach out to her later.

Another, unrelated thought came to me, then flitted away. I tried to call it back. Something I'd seen, an anomaly, pricked at me. Nothing came to mind, yet there was something, an idea or a memory, flickering just at the edge of my consciousness.

My phone vibrated. No surprise, it was Wes, texting yet again. I ignored it.

A few minutes later, Cara texted that Heather Adler, Ivan's ex-girlfriend, had called. She wanted to sell Ivan's books, and asked if I was interested in buying them. Cara included Heather's phone number.

At Prescott's, we dealt with people who'd lost a loved one all the time. Often, the process of consigning or selling that person's possessions led to dissension among friends and family, from minor tiffs to overt hostility to lawsuits. Given all the emotions at play—grief, anger, jealousy, and rivalry, to name a few—and the allure of big money, negotiations were often fraught with explosive volatility. I should have been accustomed to heirs' questionable tactics, but I wasn't. The fact that Heather hoped to sell Ivan's possessions less than twenty-four hours after his murder was to me boorish. Even thinking about it made me want to take a shower. Nonetheless, if the books were Heather's to sell, I'd buy them. I dialed her number, and she answered on the first ring, as if she'd been waiting for my call.

"I'm really sorry about Ivan's death, Heather," I said.

"Thanks," she said, sounding young and vulnerable. "It's terrible, beyond terrible, but . . . well, you got my message. I want to sell his books. Now, today. I can't stand looking them, the reminder."

"I'd love to buy them, Heather, but don't you think you should wait a few days at least, to let your loss sink in?"

"No. I know myself. Can you move them out safely in this weather?"

"Yes, I'll bring plastic tubs. I'm sorry to have to ask, but do you know if Ivan had a will?"

"No, and I think I would have known. We used to joke that there was no point in his writing a will, since he didn't own anything. If he had one, I'm sure I would have been named as his heir. He had no family. He told me that he listed me as his beneficiary on a life insurance policy Hitchens gives all their employees, even grad assistants."

"Thank you. I also need to ask . . . again, I'm sorry to have to bring this up, but . . . are they yours to sell?"

"I understand . . . yes. I bought them all and I have most of the receipts, not the flea market finds, of course, but most of the rest. I kept them for the tax deduction."

"I don't mean to add to your pain, but you asked me to tell him to come get them. That certainly implies they were his."

She exhaled loudly. "I bought them. I have most of the receipts. Do you want them or not?"

She was right. It wasn't my place to split hairs. "Yes, I want them. I'll need to see those receipts."

"That's fine."

"All right then." My watch told me it was nearly two. "How's three o'clock?"

"Good. Thank you."

Before I left the house, I texted Ellis, asking if he had any information about Ivan's will, explaining that Heather wanted to sell his books. I ended with a specific question: *Does Heather have the legal right to sell the books?*

I parked close to Prescott's front door. Police tape had been wrapped around trees to cordon off the crime scene, but the technicians and police officers had evidently finished their work, or maybe the persistent rain made continuing untenable. My phone vibrated, a call from Ellis. I stayed in the car to take it, cocooned by the foggy windows.

After thanking me for going through Gloria's files, he said, "We've gone through Ivan's documents and computer files, and we haven't found a copy of a will, or anything that makes me think he wrote one. No payment to a lawyer, for instance, or search history for a do-it-yourself legal forms website. We spoke to Heather Adler. She said he owned very little and that the books are hers—she says she has receipts. She's listed as his next of kin on his Hitchens paperwork and the sole beneficiary of a small life insurance policy."

"That's consistent with what she told me . . . thank you. That seems to cover it."

"Are the books valuable?"

"Medium. I noticed some nice leather bindings."

Before we hung up, I promised to let him know if I discovered anything unexpected, and he thanked me.

I scooped up my umbrella, ready to make a run for the office, then changed my mind. In an excess of caution, I did what I always do when I need advice only a lawyer can provide. I called Max Bixby. Ever since I'd moved to Rocky Point, Max had provided guidance and stability. He knew the law, and he had common sense. I got lucky; he was in and available to take my call.

After exchanging friendly greetings, I summarized the situation, repeated Ellis's report, and asked his opinion.

"Ms. Adler told you the books were a gift to Ivan," Max said, recapping, "yet now she's claiming ownership. For the sake of argument, let's say the books are part of Ivan's estate. A day is not sufficient to determine whether he had a will, nor is it sufficient to locate his heirs, if he died intestate. Those heirs might not even know he died."

"All good points. However, if I don't buy the books, Heather will simply call another dealer and say she has some books to sell, and here are the receipts. How about this? I buy them so someone else won't, but I don't sell them for however long you think I should wait."

"Only you know if the books are worth buying. If someone files a claim, you might be on the hook for your investment, unless you recover the money from the seller. If you proceed, waiting would be prudent. Let me give you some specific instructions here on the phone. I'll follow up with a letter for your files. I know you do everything I'm about to list as a matter of course, but let's get it in writing. Be certain to memorialize every item with video recordings and/ or photographs. Keep copies of any receipts the seller provides. Don't comingle this collection with any other objects. At the end of a year, we'll see what has transpired and determine next steps from there. How does that sound?"

"Sensible. Thank you, Max. I'll do exactly as you say."

I got out of the car, wind-whipped rain stinging my face, despite my umbrella. A member of Russ's security team stood near the tent, her eyes on me. Lenny was there, too. I waved, and they waved back. They both wore rain gear and looked miserable.

Inside, Cara reported that Sasha and Fred had fielded thirty-seven calls, emails, and in-person visits from reporters, collectors, curators, librarians, and academics wanting to know more about the Jane Austen letters described in Wes's article.

I faced Sasha and Fred, and said, "Thirty-seven inquiries? In less than a day? Wow."

Fred grinned. "Oh, yeah. We're sitting on a fire keg with this one."

"What did you two think of my idea about including tidbits about Jane Austen's life in the catalogue copy?"

"I love it," Sasha said. "Structurally, I was thinking we could use a timeline running along the bottom of each page."

"That way we can flag important moments in her life," Fred said, "but only write up those events that relate to the letters."

"Like the fact that Jane Austen was engaged to Harris Bigg-Wither for a day," I said. "Not even a day, which certainly implies she took her own advice, and wouldn't marry a man she couldn't admire."

"Can you imagine how hard that must have been for her?" Sasha said. "Jane didn't have a dowry, and without one, a woman's prospects were bleak. Also, she was almost twenty-seven. That isn't old by today's standards, but back then . . ." She shook her head empathetically. "She must have faced enormous pressure to accept his proposal."

Fred pushed up his glasses. "That's great context, Sasha. Let's add that perspective when we write it up."

"Perfect. I love that idea, Fred." I faced Sasha. "How's that expert list coming?"

"Good. I'm still developing it, and for the names I already have, I'm checking reviews, complaints, et cetera."

"Did Oliver make the cut?"

"Oh, yes." She smiled. "He's a guest expert on a popular TV show called *Josie's Antiques*, and comes very highly recommended."

I laughed. "*Josie's Antiques*! Well, then, no more need be said." I turned toward Fred. "How did the thimble taping go?"

"Good, I think. Timothy didn't talk about burning hair, though."

"I know. He wants us to sex it up."

"Sex up thimbles?"

"That's exactly what I said. In lieu of razzmatazz sexiness, we need a surprise. Have you come across an extra hidden compartment in any of the cases? Someplace to safeguard a needle or a pincushion?"

"No."

"Could we change the way we present the acorn so the fact that it's a case is a surprise?"

He thought about it for a few seconds. "I don't see how. It's obviously not a thimble, so what else could it be but a case?"

"True." I mentally ran through the other featured thimbles. "Let's put out feelers—find me a surprise!"

Fred nodded. "Will do!"

My phone vibrated. Shelley was calling from New York City.

I used to work with Shelley at Frisco's, the venerable New York City-based antiques auction house. I loved it there, until I didn't. I'd been the whistle-blower in a price-fixing scandal organized by my boss. I'd been hounded by the press, chased out of my job for not being a "team player," and deserted by my so-called friends, all except Shelley. Then my dad died, and two weeks later, my boyfriend at the time, Rick the Cretin, dumped me for being a "downer." I recalled my dad's words: When you feel as if you're at the end of your rope, tie a knot and hang on. If you can't hang on, move on. I hung on for a year, then relocated to Rocky Point to start a new life. I'd discovered the sad reality that remembered pain seared as sharply as the first time you experienced it. All I could do was endure the flashbacks and will the memories aside.

I let the call go to voicemail. I knew what Shelley wanted—she'd got wind of the Jane Austen appraisal, and she wanted in. She'd lobby hard to let Frisco's take the lead, talking up their marketing reach. I wanted to work with her, but only on my terms. The auction would take place here, in New Hampshire, or even, if Timothy thought it was a good idea, on live TV. The auctioneer would be one we used regularly. We didn't need Frisco's infrastructure. We had plenty of phone lines, laptops, and staff to pass along remote bids. The only two things I needed from Frisco's were their endorsement and marketing clout. I would hire them after we'd finished the appraisal to review the findings and offer their stamp of approval. As part of that arrangement, which would position them as the ultimate arbiter of newly discovered Jane Austen letters, a prize they'd love to win, they'd have to agree to help me promote the auction. I needed to stand my ground without alienating them, not the easiest of tasks.

I stood by the window while I waited for Shelley's message to arrive, then listened. It was short and to the point: *Got a sec to talk?*

I laughed. I loved Shelley to bits, but she was so transparent.

Frisco's was one of the two top dogs in the rough-and-tumble world of ritzy antiques auction houses. Prescott's wasn't a newcomer to the competitive scene, but we weren't nipping at the heels of the big boys, either. We'd been successful enough over the years to have earned our rank on *Antiques Insights* magazine's annual best small antiques auction house listing for five years in a row, but most of the time, we were simply an annoyance to an enterprise like Frisco's, like a metaphorical pebble in their Dolce & Gabbanas.

As good a friend as Shelley was, she didn't care about Prescott's; she cared about Jane Austen, and what landing a deal would do to her reputation and Frisco's prestige. With Frisco's support, this auction would help us scrabble our way a little higher in the pecking order, but I wasn't prepared to jump just because Shelley whistled, and I needed her to know that. I texted her: *Good to hear from you. Hope all's well. Can't talk now. Soon!*

CHAPTER TWENTY-TWO

A fter checking in with the rest of my staff, and nabbing another gingersnap, I recruited Eric to accompany me to Heather's apartment. He loaded the van with eight clear plastic latching storage tubs filled with towels for drying them once we got inside, soft protective fabric for wrapping the books, and plastic tarps for covering the tubs when we left Heather's apartment.

We got to the Islington duplex on time and were able to park only a few houses away. I flipped up my hood and dashed to the porch, while Eric retrieved the dolly from the back and loaded the tubs. I rang the bell as Eric maneuvered the hand truck up the steps.

Heather opened the door. Yesterday, I'd described her as pretty. Today, she seemed fragile, like a translucent porcelain vase, skinny rather than slender, gaunt and pale.

She stepped back. "Come on in."

I introduced Eric, wiped my feet on the coir mat, and unzipped my raincoat. I took it off and shook it before stepping inside, then hung it on a standing walnut coatrack.

"Eric will stay here to dry the containers," I said. "He'll place them on a plastic tarp so no water will get on your floor."

She thanked me, and him, and started down the hall. Eric got to work with a towel.

I followed Heather. "Before we get started, you mentioned you have receipts. Would it be all right if I take photos of them for my records?"

"Can I email them to you? I scanned them into one document."

"Sure."

She walked into her office. I waited in the hall.

After a minute, she said, "Okay, it's sent."

I checked that I'd received it, then walked with her to the sitting room. Eric followed us, caddying the tubs. I scanned the receipts, not for the prices, since what she'd paid wasn't relevant to what I could offer without an appraisal, but for the number of volumes—I wanted to be certain she'd actually purchased all these books. Most of the receipts didn't specify titles, and many didn't specify quantities, merely stating "miscellaneous volumes" or "box of books." It was hopeless. I felt confident, though, in buying them, since Ellis seemed satisfied it was appropriate and Max had signed off on the issue.

There were two ways to buy books, by the lot or by the volume. Since Heather said she just wanted the books gone, I suspected she would be most interested in selling the entire lot, and I was right. She didn't want to consign them, which typically brought the seller a higher price, but took longer, and she didn't want me to appraise individual volumes, another delay. She was willing to accept a lower price for a quicker removal. Under those constraints, all I could do was a cursory appraisal, counting volumes within categories, and estimating the price per category.

I asked Eric to count the cloth-bound twentieth-century books, for which I could offer three dollars a volume, knowing that some, based on rarity and popularity, would sell for as much as twenty dollars, but most for only a dollar or two, and some not at all. I could offer more for the leather bindings, ten dollars a book. I didn't want the other books, the paperbacks or miscellaneous volumes, and wouldn't include them in my offer, but I would remove them as a convenience to her, if she wanted. She did.

I counted the leather-bound volumes, starting with the top shelf. Most of the volumes were octavo, 6" by 9". One book was imperial octavo, 8 ¼" by 11", and one was sextodecimo, 5" by 7 ½". Heather stood across the room, near the windows, her arms crossed, watching us work.

After a minute, she said, "Thank you again for accommodating me so quickly."

I turned to face her. "Of course."

She brushed back her hair. "Ivan stopped by yesterday. Around four, for about ten minutes." She used the side of her pinky to brush aside a tear. "To pack up more of his clothes."

Her sadness, the magnitude of her loss, was apparent. She might have ended their relationship, but that hadn't ended her love.

"He measured the books, so he could calculate how many boxes he'd need to pack them up."

"This must be so tough for you."

"More than I expected." She lowered her eyes to the floor. "What really stings is that I was mean to him. He said he'd be out of my hair as soon as he could, and I replied that it couldn't be soon enough. Isn't that awful? Why would I say something like that? Then I stomped out of the room, all attitude, no compassion."

"You said it yourself . . . breakups are always hard."

"He didn't say another word to me. When he was done in here, he just walked out. He didn't even look into my office, where he knew I'd be sitting." She raised her eyes to my face. "That's the last time I saw him."

I waited for a few seconds for her to continue, then asked, "Did he say when he planned to come back for the books?"

"Over the weekend." She shifted her gaze to the bookshelves. "He sure loved these books."

"Are you sure you don't want to wait a few days or weeks before selling them?"

"No, I know how I react to things. I need all signs of him gone." She walked into the kitchen. "I'm going to put on a pot of coffee. I'll be in here if you need me."

"I'll bring in the contract in a few minutes."

I did the math, tallying our book counts, ending with a total offer of $820. I sent the information to Cara, so she could prepare the sales documents, then, iPad in hand, I joined Heather in the kitchen.

She was sitting at her small dinette table, staring out the back window. The rain had slowed to a drizzle. A forgotten towel hung limply from a clothesline. The trees were cloaked in wispy fog, the leaves dripping steadily. The coffee aroma was strong, pungent. We both signed the receipt. I emailed her a copy, then transferred the money into her bank account via Prescott's banking app.

It took us less than half an hour to pack up all the books, each one nestled in protective fabric. Eric started with the leather-bound volumes, while I worked on the rest. When we were done, he shuttled the tubs to the front hall, one at a time, then trucked them out to the van, wrapped in plastic tarps. I stuck my head into the kitchen to tell Heather that we were leaving. She kept her gaze on the trees. She thanked me again, and asked that we please close the door on our way out.

Once we were under way, Eric asked, "Are you all right?"

"I'm fine. Why do you ask?"

Eric always found expressing himself hard. He wrestled with both ideas and words. Today, he nibbled on his lip as he considered how to communicate his thoughts.

"People are so unhappy," he said.

"Some people. Not all."

"Can I ask you something?"

"Of course," I said, my worry meter spinning onto high alert. No one asked permission to pose a question that was innocuous.

"How did you know Ty was the one?"

I relaxed. Context is all. Eric had been dating a lovely young woman named Grace for years and he wanted my opinion on whether she was "the one," on whether he should propose to her.

From past conversations, I knew that Grace wanted to get her career on track before she married. She was a teacher's aide, finishing her degree at night, so she could become a full-fledged teacher. I also knew that Eric lived with his mother, who was, from what I'd observed, utterly unlovable. She acted like every bump in the road had been placed there on purpose to trip her up. She had an ugly word for anyone who crossed her path, and that was on a good day. On bad days, she could make an optimist weep. I'd often wondered how Eric could have become such a kind and empathetic young man having been reared by such a malignant malcontent. One of the mysteries of life.

I swallowed a glib answer, "You just know," although I thought there was some truth to it. "I don't believe in one and only," I said. "I think that there are a lot of people any of us might find to love, who'd love us back. It's a matter of timing, I guess, and openness—being ready, being emotionally available. The only thing I know with any certainty is that to be loved, you have to love. I know how trite that sounds, but I mean it quite sincerely, quite literally."

"So you just take a chance?"

"I wouldn't put it that way. 'Take a chance,' makes finding love or getting married sound like gambling, and I don't think of it like a lottery. It's not random, based on luck. It's knowing yourself, your values, your expectations, and what your overall life goals are. If you value a woman for who she truly is, and she values you for who you truly are; if you like spending time together whether you're doing something fun or exciting or nothing in particular; if there's chemistry between you; and if you share life goals, like whether you want children or how you feel about religion, that sort of thing, I think you've found a keeper. At that point, it becomes an issue of nothing ventured, nothing gained." I turned my head so I could see his profile. "Are you thinking of asking Grace to marry you?"

He gripped the steering wheel so hard his knuckles turned white. "Do you think I should?"

I laughed. "Only you can answer that question, Eric, but I'll tell you what I've noticed. Grace is sweet and sincere, and she seems to adore you." His lips turned up, the start of a smile. "I've seen her look at you as if you're all she needs to be happy. And you look at her the same way." The more I talked, the more his smile grew. "I also admire her. She's a hard worker and goal oriented. Teachers are among my favorite people. They change lives."

Ten minutes later, when Eric turned into Prescott's parking lot, he was still smiling.

As soon as I stepped into the front office, Fred leaned back in his chair, and gave me his "you're gonna love this" look.

"I have news," he said.

"Tell me," I said.

He stood, his eyes signaling his delight. "Follow me."

We traipsed through the warehouse to a workstation by the kitty domain. A six- or seven-inch-tall mother-of-pearl egg mounted on an ornate brass stand stood on a black velvet pad.

"That's lovely," I said.

"Guess what it is."

"A nineteenth-century French objet d'art."

"Right country, right era. It's called a *nécessaire*."

He handed me a loupe and turned the object upside down to show me the maker's mark. The mark ran around the circular stand. It read *Pierre Lunardi, 1850, Paris*. Fred unlatched a clasp hidden at the top of the egg and the two delicate halves opened like petals.

"Voilà!"

Inside, a thick gold central column rose from the stand. It was elegantly fluted and bisected by a gold circular shelf. Suspended through small cutouts were an awl, a pair of scissors, a package of needles, and a long red velvet-covered pincushion.

"What's missing?" he asked.

"Hmm," I said, tapping my chin, playing along. "A thimble?"

Hidden in one of the grooves was another hidden clasp. When Fred unlatched it, a door swung open. Inside was a shelf, and on the shelf sat a gold and brass thimble, adorned with twenty-four small diamonds.

"Oh, it's beautiful!" Light glinted off the jewels. "I'm guessing that it gets its own spot because of the diamonds."

"That's what I think, too. So what do you say? Will Timothy's hair catch fire?"

"Definitely. Timothy wanted sexy . . . you're giving him sexy!" I play-punched his arm. "Well done! And so quickly! Where did you find it?"

"You know Byrd's Antiques, that little shop in Eliot?" he asked, naming a town just over the Maine border.

"Sure. We've never found anything there."

"We have now! I called all the local shops from Maine to Massachusetts, and was about to give up, when I said, you know what, let me try Byrd's one more time. The owner, Pauline, had bought this piece as part of an estate sale.

She had the diamonds appraised and she researched the mark. She asked for five thousand. I offered four, and she took it."

We never wanted to pay more than a third of what an antique would sell for, to account for the costs of research, cleaning, and marketing, to say nothing of overhead.

"Do you really think it will sell for twelve thousand dollars?"

"Oh, yeah. Frisco's sold a Pierre Lunardi *nécessaire* three years ago for thirteen-five, and their thimble didn't have diamonds."

"Excellent!" Anything we realized over the two-thirds markup was profit. "Did you pick it up?"

"She drove it over, I handed her a check, and *boom*! Timothy's hair's a-burnin'!"

I told everyone I'd see them in the morning, put my raincoat back on, and walked through the lingering fog to the studio. It was cold, and I was glad to reach the tent, where portable heaters were doing their thing. I greeted Lenny and walked inside.

A dozen crew were on the set, testing the audio, experimenting with lighting, sweeping up. I found Starr in the back talking with one of the camera operators. She told me Timothy was in his office. I walked through the crew lounge to his private suite, and knocked.

"Enter!" he called.

Timothy's office suite was designed more like a studio apartment than an office. The layout included a separate kitchenette and full bathroom. He could have slept on the pullout couch, but he refused to do so, explaining he hadn't laid his head on a sofa since he'd arrived in New York City from Indiana right out of high school. Back then, he'd been dependent on the goodwill of acquaintances to keep him off the streets, and he said with his quirky grin, he didn't plan on reliving those memories anytime soon. He'd stay at the Austin Arms, Rocky Point's finest hotel, thank you very much.

The sofa was long and upholstered in barn-red corduroy. The entire wall in back of it was covered by wallpaper that had been custom created to Timothy's specifications from a panoramic photograph showcasing New York City's skyline. Another wall featured a mega-size flat-screen TV. His desk was a slab of black quartz dotted with flicks of mica supported by thick steel legs. The arched window, designed to match the one in the TV studio, was, as always, hidden behind thick drapes.

Timothy leapt up from his desk and walked toward me, his hands extended. "How are you? I've been so concerned."

I took his hands and squeezed, then plopped down on the couch. "Thanks, Timothy. I'm fine, but I've got to tell you, you're a sight for sore eyes."

"Why are your eyes sore?"

"I'm exaggerating."

Timothy sat at his desk. "I've told you a million times not to exaggerate."

I smiled. "I really am okay. It's just that I'm on the edge of overwhelmed. Not to worry. I'm not there yet. Actually, I came to give you some good news. We got you a sexy thimble."

"Set me on fire, girl!"

I described the *nécessaire*, highlighting the secret compartments, sharing the delicious surprise I'd felt when Fred opened the column to expose the diamond-embedded thimble, suggesting we replicate the experience on the show.

"I can feel the singe!" Timothy said, patting the back of his head. "That's a very sweet reveal. Our viewers will love it."

"Thanks. Where are you with the script for tomorrow?"

"Finished, I think. I was going to read it over one more time, then send it to you, but what the hey . . . I'll send it to you now." He tapped a few buttons on his laptop. "If need be, we can tweak it in the morning. Starr talked to Oliver and he's good for an eleven o'clock call. Do you have time to read it now? It's only three pages."

I pulled my iPad from my tote bag, downloaded the script, and started reading. It was masterful, an elegant weaving together of the facts about Gloria's appraisal process that had been mangled in the audio mixup and a tribute to her capability and accomplishments. A nod to Ivan was included, too, referencing his role as Gloria's assistant. The script had Oliver and me chatting, as if we were engaged in a real conversation.

"It's wonderful," I said. "A perfect balance of science and emotion."

"I'll tell Nancy," he said, referring to the writer assigned to the show.

"She'll be pleased. I'll email it to Starr so she can get it loaded onto the teleprompters. She'll send it to Oliver, too."

I slid my iPad back into my tote. "I'll call him before I head home to see if he has any questions. He's got to be reeling, between two colleagues' deaths and a last-minute TV slot."

"Anything you can do to stabilize the situation is appreciated."

"With pleasure." I stood. "Speaking of a lack of stability . . . how are you doing, stuck up here for so much longer than expected?"

He waved it away. "We're all good. We'll work tomorrow morning, then vamoose. Your call is at ten. We'll try to get some of the segues finished before we bring in Oliver. Next week, you and I can put our heads together about how to finish up the rest. Maybe I can entice you down to the city for a day or two."

I thought of Ty's potential new job and how convenient it would be to stop in New York en route to DC from New Hampshire.

"No enticement needed," I said, standing. "All you have to do is tell me when to be there."

"Have I ever mentioned how you are the best person in the world to work with?"

I laughed. "All the time. Say it enough, and I'll begin to believe you." I blew him a kiss and left.

The sky remained solidly pewter, but faint hints of silver told me the sun was trying to break through. My phone vibrated as I was latching my seat belt. Ty had landed at Logan after a short delay—yay!—and he expected to be home in a couple of hours, by six thirty. I told him I couldn't wait to see him.

I'd planned to call Oliver from my car, but changed my mind. Since Ty wouldn't be home for a while, I thought I might as well stop by his shop.

Ellis called as I was backing out of my space, and I stopped to take the call.

He said Ivan's office had been cleared by the crime team. "Can you help us out again by going through his files?"

"Now?"

"Tomorrow. Early, if possible."

"Yes . . . how's eight?"

"Done. Officer Meade will meet you there. The same procedures will apply."

I told him that was fine, and set out.

Crenshaw's Rare Books, Prints and Autographs was located in Portsmouth, another coastal community, about ten minutes south of Rocky Point. As I drove, I had the same sensation I'd experienced earlier when I'd struggled to recall something I'd seen or heard that was relevant to the investigation or the Jane Austen letters. I posed questions to myself about motive, means, and opportunity related to the murders and Veronica Sutton's decision to hand deliver the box, then refuse to talk to me, hoping to recapture the elusive memory, but it continued to elude me. All I was left with was a nebulous and annoying irritation, like an invisible rash.

CHAPTER TWENTY-THREE

renshaw's Rare Books, Prints and Autographs occupied a double-wide storefront on Market Street, one of Portsmouth's main drags. I parked a few doors down, and left my coat in the car.

I paused in front of the shop. Two big windows located on either side of the center entrance featured themed displays. The left window was dedicated to highly collectible middle-grade fantasy books, represented by posters and stuffed characters. The right window housed rare maps, signified by an old-style spinning globe. No actual books or maps were included. I was used to viewing the displays, which changed every couple of weeks, with sheer curtains and venetian blinds behind them, designed to block sunlight from entering the store, but they'd been removed. I was astounded that Oliver would risk it, since sunlight was anathema to antiques, especially fragile paper and fugitive inks, those that fade or darken or disappear completely when exposed to light or other elements. I could see into the shop, the bookshelves and map and print display cases arranged on the diagonal, and Rory, sitting behind a Sheraton schoolmaster's desk off to the side. Pumpkins lined the window ledge and diaphanous cobwebs hung from the ceiling.

I pushed through the front door, sleigh bells jangling a friendly welcome. "Hi, Rory!"

"Well, look what the wind blew in. How ya doing?"

"Good, good. How's that knee of yours?"

"Coming along. *Not*. If you're looking for Oliver, he's in the back. If you're looking for me, you found her."

"I'm hoping to talk to Oliver for a minute, but of course I'm glad to see you, too."

"Ha," she said. She used an old Princess phone to call to the back. She told him I was in the shop, listened for a few seconds, then replaced the receiver in the cradle. "He'll be right out." She scanned my face. "You're bringing trouble, I can tell."

"Not at all. Why would you think that?"

"I always expect the other shoe to drop, and it usually does."

"Not today. Not from me. I'll just look around a little while I wait."

I walked toward one of the locked cases, which contained elegant leather bindings, then strolled through the aisles. All the shelves were intact and organized, but everywhere I looked, I saw disarray. Tarps were spread out on the floor. The old venetian blinds, yellowed with age, were stacked beneath the windows, the slats in one heap, the ropes in a coil, the valances in a barely balanced pile. Two five-gallon buckets of paint stood in the corner. I smiled at Rory. "The shop's getting a do-over."

"More like a cover-up. I wanted to freshen the look by adding a woman's touch, but Oliver didn't warm to the idea."

"Call me crazy," Oliver said, entering from the back room, "because I didn't want hubcap light fixtures and leather walls."

I turned toward Rory, awed. "Light fixtures made of hubcaps?"

She flipped open her hands. "And black leather on the walls. Oliver has no taste."

I laughed, then turned back to face Oliver. "What color paint did you choose?"

"Pale gray, but don't tell my mother. She hates neutrals."

"I won't breathe a word." I paused for a moment to shift topics. "Thank you for agreeing to help eulogize Gloria."

Oliver's jocosity receded, replaced by gravity. "It's a terrible loss for us all, and for the industry. Now Ivan, too."

"It's beyond horrible." I paused for another moment. "The reason I stopped by was to make sure you got the script and to see if you have any questions about tomorrow."

"I read it. It's moving and beautifully written. I hate that we're in this situation, but you did Gloria proud. You're doing her proud."

"I couldn't agree more. I'll let the writer know."

"I saw the announcement about the Jane Austen letters. You must be inundated with media attention."

"It's attracted a little notice."

Oliver smiled knowingly. "'A little.' Right. Did you find Veronica Sutton?"

"Yes. I haven't asked her anything, though. It's a ticklish situation. I'm still thinking it through."

His eyebrows lifted, silently asking for more information.

"It seems she doesn't want to talk to me," I said. "I don't know why."

"You should leave her alone," Rory said. "People should be allowed to keep their secrets."

I nodded. "You may be right."

"But you won't," Oliver said. "No antiques appraiser worth her salt would let this sleeping dog lie."

I laughed. "You know me too well. I understand her reticence, and I'll do my best to respect her limits, but I can't just let it go. Even if all she can tell me is the name of the shop where my dad found the portfolio, that would be a huge step forward. With any luck, she has the receipt. We'll see. I don't know how I'll get her to talk, but I'm confident that I'll find a way."

Oliver held up his hands in surrender. "I believe you because I know you."

"Let's hope I can pull it off." I faced Rory. "I hope your knee feels better."

"That makes three of us. When I can't ride my bike, I get crabby."

"You, crabby? I can't believe it."

"Sure you can."

I laughed again, told Oliver I'd see him in the morning, and set the sleigh bells tinkling on my way out.

I got home at twenty after five. I greeted a security guard walking to the front along the side pathway, wishing I didn't feel it was sensible to keep the guards on duty. I'd ask Ty whether he thought it was necessary, but the truth was that I still felt jittery. There was too much I didn't know, too much I didn't understand—and two people had been murdered.

After changing into my bathing suit, I poured myself a martini, started up the hot tub, and texted Ty, letting him know where he could find me.

I leaned back, resting my head on the built-in padded pillow, trying to relax, to will the amorphous memory that haunted me to take shape. I went back to the first moment Gloria and Ivan walked into the studio and replayed my conversations, then switched to Veronica Sutton, and replayed that conversation, too. I tried to tackle the process methodically, but my mind kept jumping from one fragment of a conversation to another, from one specific picture to another. All I got out of the endeavor was frustration.

I sat up and had a sip of my drink, then sat back and closed my eyes. Instead of replaying conversations, I tried instead to identify a pattern among the many anomalies and oddities that seemed to be in play. Specific moments came to me like still shots in a slide show.

Veronica's sudden appearance and abrupt disappearance.

Dutch prowling around Prescott's.

Rory berating Ivan in the TV studio.

Gloria's corpse.

Gloria's car at the church. Her purse. A gun. Her portfolio.

I sat up again, and opened my eyes, stunned.

The memories came flooding back. I'd watched when Ellis opened Gloria's portfolio. I'd seen him lift the flaps. Other than a few business cards and a pad of paper, the portfolio was empty. Why? Where were her notes for the show? Why would someone take them? The notes didn't contain anything unexpected, groundbreaking, or scandalous.

I didn't have the answer, but at least I had the question. I felt inordinately relieved. It was as if I'd finally found a way to scratch an itch I hadn't been able to reach. I leaned back again and closed my eyes, relishing the feeling of quiet satisfaction.

"Hey, gorgeous."

I sat up. "Ty!" I opened my arms.

He did the same and blew kisses. "I want to rinse off the travel dust. I'll be right back."

"Hurry! I need a kiss."

Twenty minutes later, he placed his can of Smuttynose pale ale on his side table, and lowered himself into the water.

"Heaven," he said. "A beer. A hot tub. The most beautiful woman in the world demanding a kiss. Life doesn't get any better than this."

He swam to my side of the spa, one stroke, and enveloped me in his arms. He kissed me, and I kissed him back.

"I love you," he whispered.

I traced the line of his jaw with my index finger. "I love you, too."

"We have a problem, though."

"What's that?"

He pointed to his beer. "My beer . . . it's so far away."

"I'm confident you'll come up with a viable solution."

He drifted back to the other side of the spa and drank. He rested his legs on my lap.

I stroked his calf. "How did it go?"

"I'll tell you, but first, how are you doing after yesterday's attack?"

"Physically, I'm fine. Emotionally, not so much. Two people I was working with have been killed, and the weight of that horrendous loss is crushing." I paused for a moment. "And I'm scared, without knowing why. Do you think I'm being stupid to keep the guards patrolling?"

"You're asking the wrong question. Stupid doesn't come into the equation. You're among the smartest people I know, so nothing you do or don't do comes from being stupid." He lowered his legs, and lifted mine onto his lap. "You're asking me if you have any rational reason to be scared."

"Yes."

"I don't know. And it doesn't matter. You feel as you feel, and what you feel is frightened. So we keep the guards on duty."

"Have I ever told you that you're wonderful?"

"All because I said it was okay to feel frightened?"

"Yes."

"You're welcome."

I raised my glass. "I have a toast."

He raised his beer can.

"To you."

"To us."

"To us."

We clinked, plastic tapping aluminum.

I took another sip. "Tell me about DC."

"My choice is binary. I take the promotion and we move, or I don't take the promotion and my current job is mine for as long as I want it, assuming I don't screw up."

"Did you make a decision?"

"Yes. I don't want to move to DC for that job. Except it's not that simple. It's career suicide to pass up a promotion."

"What happened when you put out feelers at FEMA? What did Sheila say?"

"The agency is considering a major reorg for next year, so no division heads or deputies will be hired until and unless."

"Bummer."

Ty tipped his head back to drain the last of his beer. "That's one way of putting it."

"Now what?"

"I guess I should think about going corporate side. CSO, that sort of thing."

"Chief security officer. Would you like that job?"

"I doubt it. By definition, positions like that are strategic in nature, which is interesting, but far removed from operations, which is my first love."

"This is a real dilemma," I said. "You're so good at all things training that you qualify for a job you don't want. If you were CSO of a corporation, you wouldn't be able to use the capabilities that led to your getting the job."

"Rock and a hard place."

"I'm sorry," I said.

"Me, too."

"There's nothing you can do to get your boss to agree to let you stay here?"

"No."

"And you really don't want to move?"

"I really don't."

"You should stay with operations, do more research, analyze it, and write a book."

"On what?"

"*Emergency Management Training Strategies that Save Lives.* That's not a good title, but that's what you should write about."

"I don't think that's a bad title," he said. "That's an interesting idea."

"Speaking of interesting ideas, what does a girl have to do around here to get some dinner?"

"Ask."

I laughed. "Okay . . . I'm asking." I stood up. A gust of wind hit me, and I shivered. "Brrr. See you inside!" I got myself wrapped in my robe, scooped up my flip-flops, and ran for the door.

As I showered, I reflected on Ty's quandary. I hoped he would write that book, or, more specifically, a book proposal, since I knew that was how most nonfiction was sold. The book would have real and meaningful value, helping the people responsible for emergency management make smart, evidence-based decisions. Also, it would position him as an expert, opening doors he didn't know existed. That logic was the impetus behind my offering to write a monthly column for *Antiques Insight* magazine, and it had worked. I was frequently the go-to expert national news outfits called on when they needed a quote about an antique for publication. It would work for Ty, too. A marketing strategy began to evolve in my mind. He should teach a college course, so when he was ready to sell the book, he'd have the dual imprimatur, in-the-field expert and professor. Hitchens University offered a well-respected degree in criminology through its sociology department. Ty had participated in a panel discussion on "Criminology in the Real World: Field-based Training Tactics." The chair, Dr. Patrick Healy, had invited Ty, and after the panel, he'd written him a lovely thank-you note. I wondered if they might need an adjunct professor. I suspected they'd already finalized their spring course schedule, but maybe they hadn't assigned all the instructors. Since I was going to Hitchens in the morning anyway, it wouldn't do a bit of harm to chat with the department admin and ask how the hiring process worked.

After eating Ty's perfectly grilled chicken, I spoke to Gretchen, who told me the phone was ringing off the hook and the email in-box was nearly full with press inquiries about the Jane Austen letters. Zoë called to check on me, too. With Ty home, my shadowy fear had waned, but when Russ called to report that everything was quiet, both at Prescott's and the Gingerbread House, I told him to continue the patrols anyway.

I believed that sometimes things really do go bump in the night and there really are monsters under the bed.

CHAPTER TWENTY-FOUR

F riday morning, I arrived at Hitchens early. I walked the quiet halls and arrived at Ivan's office at seven fifty. Officer Meade was already there, with the video camera angled toward the file cabinets.

The office looked about the same.

"Has Jonathan been relocated?" I asked.

"Yes, but not the contents of his desk. That's part of the crime scene."

Ivan's desk was a mess. A two-foot mountain of paper sat on the right side. Single sheets covered the rest, lying this way and that in a disorganized heap, along with a scattering of loose pens, paper clips, pads of sticky notes, and rubber bands.

"Before we start," I said, "I have a question. May I go through the papers on Ivan's desk?"

"I'll check." She sent a text and received a reply within seconds. "Yes, with the camera on and wearing gloves."

"Of course."

She moved the tripod so the video camera faced Ivan's desk. Officer Meade stood next to me, facing the camera. She used the remote to start recording, introduced herself and me, stated the date and time, explained why I was there, replicating Ellis's wording, and stated that she would be observing in person. She added that I would start with the desk, then move to the file cabinets, and that the camera would remain on through the entire process. She stepped aside, and I got to work.

I attacked the stack first. The top papers related to Lord Byron's letters to Alexander Scott. The middle section included notes for a compendium of the various ways publishers signify a book is a true first edition. I could have happily read the entire dossier; instead, I contented myself with going through each page to ensure no errant material had found its way in. None had. The bottom papers reviewed methodologies for authentication of holographic wills. I didn't find any unrelated information in the single sheets, either. They included a printout of Hitchens's academic calendar, his receipt for renting unit number 287 in the men's locker room in the Pease Building, his course schedule, and various notes from his students.

I read the specifics to the camera, then spoke to Officer Meade. "Someone should check his locker."

She thanked me and sent a text.

I moved to the file cabinets, starting on the right, the unit closest to the wall. The top drawer contained men's underwear and socks. The second, shirts. The third, jeans and slacks. The bottom drawer held shoes. After Heather and Ivan broke up, he must have decided to move into his office.

Ivan's second file cabinet had been scantily used. I counted eight folders, seemingly randomly placed. They weren't filed alphabetically, or by date. Within the folders, a few pages were filed backward and upside down, as if they'd been shoved inside in a rush. I itched to neaten things up, but resisted.

"Nothing stands out as a problem," I said.

Officer Meade switched off the camera, but before she spoke, Ellis walked in.

"Good," he said. "I thought I might have missed you."

"I just finished." I told Ellis about finding Ivan's clothes. "I think he was planning to live here."

"It looks that way. He had a sleeping bag rolled up in a suitcase."

"Which was under his desk."

"Right."

"He probably planned to shower at Pease, which is why he joined the gym."

"We'll know soon enough. I'm getting a search warrant for the locker. Thanks for flagging it. Obviously, we missed it during our review."

"That would explain . . ." I turned to face the window.

After a minute, Ellis called my name and I swiveled back to face him. "Sorry. I was thinking about something."

"You said that would explain—and then stopped."

"Right . . ." I waved at the desk and file cabinets. "This mess got me thinking.

I realized last night that Gloria's portfolio, the one you found in her car, was empty, yet Gloria always kept her notes handy. Just now I realized that the notes related to Gloria's Thomas Jefferson authentication are missing, too. The only one of Gloria's folders to *not* include her handwritten notes was the one referencing the Thomas Jefferson case. At the time, I assumed that once an article was published, she didn't keep her notes, but that's not true. Lots of folders contained articles and essays from various magazines and journals, and those notes are intact."

"You're saying someone stole them?" he asked.

"Yes, but why? Presumably the salient information in her notes made it into the article. Why steal them now? And there was nothing scandalous or even surprising about her Beatrix Potter notes. In both cases, the thief must have thought they related to something else. Or there's more to the story than we're aware of."

"You're conflating these two sets of missing notes into one incident."

"Yes, but I don't know how they connect or why." I surveyed the disarray. "If it had been Ivan whose notes were missing, well, we wouldn't think anything about it because of the mess, but that logic doesn't apply to Gloria. She was more than organized; she was painstaking. Possibly it's a case of cause and effect. Someone stole Gloria's notes from her file, but didn't find what he was looking for, so he killed her, certain he'd find them in her portfolio." Our eyes met. "It can't be a coincidence. Something about some notes led to murder. Maybe the police officers who searched her apartment didn't realize the significance of the documents . . . you said there were only a few bills. Are you sure the searchers didn't miss something, like the Pease locker just now?"

"There were no papers there. Nothing. None. No in-wall safe or hidden compartment anywhere. We looked. According to colleagues, Gloria was not one to take her work home. She came to campus when she wanted to work. We searched her office and her car, as you know, plus her books, her apartment, and her home and work mailboxes, and we came up empty. When I called over to Pease to confirm Ivan's locker for the search warrant, I asked whether she had one. She didn't. We also called every gym and spa in town. Nothing. Where else should I look?"

"How about Dutch? If she didn't take work home, she probably wouldn't have taken it to his place, but if she did, he'd never mention it. He'd keep it."

"Why?"

"Because he's beguiled. If she touched it, he'd want to hold it close."

"Where else?" he asked.

"Did you find Gloria's mother?"

"Not yet. Other thoughts?"

"No."

Officer Meade's phone vibrated and we watched as she read something. "The warrant is on the way," she said. "Griff will meet you at the locker room."

"So quick!" I said.

"When there's a possibility of a serial killer on the loose, police and judges move fast."

"A serial killer," I said.

"A *possible* serial killer," he corrected. "If Griff is on his way, I'd better get over there."

I glanced at my watch. It was nine twenty. "I have to go, too." I stripped off my plastic gloves.

Ellis thanked me, adding, "I'll call Larkin while I wait for Griff. I remember President Jefferson . . . who was the other person you named?"

"Beatrix Potter, but I wouldn't name either of them. I'd keep it vague: 'We don't have all of Gloria's notes and we'd like to stop by to inspect any you have,' that sort of thing."

Ellis cocked his head. "You're picking up on my techniques."

"You excel at seeming nonthreatening." I raised my chin and lowered my voice to mimic Ellis's baritone. "It's all part of the routine, sir, a box I need to check."

He laughed and thanked me again. I said my goodbyes, and left.

I stopped by the sociology office on my way out, but it was closed, and not scheduled to open until ten. I was sorry not to be able to talk to the admin about hiring, but I found what I was looking for regarding scheduling and degree requirements in a wall-mounted rack next to the door. I took one of everything.

I got to my company at twenty to ten, and waved to Lenny and the guards.

One of our facilities team was blowing sodden leaves off the asphalt into the woods, and the noise was deafening. The trees weren't bare, but they'd lost a fair number of their leaves in yesterday's downpour. I understood that wet leaves were a hazard, but I hated the noise.

I went into the front office to say hello, then crossed the parking lot to the tent, taking the outside route. It was a beautiful morning, crisp and sunny.

A pickup truck pulled into the lot, parking near the front, and I stopped to see if I knew the driver. I was always glad for the opportunity to greet a customer. Dutch Larkin stepped out and stood by his vehicle.

We walked toward each other and met in the middle of the lot.

"Do you have a minute to talk?" Dutch asked, speaking loudly and leaning in close to be heard over the lawn blower.

"Yes, but not much more."

Something in back of me caught his eye, and I glanced over my shoulder. Lenny was staring at us. One of the guards came out from behind the building and paused to stare, too. I turned back to face Dutch, and waited for him to speak.

He lowered his eyes to my face. "I'm not even sure why I'm here, except that you came to see me to ask about Gloria. I'm doing the same. You were one of the last people to see her, and I was thinking, *hoping*, you would tell me what she talked about . . . how she looked . . . anything." He drew in a deep breath. "I know how I must sound. Grief isn't for the weak. I'm struggling, and I don't mind admitting it."

Compassion washed over me. "I'm so sorry. I only met Gloria that one time. I liked her very much. I really felt a connection. Mostly we talked about our work. I spoke a little about a charity I'm involved with." I raised my shoulders an inch, then allowed them to drop. "I wish I could tell you more."

"What was she working on?"

"For the show, an appraisal of *The Tale of Peter Rabbit*. She mentioned a presidential letter she'd just bought."

"Garfield."

"That's right."

"She said she couldn't wait to get it under a microscope," Dutch said. "She paid fifty-seven hundred dollars for it."

I could imagine people's astonishment on hearing the number, but it's not how much you charge, it's how much you make. Civilians, when they hear us dealers bandy about numbers like $5,700, assume we're all rolling in it. For all I knew, Oliver paid $5,000.

"That's a big number," I said.

"Her research would benefit, so she bought it."

"She was a professional through and through," I said. "I was wondering . . . do you know where Gloria's mother lives?"

"Sure. In a cottage on the beach with a full-time caregiver."

"Who Gloria paid in cash."

"Every month."

I used the flat of my hand to shield my eyes from the sun's glare. "What's the caregiver's name?"

"Melissa Rogers. Why?"

"Some documents are missing. I know the police were wondering whether Gloria left them at your place, and it occurred to me just now that she might have left them at her mom's."

"She wouldn't. Her mother has Alzheimer's, and Gloria was having a hard time seeing her like that, when she didn't even recognize her. She only went to visit once a week or so, and she never stayed long."

"That's so sad," I said. "Did she ever leave work stuff at your place?"

"No." Dutch's eyes welled up and he turned his head toward the woods. "The only thing of hers I have is her hairbrush."

"A hairbrush," I said, deeply touched. "I wish I could tell you more, Dutch, but I can't. I'm really sorry for your loss."

He didn't comment or react in any way, and after a few seconds, I turned and walked to the tent.

Lenny stood inside the tent, chatting with one of the caterer's team. As I reached the entry, I thought I saw something moving in Greely Woods, and paused to look. Whatever it was disappeared. A deer, probably.

I stepped into the studio and shut the soundproofed door. The silence fell swiftly, as if I'd stepped into an ancient tomb. The quiet was welcome, but after a moment, my ears adjusted to the change, and I realized the studio wasn't quiet at all. Murmurs and subdued laughter mixed with the steady soft whirr of the HVAC system, everything buffered by acoustic material and professional restraint.

I greeted the team. Jackie had my outfit ready, and once I'd changed, Marie set to work on my hair. She chatted about a movie she was eager to see. After she was done, Timothy came up to talk and Marie started applying foundation with a sponge.

"All your segues have been loaded into the teleprompter," Timothy said, "so we'll get started with those. When Oliver gets here, we'll switch to your conversation about Gloria, nail that down, then pick back up with your solo work. I'd love to get this segment in the can."

"What about the thimbles?"

"The beauty shots on the sexy thimble are done—and it is hair-on-fire sexy! Once you and Fred prepare the script we'll finish that segment, too, maybe back here, maybe in New York."

"That's terrific. We're making progress."

"'Progress' is a relative term. This show is an insatiable beast, never satisfied, never tamed."

"You want more."

"The show demands more, and I live to serve the show."

I wrinkled my nose as Marie wielded her powder puff. "Like the Jane Austen letters."

"Like those, yes."

"I'm working on it."

"Good." He squeezed my hand. "We'll go in ten."

When Marie finished, I dragged the tall director's chair with my name on it to the wall next to the window, a seat with a view. The foliage was putting on quite a show, pink and orange leaves shimmying in the gentle breeze. I pulled my earbuds from my tote bag and hoisted myself up into the chair. I was soon immersed in the stirring sounds of spring from Vivaldi's *Four Seasons*. I checked my phone for messages and found a dozen that needed attention, but nothing that was urgent.

A glint of silver startled me. I knew that glint.

The first bullet struck the glass about four feet up from the floor with a sharp clap, then slammed into the wall, missing my torso by an inch. The bullet left a hole in the glass the size of a man's fist. Spidery cracks spread like a deadly web.

I hurdled down from the chair, dropping to the ground.

The second bullet enlarged the hole.

Screams, muted because of my earbuds, came from all directions, indistinguishable voices screeching indecipherable pleas and admonitions.

"Gun!" I shouted. "Stay back!"

I rooted through my tote bag for my pistol, disengaged the safety, then stayed low to the ground and elbowed my way to the side wall to get myself out of the line of fire.

I stood, ignoring the strident hollering behind me.

Given the quantity of trees, the impenetrable brush, and the knots of hanging vines, I couldn't see the shooter, but I could follow his progress by watching the sunlight winking off the silver barrel. A gleam showed him raising his weapon.

I eased myself forward an inch, then two. I could take a shot, but it would be tough, angled through the hole in the glass. Given the refracted light, I couldn't tell where the shooter was standing, to the left or right of his weapon. Instead of aiming at a body I couldn't see, I aimed at the weapon itself, using both sights, exactly the way my dad had taught me, exactly the way I'd practiced ever since. I fired. The gun skittered out of the attacker's hand, jetting up, then spiraling to the ground. I kept my eyes on the silver barrel, barely visible through the low-growing shrubs and ferns. A nearly imperceptible hand scooped up the weapon, and in the bat of an eye, the silver shimmer was gone. Since I had no way of knowing if the shooter was regrouping or escaping, I stayed frozen in place, my eyes fixed on the jumbled growth. Nothing moved. After a minute, I took one last, slow look, then stepped back and leaned against the wall. It was over—for now. After another minute, I sank to the floor, aghast, the sanctity of the studio shattered. My favorite piece of classical music would be forever linked to this experience. I pulled out my earbuds and tossed them aside. Hysterical booming voices besieged me.

Muscle memory took over, and I reengaged the safety catch, but then a wave of nausea washed over me, and I lay down.

I couldn't fathom what had just happened. Someone had shot at me. Someone had tried to kill me.

And for the first time in my life, I had shot at a person.

Timothy flung himself over me, arms spread protectively. He turned his head and yelled to close the blackout curtain, and within an instant, night descended throughout the soundstage. I blinked, my eyes adapting to the diffused inside lighting. Timothy spun off me and called to Starr to dial 9-1-1, to get Lenny, and to alert the outside guards.

The thought of how ridiculous I must look struck me, and I began to laugh. "Look at me."

Timothy stared at me, sprawled on the floor, gun in hand, and he guffawed. I sat up, still laughing, gun still in hand.

"Thank you," I said, after our hysterics subsided. "You almost saved my life."

He burst out laughing again.

"Well, it's true," I said between gales. "Not everyone is an almost-lifesaver."

"Stop," he managed. "Don't set me off again."

Lenny charged in, heard the ten-second version from Starr, and tore out again.

Soon, sirens blared.

Timothy clambered up and helped me to my feet.

"Should you put that thing away?" he asked, wiggling his fingers at the Browning, as if he hoped it would flutter out of sight.

I suspected the polite thing to do was to slip my handgun into my tote bag so people wouldn't feel frightened, but I wasn't willing to put it away. I wanted it in my hand. "The safety's on. It's pointing down. It's fine."

Starr, Marie, Jackie, Greg, and a bunch of other crew huddled around us, asking if I was all right, what happened, who did it, did I shoot someone, had someone really shot at me? I stood still, pummeled by their questions, not saying a word. I suppose I was in shock.

Timothy hushed the crew.

"Oh, Josie," he said, once he'd chased them away.

The sirens grew louder.

"Are you okay?" he whispered.

I didn't know how to answer. I hadn't been shot. The tempered glass hadn't shattered, covering me with deadly shards. But how could I say I was fine, just fine, when someone had tried to kill me, when someone wanted me dead?

CHAPTER TWENTY-FIVE

I stood alone near the director's chair, doing nothing.

Ellis arrived about ten minutes later. He said something to Timothy, then spoke to Starr, then walked in my direction. Everyone's eyes followed his progress as he threaded his way through the clusters of crew members.

"How are you?" Ellis asked in a near whisper when he reached me.

"Fine."

He snapped on plastic gloves. "I need to collect your weapon."

I hid it behind my knee. "Why?"

"Pro forma in any shooting. You'll get it back."

"I'm not ready to turn it in."

"You don't really have a choice."

I exhaled loudly, then handed it over, knowing it was futile to argue the point. "This is the first time I've ever shot at a living thing."

He removed the clip and the round in the chamber, dropping each into its own evidence bag, then lowered the gun into a separate bag.

"Shooting at a person is different than shooting at a target," he said.

"That's the weird part. It didn't feel different, maybe because I couldn't see the person. I used the sights just like I've practiced all these years, lining up the only thing I could see clearly, the weapon. I didn't think about the humanity of the situation at all. Obviously, my training kicked in. My universe narrowed to the singular task of stopping him. My goal was to hit the target, period, and the target I chose was the weapon. I did a good job. I shot the gun out of his hand. When you find it, I bet it's dented all to heck."

"We're searching now."

"You won't find it around here. I saw the gun fly through the air and land on the ground. I know because the barrel is silver and when the sun hit it, there was a strong glare. Seconds later, the light disappeared. Since he didn't shoot again, he must have scooped it up and hot-tailed it out of the woods."

"Maybe he holstered it or tossed it under some leaves."

"And then what? He sauntered off to the parking lot and waved goodbye to the guard as he drove out of the lot? No, he ran deeper into Greely Woods heading to Highbridge, the development on the other side of the forest. It's not that far away. Any other plan, like running through Carter's Forest, would bring him into view of the guards—or it might."

"You're right. I just met with one of your security guys. He brought up a video feed showing me this morning's images from all your cameras. We fast-forwarded through the output. No one snuck into Greely Woods from your parking lot or from Carter's Forest, and no one left that way, which limits the search."

"You should tell your team to look for broken twigs and such because he didn't have time to pick his way through."

"Trackers have already been deployed." Ellis shifted position. "Can you describe anything else about the weapon? Barrel length, sights, anything?"

"No, all I saw was the silver of the barrel."

"How about you?" he asked. "Are your ears ringing?"

"No. I had my earbuds in. Noise canceling. I got lucky."

"Emotionally?"

I wasn't in the mood for banalities. "How should I feel?" I asked, and then, when I heard how snippy it sounded, I added, "Sorry. I'm not myself."

"I'll ask again . . . how are you feeling?"

"Upset, scared, appalled . . . mostly, though, angry. I'm more than angry. I'm out-of-my-mind furious." I aimed my index finger at the blackout curtain. "How dare someone shoot at me?"

Ellis scanned the studio. People had dispersed, forming smaller groups. "I don't want you outside, even with a guard, until we know what's what. How about going to your office? I can use my tablet to record our interview."

"Sure . . . if you want, I can set up a camera."

He decided to do both.

"We can use the inside door," I said, pointing at it, "but I want to tell Timothy what's happening."

"And I need to make a call. Let's meet at the inside door in five minutes."

Timothy saw me walking toward him and hurried to meet me.

I held up a hand. "Don't ask if I'm fine. I'm upset and angry, but physically, I'm okay. I need to give the police a statement."

"We all do."

"Another day lost," I commiserated.

"As if that matters." Timothy paused, then said, "Oliver just arrived."

Oliver stood next to Starr, his eyes round with alarm. He met my gaze and raised his hands chest high, pressing his palms together, as if in prayer. I nodded to acknowledge his good wishes, then turned back to Timothy.

Timothy lowered his voice. "I think we have to conclude that Oliver is a bad luck charm."

"That's funny." I kept my next thought to myself: *I hope that's all he is.*

Ty appeared in the doorway with Lenny. Lenny pointed in my direction. Ty thanked him and walked quickly toward me. I ran to meet him.

He enveloped me in a bear hug, whispering, "Tell me you're okay."

"I'm okay."

He exhaled, and tightened his grip. "I was as scared as I've ever been. Wes's report only said there was a shooting at Prescott's."

I nestled my head in the crook of his shoulder. I kept my arms around his chest and leaned back. I went up on tiptoe and kissed him, breathing in his scent, part honey-sweet, part minty pine, the aroma of eucalyptus from his shaving cream lingering on his skin. After a moment, I leaned back again. His eyes fixed on mine, and we both smiled.

"Wes interrupted the regular programming with what he labeled breaking news," I said.

"Just the bare fact of the shooting," Ty said. "Even Wes didn't know much."

"Fancy that." I touched his cheek. "Ellis says I shouldn't go outside until we know what's going on. He's going to take my statement upstairs."

Ty used one finger to brush an uncooperative strand of hair off my forehead. "I agree. Unless . . . Do you know who shot at you?"

"No."

"The way you said that makes me think you might have an idea."

"You're so good at reading me." I paused, trying to think how to express such a complex and incomplete thought. "Not who, but I'm making progress on the why. It's related to Gloria's appraisals and her missing notes." I paused again. "My ideas are half-developed and quarter-baked."

"Do you want me to stay while you talk to Ellis?"

"There's no need."

"True, but maybe there's a want."

"There's no want, either, but thank you. There is something you can do for me, though. Will you talk to Russ? I'm sure he's tripping over himself to explain why his guards missed a sniper in Greely Woods."

"Sure."

"You look like you're going to enjoy that discussion."

"He's not."

I laughed, and it felt good to know that in the midst of such fear-laden unease, I could.

"I don't know that it's fair to expect them to catch a sniper," I said. "They're more a burglary prevention sort of company."

"They knew you were concerned about a strange man hanging around the property and disappearing into the woods. If they didn't feel equipped to handle it, they shouldn't have taken the job." Ty kissed me again. "What time should I come back to get you? We can leave your car here overnight."

"Five."

Ellis joined us and the two men shook hands. Ellis and Ty were friends, and we were couple friends, too. None of that mattered, not now.

"I'll see you at five," I said, and went up on tiptoe to kiss him again. "I love you."

"I love you, too."

He told me to wait for him to come into the office to get me, and I agreed. Neither one of us mentioned why he didn't want me to come out on my own even for a minute, even with police on the scene and guards on duty, but it was in both our minds.

Ellis accompanied me to the front office so I could reassure my staff that I was all right.

As we walked, he said, "I'm thinking you ought to shut down for a few days. Give us some time to get a handle on what's going on."

I bristled. "No."

He frowned at me. "Why not?"

"If Prescott's closes, if we suspend filming, the shooter wins. I'll arrange for whatever security you think appropriate—but my company needs to stay open and the show must go on."

"Protecting property and people from unknown threats is nearly impossible."

"Are you saying I should cower in my home? That the TV crew should hunker down in their hotels? No way."

"I'd probably feel the same way, but you need to take precautions, Josie. Don't be cavalier about this danger. Keep the security patrols in place. Follow security protocols. Don't ditch your police protection. Agreed?"

"I promise."

When we reached the front, I found everyone milling around.

"Scary times," I said, "but we'll make our way through it, same as we always do, one step at a time. I'm fine. No one was hurt. The press is going to be all over this, and who can blame them? Regardless, remember the rules . . . don't talk to any reporter about Prescott business or me. Answer any police questions honestly. Don't speculate. Don't gossip. The Sterling Security patrols will continue for as long as we need them to. Yes, they missed this shooter, but I'm confident they won't miss anything again." I asked Eric to oversee getting the window replaced, this time with bulletproof glass, and since it had to be custom-ordered, to have the bullet-riddled window boarded up. He told me he would take care of it.

Fred stood. "May I ask something?"

"Of course."

"Was this an anti-Prescott's attack? Or was it specific to you? I guess what I'm asking is . . . are we in danger?"

Everyone leaned in a little closer. Fred was the one who asked, but they all wanted to know.

I turned to Ellis. "Will you address that issue, Chief Hunter?"

Ellis nodded at Fred, then addressed the group. "There's no reason to think any of you are in danger. The shooter was aiming at Josie. Our investigation is proceeding on the assumption that this shooting is related to the murders of Gloria Moreau and Ivan Filbert. Do any of you have any knowledge that supports or contradicts that idea?"

Everyone murmured no or shook their heads.

He took a card case from an inside jacket pocket and handed cards around. "In case you know something you don't want to say in public, you can contact me confidentially. I want to hear from you."

"And I'm glad to ask Russ to set up individual security for anyone who wants it," I said, "no questions asked. Let Gretchen know."

Ellis and I sat in the same places as last time, me on the wing chair, him on the love seat. I set up my company's video camera tripod. Ellis perched his phone against a toss pillow.

"Can I get you a coffee or anything?" I asked. Hank sprang into my lap, a welcome interruption. "Cara brought in some gingersnaps." Hank curled up and I petted him.

"No, thanks. How about you? Do you want anything?"

"Just water." I touched the bottle sitting on the small side table next to me. "Which I always have nearby."

Ellis stated the de rigueur facts, the date and time, the people present, the location, the reason for the interview, then said, "Let's start at the beginning. What time did you get to the studio?"

I described my whereabouts from my arrival at Prescott's to the shooting.

"Any idea about who did it?" he asked.

"Not exactly." I scratched under Hank's chin and he began purring, a deep, loud, guttural sound of contentment. "It all comes down to Gloria. She did something that set in motion the chain of events that led to her murder. Ivan either knew something or threatened something, so he had to be killed, too." I smiled as best I could. "Me, too, I guess, although I don't have a clue what it could be."

"Speculate for me. I know you told your staff not to, but I'm asking for your help. You said that it all starts with Gloria. Come up with some scenarios that might lead to her murder."

"I can think of three possible suspects, but I hate to brandish that word around."

"It's understood that this is all conjecture. You're thinking aloud to help me."

"You first. You think aloud."

Ellis shifted position, resting his right calf on his left thigh. "I told your staff that we're operating on the assumption that the two murders are connected, and that today's attempted murder is related, too. I'll ask you the same question I asked downstairs: Do you know anything that supports or contradicts that assumption?"

"No."

"So the question is who wanted Gloria dead, just like you said. Once we know that, we can follow the bread crumbs." He flipped his palms. "We can't get anywhere with means. No one we've looked at has an airtight alibi for the relevant times. That leaves us with motive, which is where I could use your help. Talk to me about the motives of the three people we won't label as suspects."

"Thank you for understanding my reticence. Okay, then. . . . One: Dutch Larkin, because he was infatuated with Gloria, and despite what he says to the contrary, she broke it off. Two: Oliver Crenshaw, because his professional reputation was at risk. Three: Oliver's mother, Rory. She's more than a mama bear—she's a mama grizzly bear. She would devour anyone she saw as a threat to Oliver."

"She limps . . . when Ivan's killer escaped, did you hear an uneven gait?"

"No, but I'm not sure I would have. I was focused on staying alive, and it was all over in a matter of seconds. And don't say she's old. If she's sixty, I'd be amazed, and she's tough as iron. She's an athlete. I said before the killer had to be strong, and I think Rory is plenty strong enough, limp or no limp."

Ellis took a notebook from his pocket, flipped to a clean page, and made a note. "Let's take them one at a time. Start with Dutch."

"I spoke to him just before I came into the studio. He asked me about Gloria." I recounted our conversation, his sadness. "It was hard to listen to." Hank grumbled and I petted him under his chin again. I raised my eyes to Ellis's face. "The bottom line is that if Gloria had left him, he might have tumbled into the heartbreak abyss—you know, you're with me or you're with no one. A crime of passion."

"Why would Dutch kill Ivan?"

"Maybe Ivan lied when he said he didn't hear any words on that ugly phone call he witnessed. Maybe he heard Dutch threaten Gloria, and after Gloria was killed, he offered to forget it for a price. Dutch didn't like the offer, and murdered him."

"And why did he try to kill you?"

"There could be any number of reasons I haven't thought of, but here's one idea that is certainly possible, and it applies to all three of them. What if Ivan's killer, whoever it is, thought I saw them in the office immediately after Ivan's murder? It was all over the news that I hit my head, which the killer might have thought accounted for my memory loss. If he did a two-minute internet search, he'd learn that in cases of traumatic amnesia, memories usually come back, but no one can predict how quickly. Think about that . . . the murderer must be on tenterhooks waiting for the police to come calling. Day after day, maybe hour after hour, the killer's fear grows, anxiety mushrooming into terror, until he's convinced himself that his only hope of avoiding spending the rest of his life in prison is to tie up any loose ends—myself included."

"Why would the attacker shoot at you through the window? Why not simply shoot you out in the open?"

"Here or at my house, security cameras and guards. He could have killed me, but no way could he escape."

"And for everywhere else," Ellis said, "like at the grocery store or gas station, not only are there likely to be security cameras, there are potential witnesses."

Hank licked my hand, then jumped down. "Thank you, Hank." I drank some water. "Another possibility, this one is specific to Dutch, relates to our last conversation. He was patently disappointed that I couldn't tell him more about Gloria. Maybe what I perceived as disappointment was something stronger, something like despair. If he didn't believe me—if he thought I was holding out on him because I was busy or uncaring and simply blowing him off—who knows how he might have reacted?" I raised my shoulders, then let them drop. "On the one hand, that motive seems far-fetched. On the other hand, it might have been the straw that broke the camel's back. There's no question in my mind that Dutch is genuinely suffering." I drank some more water. "Oliver is easier—and harder. It's easier to come up with a motive, but harder to believe he could be a killer. I barely know the other people involved, but Oliver I know well. I like him. He's smart and competent, a valued colleague."

"Duly noted," Ellis said. "And his motive?"

"For Gloria, jealousy, as previously explained. For Ivan, the same blackmail scheme might apply. As for why Oliver might want to kill me, beyond that he might fear I saw him in Ivan's office, maybe he thinks I know what Gloria was baiting him about—I don't, but he might have worried that I'd deciphered her taunts. If they were sufficiently veiled, they'd go over my head, but not his. That alone might have put him in a panic. Remember that someone stole the notes out of Gloria's portfolio; ergo, we can conclude the killer knew Gloria had notes he wanted, and he was determined to get his hands on them."

"But he didn't know they wouldn't be in the portfolio."

"Maybe that was another taunt—I'll bring the notes with me so you can refresh your memory about what you did."

Ellis crossed his ankles. "That's harsh."

"And dangerous. You know what they say about cornered rats. It's also possible that the notes the killer were after don't implicate anyone, but present an opportunity, a new research technique Gloria was about to announce to the world." I sipped some more water. "Ivan was in the process of validating a new document authentication metric, what he called writing hesitations. He explained they were a subtle indicator of individuality. I suppose it's possible Gloria planned to take credit for his new protocol, just like she allegedly took credit for his work on two articles." I paused for a moment, gathering my thoughts. "Oliver and Rory acted as if they were certain that Ivan did all the heavy lifting, that Gloria was using him. It's easy to dismiss their grumbles as sour grapes, except that Heather said the same thing. Maybe it was true. Regardless, it's possible that Oliver decided it was his turn to shine, so he needed to get his hands on those notes. That motive could apply to either Oliver or Rory, at his behest or on his behalf."

Ellis's eyes narrowed. "You're saying that if Oliver got hold of the notes, he could submit Gloria's or Ivan's work as his own?"

"It's feasible. The only people who'd know the truth were Gloria and Ivan."

"So they had to die. And if Oliver found out that you went through Gloria's and Ivan's files, he'd assume you found evidence of whatever he was after or located, and that you'd recognize it when he published it. Is this possible?"

"Theoretically. Except—" I broke off, a memory setting off sparks in my brain. I lowered my gaze to the carpet, trying to recall more details, then looked up. "I didn't find any notes about writing hesitations on Ivan's desk or in his files."

Ellis nodded slowly. "More missing notes. It can't be a coincidence. Let me check with my tech team." He texted someone.

While we waited for a reply, I closed my eyes and rested my head against the chair's wing. I thought about Ivan, so earnest, so hardworking. I hoped his ideas wouldn't die with him.

"Ivan had a folder on his Hitchens's laptop labeled 'Writing Hesitations,'" Ellis said, reading from his phone. "It was backed up to the cloud."

I opened my eyes. "Did he have another computer? A personal one?"

"No, Heather Adler said he did everything on his school laptop. The information includes examples he'd analyzed and bulleted notes, but no narrative text." He looked up. "That sounds like he was at the beginning of the process."

"Which is consistent with what Ivan told me—Gloria didn't think he had enough examples."

Ellis extracted a notebook from his pocket, flipped to a fresh page, and jotted a note. He asked, "What do you think about Ivan's new method?"

"Nothing. I mean, I don't know anything about it."

"What about Rory?" he asked, pocketing his notebook. "Anything unique to her?"

I thought about Rory for a few seconds. "Let's not forget that mama-grizzly-bear-protecting-her-cub thing. Other than that, I don't know. I'm just going in circles, making stuff up."

"Sometimes when you feel as if you're going in circles," Ellis said, "you end up in the center of the maze."

"That's one of your best qualities—when you're in information-gathering mode, you don't judge, you simply listen, taking it all in. It makes you easy to talk to. Thinking back to Rory's comments at the TV studio, the issue isn't whether Gloria was trying to make Oliver look bad; it's whether Rory thought she was."

"Anything else about motive?"

I told him no, then asked, "Any news from the canvass?"

"We've just begun."

"The shooter could have parked in Highbridge."

"We're checking it now."

"Everyone will be at work."

"Not everyone. There are some stay-at-home moms and retirees, and some folks work from home. Plus, lots of people have security cameras. We might be able to get some footage from them."

"Only if they turn the systems on."

"We're checking the city-owned security cameras, too. No one working here, including the guards, saw anything. It's early days, but so far, it looks like the shooter got lucky."

"That's not luck—that's planning. Whoever did this hid in the woods, waiting for the patrol to pass and for me to stand in front of the window." My anger deepened. "He knew I'd be filming this morning."

"Who had your schedule?"

"All the crew and my staff, of course, plus Dutch and Oliver, and by extension, Rory."

"Who else?"

"No one that I know of," I said. "Did you learn anything from the contents of Ivan's locker?"

"Just more evidence that he was planning to live in his office."

"In other words, you're nowhere."

"You know these things take time, Josie."

"Which, when someone is trying to kill you, isn't the least bit comforting."

Ellis spoke in a low, somber tone. "I know."

CHAPTER TWENTY-SIX

As soon as Ellis left, I went back to my office, glad for the respite. I walked to the corner curio cabinet that held my mother's rooster collection and sat on the floor, my back to the wall, my eyes on the colorful porcelain and ceramic statues.

"I love you, Mom," I whispered.

I wondered how long after my mother died my dad and Veronica Sutton had met. My mother had been gravely ill for two years before she passed away, from when I was eleven until I was thirteen. My dad had been only thirty-three when cancer finally killed her. Was it possible that their relationship started *before* my mother's death? The mere thought of it hit me like a punch. I shut my eyes. *No.* My father would never do that. *Never.* I opened my eyes. After a minute or two, my jitters quieted enough so I could make my way to my desk.

Knowing work would further calm me, I replied to a customer's request for a consignment proposal and approved Cara's budget request for office supplies. When I felt ready, I read Wes's texts. He'd sent three demands for info, one including a teaser: *I've got an info-bomb*, and one simple message that touched me: *I'm worried. You ok?*

I texted back: *Thx. I'm ok. Can you come to my office? I'll buy lunch.*

Seconds later, he replied: *20 min.*

I buzzed Cara on our intercom to tell her Wes was coming for lunch. I asked her to take him to the buffet in the tent and let him choose whatever he wanted. When she asked me what she should bring me, I thanked her and said I wasn't hungry.

I turned back to my phone. Mixed in among the score of texts and voicemail messages from the press and worried friends, including Zoë, was one from Cara. Heather Adler, Ivan's ex, had called this morning at nine.

I called Cara back. "I see that Heather Adler called. Did she say what she wanted?"

"No. It was a very brief call. I told her you weren't available, and would be hard to reach all day because you were filming. She said it wasn't important, and she didn't want your voicemail."

I thanked her, then dialed Heather's number. "I'm sorry I missed your call this morning," I said, when I had her on the line.

"Thanks for calling back. I heard about the shooting. Are you all right?"

There was that question again, the one I didn't know how to answer. "I'm fine, thanks. Is there something I can do for you?"

"No, no, I just wanted to apologize for being such a Debbie Downer when you were here picking up the books."

"You have nothing to apologize for. I understand completely—you're grieving."

"I guess that's right. Still, I'm sorry."

"No problem. Let me know if I can do anything."

After we exchanged goodbyes, I still had a few minutes to spare before Wes arrived, so I used the time to locate the February 2002 article that had launched Gloria's career in the *Antiques Insights* magazine archives, and downloaded it to my desktop.

Rereading it, I was, again, dazzled at her creativity. Everyone who appraises or validates documents knows that no two signatures from any individual are identical. Each time you sign your name there are subtle and sometimes not so subtle differences. Using the two Thomas Jefferson letters as a case study, Gloria demonstrated that while it's reasonable to expect to see these well-understood differences, the pressure people apply to various parts of their names remains constant. Specifically, President Jefferson applied equal pressure to both of the letter *f*'s in his last name. The forger, however, applied more pressure to the first *f* in Jefferson than the second *f*. Under a microscope, the deeper, darker, thicker indentation was evident. Gloria explained that after examining the forger's own signature, she discovered this same telltale pressure point. Gloria concluded that very few forgers were capable of signing someone's name so that it both reflected the expected subtle changes and duplicated the signer's pressure points—and this one was no exception. He got the subtle differences right, but not the pressure point. Thus, she would expect that every signature executed by this particular forger would show this same idiosyncrasy. An asterisk led me to a footnote, which explained that the forger had been arrested, a deal struck, and the proceedings sealed.

One of the two sidebars described her process, step-by-step. The other one detailed her conclusion that the forger was either new to the game or so good he'd escaped notice until now. She issued a call for forgery examples that matched this particular profile—someone who excelled at matching the ink, paper, weight, thickness, and ink saturation of known signatures, and included this same pressure point differential between the third and fourth letters of the last name. Within weeks, scholars and nonacademic experts produced a flurry of supporting examples. Within months, sequential pressure points became a benchmark, the metric by which all signature authentications were judged.

I swiveled to face the window. What did the murderer think I knew that made me such a threat? I racked my brain, but came up dry.

I needed to stop myself from turning into a hamster on a wheel, going over the same material, asking myself the same questions again and again, until my recollections and reflections blurred like an impressionist painting.

Instead of thinking about who wanted to kill me, an issue that could consume me if I let it, and about which I could do nothing, not yet, I turned my attention to something I could make progress on—Veronica Sutton.

I took a sheet of notepaper and wrote two headings: "Know" and "Want to Know."

Under "Know," I wrote:

- *Lives in Parker Mews, in Ginny Carson's guesthouse. Moved there two months ago.*
- *Left New York City for Sarasota, Florida, in October 2001. Bought a house. Started a children's clothing line.*
- *Doesn't want to talk to me.*

- *Has info about my father.*
- *Might have info about the Jane Austen letters.*

Under "Want to know," I wrote:

- *Why she doesn't want to talk to me.*
- *Whether the green box was my father's.*
- *Why she gave me the green leather box.*
- *Why she gave me the green leather box now.*
- *Why she gave me the green box in person.*
- *Why she moved to New Hampshire.*
- *How she knew Ginny Carson. Was Ms. Carson her landlady? A friend? A relative?*

I smoothed the paper, running my index finger down the list, as if somehow that physical act could bring me closer to the answers. I was shocked at how little I knew, and more than shocked at how little I thought I needed to know. I folded the paper and dropped it into my tote bag.

Cara called to let me know that Wes had arrived, and a few minutes later, I heard their footsteps.

I relocated to the round guest table and thanked Cara for escorting him up.

Wes had chosen a turkey sandwich and a bottle of sparkling water, a real step up from the bad old days when lunch was a double order of bacon and a Coke. Cara brought me a cup of chicken noodle soup and a small salad. She'd also brought us a small plate heaped with gingersnaps.

"You should have something," she explained.

"You're right," I said, grateful. "Thank you."

"You've been ducking my calls," Wes said as soon as she left.

"I'm fine, thanks."

"I know that," he said impatiently. "You texted me, remember?"

I skipped it. "I haven't been ducking your calls. I've been otherwise occupied."

"Tell me everything."

"I can't." I opened a packet of crackers. "What's your info-bomb?"

"You first. Did you locate that Veronica person?"

"Yes."

"And . . ." he prompted.

"And nothing. Thank you again for your help."

He shook his index finger at me. "Pony up. Give me something I can use."

"You owe me for that exclusive, Wes, not the other way around. The story was picked up by the national media because of the Jane Austen connection. It's going viral. You and your paper will be famous. So you pony up—who shot at me?"

"The same person who killed Gloria and Ivan."

"That much I already knew. Do the police have any suspects?"

"You should know better than me. You've been closeted with them ever since you pulled the Annie Oakley. Nice shooting, by the way."

I smiled. "My dad taught me well."

"Your dad taught you to shoot a gun out of a bad guy's hand?"

"He taught me to hit my target."

"How good a shot are you?"

I tilted my head and half smiled, my sassy look. "I've got game."

"Who knew? So what do the police say?"

"Nothing to me. I answered questions, that's all. What's your info-bomb?"

"I have two—both shockeroonies."

"Number one?" I prompted.

"Gloria wasn't strangled with her scarf."

"What are you talking about? I saw it."

Wes chuckled, pleased at my reaction. "Which tells you everything you need to know about eyewitness testimony. Gloria was strangled with rope—the scarf was wrapped around her neck afterwards."

"Are you serious? That's crazy."

"You called the killer neat because of the way the scarf was positioned, remember? What do you call him now?"

"Maniacal. What kind of rope?"

"That's my second info-bomb . . . it was the same kind of rope used to kill Ivan."

"The same? As in different lengths of the same skein?"

"Not knowable," Wes said, "but it was produced by the same manufacturer at the same time and used in the same manner. Both pieces were quarter-inch thick, braided cotton rope, frayed and yellowed from dust and oxidation over a lot of years."

"Do the police know where it came from?"

"No. It could be from anywhere. It's the kind used for everything from attaching life rings on boats to tent lines to securing a load in a pickup."

"What did the ME decide about Gloria?" I asked. "Was she killed in the woods?"

"Yes, but not necessarily at that spot. They found drag marks from close to Trevor. The ME says she was murdered Wednesday morning between six and noon, but the window's actually narrower than that. Oliver was the last person to talk to her, just after seven for a minute or so. And you called it in at nine after ten."

"How do they know Oliver didn't kill Gloria, then dial her number? He could have answered her phone and left the line open for a little while."

"Cell tower triangulation—they can prove his phone was in Portsmouth when he called her, and that she answered here in Rocky Point."

"So she was killed between seven and ten."

"Right."

We ate in silence for a minute, then I said, "I can pass along a little info. It's a nice story, sort of. You know that eight thousand dollars Gloria withdrew each month? I know what she did with it." I repeated what Dutch told me about Gloria's mother. "Gloria did what she could to help her."

"Except spend time."

"That's not fair, Wes. It hurt her to see her mother failing. She did her best."

"You're too nice."

I laughed. "What kind of comment is that?"

"You always see the good in people, the bright side. You skip the rest as if it didn't exist."

"Thank you."

"It wasn't a compliment."

I resisted the urge to ask for an explanation. The last thing I needed was to hear Wes's read of my character flaws. Instead, I said, "Dutch said Gloria wouldn't stash documents at her mom's place. Maybe he's wrong."

"Good, good," Wes said, extracting his notebook to make a note. "You said the caretaker's name is Melissa Rogers, right? I'll check."

"The police found a handgun in Gloria's bag. Were they able to trace it?"

"Yup. She bought it at a gun shop near Hitchens last week, all totally legal and aboveboard."

"I wonder if Melissa Rogers knows why Gloria bought a gun."

Wes jotted another note. "I'll ask. The police were hoping she might have mentioned why she was in the market for a gun to the dealer. He remembered her because she was so beautiful, but all she said was that she needed it for personal protection."

I shook my head. "She was right."

I walked Wes out, then returned to my office. I read an email from Sasha. She'd identified five document authenticators she felt comfortable recommending, and if I approved the list, she'd proceed to the next step in the vetting process, soliciting current references and analyzing examples of their work in detail. She included two people from England, one from Japan, and two Americans, including Oliver. I was pleased he made the cut.

The other American was a woman I greatly admired, Dr. Lucia Hart. I'd heard Dr. Hart speak at conferences, and recalled well her presentation, "White Paper: A Nineteenth-century Sign of Love." During that era, "white paper" referred to the highest quality paper available. To write that a lock of hair had been wrapped in "white paper," as Jane Austen did in *Sense and Sensibility*, signaled far more than the paper's color. When the book was first published in 1811, readers would have understood that only the most revered possessions would be worthy.

In a separate email, Sasha sent the list of media outlets asking for an interview, a hundred and fourteen so far and counting. Two reporters had shown up in person, a freelancer from New York, and a staff reporter from a Boston lifestyle magazine. In my reply to Sasha's first email, I authorized her vetting plan. To the latter, I sent a happy-face emoji. Fred had sent an email, too, letting me know that the list of bookstores and galleries doing business in 2001 was complete; however, they were having trouble locating most of the companies or the owners. Fred had asked Cara to check business licenses as an alternate approach to determining a company's current status, adding that he could always visit the old addresses in person to see if anyone there knew anything relevant. I told him to keep me posted.

I felt too antsy to sit and respond to any more messages. Instead, I paced, thinking about Veronica Sutton. On my third turn, a glimmer of an idea came to me. I played devil's advocate with myself, trying to consider everything that could go wrong with it—objections I might face, obstacles I might need to overcome. When I was done, I felt ready, more than ready. I had a plan, and executing that plan had become an imperative.

I walked to the window. A Sterling guard walked by. He peered into Mimi's Copse for a moment, then gazed into Greely Woods. When he rounded the corner, I lost sight of him.

I needed to be careful. Just because I'd succeeded in shooting the gun out of the attacker's hand didn't mean he'd give up. And I no longer had possession of my weapon.

My car was where I'd left it, by the front door. I was as certain as I could be that nothing would happen to me on my own property, not again, not in broad daylight, not outside in full view of half a dozen security cameras. What I needed to know was whether someone was hiding just out of sight, waiting for me to drive by.

I called Rocky Point Quarry and asked to speak to Dutch.

"I'm sorry," the young woman who answered the phone said, "he's with a customer. Can I help you?"

"When do you think he'll be available?"

"He just started a design consultation, and he has appointments lined up, back to back, all afternoon. Would you like to leave a message?"

"That's all right. I'll call again later."

One down; two to go. Oliver was next on my list, and for verisimilitude, I needed information.

I rang Timothy. He told me they were calling it a week, that he'd talked to Chief Hunter, who expected to give them an all clear by noon, so the crew could head back to New York.

"We all need a break," he said. "After we've had a little R and R, we'll come back to the project with clear eyes and a pep in our step."

"I think that's smart. How about if we bring Oliver and Fred down to the city for the day? We can finish both the Beatrix Potter and the thimble segments in one fell swoop."

"And this is why I love you."

I smiled, pleased at his tribute. "Do you want to pick a day now?"

"I'm thinking Tuesday, week after next, but let's write that in pencil, not ink. I don't want you doing anything until this situation is resolved. No undue risk, no sleepless nights."

I thanked him and promised that Fred and I would finalize the *nécessaire* copy by the time we got to New York.

"I'll call Oliver," I said, "and tell him he'll hear from Starr about travel arrangements."

He thanked me again, and we promised to be in touch soon.

Oliver answered his bookstore's phone on the third ring. After reassuring him that I was okay, I told him about the filming plans. "Are you okay with a trip to New York?"

"Oh, no, I hate going to the best city in the world." He laughed. "Tell me when and where, and I'm there."

I gave him the tentative schedule, said Starr would be in touch, then asked, "Is that your mom I hear in the background?"

"No . . . it must be one of the painters grumbling about something."

"Oh, that's good . . . you're making progress on the refresh."

"With luck they'll be done today."

"How's your mom's knee?"

"She's in week five of a projected fourteen-week treatment plan. Her knee is coming along fine. Her mood is not."

I laughed. "Does the treatment plan include anything besides physical therapy?" I asked, hoping to discover her current location without making him wonder why I was asking.

"She's supposed to do as much low-impact exercise as she can. She swims daily at the Y, freestyle swimming and a water ballet class. She's there now."

"Water ballet! What a great idea."

"All hers. She's a force to be reckoned with."

"On many levels. I'll be in touch once we confirm the filming date."

Mission accomplished, I thought.

CHAPTER TWENTY-SEVEN

I told Cara I had an errand and pretended not to notice how her eyes widened with fear. I ignored the guard who started fussing at me when I stepped outside.

I drove to Ginny Carson's lavender and yellow house and parked on the street. I walked up the path, and rang the bell.

The door was opened by a girl of about ten. She bounced up and down, sending her shoulder-length braids swinging. She had a smear of grape jelly on her chin.

"Hi," she said. "I'm Fiona."

"Hi, Fiona," I said. "I'm Josie." I could see into the kitchen. Two boys and a girl, all younger than Fiona, stood around the center island, laughing. "Is Ginny Carson here?"

A woman of about thirty appeared from somewhere on the right. "I'm Ginny."

She was tall and slim, with short caramel-brown hair and hazel eyes. She wore a teal sweater and brown jeans.

"Hi. I'm here about an antiques appraisal. I own Prescott's Antiques and Appraisals." Reading the skepticism in her expression, I added, "I'm not selling anything."

She stepped back, inviting me in. Fiona ran back to the kitchen.

"I shouldn't leave them alone too long," Ginny said, facing the kitchen. "God only knows what havoc they'll wreak."

"You have four children?"

"Five . . . the baby's napping."

"That's a lot of kids."

"Luckily, I love kids. What can I do for you?"

"It's about Veronica Sutton."

Her eyes half closed. "I thought you said it was about an antique appraisal."

"It is. I have two letters that are alleged to have been written by Jane Austen—I know, unbelievable, right? Ms. Sutton has information about them. I need that information."

A loud crash emanated from the kitchen.

"Pot down!" Fiona called.

"Follow me," Ginny said.

She marched toward the kitchen. I closed the door.

She picked up the pot, told the kids to get into their sweaters or jackets, then scooped up a baby monitor from the counter and herded them outside. Once they were out, we followed. A huge swath of land had been fenced in, separating the children's play area from the rest of the acreage. We sat on plastic lawn chairs on a paved patio in the shade of a hundred-year-old chestnut tree. In the center of the cordoned-off area, there was a multilevel, redwood play structure with a ten-foot curved slide, a captain's wheel, a telescope, a rope ladder, a tire swing, a sundial, and lots of other stuff. All four kids were on it, in it, or hanging off it. I was fascinated.

"That's the biggest, more beautiful swing set I've ever seen," I said. "Except calling it a swing set is like calling the ocean wet. It's true, but misses the point."

Ginny laughed. "Aunt Ronnie bought it for them when she moved into the carriage house."

I turned to face her. "Aunt Ronnie . . . Veronica. She's your aunt."

"That's right."

I turned back to the wooden structure. "I've never seen anything like it."

"I homeschool the kids. This is part science, part phys ed." After a moment, she added, "What makes you think Aunt Ronnie has information about your Jane Austen letters?"

I didn't want to tell her about my father's note. If Veronica Sutton had wanted Ginny to know that she had been a good friend of my father's, she would have told her herself. It wasn't my secret to share. I followed my own advice: Tell the truth. Keep your answers short. Don't speculate. Don't gossip.

I met Ginny's gaze. "She gave them to me."

She tilted her head. "I'm not following you."

"I don't mean to be mysterious. I don't understand it, either." I watched one of the boys tackle a ten-foot-high rock wall, then turned back to face Ginny. "Your aunt refuses to talk to me, I don't know why. I came to you in the hopes that you can get her to change her mind, or if not, get her to tell you the truth about the letters—how they came into her possession, whether she knows or suspects that they're real, anything and everything about those letters."

"She said she didn't want to talk to you?" she asked, sounding incredulous.

"She left a message."

Ginny looked down at the patio pavers, then up at her children. "Aunt Ronnie is getting her affairs in order." After a moment, she added, "She isn't well."

"I'm sorry to hear that."

"She's been spending a lot of time trying to lighten the load. Shredding old papers, updating her will, asking me which pieces of furniture I want after she's gone."

"Oh, my," I said.

"Giving you those letters has to be part of that process."

"And you have no information about the letters or her reticence to talk to me?"

Her eyes were on her kids, climbing and rolling, shouldering one another, jumping around, having fun. "None."

I crossed my fingers. "Will you ask her for me?"

She didn't speak for several seconds. "Aunt Ronnie likes to come over in the afternoon, to share a snack with the kids. I'll call and let her know you're here."

"If she knows I'm here, I'm afraid she won't come."

"I can't just spring you on her."

"Of course, you're right. Tell her the truth, then. I'm here about the letters, nothing more."

Ginny stood. "The phone is just inside. I can see the kids from there."

I stood, too. "Thank you."

Ginny left and I sat back down.

Fiona stood at the telescope, which she'd aimed at a tree branch. I tried to see if there was a bird or a nest there, but I couldn't. The two boys were competing on the rope ladder, which didn't seem fair, since the younger one could barely reach the lowest rung. The younger girl swayed gently on the tire swing, daydreaming.

Ginny returned a few minutes later and reported that Aunt Ronnie was on her way.

Veronica Sutton wore an emerald-green turtleneck with black slacks. She still exuded elegance, but her features were stony. It was apparent she didn't want to be here.

We were sitting alone in a small office to the right of the front door. The walls were painted seashell pink. The furniture, a small desk with matching chair, a club chair with ottoman, and a love seat with rolled arms, were all baroque in style and feminine in feel. I sat on the ottoman. Veronica Sutton sat on the love seat, her hands folded on her lap, her feet firmly planted on the ground.

"Thank you for seeing me," I said.

"You didn't give me much of a choice."

I met her eyes. "I'm sorry to intrude, but you didn't give me much of a choice, either. You can't just say you were a good friend of my father's and disappear."

She lowered her eyes to the pink carpet. "I shouldn't have told you anything. I should have shipped the box."

"Why didn't you?"

She raised her eyes. "I wanted to meet you. As soon as I did, I knew it was wrong. Since I can't answer your questions, I shouldn't have told you anything."

"Can't? Or won't?"

"Does it matter?"

"Yes."

She nodded, acknowledging that her motivation mattered to me. I appreciated her forbearance.

She took a moment to gather her thoughts. "I can imagine how harsh this must seem to you. I truly am sorry, but my hands are tied—I made a promise."

Her eyes were as empathetic as her words, and intellectually, I could appreciate her position. I understood it, but on an emotional level, I was simply enraged. I didn't want compassion. I wanted information. The anguish of knowing I would never get the answers I sought hit me with dagger-sharp clarity. I had to face the fact that there was nothing I could do or say to change her mind, which meant I had to let the dream of finding a new connection to my beloved father go. I tipped back my head and rolled it from side to side, willing myself to relax enough to speak. I had to focus on what I could do, not on what I couldn't.

"I wish I could change your mind, but I understand keeping promises. Will you tell me about the letters? Please."

She raised a hand as white as paper. "I can't."

"How did they come into your possession?"

"Please—I can't answer *any* questions."

"Why not?"

She stood. "I told you this would be a waste of time." She took a step toward the door, then turned back to face me. "I really am sorry."

"At least tell me if the letters are authentic."

She walked out, leaving me alone in Ginny's pink office. I struggled to hold my emotions in check, breathing in through my nose and out through my mouth, blinking back tears. I sat there trying to think, not feel, amid the laughter and high-pitched gleeful squeals coming from the kids in the kitchen.

After a minute, I felt calm enough to leave.

Ginny was waiting for me in the hall. "I'm sorry it didn't work out."

"Thank you for trying." I extracted a business card from my tote bag and handed it over. "If your aunt changes her mind, perhaps as part of lightening that load you spoke about, please call. I was told the Jane Austen letters were in a portfolio of sketches. I suspect she has the portfolio. If she agrees to let me see it, I'll meet her wherever she wants—at her house, here, my office, the public library, anywhere she feels comfortable. I will wear gloves. I won't damage it in any way. If you can help make that happen, I'd be most grateful."

"It's not my place."

I nodded. "Thank you anyway."

I drove around the corner, out of sight of the house, nowhere near the mews. I'd expected my conversation with Veronica Sutton to be difficult, but I hadn't expected it to be harrowing. I leaned against the steering wheel and cried. It was all just too much. After my tears petered out, I told myself to pull it together, and I did. I drove away, and I didn't look back.

Mozart's Serenade No. 13 in G major, *Eine kleine Nachtmusik,* was playing on Hitchens's classical station, and listening to it helped me regain my equilibrium. Jess Rubin, the radio show host, was describing the connection between Mozart's composition and Stephen Sondheim's musical *A Little Night Music* when she interrupted herself to announce that Wes Smith, from the *Seacoast Star,* had some breaking news.

"Thanks, Jess," Wes said. "According to a high-level police source, the forensic team found touch DNA on Gloria's scarf. The DNA belongs to Oliver Crenshaw, the owner of Crenshaw's Rare Books, Prints and Autographs. I'll be back with more details as they become available."

A flash of memory came to me. "No!" I shouted aloud.

I texted Wes: *Oliver not guilty . . . call me.*

I turned off the radio, pulled onto the shoulder, and set my flashers.

Two minutes later, Wes called. "Whatcha got?"

"You really stepped in it this time, Wes. I know how Oliver's DNA got on Gloria's scarf, and it's not the least bit incriminating. Gloria changed into that outfit after we finished filming the day before she was killed, and she dropped her scarf in the green room. Oliver picked it up for her."

"Do you have any corroboration?"

I laughed, not bothering to feel insulted that Wes didn't think my word was good enough. "Starr, my TV show's assistant director, saw it, too. It looks like your source isn't as high level as you think, Wes. Or he isn't as high level as you said."

"Oh, my source is plenty high level. Maybe there's a good reason to plant a seed about Oliver as a suspect, knowing it could be easily contradicted."

"Like what?" I asked.

Wes chuckled. "I don't know. It sounded good, so I said it out loud. What would be a reason a high-level person would pass that info along?"

I thought about it for a few seconds. "To lull the killer into complacency by implying Oliver is in the crosshairs."

"Good one, Joz!"

"But it isn't good for Oliver. You should go back on the air and quote me about how Oliver's DNA got on Gloria's scarf."

"Give me something else, maybe about Ivan's murder, to change the conversation."

"That's a good idea, but I don't know what I can tell you."

"How about a fact related to Ivan, even if it's not related to his murder? That would really switch it up."

"His ex-girlfriend Heather sold his books, including some with nice leather bindings."

"That's all human interest stuff. I need hard news."

"I don't have any."

"All right. I'll pull something together."

In typical Wes fashion, he was back on the air with an update in ten minutes. In explaining why the touch DNA wasn't relevant, Wes cited an anonymous source who'd witnessed Oliver pick up the scarf. He also quoted me as saying I'd bought Ivan's book collection from Heather Adler, Ivan's ex-girlfriend, lacing the announcement with innuendo by adding that the purchase occurred soon after Ivan's murder. He finished up with a reminder that the police were urgently seeking anyone who'd been in the Highbridge community between nine and eleven that morning, or otherwise had information about the attempted murder of Josie Prescott.

Not bad for an on-the-fly recovery effort.

CHAPTER TWENTY-EIGHT

Wes's words stayed with me: *The attempted murder of Josie Prescott*. Ty would be furious with me for going outside alone, no matter how deft I'd been in confirming none of the suspects were nearby, and I couldn't say I'd blame him. I felt like the heroine in one of those Gothic novels who finds herself alone in a decrepit mansion on a lonely moor. She hears clanking in the attic and decides to investigate. As a reader, I always shout, "Don't go up the stairs!" Yet, on a less dramatic level, that's just what I'd done. Denial was powerful.

I slowed to a crawl as the entrance to my company's parking lot came into view. The tent was down, the truck and crew rental cars gone. I recognized my staff's vehicles. Others probably belonged to the Sterling Security guards.

I parked in the same place I'd vacated earlier, and dashed inside.

"Oh, I'm glad you're back," Cara said.

I smiled to reassure her, told everyone hello, and pushed through into the warehouse. I was safe.

I walked to the kitty domain and sat on the dark green carpet next to Angela. She was curled up in her kitty bed. Hank was elsewhere, on an important errand, no doubt. I kneaded her shoulders, a mini-massage, and she began purring in her sleep. I closed my eyes, and felt the knots in my shoulders loosen, just a bit. As I petted Angela, I told myself that I'd done the best I could with Veronica Sutton, that my heartache would fade. To distract myself, I tried to understand, once again, why someone had stolen Ivan's notes on writing hesitations and both sets of Gloria's notes—the ones in the folder relating to her decades-old *Antiques Insights* article about Thomas Jefferson's signature's pressure point, and the ones from her portfolio relating to the Beatrix Potter book. Or were they simply misplaced? Misfiled? No way would Ivan destroy his work. Had Gloria destroyed hers for some reason? No. It didn't make sense, and if it didn't make sense, it wasn't true. What, I asked myself, did those three sets of notes have in common? Nothing beyond the obvious—they all related to document authentication. Two were scholarly, the third written for a lay audience. One was a work in progress, the second contained new at-the-time findings, and the third, while entertaining and intriguing, didn't include original research.

Why *those* notes? Why was everything else intact and in place?

My eyes flew open and I sat up with a jolt.

Everything else *wasn't* intact and in place. The Garfield letter Gloria had just purchased was missing, too.

There was only one possible explanation. Ivan must have stolen the Garfield letter and Gloria's notes when he went to Hitchens Tuesday morning to fetch the script Gloria had left in her office. Gloria gave him her key, presenting him with a rare opportunity. He had to have expected to sneak everything back, though, after copying the notes and studying the letter. Otherwise, she'd catch on to the theft. This realization led to a singular and inevitable conclusion: Ivan had made a copy of Gloria's office key.

There was more: Since we hadn't found those documents or the key, and I was certain that Ivan was the thief and equally certain he hadn't destroyed them, he must have hidden them somewhere it hadn't occurred to us to look—perhaps along with his own missing notes. Maybe Ivan had been afraid he would be expelled by Dr. Shield, the department chair, for whatever transgression Gloria planned to bring to his attention, so he decided to get his most important work—his original research on writing hesitations—secured. He printed it out and took it away with him. I could see the campus police escorting him off the premises, brusquely informing him that he couldn't take his laptop since it was Hitchens's property, and that the contents of his office would be packed for him after a review to ensure that all the materials were, in fact, his property. Three sets of notes and one presidential letter, all missing—where would Ivan have secreted them?

I kissed Angela and told her she was a good girl, then went upstairs to my office to call Ellis.

I explained what I'd realized, and said, "Can you check with locksmiths?"

"Yes. What else?"

"We need to look for things like a fake bottom in his suitcase or an envelope taped to the bottom of a file cabinet drawer."

"Already done," Ellis replied. "Part of our routine. We also examined Jonathan's desk and file cabinets. We checked Ivan's classroom desk, his locker in Pease, and his car. Heather says Ivan didn't give her anything to hold. Ditto Jonathan. Ditto Arlene Stevens, the department admin. Where else should we look?"

"Anywhere he went, I guess. He probably ate in the cafeteria."

"Done. There's no evidence he hid anything there."

"Another colleague."

"Not so far as we can tell."

"Ivan went to Heather's apartment to calculate how many boxes he'd need to move his books." I walked to the staircase landing and looked down at the roped-off area where Ivan's books were stored pending cataloging. "I bought them all. They're here. Slipping documents between the pages of a book would be a canny place to hide them. I'll look now and let you know if I find anything."

"I'll come watch. Give me half an hour."

I set up the video camera and moved standing lamps closer to the plastic tubs containing Ivan's books. Given Ivan's predilection for the early nineteenth century, I thought I'd start with his leather-bound volumes. Before I could sort through the tubs, though, Cara's voice crackled over the PA system, telling me Oliver Crenshaw was on line two.

I took the call at the nearest workstation.

After exchanging hellos, Oliver said, "I heard on the news that you bought Ivan's book collection. You were sure Johnny-on-the-spot this time around. How does it look?"

"I haven't gone through anything yet, let alone catalogued it," I said, beginning the seller's two-step. You have to give a little to get anything at all, and if you're any good at the dance, you learn more than you reveal. "There are some bindings that look decent."

"I noticed that volume he was reading. Is that the quality we're talking?"

"At a glance, yes, but I don't know anything about rebindings, repairs, edition, rarity . . . nothing."

"Can I come look? I'm interested in the lot."

"Including the modern paperbacks?"

He laughed. "I'll take them off your hands."

"I'm sorry, Oliver, but I need to see what I have first."

"Let's do it together and settle on a price. I have a buyer eager for bindings."

"An interior designer?"

"She wants ten yards."

"Ivan would turn over in his grave."

"I can pay top dollar."

There was no point in telling him I wouldn't be selling them for a year. "I'll call you as soon as I set a price."

Oliver didn't want to let it go. I wondered if his persistence was simply business as usual—let an antiques dealer get a whiff of quality objects, and he turns into a pit bull—or whether he suspected, or even knew, that the books might contain priceless documents. Assuming the former, I understood, and I even sympathized. It took me two minutes to get off the phone without being rude.

Ellis balanced his tablet on top of Prescott's professional quality video camera and started his video. I used the remote to start mine. He stood out of the camera view.

I followed Prescott's protocol, wearing gloves, and annotating each object with my observations, which aligned with my lawyer Max's suggestions, in case a will or heir turned up. I recorded all sides of each book, including the copyright page, then I gently fanned the pages of each volume, hoping a document would flutter out. Forty-five minutes later, with all books recorded, I tapped the video's OFF button.

Ellis's phone vibrated and he tapped the screen. "I got a text—Murphy's Hardware."

"Ned Murphy, locksmith extraordinaire. That's where Ivan had the key copied."

"Two copies."

"In case he lost one."

Ellis laughed. "A cautious thief."

"I bet this is the first time he's ever done something like this."

"Why would he?"

"Rory's criticism stung. Heather's, too. He wanted to prove he could man up with the best of them."

Ellis laughed again. "Real men steal?"

We started toward the front.

"He wouldn't have thought of taking the documents as stealing. If he thought Gloria was treating him like a flunky, taking her work was simply leveling the playing field, not stealing. Besides, he wasn't after her content; he wanted to copy her methods so he could apply them to his own writing hesitation work. To say nothing of a secondary goal—the best way to even the score was to land the Jane Austen appraisal before Gloria even noticed he'd submitted a proposal. It's amazing the justifications people come up with to do the wrong thing."

"Like going out on your own today."

"How on earth do you know that?" I demanded, stopping short.

"I assigned an officer to stick close to you."

"I didn't notice anyone following me."

"Did you check?" he asked.

"It didn't even occur to me."

"You'll see someone following Ty's vehicle on your way home today and again in the morning when he drives you back."

"We haven't finalized our schedule yet."

"We'll be sitting on your house all night. I think it's excellent that you're keeping the Sterling guards on duty. The more eyes the better."

"I understand," I said.

"It doesn't sound like it."

"I shouldn't have gone out on my own. I really do understand."

"And you'll take the threat seriously?"

"Yes."

"Good," he said. "You haven't asked about the investigation into the shooting."

"I didn't want to hear that you have no clue what's going on."

"We finished the canvass. A woman raking her yard noticed a blond person, she thinks a man, coming out of Greely Woods in the right place at the right time."

"Dutch Larkin!"

"Maybe. All that stood out was the very blond hair."

"Driving a pickup?"

"She didn't see a vehicle. She bagged some leaves, and by the time she looked up again, he was gone." Ellis pinned me with his eyes. "I'm sharing this information because I want to stress to you that we don't yet know who is behind the murders and shooting, but based on the attacker's moxie and adaptability, you need to be very, very careful."

His warning sent prickly spiders running up my spine.

"I get it."

I escorted him into the office, promised to send him a link to my video, then repacked Ivan's books, returned the camera and tripod to the case, and went upstairs to retrieve my tote bag.

I was scared and confused, and I wanted to go home.

While I waited for Ty, I asked my staff how everything was going, hoping for something that would take my mind off of the anxiety smoldering just below the surface of my consciousness.

Cara told me she was still researching the list of shops that had been open in 2001, but that it was slow going tracing the owners. Sasha said she was making good progress with the background checks of the potential appraisers, that she hadn't found any problems yet, and had found a lot of good news. She added that we'd used three of the people on the list in the past, with good results. Fred said he was ready to submit his estimate for the thimble collection.

"Give me some highlights," I requested.

"I estimate the *nécessaire*, which is the only object not part of Sally's collection, at fourteen to fifteen thousand. Most of Sally's Meissens will sell for four- to six thousand dollars each. The harbor scene, well, you know how rare those are . . ." He grinned, and I grinned with him. He was a master at wringing every ounce of drama from an auction estimate. "I'm thinking somewhere in the neighborhood of twenty big ones, baby!"

I let my mouth hang open. "Twenty thousand dollars! For one thimble?"

He held up his index and middle fingers. "And she has two of them. Plus eight thousand for the Paul Revere."

"What about the acorn and squirrel?"

"Only eighteen hundred. Molded production doesn't stack up to custom craftsmanship, no matter how cute it is."

"For a grand total of . . . ? Wait, let me do a drumroll." I tap-tapped my index fingers on the table for a few seconds. "I'm ready."

"A quarter million cash money, give or take."

I offered a palm for a high five, and he slapped it. "Well done, Fred!"

Once Ty and I got home, I changed into jeans and a sweater and made a fresh pitcher of Third Degree martinis. I placed the pitcher on a tray with a glass for me, a beer for Ty, napkins, and a bowl of peanuts, and carried it upstairs to the porch. I set the tray down and flipped on the orange lanterns. Ty sat, staring out toward the horizon.

"You look deep in thought," I said.

He opened his beer. "I was glad to see the police presence on our drive home."

"Ellis told me he was going to keep a car here all night." I recounted the canvass results; reported that Ivan had made two copies of Gloria's office key; described how I'd come to realize that Ivan's notes were missing, too; detailed how I went through every book in a failed effort to find the missing documents; and explained how I'd ensured I could safely visit Ginny Carson.

"I bet Ellis had an opinion about your venturing out alone."

"He did, and he wasn't shy about sharing it."

Ty took my hand. "I agree with him."

"Me, too, now that I'm out of my funk. It isn't that I dismissed the risk exactly. It's that I thought I was managing it."

"The killer is showing some flexibility. What do you make of the blond person seen by the woman raking leaves?"

"Dutch is the only blond . . . Wait a second." I inhaled sharply and sat forward. "Wait! Oliver told me he's going to a Halloween party dressed as Andy Warhol."

"Andy Warhol had blond hair."

"Platinum," I said, "and he wore it in a distinctive style: long, shaggy, straight, so from a distance the person's gender would be unclear. Any Halloween costume would come with a wig."

"You should tell Ellis."

"I don't want to get Oliver in trouble."

"You won't. You can't. If he didn't do anything, he won't be in trouble. If he did something, any trouble he finds himself in is all on him."

"I know . . . still."

Ty squeezed my hand. "You won't be working the tag sale tomorrow—agreed?"

"Agreed."

Typically, we all worked Saturdays because the weekly tag sale was our busiest retail event. Tomorrow, though, I'd keep out of sight. After a few minutes lost in thought, I realized Ty was lost in thought, too.

"What's wrong?" I asked.

He turned to face me. "Nothing."

I saw the tension in his eyes. "Don't keep something to yourself because you're worried about me." I stroked his arm. "Please."

He raised my hand to his lips. "I'm a little discouraged, that's all."

"Because you don't know what you want to do?"

"Because it never occurred to me that at this point in my career I'd be unsure about my next step."

"Hold that thought for a sec." I'd left my tote bag in the bedroom, so it only took me a minute to extract the course catalogues and degree requirement flyers I'd picked up at Hitchens. Back on the porch, I sat down. "I had a thought . . . two, actually. First, ask the sociology department chair, with whom you have a good relationship, whether you can teach a course. Stick your toe in that water. Why not? You're a world-class trainer. Those capabilities should adapt nicely to an academic environment."

"That's an interesting idea."

"My second thought is to kill two birds with one stone. That book we talked about you writing?"

"What about it?"

"Make it your dissertation."

"A dissertation? That's what you write for a doctorate degree."

I handed over the catalogues and flyers. "I'm a smart cookie."

He laughed. "Do you seriously think that I should pursue a Ph.D.?"

"Start with one course. Teach one. Take one. Tell the chair you're considering applying for the doctoral program and would like to take a course to see what you think, that you've been out of school for a lot of years, and want to be certain you're moving in the right direction before you enroll full time."

"I love you, Josie."

"I love you, too, Ty."

Ty closed all the blinds and drapes on the first floor. He didn't need to explain why. I got the message, but it frightened me afresh. I felt utterly powerless.

Fred, who often worked late to match his wife's schedule as general manager of the Blue Dolphin, my favorite restaurant, emailed a few minutes before seven p.m., while my mother's pomodoro sauce was bubbling away on the stove. *Sasha asked me to tell you that Dr. Lois Hart is our number one recommendation. She helped authenticate some of the Jane Austen letters at the Morgan Library, and she's an expert on paper and ink.* Fred listed her office and cell phone numbers, and her email address. Dr. Hart owned a Boston-based document-authentication consulting company.

Dr. Hart's reputation was impeccable. If we brought her in as the lead consultant, with the right to bring in anyone else she thought she needed, the process could serve as a professional development opportunity, too. Timothy would want to videotape the entire appraisal, and Sasha, Fred, and I could learn through observation, start to finish. Oliver would be disappointed, but I'd discovered early on in my career that I had to make business decisions based on what was good for the business, and nothing else.

For a good ten minutes, or so, while I cooked the pasta, sautéed the aspara-gus, toasted the garlic bread, and tossed the salad, I didn't think of murder once. As soon as I sat down with a glass of Chianti, though, the memories and fear returned. That I had a plan for appraising the Jane Austen letters and had made a nice dinner didn't change the fact that for one fleeting moment, I'd had hope that I would learn more about my father, only to have that hope dashed forever. It also didn't change the fact that someone had murdered two people and tried to kill me.

CHAPTER TWENTY-NINE

F irst thing Saturday morning, before the staff relocated to the tag sale venue, I gathered them together to tell them I wouldn't be working with them today, but would be around.

I congratulated Sasha and Fred on their outstanding work preparing for the Jane Austen appraisal, and Cara, too, for building the 2001 shop list. I authorized contacting Dr. Hart to begin the process of retaining her services, reminding Sasha that we needed everything done on site and on camera, and that at least one of us had to be present for every step.

Prescott's always provided pizza for the entire staff on Saturdays, a small perk, and before I pushed into the warehouse, I asked for mushrooms on mine.

The workstation nearest the walk-in safe was equipped with a microscope, probes, tweezers, and other tools of the trade. I perched on a high stool and read Gloria's *Antiques Insights* article about the two Thomas Jefferson letters again, this time jotting notes about her key findings as I considered how we could apply her methodologies to the Jane Austen letters.

- *Paper—laid, with a watermark from Richard Auvergne, indicating the sheets dated from Jefferson's years in France*
- *Ink—made from the most commonly used ink at the time, iron gall, expected to fade to brown, which these both had*
- *Writing implement—goose quill*
- *Content—subject matter known to be of interest to both the writer and the recipient, in this case, Barthélemy Faujas de Saint-Fond*

- *Condition—crease marks, stains, foxing, rubbing, and slight tears, all age appropriate*
- *Signature—similar to known exemplars, but not exact replicas, indicating the signatures weren't traced, photocopied, or otherwise artificially generated*

I went back to *Antiques Insights'* archives and found high-resolution digital files of the two letters Gloria had studied and a half dozen of the examples other scholars had submitted in support of her research. I printed all of them on top quality paper. Using the printouts to try to duplicate Gloria's work was a specious exercise, of course, since Gloria's discovery related to a three-dimensional observation, which couldn't be replicated on a two-dimensional plane, but I hoped that I could see what she'd referred to.

I viewed them under the microscope, one at a time. I adjusted the focus and sought out indications of the pressure point Gloria had described in the article—and there it was, time after time. I never would have recognized the pattern on my own, but once I knew what I was looking for, the difference between the third and fourth letters of the signers' last names was apparent.

I retrieved the Jane Austen letters from the safe and put on white cotton gloves. Removing the letters from the protective sleeves, I examined them under magnification.

The disparity in darkness and thickness in the third and fourth letters of Jane Austen's signature in the letter to Cassandra showed the same aberration as the documents Gloria and her colleagues had identified as fakes. The letter to Fanny did not.

I couldn't believe it, but there it was.

The letter to Cassandra was a forgery, executed by the same forger Gloria had identified in 2002. The letter to Fanny was either authentic or it had been forged by a different hand.

I swiveled away from the microscope, thunderstruck.

I recalled Gloria's seemingly playful remark about the Garfield letter—she said she couldn't wait to get it under a microscope.

"When Gloria examined the Garfield signature with a loupe at Crenshaw's," I said aloud, "she recognized the pressure point variance between the third and fourth letters—that's why she bought it."

It seemed impossible that Gloria had been able to spot the discrepancy under those conditions, but that capability was what distinguished a journeyman from a virtuoso.

Oliver and Rory had been in the TV studio when Gloria made the suggestive comment. So had Ivan. If one of those three people had forged the Garfield letter, they might have heard Gloria's comment as a threat.

Regarding Oliver and Rory's possible involvement, there were two possibilities, both ruinous: First, if they'd sold it knowingly—whether or not Oliver or Rory had actually created the forgery—exposure would destroy their store's reputation and Oliver's status as an expert. They'd probably go to prison, too. Second, if Oliver or Rory had themselves been duped, no one in the industry would ever trust them again.

Thinking about Ivan, I could see him trying his hand at replicating one of Byron's letters, not for sale, but rather to get close to a hero, to discover what it felt like to write those words in that style holding a quill in just that way. If Ivan had discovered he possessed a talent for copying Byron's handwriting, he might have experimented with other authors. If his forgeries were good enough, he might have sold one or two. According to Heather, he was neck-deep in debt when he died, so his involvement couldn't be current. But if he'd sold a few forgeries when he was in college, well, the proceeds might have paid for his undergrad education. Then he got caught, got lucky with a plea deal, and stopped cold turkey.

Except it couldn't have happened that way.

Gloria knew the forger's identity, and there was no way she would have allowed him anywhere near her work. Oliver or Rory might be behind the scheme, as forgers or buyers of forgeries, but so too could anyone else. Just because Oliver and Rory had been in the studio when Gloria made her remark about looking at the Garfield letter under a microscope didn't mean they were the only suspects. Her comment could have been innocent, not jousting, and anyone with knowledge, brains, technical skills, and a steady hand could be the forger. I needed more information.

I tried to locate the court proceedings that named the forger by searching official records. I entered various keywords and Gloria's name, all without luck, so I called Max Bixby, my lawyer. Since it was Saturday, I didn't expect him to be available, and he wasn't, but Marcus, the paralegal on duty, knew exactly what I wanted before I'd finished my request, and he told me he'd get back to me within an hour.

Marcus found the case. The forger pled nolo contendere, no contest, to a single Class B misdemeanor charge of forgery with no criminal intent, and as part of the plea arrangement, the records were sealed, then annulled, New Hampshire's version of expungement.

My heart sank. "Oh, no! So I can't see the records?"

"Actually, you can. New Hampshire has a Right-to-Know law, our version of the Freedom of Information Act. All you have to do is request them."

My brows drew together. "Doesn't this defeat the purpose of expungement?"

"You'd think so, wouldn't you? What can I tell you? In 2016, the New Hampshire Supreme Court ruled that criminal records weren't exempt."

"Amazing. How soon can I get the file?"

"The clerk is required to respond to the request within five days, but a response doesn't mean you'll get the records that quickly. Usually it's a simple acknowledgment of the request issued to comply with the statute. The quickest way is to use an expeditor, someone who knows the best wording to use on the letter, hand delivers it to the right person, pays the fees on the spot, and so on. It still takes time, since every request has to be vetted, but it's much faster than simply filing it yourself."

"Can you do it?"

"Sure. We'll get it filed first thing Monday morning."

I tapped the END CALL button, as another piece of the puzzle snapped into place.

I called Ellis, and when I had him, I said, "I don't know who the killer is, but I have an idea about how you might be able to figure it out. I can't explain on the phone . . . I need to show you something."

He said he was on his way.

"I don't mean to sound quixotic," I told Ellis, once he was standing in front of the microscope, "but Gloria has set us on the path to solving her own murder."

"I'm listening."

"It was the signatures that gave it away. The technical explanation can wait for the experts, but here's the point: Years ago, Gloria discovered a new metric for authenticating signatures. She proved one of two Thomas Jefferson letters was a fake. She got a bunch of other experts to send her examples, and soon, she had enough evidence to prove the documents were fakes, and that they'd all been produced by the same person. As soon as she looked at the fraudulent Garfield signature, she recognized it as the work of that same forger. This particular forger can replicate a signature beautifully, but he can't change the pressure he applies to certain letters when signing. It's a tell, like in poker, where over time you learn that when a certain player tugs on his left earlobe or rubs his neck before raising your bet, or whatever, he's bluffing. In this case, the forger applied extra pressure in the same manner in the discredited Jefferson letter, the Garfield letter, a bunch of documents submitted in response to Gloria's call for examples, and in one of my Jane Austen letters. They're forgeries, executed by the same person."

"That's one heck of a coincidence."

"It's not a coincidence—it's a pattern of behavior. See for yourself."

I handed Ellis a pair of white cotton gloves, eased the Jane Austen letter I was certain was a fake onto the microscope stage. I took a look to ensure the signature was lined up with the lens.

Ellis put on the gloves and tuned the focus. I described what he was seeing, the deviation in pressure between the *s* and the *t*, the third and fourth letters of her last name. When he finished his examination, I slipped the fake Austen letter into its sleeve, replacing it with the genuine one.

"I see the difference," he said, "but I don't see the point. No one signs their name the exact same way twice."

"That's true, and that's what previous examiners had assumed about the President Jefferson signatures that Gloria studied when she was in grad school. Her breakthrough was to prove that pressure points are unique, like fingerprints."

Ellis took off his gloves and laid them neatly on the worktable. "Do you understand this?" he asked in the tone I might use with an astrophysicist who's trying to give me a one-minute explanation of the string theory of the cosmos.

I laughed. "Yes."

"Can't scientists check the paper and ink and so on?"

"Absolutely, and those are straight-ahead tests, and contribute to credibility, but they aren't definitive. For example, both Jefferson letters were written with iron gall ink on laid paper produced by Richard Auvergne, proving only that the forger was able to acquire a supply of old paper and produce the ink."

"It seems, I don't know . . . whimsical. Can you prove it to a jury?"

"Me, personally? No. I wouldn't qualify as an expert witness, but I'm right, I know it, and certified document appraisers will concur. They agreed with Gloria when she originally set out the protocol, and they'll agree now."

"And you're saying the forger is the killer?"

"Maybe. You commit fraud for the money. You kill to cover up the underlying crime." I told Ellis I planned on filing a request for the court records on Monday, then asked, "Can you get a search warrant?"

"I don't know. What, exactly, would I be looking for?"

"Nineteenth-century paper and an inkwell that might or might not be full of iron gall ink. You should also look for oak galls, which may be dried or crushed into a powder; ferrous sulfate or another vitriol; and gum, probably gum arabic. Mix those three components with water, and you get the ink. And, of course, a quill pen, probably from a goose, and probably without the feathers; a length of rope; and for everyone except Dutch, a blond wig."

"You think Dutch is capable of this? Aren't we looking for someone with artistic talent?"

"Dexterity, precision of eye, and technical skills are more important."

"I can't go on a fishing expedition."

"You won't need to. We have a finite number of suspects: Dutch, Oliver, and Rory. I have an idea how we can narrow the field to one."

Ellis and I walked to a supply cabinet attached to the wall near the door that led to the front office. I slid a dozen sheets of Japanese-made artist's paper, manufactured with 20 percent real cotton, into a folder, and gave it to him.

"Organize a photo array of blond men," I suggested. "We'll tell the suspects that you're trying to ID the person who shot at me. Have them sign a form printed on this paper stating whether they recognize anyone. Presumably they'll say they don't. It doesn't matter—all we want is their signature."

"Why this paper?"

"It's absorbent and fast-drying. I'll be able to identify the signature pattern." I met his eyes. "I need to come."

"Forget it, Josie."

"I might be able to tell something from how they hold the pen, which way they lean, and so on."

"You're making that up."

"No, I'm not. We'll go to their locations, so that signing the form feels as natural as it can. If they ask why I'm there, I'll say I'm determined to help find the man who tried to kill me, and I came to personally ask them to help, to look at the photos."

"And when they ask why them?"

"You'll say you're asking everyone. If you're worried about my safety—don't be. The person who tried to kill me might be desperate, but he's not stupid. He's not going to try to murder me when I'm with the police chief."

Ellis reluctantly agreed, then made some calls to ask Detective Brownley to find appropriate photos. While I waited, I texted Gretchen that I was leaving with Ellis, then tried to decide how I'd handle the document aging process if I were a forger. Was it better to use an iron, Oliver's idea, or a smoker, Gloria's contribution? I decided on the iron—I'd be able to exert more control.

When Ellis was ready, he hustled me into his SUV and drove to the police station, a one-story building across from the beach on Ocean Avenue. The shingles had weathered to a soft dove gray. The trim was painted snow white.

He left me in his office, telling me to stay away from the window. The office looked the same as the last time I'd been there, with blond wood furniture and beige industrial carpeting. Three framed Norman Rockwell illustrations adorned the wall.

I sat at the guest table, as far from the window as I could get.

A few minutes later, Cathy, the civilian admin, popped her head in to ask what I wanted for lunch, explaining that Chief Hunter said he needed to take care of some things, so I might as well eat. I fought the impulse to protest against the delay, and ordered a ham and cheese sandwich, and a ginger ale.

I had no idea what the holdup was, and no way of knowing. I told myself that an hour's delay was irrelevant—the forger was doomed.

To calm myself, I thought about love seats. I hoped Ty would agree that we should choose based on comfort more than style. No one would see it but us. I wanted something cushy. And orange, to match the little lanterns. I texted Ty my ideas, garnering as much pleasure from the planning as I would from the purchase.

Cathy delivered my sandwich and drink and I ate, but I didn't taste a thing.

Thirty minutes later, Ellis returned with a photo array of blond men and forms asking whether the signer recognized any of the men in the photographs, printed on the Japanese paper.

CHAPTER THIRTY

We went to Rocky Point Quarry first. Dutch stood between two ten-foot-high stacks of granite, telling a burly workman where to place another load.

The workman set off, and Dutch, seeing us head his way, took a step toward us, then stopped. When we reached him, Ellis explained why we were there.

Dutch squinted a little in the sun. "I didn't see anyone when I was there."

"You didn't *notice* anyone," Ellis corrected. "I'd appreciate it if you'd take a look."

Dutch took the photo array and took his time, examining each face carefully. "I've never seen any of them."

"Thanks for looking. If you'd just sign this, we'll be out of your hair."

Dutch accepted the paper Ellis proffered, and read it slowly. When he was done, he laid the paper on a slab of polished granite, and used a Rocky Point Quarry-branded pen to tick the NO box and sign his name.

"How are you doing?" I asked Dutch as we prepared to leave.

"The love of my life just died. How do you think I'm doing?"

Without waiting for a reply, he marched toward the back of the quarry.

Ellis had asked for a Portsmouth police officer to accompany him to Crenshaw's, since he was calling on a suspect out of his jurisdiction. Dawn LeBlanc met us on Bow Street, about a block away from the shop.

I knew Dawn fairly well. She'd gone undercover to help with Rocky Point investigations a couple of times. She was short and plump, with a dusting of freckles on her cheeks and nose. Her brown hair was shorter than I recalled, and she'd updated her glasses to a pair with platinum-tinted translucent frames.

The three of us entered Crenshaw's together, setting the sleigh bells ringing. Oliver stood by one of the display cases, talking to an older man. He nodded at us. Rory sat at the schoolmaster desk, processing a credit card purchase for a young woman.

Ellis walked me to the rear, away from the windows. Dawn stood nearby.

"I'll leave you to look at it," Oliver said to the man. "If you have any questions, please ask."

He greeted us warmly. "I know you!" he told Dawn, offering his hand for a shake. To me and Chief Hunter, he added, "Dawn is killer on the ball field. I played a couple of seasons in the merchants versus frontline heroes invitational. I couldn't throw a pitch she didn't hit. How you all doing?"

"I didn't know you were a softball player," I said.

He laughed. "I'm not. That's why I only played a couple of seasons."

We all joined in some good-natured ribbing, and after a lull in the repartee, I pointed to a wall and said, "The paint color looks great."

"Thanks," Oliver said. "I'm getting there. Mom will be rehanging the cobwebs soon. It killed her to take them down for the painters." He turned to Ellis. "I assume this isn't a social visit. Can I help with something?"

Ellis thanked him, described the situation, and handed over the photo array. "Have you ever seen any of these men?"

Oliver studied the photographs. "No."

"Thanks again!" the young woman customer said, and left.

Rory limped over and nodded curtly at Dawn.

Oliver handed his mom the photos. "The police are trying to ID this guy. I don't know him . . . do you?"

Rory took the array, but didn't look at it. She turned to face me. "Officer LeBlanc is here because of protocol. I get that part. What about you? Do you stop at car accidents, too? The bloodier, the better?"

"You sure have a way with words, Rory," I said. "We're trying to find the person who shot at me. I have a vested interest in our success. Your help would be appreciated."

"That was a bad thing." She held my gaze for a few seconds longer, then studied the images. "I don't recognize any of them." She handed it back to Ellis and kept her eyes on his face. "If you have suspects, you must be close to catching him."

"We're making real progress." He extracted two forms. "If you'd each just sign that you couldn't make an ID, we won't have to take any more of your time."

Rory took her copy, returned to the desk, and sat down to read it.

Oliver barely glanced at the form. He rested the paper on the window ledge, took a fountain pen from his pocket, checked the NO box, and signed on the dotted line.

I turned toward Rory. She held the paper in front of her long enough to read it twice, then took a gold-tone ballpoint pen from a rosewood stand, ticked no as well, and signed her name.

"I better see if my customer has any questions," Oliver said, glancing over his shoulder at the older man, still standing by the display case. He lowered his voice. "With any luck, his only question will be, 'Do you take Amex?' Good seeing you, Dawn."

Ellis accepted his form, then Rory's. Oliver crossed the shop to his customer and Ellis thanked Rory for her cooperation.

"You call it cooperation. I call it acquiescence."

"I can't tell if she's trying to intimidate me, or if she's just mean," I said, once we'd parted company with Dawn and were en route back to my office.

"Don't bother analyzing her intentions. Analyze her signature instead."

I said hello to my staff as we passed through the front office to the warehouse. When we reached the workstation equipped with the microscope, I examined the forms, taking my time, and spotted the anomaly easily. The pressure-point tell was evident.

When I was done, I stepped aside so Ellis could take a turn.

He brought the microscope into focus. After he examined all three signatures, he said, "There's no question." He looked me dead in the eyes. "I'll call for a search warrant."

At my suggestion, Ellis arranged for the warrant to include the dumpster outside Crenshaw's, in addition to the shop itself, and Oliver's and Rory's vehicles and homes.

While we waited for word that the warrant had been approved, Ellis asked me how the search team could recognize gall nuts and know which paper was which.

"You can't. You need to bring me."

"No way. It's too dangerous."

"Not if I'm with you and stay away from windows."

After a moment's reflection, he agreed, not because he wanted to, but because he needed my expertise.

After receiving the warrant, another warp-speed accomplishment, Ellis and I entered Crenshaw's with Dawn, the Portsmouth police officer assigned to the job, and three Rocky Point police officers: Griff, Meade, and Darryl.

While Ellis served the warrant, Officer Meade got me settled on a chair near the back office. Angled bookcases blocked my view of the front windows, which meant no one could see me from the street.

The back office was designed for work, not display. There was a big worktable, a sorting bookcase, a computer table, file cabinets, and four wall-mounted shelves, keeping various supplies within easy reach. Griff stepped past me and began his search.

Rory was in Ellis's face, arguing, stomping her foot. Her message was clear—she was outraged, and if Ellis knew what was good for him, he'd clear out now. Ellis stood with his feet apart, buffeted but stable, like a buoy standing tall in gale force winds.

Oliver slouched against the wall in back of the schoolmaster's desk, with his hands stuffed in his pockets, his forehead scrunched, his lips compressed into one thin angry line, watching the police work. The officers, ignoring Rory's protests, began searching the shop itself. They put on plastic gloves and moved every book, opened every cabinet and drawer, and found nothing.

Rory's ranting continued unabated.

Dawn perched on a low stool by a tall bookcase, reading something on her phone, uninvolved.

Griff beckoned Ellis to the back and Ellis excused himself to Rory. Without an audience, Rory's diatribe fizzled out. A minute later, Ellis asked me to look at the supplies of paper Griff had located. I stood near the worktable.

Ellis straddled the threshold between the back office and the shop, watching me assess the reams of letterhead; multiuse printer-copier paper; acid-free paper; and heavy stock appropriate for catalogue notes.

"No," I said.

"Thank you," Ellis said.

Ellis touched his ear, and I saw an earbud. He listened for a moment, then stepped past us, and exited through the rear door.

Griff returned to the shop and joined the search there. Rory stood near the front door with her hands on her hips, out for bear. Oliver maintained his position against the wall.

The back door was solid-looking, with a small window near the top. I dragged a low stool, a match to the one Dawn was sitting on, positioning it to the right of the door, out of view of anyone peeking in. By standing on the stool and aiming my eyes on the diagonal, I could see a long stretch of alley.

Darryl was displaying the old venetian blind cords I'd seen inside the shop. Ellis said something I couldn't hear, then Darryl dropped them into an evidence bag. Ellis turned toward the rear door, and I stepped down and slid the stool aside.

I sat back down.

I heard the rear door open, then close. A moment later, Ellis joined me at the threshold, observing.

Oliver still hadn't moved. Rory was seated behind the desk, glowering.

Griff did a slow 360, then caught Ellis's eye. He shook his head, communicating that he hadn't found anything, and doubted there was anything to find.

"Nothing?" I asked.

"He probably works out of his house. I have a team there now."

"Did you look in the desk?"

"Sure. The drawers are filled with regular stuff: letterhead, paper clips, pens, pencils, Scotch tape . . . stuff."

"I'm talking about the hidden compartment."

Ellis stared at me.

"That's a Sheraton schoolmaster desk. The center section lifts up. It's big, so the teacher had plenty of room for books and such."

"Wait here."

Ellis strode into the shop and crossed to the desk. He said something to Rory, and she shook her head, no, no, no. Ellis started to reach for the center section lid and she collapsed over it, clutching the front edge, refusing to budge.

"No!" Rory shrieked. "No!"

It was like watching a car crash in slow motion, horrifying and sickening. "No! No! No!"

Ellis remained by the desk, watching her with professional detachment, while the officers stood a few paces away, awaiting instructions. Oliver, still leaning against the wall, gazed at the ceiling, remote, removed from his mother's anguish.

Rory threw back her head and screamed again, her torment palpable. "No-o-o-o!"

I stood. "Oliver," I said quietly.

Oliver turned his head toward me. "How did you get onto me?"

"It wasn't just one thing."

He stepped forward and touched Rory's shoulder. "Mom . . . it's over."

She wailed.

Oliver disengaged her hands from the desk and rolled her chair backward. She turned sideways, hugging his waist, burying her head in his side. He rubbed her back, gentling her into submission.

Ellis lifted the desk's center lid.

It was all there, paper in a protective folder, a small terra-cotta bowl filled with gall nuts, small sealed glass jars containing powders and crystals, half a dozen quills, thin white cotton gloves, and magnifying glasses.

"My mother had nothing to do with it," Oliver said. He disentangled himself from her clench, leaned down, and kissed her cheek. "I'm the forger."

"And the killer," Ellis said.

"Me?" Oliver said, staggered. "No way."

"We found the rope, from your venetian blinds."

"Test it . . . you'll see. Unless the murderer stole it from my dumpster, of course. As for me . . . I've never killed anything in my life, except an African violet once, but that was years ago, before I learned how to garden."

I believed him.

CHAPTER THIRTY-ONE

After Rory and Oliver were taken away—Oliver in handcuffs, Rory spitting fire—Ellis thanked me for my help.

"Do you want me to come to the station, too?" I asked.

"No, we're good."

"I can help frame some of the antiques-related questions."

"If I need help, I'll ask. As of now, we're fine."

"I want to come."

"I can tell."

"You're not listening to me," I grumbled.

"Just because you don't like the answer doesn't mean I didn't hear the question. I listened. I said no." He paused to see if I had a comeback, and when I didn't, he added, "I'm leaving the patrol as is. Griff will escort you to your place."

"Thank you," I managed. "Can I ask you one more thing?"

"Sure."

"Did you believe Oliver when he said he didn't do it?"

"I neither believe nor disbelieve him. I deal in evidence, not beliefs."

Griff appeared from around the corner.

"I'll be in touch," Ellis said. "Thanks, again."

Ty and I spent the rest of the weekend in lockdown in our home, something we'd never done before. We didn't go out for dinner or brunch. We didn't go for a walk on the beach or a hike in the mountains. We didn't go shopping. We didn't go to a play or the movies. We didn't go into our own hot tub. We kept the first-floor curtains drawn and the blinds down. Except for my rampant curiosity and lingering fear, I had a wonderful time. We played backgammon and Scrabble, read books and magazines, did a little work, watched old movies, and talked.

Sunday afternoon, during one of my frequent checks of the *Seacoast Star*'s website for updates, Ty asked, "Any news about Oliver?"

"Just the formal police statement that on advice of counsel, he isn't answering questions at this time. He's probably counting on getting another sweet plea deal."

"Why do you think he isn't the killer?"

"No reason the police would accept. I know him, that's all. Not to be glib, but he's a lover not a killer. He charms his way out of bad situations and into good ones. If something doesn't work out, he shrugs and moves on. I can see him as a forger. He'd enjoy pulling the wool over people's eyes because it would make him feel cleverer than everyone else, but he'd never attack them, no matter what."

"Not even if Gloria or Ivan threatened him with exposure?"

"I can't see it. I threatened him with exposure, and what did he do? He confessed. If Gloria told him to back off from accepting the Jane Austen letter appraisal to give herself a leg up, he'd back off. If Ivan tried to blackmail him, he'd pay."

Ty stretched out his legs. "So you think Oliver got his hands on an authentic Jane Austen letter, and used it as a model to forge one. Why didn't he just sell it? From what you've told me, he could have made a bundle."

"First, there's no reason to think the Jane Austen letter Oliver used as a guide was real. He could have created a fake based on an earlier forgery. Second, he was what ... fourteen, fifteen? Something like that. He wasn't thinking about money. To him, it was a game, a private competition to see whether he could pull it off. Evidently, he could. The Thomas Jefferson letter he forged, for instance, was accepted as authentic until Gloria got hold of it. By the time he needed cash, nearly twenty years had passed, and he'd forgotten about the Jane Austen letters."

Ty laughed. "How do you forget something like that?"

I laid the book down. "I'm making this up, obviously, but here's one possible scenario: Oliver finds a letter signed by Jane Austen, which may or may not be genuine. He doesn't care. He creates a fake letter, not a replica. Oliver's forgery showed a significant awareness of Jane Austen's life and the era in which she lived, an astonishing accomplishment for a kid."

"And he did it on his own?" Ty asked, sounding skeptical.

"So it seems. Now picture him, sitting in the shop, his forgery complete, admiring his handiwork when his mom walks in. Quick like a bunny, he slips the two letters into a nearby portfolio of sketches, and smiles like the loving son he is. Later, when he goes to retrieve them, he can't find the portfolio. Someone bought it. Oops! Years go by. Then—*boom*—I announce I have two Jane Austen letters. He must be a whiz at Texas Hold'em because I didn't have a clue he had inside knowledge he was trying to hide."

"You think your dad bought the portfolio at Crenshaw's?"

"It sure looks that way. I know Oliver forged one of the Jane Austen letters and I know the portfolio ended up in my father's possession. What I don't know is how Oliver got his hands on the original Jane Austen letter. Probably it's nothing more than happenstance. Remember when we found the van Gogh in a box of old paintings someone brought in after they'd cleaned out their attic? They didn't want an appraisal—they wanted cash. Same thing happened to me with Heather. She simply wanted Ivan's books out of the house. It occurs all the time—not every day, of course, but frequently enough that I established the policy that we videotape every single object that comes to us, no matter how, no matter if it's purchased as a single unit or as part of a collection. You just never know what will walk in the door."

"Let me get this straight," Ty said. "Oliver's dad buys this miscellaneous lot and leaves it to Oliver to sort through." He laced his fingers behind his head. "Which brings us back to where we started—who's the killer?"

"If I knew that, we wouldn't be sitting here on a beautiful autumn Sunday afternoon. We'd be out hiking."

"We might have to play hooky one day soon. It would be a shame to miss the foliage."

"Count me in, big fella."

Ty smiled.

I picked up my book and Ty resumed typing.

Ellis called at about five and asked to stop by.

We went into the dining room because Ellis had said he needed to spread out a little. Ty sat next to me on one side of our long farm table. Ellis sat across from us.

"Thank you again for forwarding Ivan's internship application. He listed Gloria and two other professors as references. They both spoke highly of his intellect and had nothing much to say about his personality and communications skills."

"Is Oliver going to get a deal?" I asked.

"Yes. He got himself a good lawyer and they're ironing out the details. He's in some real trouble over the forgeries because the dollar amounts are high. He'll do jail time. But he swears he had nothing to do with the murders or the attempt on your life."

"Did the venetian blind cord match?"

Ellis shifted position. "No."

"How's Rory handling things?" I asked.

"As expected. She'd tear the house down if she could."

"I read about a woman who lifted a two-thousand-pound car to save her child. Maybe Rory could have made it through the woods after all."

"That's actually why I'm here. The red-light camera at the entrance to Highbridge captured three people driving in and/or out during the relevant time period. I brought the photos to see if you recognize anyone."

Ellis opened an envelope and extracted three eight-by-ten photographs, all in black-and-white. He laid them out along the table in front of me.

One of the three showed a man, past retirement age, in profile. I didn't recognize him. One of the two women was in her twenties. I didn't recognize her, either. The third photo showed a woman wearing a big floppy hat that hid most of her face. A tendril of blond hair straggled down her neck. The car window was down and her elbow jutted out.

"I can't see her face," I said.

"And this is the only shot we have of her. No one we asked, including the woman who was raking, recognizes her."

"From the angle, I infer that this shot was taken when she turned into the development. How about when she left?"

"She must have driven out the other exit, and there's no camera there."

I picked up the photo and studied it. And then I saw it. I inhaled sharply and looked up, meeting Ellis's eyes. "I need to see a blowup."

He tapped something on his tablet, then slid the device across the table.

I pinched the screen to enlarge the image and examined her arm. "I can't believe it! I just can't. This is Heather Adler, Ivan's ex." I slid the device back. "Look at the tattoo. It's hard to read because it's in white ink. And she's not a blonde, but she had a Marilyn Monroe wig on her wall . . . for inspiration, she said."

Ellis fingered the printed photo toward his side of the table and stared at it for several seconds, then turned to the tablet and leaned in close. "What does the tattoo say?"

"Be bold."

He studied the photo for another minute. "I don't see a sex kitten wig."

"She could have tucked the excess hair under her cap. Poof! No more sex kitten, but you're still a blonde. That would be a better alternative than buying a new wig that maybe could be traced." I paused for a moment. "Heather called me. Cara told her I wasn't available, that we were filming. When I called her back, she said she wanted to apologize for being down. I didn't think anything about it at the time, but Heather doesn't strike me as a person who calls to apologize for being in a bad mood."

"You're saying she called to suss out where you were."

"And it worked." I shut my eyes and went back over my conversations with Heather, picturing her, recalling her apartment. The front hall and the corridor leading to the sitting room. The layout, providing an unobstructed view through the kitchen window. And the bookshelves with the leather bindings lovingly displayed. "Oh, wow." My eyes flew open. "I just remembered something, two things. There's a clothesline in Heather's backyard. And the first time I looked at Ivan's books, there was a red leather folio, but it wasn't included in the collection I bought."

"A folio?" Ellis asked.

"The term refers to a book's size. It was the largest book in Ivan's collection, twelve by fifteen. That's plenty big enough to protect documents or notes slipped between the pages. She must still have it. That's the main reason Ivan went to the apartment that day—not to measure the books so he'd know how many boxes to bring, like he told Heather. He wanted to hide the notes and Garfield letter he stole from Gloria, and his own notes on writing hesitations, in case he summarily got the boot from Hitchens."

"From what you've told me about her," Ty said, "I wonder if Heather was the brains behind the whole operation."

"That wouldn't surprise me a bit," I agreed. "Heather was desperate for Ivan to succeed. If he told her that he needed Gloria's notes to adapt her process to his writing hesitation metric, she would have goosed him to ... ahem ... *borrow* them. Can you find out if he called Heather en route to Hitchens to pick up Gloria's script? I bet he did. Heather would have told him to detour to Murphy's and make a copy of Gloria's key so he could get Gloria's notes back after he copied them without anyone being the wiser. Remember, he needed more examples for his analysis of writing hesitations. That's why he took the Garfield letter. It isn't every day a grad student gets to work with a presidential letter."

"That's enough for me." Ellis gathered together the photos. "I should be able to get a search warrant. Will I be able to recognize that book?"

I smiled. "No way."

He smiled back. "Then you'd better come along."

Heather opened the door. Her gaze took in the platoon of police lined up on the porch, and she tried to shove the door closed. Ellis held it open with one hand and proffered the search warrant with the other.

She glanced at it, then met Ellis's eyes. "What's going on?"

Ellis explained.

"No," she spat, and thrust her shoulder against the door, putting energy behind the move.

He overpowered her easily, and we all tramped in. I brought up the rear.

Heather stood with her arms crossed, glaring. "This isn't right."

Ellis told Officer Meade, "Stay with Ms. Adler." He directed Griff to bag the Marilyn Monroe wig, hanging gracefully on the wall.

I walked to the sitting room, as Ellis and I had previously arranged. I wore plastic gloves, but had promised not to touch anything. Darryl was assigned to observe my every move.

The folio wasn't visible. I asked Darryl to open the closed cabinet doors on the media center. He did so. There were stacks of old copies of *InDesign* magazine and a few DVDs. Searching under couch cushions could wait. It was more likely Heather had hidden the book in a cupboard, someplace out of sight, but easy to access. In the kitchen, I asked Darryl to open each cabinet door. We started on the bottom units. In the third one, a tall rectangular-shaped object covered by a white pillowcase stood behind an old-style standing mixer.

"We should look at that," I said.

Darryl spoke into his collar mic and within seconds Ellis and Detective Brownley came into the kitchen. As they moved forward, I was elbowed back. Ellis asked Darryl to man the video camera and record everything from this point forward. Ellis eased the object out and positioned it on a small plastic tarp Detective Brownley draped over the dinette table. We all huddled close as she lifted the pillowcase up and off, revealing a folio-size book. The dark red leather binding was embellished with gilt tooling.

"It's not a book," I said, pointing at the hard sides, artfully painted to replicate gilt-tipped pages. "It's hollowed-out. Viewing the spine, it looks like a regular book, but it's not."

Ellis lifted the cover. Inside was a steel safe.

"A three-digit combination lock," he said.

"No problem. I'll have it open in about a minute."

"You know how to pick locks?"

"Sure. This lock is nothing special, designed to keep little kids out, not pros. We open lockboxes featuring this kind of lock all the time, and, sadly, they're usually empty. Don't you know how to do it?"

"Yes, but I'm a cop."

Still wearing the plastic gloves he'd given me, I tested all three rows to find the one that offered the most resistance, then turned the dial, one digit at a time, listening for the click. The tighter the resistance, the louder the click. The middle row won that contest, clicking at three. The bottom row was the next most resistant, and the click came at four. The top row clicked at one.

"Ivan's office number," I said. "Three-four-one. Did you time me?"

"No. I wanted to, but you were done before I could set the timer."

I laughed. "May I open it?"

"Yes."

I unlatched the door. Four plain white ten-by-thirteen envelopes sat inside the cubbyhole.

"May I take a photo?" I asked.

Ellis gave a hint of a smile. "Yes."

When I was done, Ellis lifted the envelopes clear of the box. At the bottom, sat a dinged-up silver-barreled pistol.

"Wow," I said.

"That's an old Baby Browning," Ellis said.

"May I take another photo?"

Ellis's smile broadened. "Yes."

He removed the magazine and the bullet in the chamber.

None of the envelopes was sealed. The top one contained the Garfield letter, still in the Crenshaw-branded acid-free sleeve. The second one contained a sheaf of handwritten notes. The handwriting was similar to documents I'd examined in Gloria's files. Scanning the pages, I saw the name "Jefferson" repeated a dozen times. The third one contained Ivan's typed notes. Flipping through the pages, I spotted several mentions of "writing hesitations." The bottom envelope contained a printout of Gloria's script for my TV show—the notes stolen from her portfolio.

"Go ahead," Ellis said. "Wes likes photos."

I ignored his comment and snapped away, then leaned in to look at the documents closely. "May I take the Garfield letter back to my office for analysis?"

"Not now. We need to do our due diligence first."

The pillowcase, the gun, the magazine, the bullet from the chamber, and the envelopes were sealed in individual evidence bags. Ellis closed the book safe and lowered the folio into its own jumbo-size bag.

As soon as he sealed the last bag, he told me to wait in the kitchen, and asked Darryl to follow him out back, to record him packing up the clothesline.

They returned a few minutes later, and Ellis said, "You can switch off the video now." When the red dot went out, Ellis turned to me. "I'm going to put a rush on our analysis. With any luck, I can get the letter back to you tomorrow afternoon or Tuesday morning."

"Thank you." I paused for a moment. "I still can't believe that someone who had so much going for her is a killer. I guess it shows the power of perception. I looked at Heather and saw a competent, successful woman. She looked at herself and saw a failure—she failed in getting Ivan to live up to her ideals."

"People can only be pushed so far before they snap."

"Not everyone snaps."

"Sure they do, in their own way, in their own time."

"I'm going to have to think about that."

Back in the front hall, I stood in the corner, near the shadow puppets, as Detective Brownley placed Heather under arrest.

Heather's face was whey-pale, the muscles in her neck and shoulders as stiff as brittle.

Officer Meade opened the front door. The detective kept her hand on Heather's elbow, ready to propel her out, to ensure compliance.

Heather took a step toward the door, then stopped and looked over her shoulder at me. She spoke softly, without affect, as if she had been drugged. "Did you see who killed Ivan?"

"No."

They led her away. I stepped out on the porch to watch.

Just before the patrol car door closed, Heather turned toward the house, her eyes finding mine. Tears trickled down her cheeks.

Darryl drove me home, and as soon as I was inside, I called Russ at Sterling Security to cancel the patrols at both my house and my company.

I found Ty in his second-floor office, still tapping away on his laptop.

"It's over," I said. "Let's get in the hot tub."

CHAPTER THIRTY-TWO

Wes was waiting for me when I pulled into my company parking lot just after eight Monday morning. His primary gripe was that I hadn't taken photos of Oliver or Heather in handcuffs.

"If you don't stop fussing," I said, "I won't send you the photos I did take."

"Of what?" he asked, his interest piqued.

"Wouldn't you like to know."

"Josie!" he whined.

"Heather's secret hiding place—a book safe—and what was hidden in it, including the gun she used to try to kill me."

Wes nearly salivated, but he made a quick recovery and demanded, "Why didn't you send them yesterday?"

"Because I was enjoying a spell of freedom. Ty and I stayed in the hot tub without a care in the world until we were pruney." I didn't mention the hours I'd spent brooding about Veronica Sutton and my father. "Did you talk to Melissa Rogers, Gloria's mom's caregiver?"

"Yup. She's a nurse, a nice lady. She owns the cottage and takes in one patient at a time, private nursing. She never saw any documents, but you already know that because you found them—you're a hot banana, Joz! Gloria mentioned she had an ex who was on her like a tick, so she got herself a tool of persuasion. She showed Melissa the gun. That's what Gloria called it, 'a tool of persuasion.' Melissa was irked that Gloria brought the weapon into the house. She told me she hates guns. She told Gloria to be careful, and Gloria laughed, saying she wasn't the one who needed to be careful."

"So much anger!"

"In all directions."

"I'm not angry at you," I said.

Wes grinned. "Then I'm not doing my job right."

I laughed. "Wes!"

"So why did Heather kill them and try to kill you?"

I thought for a minute. "To try to salvage her future. Ivan stole Gloria's notes and documents, and he got caught, probably because he let something slip while Gloria was rehearsing at my studio, something he would have had no way of knowing unless he'd seen her original notes about the Thomas Jefferson letters. That Oliver was the forger, for instance. Gloria would have gone ballistic. That one misstep set everything else in motion."

"Why did Ivan steal the notes? I mean, didn't he think Gloria would notice?"

"Desperate people do stupid things. He'd planned on copying them and sneaking them back into the file, but it was still a risky proposition. He'd been in a pressure cooker for months, for years—and finally, he broke under the strain. He wanted to make a splash the way Gloria had when she was in grad school. He had his own idea, 'writing hesitations.' He wanted to study Gloria's original research into the Thomas Jefferson letters to see how he could replicate her success. Ivan had access to the sanitized version of her research published in the magazine, the same as anyone, but he wanted her actual in-the-trenches findings—that's why he stole her notes."

"Jeez . . . that's dunce cap stupid. So he got busted—then what?"

"Gloria told him she was going to report him to Dr. Shield, the head of the department. Ivan tried to convince her to give him a second chance. She would have refused point-blank. Gloria told me how she'd worked like a demon to get where she was. I guarantee she would have been in no mood to give a cheater a break. So he runs to Heather."

"And confesses that he's a thief?" Wes asked. "She's one forgiving woman."

"I doubt forgiveness had anything to do with it. Heather was totally fixated on rescuing Ivan to save her own dreams. I'm conjecturing, of course, but nothing else makes sense. Heather told Ivan to stop being so spineless, to fix it. He flailed around, not knowing what to do, so she said she'd take care of it. Ivan probably assumed Heather meant she'd persuade Gloria to change her mind. Maybe Heather tried, but Gloria wouldn't even listen, so she killed her.

Let's not forget, though, that Heather had brought the clothesline with her—that shows premeditation. Then she drove Gloria's car to the church to give herself time to get away—she couldn't just leave it on Trevor, where it would be seen right away by anyone going to my company. When Heather told Ivan what she'd done—that she'd taken care of the problem—she expected him to be grateful that she'd cleaned up his mess so efficiently. Instead, he was aghast, and broke off their relationship on the spot. Heather must have been mortified. She kills for him and he dumps her. It didn't take her long to conclude a man that weak would eventually turn her in. Which meant he had to die, too. She gets to his office, has him show her his notes on his writing hesitations, then kills him, grabs the notes, and I breeze in."

"He was no shrimp. How did she pull it off?"

"I doubt it even occurred to him that he might be in danger—he turns his back to her for one second, she tosses the rope around his neck, twists it tight, and waits ten seconds, which is roughly how long it takes for a person to lose consciousness."

"She's flexible—she strangles two people, then switches to a pistol."

"She's an opportunistic killer. She would have strangled me, too, probably, if she could have gotten me alone."

"What was she going to do with Ivan's notes?"

I pursed my lips, thinking. "I don't know . . . sell them, maybe. Ivan thought they were his ticket to success. Heather probably reasoned that on the off chance he was right, she ought to keep them."

"Back to Gloria . . . How did Heather manage to arrange the last-minute meeting so early in the morning?" Wes asked.

"Heather used Ivan's phone. Gloria would recognize the number and take the call. Gloria was mad at him, but they were still working together. Heather said something to get Gloria to agree to meet, maybe that she had important information about Ivan that Gloria needed to hear. They met on Trevor Street, which, as you know, has almost no traffic, especially at that hour. Gloria was going that way anyway, to get to my place, so it wouldn't inconvenience her. Strangling her took presence of mind, but more determination than strength. She did the same thing with Gloria as she did with Ivan—throw the rope over her head, twist it, and hold it taut. Once Gloria was dead, Heather towed the body into some low brush and drove Gloria's car to the church parking lot. An easy jog brought her back to her own car, and she was on her way in minutes. No fuss, no muss."

"Why did Heather arrange the scarf so carefully?"

"That's a good question. I don't know. Why do you think?"

"Beats me. It's crazy." Wes held up his notebook. "Give me some ideas I can play with."

"To delay discovery of the rope. To confuse the investigation. Because she was in shock and is an artist, so she automatically tidied up the design."

Wes scribbled a note. "Why did she go after you?"

"By that point, Heather was little better than a maniac. She'd gone from happy and secure in her relationship to twice a killer in a matter of hours. I've been thinking from the start that she was afraid my memory of having seen the killer would come back . . . probably that's the reason. When they arrested her she asked me if I'd seen the killer. Fear festers."

Wes's expression softened. "I don't want to turn all schmaltzy or anything, but I'm glad she missed her shot."

I patted his arm. "Thanks."

"What else ya got?"

"Nothing."

He started toward his car, then paused, turned back, and shook his finger at me. "Send me those photos." He got behind the wheel, and drove away.

I emailed the photos, adding a two-sentence explanation about them and a one-sentence quote. Wes would be a happy man.

A man named Giles Lipp called at ten. He explained he was a lawyer with the firm of Corwin Gresham Blaine, LLP, representing the estate of Veronica Sutton.

"The estate?" I exclaimed. "She's dead?"

"I'm afraid so. She died Saturday afternoon. I might add, her passing was peaceful. As you may be aware, she'd been ill for some time."

"I didn't know things were so serious."

"Yes, well, the reason I'm calling is that by the terms of her will, we are to deliver a certain package within forty-eight hours of her death. That means I need to get it to you by this afternoon. Would it be possible for me to deliver it now?"

"Veronica Sutton left me something? Is that what you're saying?"

"Yes. Is now convenient? I could be there in half an hour."

Utterly mystified, I told him to come on ahead.

Giles Lipp was in a hurry. He didn't want to chat or sit or answer any questions. All he wanted was for me to sign for the cardboard banker box he placed on the guest table, so he could leave. The form was simple, acknowledging receipt as part of the distribution of Veronica Sutton's estate. The box was heavy, forty pounds or so, and sealed with a plastic strap. I hoisted it onto a cart and wheeled it to a worktable in the warehouse. I used a razor to slit the strapping.

For a week, I'd been trying to learn about Veronica Sutton's relationship with my father. Now that I had the opportunity to discover something, I found myself shying away from lifting the lid. *Be careful what you wish for.* After a few seconds, I opened the box.

A notecard-size envelope sat on a legal-size manila folder, which in turn, rested on two stacks of leather-bound books. I opened the envelope and eased out a cream-colored notecard.

The note was dated last Friday, the day I'd spoken to her at her niece's house.

Dear Ms. Prescott,

I promised your father I would never reveal our relationship to you. He thought you would resent it, resent him. I disagreed with him, but I deferred to his judgment. I promised him I would keep the secret for as long as I lived, and I have done so.

I suppose I shouldn't have visited you, but I have learned that at the end of life, one cares less about form and more about function. It was bad form to suggest that I had knowledge of your father, then refuse to answer your questions, and for that I apologize. But I needed to meet you, the daughter your father loved so much, and that function was fulfilled. It was a selfish act. I hope you can forgive me.

I'd had the feeling she was an actress playing a part, and I was right.

I am days or weeks away from dying. With my death, comes an end to the secret. Perhaps I should take it to the grave, but if I were in your place, I'd want to know just as much as you seem to. Here, then, is the information you seek. I will arrange for it to be delivered immediately upon my death in the hopes that some of it will help with your appraisal of the Jane Austen letters.

Your father thought you were the best daughter a man could ever have. Truly, he adored you, but you know that. Don't judge him too harshly.

Sincerely,
Veronica Sutton

I set the note aside and opened the folder. Inside was a faded cardboard portfolio containing six watercolor landscapes and seascapes, and a receipt. I went through the sketches. I didn't recognize the artists' names. One of the ocean scenes was powerful, the sky minacious, the ocean roiling. There was nothing that related to or referenced the Jane Austen letters. The receipt was printed on Crenshaw letterhead, indicating a sale of one portfolio of miscellaneous sketches for $35, cash, dated September 6, 2001. The receipt was signed "Brian Mayhew."

There were ten books, all the same, the size of standard hardbacks, bound in brown leather. None bore a title. I extracted the one on top of the left-hand stack. It was a journal. The first entry was dated February 12, 1985, two months after my mother's death.

Dear Diary,
I've decided to start a diary! I know, I know, whoever heard of a thirty-one-year-old woman starting a diary for the first time in

her life? It's all Ryan's fault. I want to remember everything, every mood, every touch, every conversation, and this will help me do so. It will also let me be with him, metaphorically, at least, when he can't be with me. We'll see how it goes.
RS

Ronnie Sutton, I thought. She called herself *Ronnie*. My father must have done so, too.

I closed the journal. I couldn't read it. Not now. I couldn't bear it. As soon as I'd suspected that Veronica Sutton and my father had been involved romantically, I'd tried to understand why he hadn't told me about her, about their relationship. Now I knew why. He'd feared that I would have been distraught to learn that he started dating within weeks of burying my mother, and he would have been right.

I placed the receipt in my tote bag and everything else back inside the box. I moved the box onto the cart, and wheeled it to my car. After wrestling it onto the back seat, I brought the cart inside, and told Cara I had an errand, that I wouldn't be long.

At home, I used a luggage cart we kept in the basement to maneuver the box inside. I brought it to my study. I picked up one of the photos I kept on my desk, of me and my dad on a hike. I'd just finished a six-month internship at a SoHo gallery and landed the job at Frisco's. We looked happy and carefree, standing amid soaring fir trees. I didn't remember who'd taken the photo—another hiker, I supposed. While my dad stood beside me, looking and acting the same as always, he'd been involved with Veronica Sutton for eight years, and I hadn't had a clue that something was up.

Of course I would have been horrified that my father had started a new relationship so soon after my mother's death, but I would have gotten over it. Why didn't my father know that about me? I touched my dad's arm through the protective glass. In suggesting that we go away for that weekend, I'd thought I was offering solace to a man still grieving his long-dead wife. He'd thought I was expressing a need to be with him, just us two. The lies we tell to protect the people we love—or more to the point, the lies we tell when we think the people we love need protecting. And with both Veronica—Ronnie—and my dad dead, there was nothing I could do to fix it.

I got back to the office at noon. I greeted everyone quickly, and retreated to my private office. I felt odd, out of sync, as if I were lost in a meadow of tall grass, unable to find my way out. I felt baffled and confused, and utterly overwhelmed. Finally, after sitting like a lump for far too long, I checked my messages, just for something to do.

Marcus, the paralegal I'd spoken to over the weekend, had left a voicemail that the Right-to-Know paperwork had been submitted. Sasha had sent an email saying Dr. Hart was eager to take on the project and would drive up from Boston to discuss the specifics today at two. I replied, saying I had the receipt for the portfolio, so she could suspend Cara's work trying to find the shop or gallery where it had been purchased. I scanned in the receipt and attached it.

I sent out for lunch, but had no appetite. I was tempted to go home, to crawl into bed, but I knew that wouldn't help, so I toughed it out. Somehow, I found the wherewithal to jot some notes for the meeting with Dr. Hart.

Cara called up that Timothy was on line one.

"I bet you called to tell me you don't think we should use any footage from either Oliver or Gloria," I said.

"You're right. Someone put a hex on that episode. Should we abandon poor little Peter Rabbit?"

"I don't think we need to go to that extreme. Let's just not make it a battle . . . I'll go solo. We did a full appraisal here, so we can use our own work, as usual. Maybe Nancy can draft something for me to review."

"Perfect. With any luck we can get the script retooled by the time you're here in the city."

"By the way," I said, "I owe you a thank-you. I've discovered I love Third Degree martinis. You are a magic man."

"Oh, honey, you don't know the half of it."

I laughed, thanked him for everything, and we promised to talk soon. The momentary reprieve talking to Timothy had provided dwindled, leaving me alone again with my addled mind. I had to work. I had to.

Someone named Brian Mayhew had signed the portfolio receipt. I googled his name, searching in New Hampshire, and found him easily through his LinkedIn profile. He listed Crenshaw's as an employer during his junior year in college. He was a librarian now, working in Manchester.

I still had twenty minutes before Dr. Hart was scheduled to arrive, so I called the library. After a long wait, he came on the line.

I introduced myself, explained I was contacting him as part of an antiques appraisal, and apologized for bothering him.

"You're a welcome change of pace. I'm working the reference desk today, and it's midterms. Panicky students have their own charm, but, well, let's just say, I'm *thrilled* to talk to you."

Brian had a deep voice, a radio voice. His wry humor provided a pleasant change of pace for me, too, enabling me to set aside my angst-riddled regrets.

"You're not going to remember this," I said, "but on September 6, 2001, you were working at Crenshaw's Rare Books, Prints and Autographs. You signed a receipt for a portfolio of sketches."

He gave a bark of laughter. "You better believe I remember it. I nearly got fired because of it."

"For selling the sketches?"

"For selling the portfolio. The customer, a man, if I remember right, went through the portfolio on his own, one sketch at a time, then said he wanted to buy the whole kit and caboodle. A couple of days later, Oliver, the owner's son, was back in the shop, and asked where I'd put the two Jane Austen letters. I told him I had never seen them, that I had no idea what he was talking about. Apparently, he'd slipped the letters into the portfolio backwards behind a sheet of blank paper. Anyone flipping through would simply think there were a few sheets of blank paper in the back."

"How did he explain putting them in such an odd place?"

"He said he wanted them safe from any mishaps and the portfolio was handy. It never occurred to him that anyone would look through those sketches, let alone buy them. He went insane. To tell you the truth, Oliver's dad seemed more upset that this was the first he was hearing about those letters than that the letters were gone."

"Did they try to contact the buyer?"

"They wanted to, but they couldn't because it was a cash transaction.

Thirty-five dollars. Can you believe I remember the amount? That goes to show what a traumatic event does to you. It sharpens your wits and your memory. I thought there was a chance the customer had signed the guest book, but he hadn't, and as far as I know, that was the end of it. I lasted a couple of days longer, but the tension was so thick, you would have needed a machete to bushwhack your way through, so I quit. I started tending bar. Far less stressful."

"Did you ever learn where the letters came from?"

"Yes. Mr. Crenshaw bought a box of miscellaneous ephemera at Brimfield, the big flea market, and he'd spotted one of the letters in that box. He hadn't sorted through things yet, and he was mad as a hornet that Oliver had taken it on himself to do so. Then Oliver's mom came in." Brian exhaled with a soft whistle. "As soon as she caught the gist of things, she dragged Oliver out by his earlobe. The whole situation creeped me out. That's when I quit."

"I can't thank you enough for telling me all this."

"You're welcome. Back to anxiety central for me!"

I searched for the 2001 dates of the Brimfield Antiques Flea Market, then called Ellis and got him on his cell phone.

"I think the Jane Austen letter was part of a box of ephemera Alfred Crenshaw bought at the Brimfield flea market in May or July 2001. May I look for the receipt?"

"The DA is organizing a forensic accountant to go through the books, but not that far back. They're only considered potential crimes within the statute of limitations."

"Are the files well-organized?"

"Yes. About two years ago, they converted all their records to a digital format. Actually, it's a searchable database. Hold on . . . I'm in my office and can check in now." I waited impatiently. "Give me a keyword."

"Brimfield."

"Got a bunch. Now what?"

"2001."

"There were two purchases, one a set of old leather bindings for five dollars, the other—here it is—in July, that box of ephemera you mentioned, for eight dollars."

I crossed my fingers. "Who sold the box?"

"Mom's Junque," he said, spelling the name, "out of Groton, Connecticut."

He gave me the phone number, and I thanked him. "Can you tell me anything about Oliver?"

"Not at this point. There's a bunch of directions this might go, including charges for mail fraud because some of his forgeries were shipped out of state, which could get him twenty years. We're letting Rory camp out in the lobby. For now."

"What a mess."

"It's all of that, and then some," Ellis said.

"Do you have an update on when I'll get to look at the Garfield letter?"

"Tomorrow morning is realistic. I'll stop by around ten."

I told him that was fine, and thanked him again.

Mom's Junque's phone number was answered by an engineering company. The receptionist told me they'd had the same number since the company's inception, fifteen years earlier. Information didn't have a number for Mom's Junque, and a quick search of Connecticut business licenses didn't turn up anything. Probably we were out of luck, but we couldn't give up. Although I'd demonstrated that the Cassandra letter was probably a fake, I still needed to confirm the provenance of the Fanny letter in case it was real, and as Ivan had said, when you run into a brick wall, you take it apart brick by brick. I'd removed two bricks, verifying that my dad had bought the portfolio at Crenshaw's, and discovering Crenshaw's had bought it from Mom's Junque. Dr. Hart's team could take it from there.

Sasha, Fred, Dr. Hart, and I sat in a loose circle in my office's conversation area.

Dr. Hart, who asked us to call her Lois, was about sixty. She had shoulder-length gray hair, dark blue eyes, and a creamy complexion. She wore a white button-down shirt and a black skirt, with a red belt and black knee-high boots.

Fred had carried up a silver tray with a coffeepot, teapot, various accoutrements, and Cara's gingersnaps.

I sipped a cup of strong black tea from the Minton china we used with guests, and listened as Sasha and Fred described the project and our expectations. I explained that sometimes there would be a TV crew on site, but most of the time, we'd simply set up video recorders, and that the producer would splice the footage together in the editing process.

Lois asked smart questions about the limits of her authority and the time line, then said, "I'd love to take it on, and I'm fine with doing all the work here, the TV recording, and having one or more of you participate at every step. I'm also glad there's no great urgency, so that we can be guided by the science, not an arbitrary timeline."

We settled on her fee, and I said, "I have a bit of new information, relating to provenance." I told them about the receipt I'd received from Veronica Sutton, my conversation with Brian, and Mom's Junque, which I suspected would prove to be a dead end.

"That's wonderful, Josie," Lois said. "Not that it might be a dead end, but that you made such progress, so quickly."

I laughed. "You, my friend, are a glass-half-full kind of gal!"

She smiled. "Always. One more question . . . do you have any consultants you want me to use, or do I have free rein?"

"That's an interesting question," I said. "You have free rein, with one caveat. You can choose your own team, but I'd like us to have the opportunity to vet them before you retain them—better to have an extra layer of security than not enough. Also, I have a contact at Frisco's. I was thinking of bringing them in after you submit your final report to validate your findings. With that cachet, we'll be in the catbird seat, in terms of auction potential."

"That's an excellent strategy."

I described our idea for the catalogue, to integrate stories about Jane Austen's life and connect them to a timeline.

Lois thought that was an intriguing approach. "In thinking about the 1814 letter to Fanny, we could discuss how in *Sense and Sensibility*, Elinor Dashwood's attitude toward marriage might have been informed by Jane's own experience with failed romances. Elinor thought that tying yourself up with a man you don't love is 'the worse and most irremediable of all evils.'"

"How about something to do with *Mansfield Park*?" Fred suggested. "That book was published that year."

"Yes," Lois agreed. "For instance, *Mansfield Park* was ignored by reviewers, but sold out within six months."

Sasha leaned forward. "I was thinking we could explain how Jane changed the title of *First Impressions* to *Pride and Prejudice*, to avoid confusion with a book of the same title that had been published in 1800."

"We could do the same with *Sense and Sensibility*," Fred said, "which was originally titled *Elinor and Marianne*."

"These are all great ideas," I said.

Lois laughed. "Choosing these stories will be enormous fun!"

"Sasha, you and Fred should start a file, so we don't lose track of any of these gems." I asked if anyone had anything else, and when no one did, I stood, signaling the meeting was over. I smiled at Lois. "I'll call Max Bixby, our lawyer, and get him going on the contract. With any luck, we'll be up and running in a week or so."

"May I see the letters?" she asked.

"Yes, of course." I asked Sasha to arrange the showing.

They left, and I sat back down.

The internal turmoil I'd sublimated rushed back. I tried to think of what to do, of how to be productive, but my mind was blank. If I couldn't trust my assessment of my relationship with my father, I couldn't trust anything. What else had I misjudged? What else had I romanticized? I was saved from sinking into a pitiful depression by the realization that Veronica Sutton's diary entries might have included one on September 6, 2001, the date Brian signed the Crenshaw's receipt.

I grabbed my bag and ran to my car.

CHAPTER THIRTY-THREE

I arranged Veronica Sutton's diaries by date, spreading them out on the floor. The last volume started on December 28, 2000, and ended on September 11, 2001. The entry from September sixth read: *I flew up to join Ryan in New Hampshire, and we spent the afternoon browsing in Portsmouth shops. It was a beautiful, sunny day, a perfect day, but I didn't like the sun on my face, so Ryan bought me the most beautiful Saint Laurent two-tone straw large brim hat. Such fun! We had lunch at the Blue Dolphin, including a bottle of Sancerre. He found a portfolio of sketches in Crenshaw's, where we always stop. I didn't think much of the artwork, but he thought one or two of them were worth thinking about. What a heavenly man—he thinks about art.*

Tears stung my eyes. I packed everything up, closed the box, and shoved it under my desk, out of sight.

I took a step, but found myself too wobbly to continue. I sat on the floor, leaning back against the wall. I was still sitting there when Ty got home.

He took one look at my face, sat beside me, and took my hand in his. He didn't ask any questions. He didn't speak.

I appreciated his forbearance.

After a few minutes, the absurdity struck me, and I laughed.

"I'm a mess," I said. "It's perfectly logical that I'm sitting on the floor doing nothing, but there's no reason for you to waste time like this."

"Anywhere you are, I want to be. Why are you sitting on the floor doing nothing?"

"I don't want to talk about it."

"Okay." After a minute, he added, "Do you want to sit here doing nothing? Or are you here because you're too upset to do something else?"

"The latter."

"I don't necessarily have a cure," he said, standing. He helped me up. "But I have a recommendation. It involves a martini, a hot tub, and a conversation when you're ready."

"I guess I should do as you suggest. After all, you are an expert in emergency management." I stopped, and he stopped, too. "You're happy."

"You state it like an accusation."

"Well?"

He opened his arms wide. "I am happy, and it's all because of you. I met with Patrick Healy at Hitchens today, the chair, and he signed me up to teach an online course called 'The Basics of Emergency Management.' Because it's online, I can teach it from anywhere, so my travel schedule won't be an issue. I also enrolled in a Ph.D. level course called 'Data-driven Investigations.' If I decide to apply for a doctorate, the credits will apply. It's online, too."

I gave a little shriek of joy, and threw my arms around his neck. "I'm so proud of you! I can't believe you did all this today."

"I did all that this morning. This afternoon I caught a speeding bullet and leapt a tall building."

I laughed. "Only one?"

Once we were settled in the hot tub and I'd had a few sips of martini, I told him about the diaries and confessed my shameful realization—I'd tried to help my father cope, but had only succeeded in keeping him from moving on. I admitted that it was wrenching reading Veronica Sutton's diaries, discovering that they'd fallen in love so soon after my mom died, hearing her reports of his devotion. It was agonizing knowing that my father had another life, one he never revealed to me because he hadn't thought I could handle it, even as an adult.

"He didn't trust me," I whispered.

"I don't think it has anything to do with trust, Josie. I suspect he was protecting you. He loved you very much."

"I'll never know how I would have reacted. But I know how I'm reacting now, and it's not good. I hate Veronica Sutton." I used air quotes and a snarky tone to add, "Ronnie."

"Are you jealous?"

"No. I'm mad. And hurt. And confused. They had a life together. I wondered if my dad had the green leather box made before he died, but it was her. She knew my dad's favorite color. She picked that shade of green. She knew everything about him. She knew him better than I did."

"She knew him differently than you did, not better."

I leaned back against the pillow. "Should I read the diary? All the volumes?"

"There's no 'should' about it," he said, placing his arm around my shoulders. "Heather hated the word 'should.'"

"I'm not very fond of it myself, so I guess I have something in common with a killer."

"What if you and I miscommunicate? What if I think I'm helping, and you don't want to tell me not to do whatever I'm doing because you don't want to hurt my feelings. Then what?"

"We'll talk about it."

"But you'll be afraid of hurting my feelings."

"I don't accept the premise of your question. I promise to tell you the truth, even if it hurts your feelings. Except about your cooking."

"You don't like my cooking?"

"I don't like your French onion soup."

"You don't? You've never told me that."

"You see? It's your mother's recipe and I didn't want to hurt your feelings."

"What's wrong with my mother's French onion soup?"

"You sauté the onions. You're supposed to sweat them."

"Guess what?"

"What?"

"You're now in charge of making French onion soup."

"Thank goodness."

I snuggled in closer. "I love you, Ty."

He kissed me. "I love you, too, Josie."

CHAPTER THIRTY-FOUR

Ellis arrived on schedule at ten o'clock Tuesday morning. I brought him back to the worktable, placed the Garfield letter on the microscope stage to study the signature, and found the same pattern: the *r* was slightly darker, thicker, and deeper than the *f,* unlike the president's actual signature.

"It's a forgery," I said.

Ellis examined it, too. "I'll tell the DA. They'll probably ask you to recommend some experts for Oliver's case if it goes to trial, although I doubt it will. It isn't signed yet, but they have an agreement in principle on a deal. Five years, full allocution, and complete restitution. He might get out in as little as three years."

"Poor Rory."

"She finally went home."

I took another look at the letter, then asked, "In Gloria's Thomas Jefferson notes, did she name Oliver as the forger?"

"Yes."

"How did she discover him?"

"He was helping his dad staff a booth at a rare document fair in New York City. He only offered the forgeries when his dad wasn't around. It didn't take her long to put two and two together. It was his bad luck she was so observant."

"It's all so sad. Sordid and sad. Were you able to access his original arrest records?"

"The annulment records, yes—it's confirmed. Oliver Crenshaw forged the Jefferson letter when he was fifteen, and he forged this now. Old habits die hard."

"He needed the money."

"And how. He was running on fumes."

"You realize what this means?" I asked rhetorically. "The forger authenticated his own forgery."

"Ironic."

As we walked back to the front, I asked, "Were you able to trace Heather's gun?"

"Her great-uncle brought it home as a souvenir from World War Two. You were right that Ivan called Heather en route to Hitchens, by the way, about ten minutes before he bought the duplicate keys at Murphy's."

"Has she confessed?"

"No."

"I don't think she will. She's rawhide tough."

"She's a killer. That's all I need to know."

Cara called up to my private office to ask me if I had time to see Eric. I said I did.

"Have a seat," I invited.

"That's okay." He stood in front of the desk, his shoulders hunched forward. "I've decided. I'm going to ask Grace to marry me."

I applauded softly. "I'm so pleased, Eric. Excellent!"

"I told my mother. I thought she'd be upset, but she wasn't. She said that when I leave, she'll move to Houston, to be with her sister. It made me think she wished I'd gotten my own apartment years ago. There I was staying in that old house for her, and there she was staying for me, when the truth was neither one of us wanted to be there."

Just like my dad and me, I thought. Another memory came to me: I'd passed up a trip to Paris because I hadn't wanted to cancel a camping trip with my dad. Now I wondered if he'd wished I'd gone to France so he could have spent the week with Ronnie.

"I'm kind of scared," Eric added. "I don't know what to say."

"Did you write something out?"

He nodded and took a sheet of paper from his shirt pocket. He handed it to me.

"Read it to me," I said.

"Now?"

"Yes."

He cleared his throat, licked his lips, and started in, mumbling. "Grace, I want you to know how much I love you." He raised his eyes from the paper. "What do you think? Is that a good beginning?"

"Yes, but don't mumble. Speak loud and proud."

"Okay." He continued, and his voice had some heft, "I love everything about you, your heart, your mind, your sweetness. You're the perfect woman. Will you marry me?"

I stood and smiled. "That's beautiful, Eric. Just beautiful."

His shoulders straightened and his eyes shone. "Really?"

"Really. Do you have the ring?"

He nodded, and pulled a small box from his pocket. "I bought it at Blackmore's. Nate said I could exchange it if . . . if she doesn't like it." He licked his lips again. "He said I could return it, too, if, you know, she says no." He lifted the hinged lid and showed it to me.

The ring was spectacular, a deep blue round sapphire with scalloped pavé diamonds in a white gold halo setting.

"Eric, I love it! It's so elegant, just like Grace. Why did you pick a sapphire?"

"It's her favorite stone."

"She's a lucky woman, Eric. You're a very special man."

Blood rushed to his cheeks. "Thanks, but I'm the lucky one. I just hope she says yes."

I was in the front office around three, when Rory stepped inside, leaning heavily on her cane.

"Good," she said. "You're here. We need to talk." I wasn't in the mood for Rory, and my disinclination must have shown because she added, "Don't worry. I won't bite your nose off."

I laughed. "I don't believe you. You bite off noses for fun."

"That's true, but not today."

"My office is up a spiral staircase. How about if we step outside? There's a bench not far away."

She agreed and I led the way. It was warm enough to sit outside, mid-sixties, or so.

"Oliver's in big trouble," she said.

"Did you know he was back to his old tricks?"

"Heck, no. And it's not like he doesn't know better. I raised him right."

She might not have been the most likable person in the world, but she truly loved her son, and she never made excuses for his bad behavior. "I'm sorry, Rory."

"Me, too. I need to sell the business. That's why I'm here. Want to buy it? I want to sell everything, lock, stock, and barrel. The name, if you want it, although who would, the way Oliver's smeared it? The inventory is worth something, although everything will need an independent appraisal, thanks to him, and I own the building, which is worth a lot. What do you say?"

I hated benefiting from someone's troubles, but I hadn't caused the trouble, and emotions shouldn't dictate business decisions. If Rory needed to sell, I needed to buy.

"Yes. I'll make you an offer." I stood. "Let me get you my lawyer's card. I'll work with him to set the terms."

Rory stood, too. "Don't think you can beat me down because Oliver got me in a mess."

"I won't."

I got Max's card from the pile we kept in a drawer, and she stuffed it into her pant pocket and limped across the lot to her car.

CHAPTER THIRTY-FIVE

At four o'clock Giles Lipp, Veronica Sutton's lawyer, called and asked me to stop by his firm. He said he had important and time-sensitive information.

He wouldn't answer any questions on the phone, so I agreed to go. I jotted down the address as he called it out, told Cara I wouldn't be back, and left.

Corwin Gresham Blaine, LLP, occupied two floors of a modern four-story building not far from the Rye border. The reception area overlooked the ocean.

I introduced myself to the receptionist, a young man with gel-spiked hair, and he gave me a curious, knowing look. Something was afoot. A minute later, a woman about my age poked her head into the reception area and invited me to follow her. She brought me into a small conference room and left me alone. I walked to the window, which also overlooked the ocean. Sun-tipped glitter skipped across the Egyptian-blue water.

Giles Lipp stepped into the room and handed me a notecard-size envelope, a match to the one I'd found in the box of diaries.

I accepted it, and asked, "What's going on?"

"Please read the note. I'll give you some privacy. When you're ready, I'll be right outside this door."

My name was written on the envelope in what I'd come to recognize as Veronica Sutton's neat hand. I broke the seal, and extracted the card.

Dear Josie,
If you're reading this note, you have a shock coming. Here it is: You have a half brother. His name is Ryan Bertram Sutton. Bertram was my father's name, and of course my son was named for his father.

I pulled one of the oversize chairs away from the conference table and sat down.

I decided to tell Ryan about you in a note, to be delivered after my death, much as I'm doing here, and to leave it to him to decide if he wants to meet you. He does—I know this because I instructed my lawyer to give you this note only if Ryan asked to meet you.

Now the decision is in your hands. Regardless of what you decide, I want you to know that your father loved his son very much.

Sincerely,
Veronica Sutton

I couldn't believe it. I didn't believe it. It was inconceivable. My father had a son. Gold specks twirled in front of my eyes, and I wondered if I was going to faint.

I read the note again, but this time, I couldn't make sense of the words.

I was hot, too hot, heatstroke hot.

I managed to stand and got myself back to the window. I rested my burning forehead against the cool glass.

My ready empathy returned as my temperature dropped. My father did what he thought was best for everyone involved. Ryan must be as shocked as I am. His mother just died, and now this.

I opened the door. Giles stood across the hall, reading from his phone.

"I'd like to meet him," I said. "How can I arrange it?"

"He's here now. I'll bring him. You can wait inside."

I returned to the conference room and stood by the window facing the door. Two minutes later, the door opened and a handsome well-built man in his midtwenties entered.

"You look just like my dad," I said, amazed.

"You don't."

"No, I look more like my mom." I paused for a moment. "I'm sorry about your mother."

"I can't believe she lied to me all these years."

"I feel the same about my dad." I sat at the head of the table. "I don't know what to do or say. I don't know what to think. I can't believe we're siblings. Half siblings."

He took the chair at the foot. "Me, either."

"How about if we exchange some facts?" I suggested after a moment's awkward silence.

"Okay. You go first."

"I'm an antiques appraiser. I own a company called Prescott's Antiques and Auctions, and I have a TV show, *Josie's Antiques*. I'm married. My husband is Ty Alvarez. He's an expert in emergency management. He works for Homeland Security. We live here in Rocky Point."

"I'm an analyst for the State Department. You know those travel advisories? I write them. I work in DC and live in Alexandria, Virginia. I have a girlfriend, Annie. She's a political writer, freelance."

"You're up here for the funeral."

"Yeah, and I'm staying a few days to help my cousin clean out my mom's house."

"I've got to tell you, I'm a little dazed. I don't even know how to begin thinking about all this."

"I feel the same."

I smiled. "I have a brother. A half brother who looks just like my dad. I always wanted a brother."

He smiled, too. "I always wanted a sister."

I handed him a business card and accepted his in return. "How long are you in town for?"

"Until Thursday afternoon."

"How about if we give ourselves a day to let all this settle in . . . want to come for dinner tomorrow night?"

"Thank you. I'd love to."

I called Ty from my car, and left him a voicemail asking him to meet me at Rocky Point Interiors.

Ty found me sitting on a gray rattan love seat with plump burnt orange cushions. My feet were up on the matching ottoman.

"What do you think?" I asked.

He sat beside me. "I like it. It's comfortable, and I like the color."

"They call this shade of orange 'Tuscan.'"

"Let's buy it."

"Okay."

While we waited for the salesperson to ring up the sale, Ty asked, "Why are we here on a Tuesday afternoon?"

"I needed normalcy. Buying a love seat qualified." I paused for a moment. "I had a bit of a shock today."

"Another one?"

"It seems I have a half brother. I met him."

"You have a half brother?"

"Named Ryan. Ryan B. Sutton. Ronnie didn't name her company for my dad. She named it for her son."

"Did you like him?"

"He looks like my father, the spitting image. I only talked to him for about three minutes. I couldn't deal with it for longer than that, so I left. He lives outside of DC, but he's here for a couple of days. I invited him for dinner tomorrow night."

Ty pocketed the receipt and we walked outside.

"I'm not coping well," I said.

"You're coping fine."

We reached my car, and I told him I'd see him at home.

My phone vibrated. Eric had texted, *Grace said yes.* More normalcy. I smiled as I typed my reply: *Yay!*

I called Ryan. "Hi, it's Josie. What's your favorite food?"

"I eat anything, but comfort food is meat and potatoes."

"For me, too. I'll make us a nice roast."

CHAPTER THIRTY-SIX

A month later, I walked onto our second-floor porch and perched on the ottoman. Ty was already there, sitting on our new love seat.

"I got a call from Lois Hart," I said, "the woman in charge of appraising the Jane Austen letters. She's certain the one to Fanny is genuine. Of Jane Austen's extant letters, five offer romantic advice to her niece, Fanny. This is the sixth."

"Congratulations."

"Thanks. I'm not going to lie . . . this is a super big deal."

I moved to the love seat, cuddling up next to him. "Lois has identified the watermarks. The Cassandra letter, the fake one, was written on paper produced by W. Turner and Son in 1810. Ellis found several sheets with that watermark in Oliver's stash, cream-colored, just like the paper Jane used. The wove paper used on the authentic letter, also cream-colored, came from J. Jellyman, and was manufactured in 1813."

"What's wove paper?"

"If you hold it up to the light you can see a pattern that looks like a window screen, a kind of fine mesh. Can you imagine? That paper was touched by Jane Austen. It gives me shivers to even think about it."

We sat without speaking for several seconds, then Ty asked, "Did you speak to Ryan?"

"Yeah . . . he can't come. He said he'll be out of the country over the holidays researching travel conditions in the Middle East, so Thanksgiving and Christmas are both out. We agreed to connect over the winter. You know what I think?"

"What?"

"I think 'analyst' is a euphemism. I think he's a spy."

"Smart, brave, loyal . . . some people with those qualities become spies. Other people with those qualities become antiques appraisers."

"Or Ph.D. candidates," I said. "Do you think my father was right to not tell me about his relationship with Ronnie?"

"Certainly when you were a kid. Later, I don't know. You would have asked how they met, and the truth about the timing would have come out. My guess is that he was afraid you'd find what he did unforgivable."

I watched the ocean for a moment, the deep blue water growing darker as the sun dropped below the horizon.

"He might have been right . . . I don't know. Regardless, it was his secret to keep, and he kept it out of love."

"He made the best decision he could with the information he had available at the time."

That sounded right. My father was a good man, a decent man. His love for me was real, which made me wonder about his relationship with his other child. The next time Ryan and I got together, I'd ask him to tell me about his father.

I took Ty's hand, and we sat quietly as the waves rolled into shore.

ACKNOWLEDGMENTS

S pecial thanks go to my literary agent, Cristina Concepcion of Don Congdon Associates, Inc. Thanks also go to Michael Congdon and Cara Bellucci.

Thanks to G. D. Peters, who read early drafts of this novel with care and diligence.

The Minotaur Books team gets special thanks, too, especially those I worked with most closely, including associate editor Hannah O'Grady, for her many insights, assistant director of publicity Sarah Melnyk, for her guidance and support, and associate director of marketing Martin Quinn. Thanks also to copy editor Sabrina Roberts, and cover designer David Baldeosingh Rotstein.